THE
CORRETTIS
Scandals

CAITLIN CREWS
MAISEY YATES

MILLS & BOON

First published in Great Britain 2013
Mills & Boon, an imprint of Harlequin (UK) Limited,
Eton House, 18-24 Paradise Road, Richmond, Surrey TW9 1SR

THE CORRETTIS: SCANDALS
© Harlequin Enterprises II B.V./S.à.r.l. 2013

A Scandal in the Headlines © Harlequin Books S.A. 2013

Special thanks and acknowledgement are given to Caitlin Crews for her contribution to *Sicily's Corretti Dynasty* series

ISBN: 978 0 263 90621 9

53-0813

Harlequin (UK) policy is to use papers that are natural, renewable and recyclable products and made from wood grown in sustainable forests. The logging and manufacturing processes conform to the legal environmental regulations of the country of origin.

Printed and bound
by CPI Group (UK) Ltd, Croydon, CR0 4YY

A Scandal in the Headlines

CAITLIN CREWS

Caitlin Crews discovered her first romance novel at the age of twelve. It involved swashbuckling pirates, grand adventures, a heroine with rustling skirts and a mind of her own, and a seriously mouthwatering and masterful hero. The book (the title of which remains lost in the mists of time) made a serious impression. Caitlin was immediately smitten with romances and romance heroes, to the detriment of her middle-school social life. And so began her lifelong love affair with romance novels, many of which she insists on keeping near her at all times.

Caitlin has made her home in places as far-flung as York, England and Atlanta, Georgia. She was raised near New York City and fell in love with London on her first visit when she was a teenager. She has backpacked in Zimbabwe, been on safari in Botswana and visited tiny villages in Namibia. She has, while visiting the place in question, declared her intention to live in Prague, Dublin, Paris, Athens, Nice, the Greek islands, Rome, Venice and/or any of the Hawaiian islands. Writing about exotic places seems like the next best thing to moving there.

She currently lives in California, with her animator/comic book artist husband and their menagerie of ridiculous animals.

CHAPTER ONE

"WHAT THE HELL are you doing on my boat?"

Elena Calderon froze in the act of polishing the luxurious teak bar in the yacht's upper lounge. The low growl of the male voice from across the room was laced with a stark and absolute authority that demanded instant obedience. And she knew exactly who he was without looking up. *She knew.*

She felt it slam into her, through her, like a sledgehammer.

Alessandro Corretti.

He wasn't supposed to be here, she thought wildly. He hadn't used this boat in over a year! He usually rented it out to wealthy foreigners instead!

"I'm polishing the bar," she managed to say. She kept her tone even because that was how a stewardess on a luxury yacht spoke to the guests. To say nothing of the owner himself. But she still couldn't bring herself to look at him.

He let out harsh kind of laugh. "Is this some kind of joke?"

"It's no joke." She tapped her fingers on the bar before her. "It's teak and holly, according to the chief steward."

She'd told herself repeatedly that what had happened during that one mad dance six months ago had been a fluke. More to do with the wine and the music and the romantic ballroom setting than the man—

But she didn't quite believe it. Warily, she looked up.

He was half-hidden in the shadows of the lounge's entryway, with all of that bright Sicilian sun blazing behind him—but she recognized him. A bolt of sensation sizzled over her skin, then beneath it, stealing her breath and setting off a hum deep and low inside.

Alessandro Corretti. The man who had blown her life to bits with one single dance. The man she knew was bad no matter how intensely attractive he was and no matter how drawn she was to him, against her will. The man who was even worse than her lying, violent, criminally inclined ex-fiancé, Niccolo.

Elena hadn't dared go to the *polizia* when she'd fled from Niccolo, fearing his family's connections. Alessandro's family, however, made those connections seem insubstantial, silly. They were the Corretis. They were above the law.

And yet when Alessandro stepped farther into the lounge, out of the shadows, Elena's chest tightened in immediate, helpless reaction—and none of it terror. Her breath caught. Her heart sped up. She yearned, just as she had six months ago, as if her body believed he was good. Safe.

"Was that an attempt at levity?" There was nothing in the least bit safe about his hard voice, or that look in his eyes. "Hilarious, I'm sure. But you still haven't answered my question, Elena."

Today the usually breathtakingly sophisticated eldest heir to and current CEO of Corretti Media and its vast empire looked...rumpled. Uncharacteristically disheveled, from his thick, messy dark hair to his scuffed shoes. His tall, muscled strength was contained in a morning suit with the torn jacket hanging open over his lean, hard chest. He had a black eye, scrapes and cuts that only accentuated his aristocratic cheekbones, a slightly puffy lip, even scraped knuckles. And that famous, cynical mouth of his was set in a grim line while his too-dark green eyes were ferociously narrowed. Directly at her.

What was truly hilarious, Elena thought then, was that she'd actually convinced herself he wouldn't recognize her in the unlikely event that they ran into each other on this yacht she'd been repeatedly assured he hardly used. She'd told herself that he had world-altering interactions like the one she wanted to forget with every woman he'd ever clapped eyes on. That it was simply what he did.

And if some intuitive, purely feminine part of her had whispered otherwise, she'd ignored it.

"I'm not trespassing," she said with a calm she wished she felt. "I work here."

"Like hell you do."

"And yet here I am." With a wave of her hand she indicated the smart tan-colored skirt she wore, the pristine black T-shirt tucked in at the waist, the sensible boat shoes. "Uniform and all."

His dark eyes were trained on her, hard and cold. She remembered the fire in them that night six months ago, the impossible longing, and felt the lack of both as a loss.

"You are…what, exactly? A maid?" His voice managed to be both incredulous and fierce at once, and she ordered herself not to react as he began to walk toward her, all impeccable male lines and sheer masculine poetry despite the beating he'd obviously taken.

Damn him. How could he still affect her like this? It disgusted her. She told herself what she felt now was *disgust*.

"I'm a stewardess. Cleaning is only one of my duties."

"Of course. And when you found yourself possessed of the urge to trade in designer gowns and luxury cars for actual labor, I imagine it was pure coincidence that made you choose this particular yacht—my yacht—on which to begin your social experiment?"

"I didn't know it was yours." Not when she'd answered the original advert, when she'd decided waitressing at the tourist restaurants along the stunning Sicilian coast was too risky for someone who didn't want to be found. And now she wished she'd heeded her impulse to keep running when she'd discovered the truth. Why hadn't she? "When I found out, I'd already been working here a week. I was told you rarely, if ever, used it."

If she was honest, she'd also thought he owed her, somehow. She'd liked the idea that Alessandro had been paying her, however indirectly. That he was affected in some way by what that dance had put into motion, no matter if he never knew it. It had felt like a kind of power, and she needed every hint of that she could find.

"What a curious risk to take for so menial a position," he murmured.

He was even closer now, right there on the other side of the bar, and Elena swallowed hard when he put his hands down on the gleaming surface with the faintest hint of a sensual menace she didn't want to acknowledge. If she'd been on the same side he was, he would have been caging her between them. She couldn't seem to shake the image—or perhaps it was that the barrier seemed flimsy indeed when the way he was looking at her made something coil inside of her and pull taut.

"It's an honest job."

"Yes." His dark green gaze was laced through with something she might have called grief, were he anyone else. "But you are not an honest woman, are you?"

Elena couldn't hide the way she flinched at that, and she wasn't sure what she hated more—that he saw it, or that she obviously cared what this man thought about her. When he didn't know anything about her. When all he'd ever known about her was that shocking, overwhelming explosion of awareness between them at that long-ago charity ball.

He couldn't know how bitterly she regretted her own complicity in what had happened that night, how her reaction to him still shamed her. He couldn't know what Niccolo had planned, what she'd very nearly helped him do. He knew how blind she'd been, sadly, but he couldn't know the truth....

But Alessandro was just like Niccolo, she reminded herself harshly then, no matter her physical reaction to him. Same kind of man, same kind of "family business," same kind of brutal exploitation of whoever and whatever he could use. She'd had a lot of time to read about Alessandro Corretti and the infamous Corretti family in her six months on the run. There was no telling what he might know about his rival Niccolo Falco's broken engagement and missing fiancée, or how he might use that information.

She had to be careful.

"I already know what you think of me," she said, keeping her voice cool. Unbothered. "And anyway, people change."

"Circumstances change." There was no denying the bitterness in his voice then, or stamped all over that battered, arrogant face. She told herself it didn't move her at all, that she didn't feel the insane, hastily checked urge to reach over and cover his hand with hers. "People never do."

Sadly, she knew he was right. Because if she'd changed at all—if she'd learned anything from these months of running and hiding—she wouldn't have found this man compelling in the least. She would have run screaming in the opposite direction, flung herself from the side of the boat and swum for the Palermo shoreline they'd left more than ninety minutes ago.

"If you don't want me here—"

"I don't."

She swallowed, fighting to remain calm. She couldn't afford to lose her temper, not when he could ruin everything with a single telephone call. It would take no more than that to summon Niccolo from that villa of his she'd nearly moved into outside of Naples. Alessandro would probably even enjoy throwing her back into that particular fire. Why not? The Correttis had been at bitter odds with Niccolo's family for generations. What was one more bit of collateral damage?

Especially when Alessandro already thought she was the sort of woman who aspired to be a pawn in the kind of games men like him played.

Think, she ordered herself. *Stop reacting to him and think about how best to play this!*

"Then I'll go, of course." Given what she knew he believed about her, he must imagine she'd be impervious to threats. Which meant she had to be exactly that. She smiled coolly. "But we're out at sea."

He shifted then, only slightly, and yet a new kind of danger seemed to shimmer in the air of the lounge, making Elena's pulse heat up and beat thick and wild beneath her skin. His dark green eyes gleamed.

"Then I certainly hope you can swim."

"I never learned," she lied. She tilted her head, let her smile flirt with him. "Are you offering me a lesson?"

"I suppose I can spare a lifeboat," he mused, that gleam in his eyes intensifying. "You'll wash up somewhere soon enough, I'm sure. The Mediterranean is a small sea." One corner of his battered mouth quirked up. "Relatively speaking."

She didn't understand how she could still find this man so beautiful, like one of the old gods sent down to earth again. Savage and seductive, even as he threatened to set her adrift. But she knew better than to believe her eyes, her traitorous body, that awful yearning that moved in her like white noise, louder by the second.... She knew what and who he was.

She shouldn't have had to keep reminding herself of that. But then, she couldn't understand why she wasn't afraid of him the way she'd come to be afraid of Niccolo, when she also knew Alessandro was far more dangerous than Niccolo could ever be.

"You're not going to toss me overboard," she said with quiet certainty.

A different kind of awareness tightened the air between them, reminding her again of that fateful dance. The way he'd held her so close, the things she'd simply *known* when she'd looked at him. That curve in his hard mouth deepened, as if he felt it, too. She knew he did, the way she'd known it then.

"Of course not," he said, those dark eyes much too hot, something far more alarming than temper in them now. Memories. That old longing. She had to be careful. "I have staff for that."

"Alternatively," she said, summoning up that smile again, forcing herself to stand there so calmly, so carelessly, "though less dramatically, I admit—you could simply let me go when we arrive at the next port."

He laughed then, and rubbed his hands over his bruised face. He winced slightly, as if he'd forgotten he was hurt.

"Maybe I'm not making myself clear." When he lowered his hands his gaze burned fierce and hot. She remembered that, too. And it swept through her in exactly the same way it had before, consuming her. Scalding her. "Niccolo Falco's woman is not welcome here. Not on this boat, not on my island, not anywhere near me. So you swim or you float. Your choice."

"I understand," she said after a moment, making it sound as if he bored her. She should have been racked with panic. She should have been terrified. Instead, she shrugged. "You must have your little revenge. I rejected you, therefore you have to overreact and throw me off the side of a yacht." She rolled her eyes. "I understand that's how it works for men like you."

"Men like me," he repeated quietly, as if she'd cursed at him. He sounded tired when he spoke again, and it made something turn over inside of her. But she kept on.

"You're a Corretti," she said. "We both know what that means."

"Petty acts of revenge and the possibility of swimming lessons?" he asked dryly, but there were shadows in that dark gaze, shadows she couldn't let herself worry about, no matter that strange sensation inside of her.

"It also means you are well known to be as cruel and occasionally vicious as the rest of the crime syndicate you call your family." Her smile was brittle. "How lucky for me that I've encountered you on two such occasions."

"Ah, yes," he said, his dark gaze hard as his cynical mouth curved again, and something about that made her legs feel weak beneath her. "I remember this part. The personal attacks, the insulting comments about my family. You need a new topic of conversation, Elena."

He didn't move but, even so, she felt as if he loomed over her, around her, and she knew he was remembering it even as she did—those harsh words they'd thrown at each other in the middle of a ballroom in Rome, the wild flush she'd felt taking over her whole body, the way he'd only looked at her and sent that impossible, terrifying fire roaring through her. She felt it again now. Just as hot. Just as bright.

And just like then, it was much too tempting. She

wanted to leap right into the heart of it, burn herself alive—

She shoved it aside, all of it, her heart pounding far too hard against her ribs. There was so much to lose if she didn't handle this situation correctly—if Niccolo found her. If she forgot what she was doing, and why. If she lost herself in Alessandro Corretti's dark, wild fire the way she still wanted to do, all these months later, despite what had happened since then.

"Far be it from me to stand in the way of your pettiness," she said, jerking her gaze from his and moving out from behind the bar. She headed for the doorway to the deck and the sunshine that beckoned, bright and clear. "It's a beautiful day for a swim, isn't it? Quite summery, really, for May. I'm sure I won't drown in such a small sea."

"Elena. Stop."

She ignored him and kept moving.

"Don't make me put my hands on you," he said then, almost conversationally, but the dark heat in it, the frank sensual promise, almost made her stumble. And, to her eternal shame, stop walking. "Who knows where that might lead? There are no chaperones here. No avid eyes to record our every move. No fiancé to watch jealously from the side of the dance floor. Which reminds me, are congratulations in order? Are you Signora Falco at last?"

Elena fought to breathe, to keep standing. To keep herself from telling this man—this dangerous, ruinous man—the truth the way every part of her screamed she should. She hardly knew him. She couldn't trust him. She didn't know what made her persist in thinking she could.

She thought of her parents—her loving mother and her poor, sick father—and what they must believe about her now, what Niccolo must have told them. The pain of that shot through her, taking her breath. And on some level, she knew, she deserved it. She thought about the unspoiled little village she'd come from, nestled on a rocky hill that ran along the sea, looking very much the same as it had hundreds of years ago. She needed to protect it. Because she was the only one who could. Because her foolishness, her selfishness and her vanity, had caused the problem in the first place.

She'd chosen this course when she'd run from Niccolo. She couldn't change it now. She didn't know what it was about Alessandro, even as surly and forbidding as he was today, that made her want to abandon everything, put herself in his hands, bask in that intense ruthlessness of his as if it could save her.

As if he could. Or would.

"No," she said. She cleared her throat. She had to be

calm, cool. The woman he thought she was, unbothered by emotion, unaffected by sentiment. "Not yet."

"You've not yet had that *great honor*, then?"

She didn't know what demon possessed her then, but she looked back over her shoulder at him as if his words didn't sting. He was lounging back against the bar, gazing at her, and she knew what that fire in his eyes meant. She'd known in Rome, too. She felt the answering kick of heat deep in her core.

"I can't think of a greater one," she said. Lying through her teeth.

He watched her for a long, simmering moment, his gaze considering.

"And because you feel so honored you have decided to take a brief sabbatical from your engagement to tour the world as a stewardess on a yacht? My yacht, no less? When Europe is overrun by yachts this time of year, swarming like ants in every harbor, and only one of them belongs to me?"

"I always wished I'd taken a gap year before university," she said airily. Careless and offhanded. "This is my chance to remedy that."

"And tell me, Elena," he said, his voice curling all around her, tangling inside of her, making her despair of herself for all the ways he made her weak when she should have been completely immune to him, when she *wanted* to be immune to him, "what will happen when this little journey is complete? Will you race back into the *great honor* of your terrible marriage, grateful for the brief holiday? Docile and meek, as a pissant like Niccolo no doubt prefers?"

She didn't want to hear him talk about Niccolo. About the marriage he'd warned her against in such stark terms six months ago. It made something shudder deep inside of her, then begin to ache, and she didn't want to explore why that was. She never had.

This is not about you, she snapped at herself then, reminding herself how much more she had to lose this time. *And it's certainly not about him.*

"Of course," she said with an air of surprise, as if he really might believe that Niccolo Falco's fiancée was acting as a stewardess on a yacht simply to broaden her horizons before her marriage. As if she did. "I think that's the whole point."

"I've witnessed more than my share of terrible marriages," he said then, a bleakness beneath his voice and moving in his too-dark eyes as he regarded her. It made her shiver, though she tried to hide it. "I was only yesterday jilted at the start of one myself, as a matter of fact. My blushing bride was halfway down the aisle when she thought better of it." His mouth curved, cynical and hard. "And yet yours, I guarantee you, will be worse. Much worse."

She didn't want to think about Alessandro's wedding, jilted groom or not. Much less her own. Once again, she fought back the strangest urge to explain, to tell him the truth about Niccolo, about her broken engagement. But he was not her friend. He was not a safe harbor. If anything, he was worse than Niccolo. Why was that so hard to keep in mind?

"I'm sorry about your wedding." It was the best she could do, and she was painfully aware that it wasn't even true.

"I'm not," he said, and she understood the tone he used then, at last, because she recognized it. *Self-loathing*. She blinked in surprise. "Not as sorry as I should be, and certainly not for the right reasons."

Alessandro straightened then, pushing away from the bar. He moved toward her—stalked toward her, if she was precise—and she turned all the way around to face him fully. As if that might dull the sheer force of him. Or her wild, helpless reaction to him that seemed to intensify the longer she was in his presence.

It did neither.

He stopped when he was much too close, that marvelous chest of his near enough that if she'd dared—if she'd taken leave of her senses entirely, if she'd lost what small grip she had left on what remained of her life—she could have tipped her head forward and pressed her mouth against that hard, beautiful expanse that she shouldn't have let herself notice in the first place.

"Tell me why you're here," he said in a deceptively quiet voice that made her knees feel like water. "And spare me the lies about gap-year adventures. I know exactly what kind of woman you are, Elena. Don't forget that. I never have."

There was no reason why that comment should have felt like he'd slapped her, when she already knew what he thought of her. When she was banking on it.

"You're hardly one to talk, are you? Remember that I know who you are, too."

"Wrong answer."

Elena sighed. "You were never meant to know I was here. Let me off when we reach port—any port—and it will be like I was never on this boat at all."

And for a moment, she almost believed he would do it.

That he would simply let it drop, this destructive awareness that hummed between them and the fact she'd turned up on his property. That he would shrug it off. But Alessandro's mouth curved again, slightly swollen and still so cynical, his eyes flashed cold, and she knew better.

"I don't think so," he said, his gaze moving from hers to trace her lips.

"Alessandro—" she began, but cut herself off when

his gaze slammed back into hers. She jumped slightly, as if he'd touched her. She felt burned straight through to the core, as if he really had.

"I've never had someone try to spy on me so ineptly before," he told her in a whisper that still managed to convey all of that wild heat, all of that lush *want*, that she felt crackling between them and that would, she knew, be the end of her if she let it. The end of everything. "Congratulations, Elena. It's another first."

"Spy?" She made herself laugh. "Why would I spy on you?"

"Why would you want to marry an animal like Niccolo Falco?" He shrugged expansively, every inch an Italian male, but Elena wasn't fooled. She could see the steel in his gaze, that ruthlessness she knew was so much a part of him. Something else that reminded her of that dance. "You are a woman of mystery, made entirely of unknowables and impossibilities. But you can rest easy. I have no intention of letting you out of my sight."

He smiled then, not at all nicely, and Elena's heart plummeted straight down to her feet and crashed into the floor.

She was in serious trouble.

With Alessandro Corretti.

Again.

* * *

It was not until he propped himself up in the decadent outdoor shower off his vast master suite that Alessandro allowed himself to relax. To breathe.

The sprawling island house he'd built here on the small little spit of land, closer to the coast of Sicily than to Sardinia, was the only place he considered his true home. The only place the curse of being a Corretti couldn't touch him.

He shut his eyes and waited for the hot water to make him feel like himself again.

He wanted to forget. That joke of a wedding and Alessia Battaglia's betrayal of the deal they'd made to merge their high-profile families—and, of course, of him. To say nothing of his estranged cousin Matteo, her apparent lover. Then the drunken, angry night he hardly remembered, though the state of his face—and the snide commentary from the *polizia* this morning when he'd woken in a jail cell, hardly the image he liked to portray as the CEO of Corretti Media—told the tale eloquently.

His head still echoed with the nasty, insinuating questions from the paparazzi surrounding his building in Palermo when his brother, Santo, had taken him there this morning, merging with his leftover headache and all various agonies he was determined to ignore.

Did you know your fiancée was sleeping with your cousin? Your bitter rival?

Can the Corretti family weather yet another scandal?

How do the Corretti Media stockholders feel about your very public embarrassment—or your night in jail?

He wanted to forget. All of it. Because he didn't want to think about what a mess his deceitful would-be bride and scheming cousin had left behind. Or how he was ever going to clean it up.

And then there was Elena.

Those thoughtful blue eyes, the precise shade of a perfect Sicilian summer afternoon. The blond hair that he'd first seen swept up behind her to tumble down her back, that she'd worn today in a shorter tail at the nape of her neck. Her elegant body, slender and sleek, as enchanting in that absurd yachting uniform as when he'd first found himself poleaxed by the sight of her in that ballroom six months ago.

Then, she'd worn a stunning gown that had left her astonishingly naked from the nape of her neck to scant millimeters above the swell of her bottom. All of that silken skin *just there*.

His throat went dry at the memory, while the rest of his body hardened as it had the moment he'd laid eyes on her at that charity benefit in Rome. He didn't remember which charity it had been or why he'd attended it in the first place; he only remembered Elena.

"Careful," Santo had said with a laugh, seconds after Alessandro had caught sight of her standing only a few feet away in the crush of the European elite. "Don't you know who she is?"

"Mine," Alessandro had muttered, unable to pull his gaze away from her. Unable to get his bearings at all, as if the world had shuddered to a halt—and then she'd turned. She'd looked around as if she'd been able to feel the heat of his gaze on her, and then her eyes had met his.

Alessandro had felt it like a hard punch in the gut. Hard, electric, almost incapacitating. He'd felt it— her—everywhere.

His.

She was supposed to be his.

He hadn't had the smallest doubt. And the fact that he'd acquiesced to his grandfather's wishes and agreed to a strategic, business-oriented marriage some two months before had not crossed his mind at all. Why should it have? The woman he was engaged to was as mindful of her duty and the benefits of their arrangement as he was. This, though—this was something else entirely.

And then he'd seen the man standing next to her, a possessive hand at her waist.

Niccolo Falco, of the arrogant Falco family that had given Alessandro's grandfather trouble in Naples many years before. Niccolo, who fancied himself some kind of player when he was really no more than the kind of petty criminal Alessandro most despised. Alessandro had hated him for years.

It was impossible that this woman—*his woman*—could have anything to do with scum like Niccolo.

"The rumor is her father has some untouched land on the Lazio coast north of Gaeta," Santo had said into his ear, seemingly unaware of the war Alessandro was fighting on the inside. "He is also quite ill. Niccolo thinks he's struck gold. Romance the daughter, marry her, then develop the land. As you do."

"Why am I not surprised that a pig like Niccolo would have to leverage a woman into marrying him?" Alessandro had snarled, jerking a drink from a passing waiter's tray and draining it in one gulp. He hadn't even tasted it. He'd seen only her. Wanted only her.

"Apparently that's going around," Santo had muttered.

Alessandro had only glared at him.

"Are you really going to marry that Battaglia girl in cold blood?" Santo had asked then, frowning, his dark green eyes so much like Alessandro's own. "Sacrifice yourself to one of the old man's plots?"

Santo was the only person alive who could speak

to him like that. But Alessandro was a Corretti first, like it or not. Marrying a Battaglia was a part of that. It made sense for the family. It was his responsibility. He would marry for duty, not out of deceit.

Alessandro was not Niccolo Falco.

"I will do my duty," he had said. He'd tapped his empty glass to his brother's chest, smiling slightly when Santo took it from him. "A concept you should think about yourself, one of these days."

"Heaven forbid," Santo had replied, grinning.

The orchestra had started playing then, and Alessandro had ordered himself to walk away from the strange woman—*Niccolo Falco's woman*—no matter how bright her eyes were or how that simple fact made his chest ache. There was no possibility that he could start anything with a woman who was embroiled with the Falcos. It would ignite tempers, incite violence, call more attention to the dirty past Alessandro had been working so hard to put behind him.

Walking away had been the right thing to do. The only reasonable option.

But instead, he'd danced with her, and sealed his fate.

CHAPTER TWO

AND NOW SHE was here.

Alessandro had thought he was hallucinating when he'd first seen her on the yacht. He'd thought the stress was finally getting to him—that or the blows to his head. *You've finally snapped,* he'd told himself.

But his body had known better. It knew *her.*

He could still feel the heat of her when he'd touched her all those months ago, when he'd pulled her close to dance with her, when his fingers had skimmed that tempting hollow in the small of her back and made her breath come too fast. He still remembered her sweet, light scent, and how it had made him hunger to taste her, everywhere.

He still did. Even though there was no possible way that he could have ignored his responsibilities back then and pursued her, even if she hadn't been neck-deep in a rival family, engaged to one of the enemies of the Corretti empire. He'd told himself that all he'd wanted after that charity ball was to forget her, and he'd tried. God help him, but he'd tried. And there'd certainly been more than enough to occupy him.

There'd been the pressure of managing his grandfather's schemes, the high-profile wedding and the docklands regeneration project the old man had been so determined would unite the warring factions of the Corretti family.

"You will put an end to this damned feud," Salvatore had told him. "Brother against brother, cousins at war with one another. It's gone too far. It's no good."

It was still so hard to believe that he'd died only a few weeks ago, when Alessandro had always believed that crafty old Salvatore Corretti would live forever, somehow. But then again, it was just as well he'd missed that circus of a wedding yesterday.

And if Alessandro had woken from a dream or two over the past few months, haunted by clever eyes as blue as the sky, he'd ignored it. What he'd felt on that dance floor was impossible, insane.

The truth was, he'd never wanted that kind of mess in his life.

His late father, Carlo, had always claimed it was his intensity of emotion that made him do the terrible things he'd done—the other women, the shady dealings and violently corrupt solutions. Just as his mother,

Carmela, had excused her own heinous acts—like the affair she'd confessed to yesterday that made Alessandro's adored sister, Rosa, his uncle's daughter—by blaming it on the hurt feelings Carlo's extramarital adventures had caused her.

Alessandro wanted no part of it.

He'd viewed his calm, dutiful marriage as a kind of relief. An escape from generations of misery. He was furious enough that Alessia Battaglia had left him at the altar—what would he have done if he had *felt* for her?

He'd felt far too much on a dance floor for a woman he couldn't respect. Far more than he'd believed he could. Far more than he should have. It still shook him.

Alessandro turned the water off and reached for a towel, letting the bright sun play over his body as he walked into his rooms. He didn't want to think about the wedding-that-wasn't. He didn't want to think about the things Santo had told him this morning en route to the marina—all the business implications of losing that connection with Alessia's father, the slimy politician who held the Corretti family's future in his greedy hands. He didn't want to think at all. He didn't want to feel those things that hovered there, right below the surface—his profound sense of personal failure chief among them.

And luckily, he didn't have to. Because Elena Calderon had delivered herself directly into his hands, the perfect distraction from all of his troubles.

He didn't care that she was almost certainly on some kind of pathetic mission from Niccolo and the Falco family, who had been openly jealous of the Corretti empire for decades. He didn't care why she was here. Only that she was when he'd thought her lost to him forever.

And he still wanted her, with that same wild ferocity that had haunted him all this time.

He'd had every intention of doing his duty to his family, to his grandfather's final wishes, and it had exploded in his face. Maybe it was time to think about what *he* wanted instead.

Maybe it was time to stop worrying about the consequences.

He found her in one of the many shaded, open areas that flowed seamlessly from inside to outside, making the whole house seem a part of the sea and the sky above. She was frowning out at the stretch of deep blue water as if she could call back the yacht he'd sent on its way with the force of her thoughts alone. He'd pulled on a pair of linen trousers and a soft white T-shirt, and he ran his fingers through his damp hair as she turned to him.

That same kick, hard to the gut and low. That same wildfire, that same storm.

His.

She looked almost vulnerable for a moment. Something about the softness of her full mouth, the shadows in her beautiful eyes. The urge to protect her roared through him, warring with the equally strong impulse to tear her open, learn her secrets—to figure out how she could want that jackass Niccolo, to start, and fail to see what kind of scum he was. How she could have felt what Alessandro had felt on that dance floor and turned her back on it the way she had.

How she did this to him when no other woman had ever got beneath his skin at all.

And there were no prying eyes here on his island. No whispers, no gossip. No one had to know she'd ever been here. There would be no business ramifications if he finally put his mouth on her. No ancient feuds to navigate, no humiliating scenes in public with his shareholders and the world looking on. Whatever game she and Niccolo were playing, it wouldn't affect Alessandro at all if he didn't let it.

No consequences. No problems. No reason at all not to do exactly as he wished.

At last.

"I told you to change into something more comfortable," he said, jerking his chin at that dowdy little uniform she still wore, not that it concealed her beauty in the least. Not that anything could. "Why didn't you?"

Clear blue eyes met his, and God, he wanted her. That same old fist of desire closed hard around him, then squeezed tight.

"I don't want to change."

"Is that an invitation?" he asked silkily, enjoying the way her cheeks flushed with the same heat he could feel climb in him. "Don't be coy, Elena. If you want me to take off your clothes, you need only ask."

His mocking words scalded her, then shamed her.

Because some terrible part of her wanted him to do it—wanted him to strip her right here in the sea air and who cared what came afterward? Some part of her had always wanted that, she acknowledged then. From the first moment their eyes had met.

Elena remembered what it had been like to touch this man, to feel his breath against her cheek, to feel the agonizingly sweet sweep of his hand over the bared skin of her back. She remembered the heat of him, the dizzying expanse of those shoulders in his gorgeous clothes, the impossible beauty of that hard mouth so close to hers.

It lived in her like an open flame. Like need.

She remembered what it had been like between them. For those few stolen moments, the music swelling all around them, making it seem preordained somehow. Huge and undeniable. Fated.

But look where it had led, that careless dance she knew even then she should have refused. Look what had come of it.

"No?" Alessandro looked amused. That sensual gleam in his dark green gaze tugged at her. Hard. "Are you sure?" His amusement deepened into something sardonic, and it didn't help that he looked sleek and dark and dangerous now, the pale colors he wore accentuating his rich olive skin and the taut, ridged wonder of his torso. "You look—"

"Thank you," she said, cutting him off almost primly. "I'm sure."

He really did smile then.

Alessandro sauntered toward her with all the arrogant confidence and ease that made him who he was, and that smile of his made it worse. It made him lethal. His shower had turned the evidence of his misspent night, all those cuts and bruises, into something very nearly rakish. Almost charming.

No one man should be this tempting. No other man ever was.

She had to pull herself together. The reality that she was trapped here, with Alessandro of all people, on this tiny island in the middle of the sea, had chipped a layer or two off the tough veneer she'd developed over the past few months. She was having trouble regaining her balance, remembering the role she knew she had to play to make it through this.

You will lose everything that matters to you if you don't snap out of this, she reminded herself harshly. *Everything that matters to the people you love. Is that what you want?*

He stopped when he stood next to her at the finely wrought rail that separated them from the cliff and the sea below. He was much too close. He smelled crisp and clean, and powerfully male. Elena could feel the connection between them, magnetic and insistent, surrounding them in its taut, mesmerizing pull.

And she had no doubt that Alessandro would use it against her if he could, this raging attraction. That was the kind of thing men like him did without blinking, and she needed to do the same. It didn't matter who she really was, how insane and unlike her this reaction to him had been from the start. It didn't matter what he would think of her—what he already did think of her. What so many others thought of her, too, in fact, or what she thought of herself. And while all of that was like a deep, black hole inside of her, yawning wider even now, she had to find a way to do this, anyway. All that mattered was saving her village, preserving forever what she'd put at risk in the first place.

What was her self-respect next to that? She'd given up her right to it when she'd been silly and flattered and vain enough to believe Niccolo's lies. There were consequences to bad choices, and this was hers.

"I should tell you," he said casually, as if he was commenting on the weather. The temperature. "I have no intention of letting you go this time. Not without a taste."

That was not anticipation that flooded through her then. And certainly not a knife-edge excitement that made her pulse flutter wildly in response. She wouldn't allow it.

"Is that an order?" she asked, her voice cool, as if he didn't get to her at all.

"If you like." He laughed. So arrogant, she thought. So sure of her. Of this. "If that's what gets you off."

"Because most people consider a boss ordering his employee to 'give him a taste' a bit unprofessional." She smiled pure ice at him. She did not think about what *got her off*. "There are other terms for it, of course. Legal ones."

He angled himself so he was leaning one hip against the rail, looking down at her. A faintly mocking curve to his mouth. Bruised and bad, head to foot. And yet still so terribly compelling. Why couldn't what she *knew* rid her of what she *felt*?

"Are we still maintaining that little bit of fiction?" He shrugged carelessly, though his gaze was hot. "Then consider yourself fired. Someone will find another stewardess for my yacht. You, however." His smile then made her blood heat, her traitorous body flush. "You, I think, have a different purpose here altogether."

Elena had to fight herself to focus, to remember. Alessandro Corretti was one of the notorious Sicilian Correttis. More than that, he was the oldest son of his generation, the heir to the legend, no matter how they'd split up the family fortune or the interfamily wars the press reported on so breathlessly. He was who Niccolo aspired to become—the real, genuine article. Corrupt and wicked to the marrow of his bones, by virtue of his blood alone.

He should have disgusted her to the core. He should have terrified her. It appalled her that he didn't. That nothing could break this hold he had on her. That she still felt this odd sense of safety when she was near him, despite all evidence to the contrary.

"Oh, right," she said now. "I forgot." She sighed, though her mind raced as she tried to think of what she would do if she really was the woman he thought she was. If she was that conniving, that amoral. "You think I'm a spy."

"I do."

No man, she thought unsteadily, should look that much like a wolf, or have dark green eyes that blazed when he looked at her that way. It turned her molten, all the way through.

"And what do you think spying on you would get me?"

"I know it will get you nothing. But I doubt you know that. And I'm sure your lover doesn't."

That he called Niccolo her lover made her skin crawl. That she'd had every intention of marrying Niccolo—and probably would have, had fate and this man and Niccolo's own temper not intervened—made her want to curl up into a ball and wail. Or tear off her own skin. But she tacked on a little smile instead, and pretended.

She got better at it all the time.

"You've caught me," she said. "You've unveiled my cunning master plan." She lifted her eyes heavenward. "I'm a spy. And I let myself be caught in the act of… stewardessing. Also part of my devious mission! What could I possibly want next?"

He looked amused again, which only made the ferocity he wore like a shield around him seem that much more pronounced.

"Access," he said easily. "Though I should warn you now, my computers require several layers of security, and if I catch you anywhere near them or near me when I'm having a private conversation, I'll lock you in a closet. Believe that, Elena, if nothing else."

He said that so casually, almost offhandedly, that smile playing around his gorgeous, battered mouth— but she believed him.

"You've clearly given my imaginary career in espionage a great deal of thought," she said carefully, as if she was appeasing a raving lunatic. "But ask yourself, why would I risk this? Or imagine you'd let me?"

His expression of amusement edged over into something else, something voracious and dark, and her pulse jumped beneath her skin.

"Your fiancé was not blind, all those months ago," he said softly. She felt him everywhere, again, as if he was touching her the way she knew he wanted to do. The way she couldn't help but wish he would. "Nor was I."

For a moment, she forgot herself. His dark green eyes were so fierce on hers then, searing into her. Challenging her. The world fell away and there was nothing but him and all the things she couldn't— wouldn't—tell him. All the things she shouldn't want.

And despite herself, she remembered.

Six months ago...

"Tell me your name," he demanded, sweeping her into his arms without even asking her if she'd like to dance with him.

Elena had seen the way he looked at her. She'd *felt*

it, like a brand, a claim, from halfway across the room. She told herself that Niccolo, who had gone to fetch her a drink, wouldn't mind *one dance*. They were in full view of half of Rome. It was all perfectly innocent.

She knew she was lying. And yet, somehow, she didn't care.

He was stunning. Overwhelmingly masculine, impossibly attractive and, she thought with a kind of dazed amazement, *hers*. Somehow hers. He looked at her and set her alight. He touched her, and her whole body burst into a hectic storm of sensation, like being dropped headfirst into freezing cold water at the height of summer.

"Your name," he urged her. His hands were on her, hard and hot, making her shiver uncontrollably. His dark head was bent to hers, putting that mesmerizing mouth of his much too close. Tempting her almost past endurance.

"Elena," she whispered. "Elena Calderon."

He repeated it, and made it into something else. A kind of song. It swelled in her, changing her. It hung there between them, like a vow.

"I am Alessandro," he said, and then they'd danced.

He swept her along, every step perfect, his attention on Elena as if she was the only woman in the room. The only woman alive. Lightning struck everywhere they touched, and everywhere they did not, and some shameless, heedless part of her gloried in it, as if she'd been made for this. For only this. For him.

She felt him in the treacherous ache of her breasts, the unmistakable hunger low in her belly and the glazed heat that held her in its relentless grip as surely as he did. She *felt him*—and understood that what she was doing was wrong. Utterly, indisputably wrong.

She understood that she would have to live with this. That this was a defining moment. That her life would be divided into before and after this scorching hot dance, and that she would never again be the person she'd believed she was before this stranger pulled her against him. But his eyes were locked to hers, filled with wonder and fire, and she didn't pull away. She didn't even try—and she understood she'd have to live with that, too.

And then he made it all so much worse.

"You cannot marry him," he said, those dark green eyes so fierce, his face so hard.

It took her longer than it should have to clear her head, to hear him. To hear an insult no engaged woman should tolerate. It was that part that penetrated, finally. That made her fully comprehend the depths of her betrayal.

"Who are you?" she demanded. But she still let him hold her in his arms, like she was something precious to him. Or like she wished she was. "What makes you think you can say something like that to me?"

"I am Alessandro Corretti," he bit out. She stiffened, and his voice dropped to an urgent, insistent growl. "And you know why I can say that. You feel this, too."

"Corretti…" she breathed, the reality of what she was doing, the scope of her treachery, like concrete blocks falling through her one after the next.

He saw it, reading her too easily. His dark eyes flashed.

"You cannot marry him," he said again, some kind of desperation beneath the autocratic demand in his voice. As if he knew her. As if he had the right. "He'll ruin you."

Elena would never know what might have happened then, had she not jerked her gaze away from Alessandro's in confusion—and seen Niccolo there at the side of the dance floor, glaring at the two of them with murder in his black eyes.

Elena was amazed that it was possible to hate herself so much, so fully. And that the shame didn't kill her where she stood.

"How dare you?" she ground out, all her horror at her own appalling actions in her voice. "I know who you are. I know *what* you are."

"What *I* am?" As if she'd stabbed him.

"Niccolo's told me all about you, and your family."

Something like a laugh. "Of course he has."

"The Correttis are nothing but a pack of violent thugs," she threw at him desperately, quoting Niccolo. "Criminals. One more stain on our country's honor."

"And Niccolo is the expert on honor, I suppose?" His face went thunderous, but his voice stayed cool. Quiet. Somehow, it made him that much more formidable. And it ripped into her like a knife.

"Do you think this will work?" she demanded, furious, and she convinced herself it was all directed at him. All *because* of him. "Do you really think you'll argue me into agreeing with you that *my fiancé*, the man I *love*, is some kind of—"

"You don't strike me as naive," he interrupted her, that fierce, dark edge in his voice, his gaze, even in his hands as he held her. "You must know better. You must."

He shook his head then, and she watched as bitter disappointment washed over him, turning his dark green eyes black. Making that fascinating mouth hard, nearly cruel. Making him look at her as if there had never been that fire between them, as if she couldn't still feel the flames, licking over her skin.

And she would never forgive herself, but she *ached*. She ached.

"Unless you like the money, the cars, the houses and the jewelry." His gaze was a jagged blade as it raked over her, and she bled. "The fancy dresses. Why ask where any of it comes from? Why face so many unpleasant truths?"

"Stop it!" she hissed at him.

"Ignorance is the best defense, I'm sure," he continued in that withering tone. "You can't be a stain on Italy's honor if you're careful not to know any of the sordid details, can you?"

None of this should be possible. A look, a dance, a few words with a total stranger—how could it *hurt?* How could she feel as if her whole world was ripping apart?

"You don't know what kind of woman I am," she told him, desperate to reclaim herself. To fix this. "And you never will. I have standards. I can't wait for Niccolo to do me the great honor of marrying me—to make me a Falco, too. I would never lower myself to Corretti scum like you. *Never.*"

He looked shattered for a moment, but only a moment. Then contempt moved over his fine, arrogant face, and made her stomach twist in an agony she shouldn't feel. He led her to the edge of the floor, gazed at her for one last, searing moment and then walked off into the crowd.

Elena told herself that wasn't grief she felt then, because it couldn't be. Not for a stranger. Not for a dance.

Not for a man she'd been so sure she'd never see again.

* * *

"I don't really remember," Elena said now in desperation, standing out on his terrace with only the sea to hear her lies. "It was a long time ago."

Alessandro only watched her, that wolf's smile sharp-edged, digging deep into her and leaving marks. He was much too close, and she hadn't forgotten a thing. Not a single thing.

"Then why are you blushing?" he asked, a knowing look on that battered, somehow even more attractive face—and her heart kicked hard against her ribs.

"I'm not spying on you," she gritted out, trying to break through the tension that gripped her. Trying to pretend he couldn't see into her so easily. "And if you really think I am, you should have let me leave with the boat."

But something had changed. His dark eyes burned. She felt the flames licking at her, seducing her and scaring her in equal measure.

"Alessandro." Saying his name was a mistake. She saw him react to it as if it was a caress, saw his intense focus on her sharpen, and it stole her breath away. "My being on your boat was a coincidence."

"Liar." Implacable. Fierce.

Elena's stomach knotted. She felt a deep kind of itch work through her, from her neck to her breasts to her core, and she felt a terrible panic bite at her then, as if she was in danger of losing herself completely.

You're supposed to be beating him at his own game! some last remnant of her self-control cried out inside her head.

"You can call me any names you like," she threw at him, desperate to find her balance again—to claw her way back to solid ground. "It won't change a thing. I met you once a long time ago. It wasn't particularly memorable."

That ruthless, cynical mouth kicked up in the corner, and his gaze turned jet black. It rolled through her, too hot to bear, shaking her apart from the inside out. Until there was nothing at all but this moment.

This. Him. Now.

"Such a liar," he whispered.

He reached out as if to touch her, but she knew she couldn't let that happen—*she couldn't*—so she threw out her own hand to catch his.

Skin against skin, after all this time. The same way their hands had touched once before, on that glimmering dance floor far away.

And they both caught fire.

The sea and the sun and the whole bright world disappeared into the blaze of it. There was only this man, who she should have run from the moment she'd seen him six months ago. This man, who had eyes like thunder and saw straight through into the heart of her. This man, who had claimed her from across a crowded room with a single, searing glance.

There was only the riot inside of her, the electricity that roared between them. *Skin to skin.* At last.

Neither one of them moved. Elena wasn't sure she breathed. This disastrous, unquenchable attraction seemed to swell and grow, radiating from his hand to hers, a hard, gnawing ache that every heartbeat only made worse. It penetrated every part of her, and made her want. Crave. *Need.*

"It haunts you," he said, a dark, male hunger stamped across his face. "I haunt you. Believe me, Elena. I know."

She jerked her hand from his. But as she did, she had a searing burst of clarity.

She wanted him. She always had. It didn't matter that it didn't make sense, that a single dance should never have affected her so much. It had. *He* had. And that wanting had ripped apart her world, changed everything. She'd been paying for it for six long months, in isolation and often in fear, moving from odd job to odd job across the whole of Italy, trying to keep herself out of sight and away from Niccolo.

All because of this. All because of Alessandro.

She had already been crucified for this crime. She paid for it every day. Why not commit it?

And if there was a part of her that knew that this was also the best way to prove to Alessandro that she was exactly the kind of woman he believed her to be, that this would cement his opinion of her, she told herself that only made the decision easier.

"This isn't a haunting," she whispered, watching the thunder roll through his eyes. "Neither one of us is a ghost." She smiled then. "I can prove it."

And then she indulged the roaring inside of her, that terrible hunger, and put her hands on him.

Not a light touch on his shoulder as she had when they'd danced, polite and appropriate. She slid her palms over the whisper-soft cotton that strained against his marvelous torso, and felt the pure, raw heat of him. The iron strength. Her head spun, dizzy and delicious.

Alessandro let out a sound that was almost a laugh, and then he tugged her closer, lifting her up against him. Her aching breasts pressed hard against his beautiful chest, sending a frantic shiver through her, and he muttered a curse. He settled her on the rail, his arms strong and hard and exquisite as they held her fast. She heard her boat shoes fall off, two loud slaps against the stone floor, and then she forgot them.

Alessandro stepped between her legs, and it wasn't enough. Her skirt kept him from pressing against her, into her, even as he leaned into the palms she'd flattened against him. She was surprised to see her hands were shaking. She was shaking. Or maybe the world was, all around them, and she didn't care.

This was finally happening. *Finally.*

He held her with one hand in the small of her back, hot and hard and *his*, while his other hand moved to her neck, her jaw, tracing patterns. Igniting her. And it wasn't *enough*—

"Look at me," he commanded her, that low voice of his snaking through her like a brushfire, making her skin seem to pull tight over her bones, and she would do anything. Anything he wanted. Anything at all.

Anything to keep them both burning like this.

His dark green eyes flashed, triumph and fire, and that wonder she knew was only theirs. Only this. His mouth looked nearly grim with need, and she knew she should be afraid. Of him. Of what was about to happen—what had always been going to happen, sooner or later.

But again, she felt only that wild passion. That desire. And that conviction that she was safer now, in his clever, dangerous hands, than she had been in months.

"Inevitable," she whispered before she knew she meant to speak, and the faintest hint of a smile moved across his mouth, then was gone.

"Hold on," he ordered her with a gruff intent that made her core seem to glow.

He moved his hands to cradle her face between them, and she grabbed his shirt in greedy fists.

At last, that voice chanted inside of her, again and again. *At last.*

And then he took her mouth with all of that ruthlessness and command, and Elena lost her mind.

CHAPTER THREE

HOT. WILD.

She was his.

And she kissed him back as if she wanted to devour him, too.

As if he'd set her on fire and this was how they'd burn, together, in this tumult of heat and glory, and her perfect mouth he couldn't taste enough.

She was better—this was better—than Alessandro had dared imagine in the middle of a hundred nights, when he'd pictured this in stark detail. When the dark fury that she could bewitch him as she had and be so much less of a person than he'd hoped didn't matter.

It didn't matter now, either. Need stormed through him, making him closer to desperate than he'd ever been before.

He wanted her skin against his, slick and sweet. He wanted his hands on those tempting breasts, her enchanting curves. He wanted to lick between her legs and stay there until she screamed. He wanted deep inside of her. *He wanted*. And every kiss, every taste, every little way she moved against him, only drove him higher.

"More," he said, and he picked her up again, yanking that damned skirt up and over her hips.

Deep masculine elation pounded through him when she lifted her legs and wrapped herself around him. And then he was there. Hard and hot against her melting heat, separated only by his trousers and the slightest wisp of material she wore. A delicate shudder moved through her, and for a moment he thought he might lose control.

But Alessandro wanted her too much, and had for too long. He took her mouth again, thrilled when she met him with a passion he could taste. She arched against him, her arms wrapped around his neck, and it wasn't enough.

It would never be enough.

He carried her to one of the loungers scattered about the terrace, then set her down. She was unsteady on her feet, her blue eyes wide and dazed, bright with need, and he wanted her more than he'd ever wanted anyone else. More than he'd imagined it was possible to want.

"Please," Elena said, her voice ragged with desire. The most beautiful thing he'd ever heard. "Don't stop."

Her hands were still on his chest, and he could feel each touch, each caress, directly in his sex. He kissed her again, deep and demanding, ravaging her mouth, and she thrilled him by returning it in kind.

Out of control. So good it hurt. Again. And again.

"These clothes need to come off," he muttered, pulling his mouth away from hers.

Alessandro moved to tug her T-shirt over her head, then hissed out a breath when he threw it aside and she stood there before him, bared to the waist. No bra to block him from her perfect breasts, small and round, with nipples like hard, ripe points. Lovely beyond reason. He nearly shook as his hands went to her skirt, working the zipper and then grabbing on to her panties as he tugged all of it down over her hips and out of his way.

And then Elena was naked. Gloriously, beautifully naked, and she was real and *here* and his. Finally his.

For a moment he only stared at her, a kind of awe sweeping through him as his body went wild, so desperate for her he could hardly bear it. He swept her up and then took her down with him, splaying her out above him as he lay back on the chaise.

Elena twisted against him, and then her frantic hands were on the hem of his T-shirt and he sat up slightly to peel it off. He brushed her hands out of the way to rid himself of his trousers, kicking them aside. And when he pulled her back into place they both sighed in something like reverence. And then she was like silk against him, all over him, soft and naked and hot.

Finally.

Alessandro's heart pounded. He was so hard it bordered on the painful, and then she rolled her hips and moved all of that slick, wet heat against the length of him, and he groaned. He traced the line of her spine down to her bottom, and then bent to take one of those achingly perfect nipples into his mouth. She made a wild, greedy sort of noise, and he couldn't wait. He couldn't take another moment of this magnificent torture.

It had been too long already. It had been forever.

He sat up, holding her against him, her soft thighs falling on either side of his. She knelt astride him, her hands moving from his chest to his shoulders, then burying themselves in his hair. Alessandro reached down between them, sinking his fingers deep inside the molten core of her.

She cried out, and he loved it. He tested her slickness, learned her lush shape, his palm hard against the center of her need. He watched her pretty face flush, felt her hips buck against his hand, and he returned to her breasts, sucking a taut nipple into his mouth and then biting down. Just hard enough.

She broke apart in his arms with a wordless cry, hot and wet in his hand, her head falling forward until her face was pressed into his neck. He lifted her in his arms while she still shook and shuddered, and then he thrust hard and deep inside her.

At last.

She was scalding hot, so deliciously soft, and still in the grips of her climax when he began to move. Alessandro held her hips in his hands and guided her into the rhythm he wanted. Slow, but demanding, catching the fire that was tearing her apart and building it up again with every stroke.

Higher. Hotter. Hungrier.

He heard her breath catch again, felt her stiffen, heard the shocked sound she made in his ear. She gripped his shoulders tight and shook all around him again, just as he wanted. He watched her arch back into the sunlight—so painfully, perfectly beautiful. This woman, *his woman*, lost to her pleasure, mindless and writhing against him, while he moved hard and deep inside of her.

He rolled them over on the lounger, coming on top of her and deeper into her. Alessandro let his head drop down next to hers, and then her arms wrapped around him, her hips meeting his in a wild, uncontrollable dance.

He felt her move beneath him, heard her gasp anew, and each hitch in her breath, each mindless cry, made him want her more. He was so deep inside of her, and they moved together like a dream—like a dream he'd had a thousand times, only much slicker, much hotter, much better.

And this time, when she began to break apart around him, when she threw her head back once more and arched up against him, Alessandro called out her name like the incantation it was and fell right along with her.

Elena came back to herself slowly. Painfully.

She was tucked up against Alessandro's side. He was sprawled out on the lounger beside her, one arm thrown over his head, looking for all the world like some kind of lazy, sated god. There was no reason he should be so appealing, even now, with his dark lashes closed, his arrogant features with the marks of the previous night's violence stamped into his skin. And yet…

She sat up gingerly, surprised her body still felt at all like her own when he'd made it his—made her his—with such devastating completeness. Her body still hummed with pleasure. So much pleasure Elena could hardly believe she'd survived it, that she was still in one piece.

Then again, perhaps she wasn't.

He shifted, and she felt his hand on her back, smoothing its way down to curl possessively over her hip. Impossibly, she felt something in her catch anew. A spark where there should have been nothing but ash and burned-out embers.

Surely this was the end of it. Succumbing to what had burned so bright between them had to have destroyed it, didn't it? But his fingers traced a lazy alphabet across her skin, spreading that fierce glow deep into her all over again, making her realize this wasn't over at all.

Elena had made a terrible mistake, she understood then. There were many ways to pay, and she'd just discovered a brand-new one. Perhaps, on some level, she'd held out the hope that what had surged between them was all smoke, no fire. That indulging it would defeat it.

Now she knew better. Now she knew exactly how hot they burned. She would have to live with that, too.

"Come here," he said, and she felt his voice move in her like magic, making her chest feel tight.

Despite herself, she turned. She looked down at him, bracing herself for a smug expression, a cocky smile—but that hard gaze of his was serious when it met hers. Almost contemplative. And that was worse, because she had no defense against it.

He reached up and traced a lazy line from her collarbone down over the upper swell of her breasts, and there was a dangerous gleam in his eyes when she caught his hand in hers and stopped him.

"Alessandro…" she began, but she didn't know what to say.

He didn't respond. Instead, he tugged her back down beside him, surrounding her once again with all that warm male strength. As if she were safe, she thought in a kind of despair. As if she'd finally come home.

When she knew perfectly well neither one of those things were true.

His gaze darkened as he watched her. He slid a hand around to the nape of her neck, but she was the one who closed the distance between them, pressing her mouth to his, spurred on by a great wealth of emotion she didn't want to understand.

This time, there should have been no wild explosion, no impossible heat. This time, she should have been more in control of herself, of all these things she didn't want to feel.

But his mouth moved on hers and something incandescent poured through her, lighting her up all over again. She felt that spark ignite, felt that same fire grow again inside of her. His kiss was tender, something like loving, and it ripped her into pieces.

She kissed him back, desperately, letting her hands learn his fascinating body all over again, letting herself disappear into this madness that she knew perfectly well would destroy her. It was only a matter of time.

And this time when he slid into her it was a different kind of fire. Slow, deliberate. It stripped her bare, made her eyes fill with tears, battered what was left of her defenses, her carefully constructed veneers. He gazed down at her as he moved inside of her, his dark eyes grave and something more she didn't want to name, as he spun this wicked fire around them.

As he wrecked her totally, inside and out, and she loved every second of it.

And then he pushed them both straight over the edge of the world.

When she woke a second time, the sun was beginning to sink toward the sea, bathing the sky in peaches and golds, and Alessandro wasn't next to her. Elena sat up in confusion, only realizing as she almost let it slide from her that she was draped in something deliciously silky. A robe, she discovered when she frowned down at it.

She pulled it on as she stood, belting it around her waist, and when she looked up she saw him.

He sat at a nearby table in the gathering dusk, a wineglass in one hand, his gaze trained on her. He hadn't bothered with his shirt. A quick glance assured her he was wearing those loose, soft trousers, low on his narrow hips. That lean, smoothly muscled body was even more beautiful from a distance and now, of course, she knew what he could do with it. *She knew.* She snapped her attention back to his face—and went still.

He was watching her with an expression that made her breath catch in her throat. She recognized that look. This was the Alessandro Corretti she remembered, brooding and dark.

And it seemed he'd remembered that he hated her.

Elena steeled herself. It was better this way. This was what she'd wanted. She ran her hands down the front of the silk robe, but then stopped, not wanting him to see any hint of her agitation.

"Sit down," he said, indicating the table before him and the selection of platters spread out across its inlaid mosaic surface. His voice was cold. Impersonal. A slap after what they'd shared, and she was sure he knew it. "You must be hungry."

The moment he said it she realized she was ravenous, and she told herself that was the only reason she obeyed him and sat. Alessandro seethed with a dark menace, lounging there with such studied carelessness, watching her with a slight curl to his lip.

She'd expected this, she reminded herself. She'd known sleeping with him would make him despise her, would confirm his low opinion of her, when he believed her still engaged to Niccolo and all manner of other, horrible things. But it shocked her how much it hurt to see it, how it clawed into her, threatening to spill out of her eyes. She blinked it away.

And then she settled herself in the seat across from him as if she hadn't a care in the world, and gazed down at the food spread out before her. A plate of plump, ripe cheeses, tangy cured meats and an assortment of thick, lush spreads—an olive tapenade, a fragrant Greek-style taramasalata—next to a basket of fresh, golden semolina bread. A serving dish piled high with what looked like an interesting take on the traditional Sicilian caponata, a cooked aubergine salad laden here with succulent morsels of seafood, rich black and green olives and sweet asparagus spears.

Elena took the wine he poured for her, a rich and hearty red, and sipped at it, letting the mellow taste wash over her, wash her clean. She tried to match his seeming insouciance, leaning back in her chair and holding her glass airily, as if she spent most of her evenings with her various lovers in their magnificent island estates. As if this—as if he—was nothing but run of the mill.

"It's quite good," she said, because she thought she should say something.

Not for the first time, she was painfully aware of how deeply unsophisticated she really was—how categorically unsuited to playing in these deep, dark waters with men like him. Niccolo had dressed her up and taught her how to play the part, but here, now, she was forcefully reminded that she was only Elena Calderon, a nobody from a remote village no one had ever heard of, descended from a long line of mostly fishermen. She was out of her league, and then some.

Alessandro only watched her. Something about that cold regard, that dark, silent fury, made her feel raw. Restless.

"Alessandro Corretti with nothing to say?" She attempted a smile. "Shocking."

"Tell me," he said in that calm, easy way that only emphasized the deadly edge beneath. "When you run back to your fiancé and tell him what you did here, how detailed a picture will you paint for him? When you tell him you slept with a man he loathes, will you also tell him how many times you screamed my name?"

Elena paled, even though she knew she shouldn't— that she should have expected this. That she *had* expected this. Her fingers clenched hard on the stem of her glass.

"Or perhaps that's how he likes it. Perhaps he enjoys picturing his woman naked and weeping with ecstasy in another man's arms." His eyes were like coals, hot and black. "Perhaps this is a game the two of you play, and I am only the latest in a long line of targets. Perhaps you are the bullet he aims at his enemies, then laughs about it later."

Elena congratulated herself on achieving precisely what she'd set out to achieve, and in spades. She told herself his opinion of her didn't matter. That the worse it was, the better. The less he thought of her, the less he'd feel compelled to betray her to Niccolo. She took another nonchalant sip of her wine, and ordered herself to enjoy her curiously bitter-tasting triumph.

"Niccolo is a man of many passions," she said, and was perversely satisfied by the flash of temper in his gaze.

"Never mind what that makes you."

She glared at him, determined not to let him see he'd landed a blow. She reminded herself that she could only be used as a bargaining chip if he believed she had some worth.

"Are you calling me a whore?" she asked softly. *This is good,* she assured herself. *This is what you want.*

But even the air seemed painful, shattering all around her. As if it was as broken as she felt.

"Is this some kind of twisted retribution for Rome?" he asked after long moments passed, no hint of green in those dark eyes of his.

"I'm not the one who started this," Elena threw at him before she had time to consider it. Not that he was the first man to think she was a whore, not that Niccolo hadn't covered the same ground extensively—but somehow, this didn't feel anything like the triumph it should have been. It hurt. "I was perfectly happy on that boat. But you had to sweep in and ruin everything, the same way you did—"

She cut herself off, appalled at what she'd nearly said. Her heart was rioting in her chest, and she was afraid to look at him—afraid of what she'd see. Or what he would.

"By all means," he invited her, his voice silk and stone. "Finish what you were saying. What else did I ruin?"

She would never know how she pulled herself together then, enough to look at him with clear eyes and something like a smile on her mouth.

"That was the first ball I'd ever attended, my first night in Rome," she said, light and something like airy, daring him to refute her. "I felt like a princess. And you ruined it."

"You have no comprehension whatsoever of the damage you do, do you?" He shook his head. "You're like an earthquake, leaving nothing but rubble in your wake."

It's like he knows, a little voice whispered, directly into that dark place inside of her where she hated herself the most. *Like he knows what you nearly let happen.*

She set her glass back down on the table with a sharp click. "I don't know what you want from me."

"I would have thought that much was clear," he replied, a self-mocking curve to that hard mouth she knew too well now. Far too well. "If nothing else. I want you, Elena. Then. Now. Still. God help us both."

Elena clenched her hands together in her lap, everything inside of her seeming to squeeze tight and *ache.* Something deep and heavy sat over the table as the sun disappeared for good, and soft lights came on to illuminate the terrace. She could feel it pressing down on her, into her, and the way he was looking at her didn't help.

"No clever reply to that?" His voice then was quiet, yet no less lethal, and it sliced into her like a jagged blade. "I don't know what lies you tell yourself. I can't imagine. But I know you want me, too."

She shook her head as if that might clear it, pulling

in a breath as if that might help. When she looked at him again, she wasn't playing her part. She couldn't.

"I want you," she said in a low voice, letting all of the ways she loathed herself show, letting it all bleed out between them, letting it poison him, too. "I always have. And I'll never forgive myself for it."

She thought he looked shaken then, for the briefest moment, but he blinked it away. And he was too hard again, too fierce. She told herself she'd seen only what she wanted to see. He sat forward, those dark, cruel eyes fixed on her, and she reminded herself that nothing shook this man. Nothing could. Especially not minor little earthquakes like her.

"Congratulations, Elena," he said, his voice a sardonic lash. "I believe that's the first honest thing you've said to me since you told me your name."

She had to wrench her gaze away from his then, while she ordered herself to stay calm. To tamp down the chaotic emotions that surged inside of her, taking her over, making her want nothing more than to sob—once again—for something she could never have. Something she never should have wanted in the first place.

Unbidden, images of what they'd done together, here on this very same terrace, skated through her mind. His mouth, those hands. The wild heat of him, his impossible strength and his ruthless, intense possession—

Something occurred to her then, slamming through her as hard and as vicious as if he'd punched her in the gut. He might as well have. It couldn't have been worse.

She had been on birth control pills throughout her relationship with Niccolo, but the past six months had been so hectic. She'd run away and run out of the pills, and she hadn't wanted to leave any kind of record of where she'd been—so no doctors. She hadn't imagined it would be an issue. And then, today, she'd simply forgotten she wasn't protected.

She'd forgotten.

"We didn't use anything," she gasped out, so appalled she could hardly get the words past her lips. She felt numb with horror.

Alessandro went still. Too still. And for the first time in their brief, impossible acquaintance, she couldn't read a thing in the narrow, considering gaze he aimed at her. She could only see the darkness.

"I'm clean," he said. Cool and concise. And nothing more.

And the caustic slap of that helped her, strangely. It reminded her who she was, what she was doing here. Why she'd decided to give in to her desire for him in the first place.

"You think I'm a liar and I know very well you are," she said, trying for a calm tone. "You'll excuse me if I have no particular reason to believe you."

Temper streaked across that arrogant face of his. "You know I'm a liar, do you?" His deceptively gentle tone made her skin prickle. "And how exactly do you know that?"

She laughed, deliberately callous. "Because I know your name."

A deep blackness flashed through his dark green eyes and over his face then, old and resigned, with the faint hint of some kind of pain, and Elena fought off a sharp stab of regret. She shouldn't care if she hurt this man's feelings. He certainly didn't care if he hurt hers. So why couldn't she stave off the bizarre urge to apologize? To trust him the way that insane part of her urged her to do?

But even as she opened her mouth to do exactly that, she stopped herself. Because their carelessness had changed everything. She knew enough about him to know that he would never send her back to Niccolo if he thought she might be carrying his baby. Not a proud man like Alessandro. Not when the blood between the Falcos and the Correttis had been notoriously bad for generations.

Which meant, after all of this, she really was as safe as she'd always felt with him.

It should have felt something more than hollow.

But she had to keep going no matter how it felt. She had to push this to its logical extreme. This was her chance to stay hidden away in a place Niccolo could never find her. In a place he'd never dream or dare to look.

"I could be pregnant," she said, steeling herself to the look on his face then, to her own intense horror at what she was doing. But she had no other option. There was so little time left, and she couldn't let Niccolo find her. She would do anything to keep that from happening, even this.

"I'm familiar with the risks," Alessandro bit out, temper still dark on his face, in his eyes, shading his firm mouth. "Why the hell aren't you protected?"

Elena eyed him across the table. "I wasn't aware that the sole responsibility for protection fell to me. Were you not equally involved?"

He muttered a harsh, Sicilian word beneath his breath, and she was perfectly happy she couldn't understand the dialect even after her time there.

She reached out to one of the platters, scooping up some of the olive tapenade with a piece of the fragrant bread and settling back to nibble at it as if she hadn't a care in the world.

"It will be fine, I'm sure," she said. She met his

gaze and allowed herself a callous smirk. "Niccolo will never know the difference."

Alessandro actually jerked in his chair. His face went white.

"Over my dead body will you pass off a child of mine as his," he said hoarsely, so furious he nearly lit up the night with it. "Over my dead body, Elena—or yours."

She smiled. It didn't matter that he looked at her as if she revolted him completely. It didn't matter that she hated herself, that she thought she might be sick from this terrible manipulation. It didn't even matter that she really might be pregnant, which she couldn't let herself consider. It only mattered that she kept herself safe, one way or another, for this little while longer. Whatever the cost.

And the truth was, she knew somehow Alessandro would never hurt her. Hate her, perhaps, but never hurt her, and after all these months that was the same thing as safe. And it was a far better bargain than being with a man like Niccolo, who had pretended to love her and would likely put her in the hospital if he caught up with her.

"Then we'll count a month from today," she said smoothly, as if she'd never had any doubt that it would end this way. That she would get what she wanted. "Plus an extra ten days or so, as these things are so inexact. And we'll see if any dead bodies are necessary, won't we?"

His jaw was tight and hard, his gaze like bullets. "Forty days. On my island. Alone. With me."

He stared at her for a long moment, and she made herself look back at him, shameless and terrible, the woman he'd always believed she was and far worse than he'd imagined. This was her protection. This brazen, horrible creature she'd become, this calculated act. This was how she'd save herself, and the things she held dear.

"Or I could text you," she offered.

His face was drawn, that serious mouth grim. And his eyes were like the night around them, haunted and destroyed. This was what she'd done. This was what security looked like.

This was one more thing she'd have to live with when all of this was done.

"Just remember," he said, threat and promise laced through that low voice, bright in his dark eyes. "You asked for this."

CHAPTER FOUR

IT WAS WORSE now that he knew, Alessandro thought days later.

Worse now that he'd touched her, tasted her, held her. Lost himself inside her. There was no unknowing her exquisite heat, her lithe body wrapped around his as if she'd been created for that alone. For him. There was no forgetting it.

Alessandro didn't understand how he could know what he knew and still want her. How she could have used their carelessness as leverage, making him wonder if it had been carelessness on her part at all—and yet, he still wanted her.

He sickened himself.

"You don't need to look at me like that," she'd said the other morning out by the pool, not looking up from the glossy English magazine he assumed one of his unfailingly efficient staff had provided for her. Better to focus on that than what she looked like in a scalding red bikini hardly big enough to lick over the curves it displayed. Better to ignore how much he wanted to lick those curves himself. "I'm aware of what you think of me. The dark and terrible glare is overkill."

"This glare is the only thing between you and my temper," he'd replied, making no attempt to cushion her from the thrust of that temper in his voice. "I'd be more grateful for it, were I you."

"And what will you do if you lose it?" Elena had asked, sounding bored. She'd angled a look at him then over the rims of her dark glasses. "Hate me even more? By all means. Try."

It had taken everything he had not to cross over to her then and there and teach her exactly where his temper would lead. Exactly where it would take them both. The hot glory of the way they could burn each other alive. Only the fact that he wanted it too badly, and was furious at himself for that shocking deficiency in his character, kept him from it.

Alessandro stood up on one of the terraces now, looking out over the sweep of land that made up the rest of the island behind his house. On the far side of the tennis court was the small meadow that ran down to the rocky shore, late-spring grasses and early-summer flowers preening beneath the June sun. Scrappy pines and elegant palm trees scraped the sky.

Stout fruit trees displayed their wares—lemons and oranges and leafy almonds. Seagulls floated in the wind, calling out their lonely little songs. And in the center of all that natural beauty was Elena.

Elena. Always Elena.

He'd been so furious that first night he was glad she'd removed herself shortly after dropping her little bombshell about her possible pregnancy—and her intention to stay here, with him. He'd drunk his way into what passed for sleep and had woken the next morning determined to regain the upper hand he never should have yielded in the first place.

She wanted to stay on his island to further some twisted agenda of her own? She wanted to play this game of consequences with him? *Va bene.* Then she would have to deal with what she'd put into action. And she'd have to face him while she did it.

"I'll expect you at dinner," he'd told her that first morning. "Every night."

She'd been walking into the cheerful breakfast room then, its floor-to-ceiling glass windows pulled back to let the morning in. She'd hardly looked at him as she'd helped herself to the carafe of the strong Indonesian coffee he preferred to the more traditional, milky cappuccinos.

"Your expectations are your own, Alessandro," she'd said almost sweetly when she'd turned back from the simple, wood-carved sideboard to face him, balancing her coffee cup in her hands.

She'd worn a huge, shapeless sundress, swaddling herself in cheery turquoise from her neck to her toes, and topped off with one of those flimsy, gauzy wrap things that served no discernible purpose at all but to conceal her figure.

He'd liked the idea that she'd felt she had to hide herself from him. That he'd got at least that far beneath her treacherous skin, that he hadn't been the only one feeling battered that morning.

"If you want to hold me captive on my own island for forty days, that's the price."

"The price is too high."

He'd smiled. "You really won't like my alternate plan. Trust me."

"I told you I'd be happy to go my merry way and let you know what happens," she'd replied, her expression cool but her blue eyes a shade darker than usual. "You were the one who started ranting on about dead bodies. I don't see why I should have to subject myself to more of the same over dinner."

"Afraid you won't be able to control yourself?" he'd taunted her. "Will I be forced to fend off your advances over pasta alla Norma, Elena? Defend what remains of my virtue over the soup?"

Her blue eyes had blazed. "Unlikely."

"Then I fail to see the problem," he'd said, still smiling, though his gaze had been a challenge and demand on hers.

Her mouth had curved slightly then, that cool slap of a smile he'd already come to loathe.

"Also unlikely," she'd replied.

He'd lounged there in his chair and looked at her for a moment, enjoying himself despite the pounding in his head, the stark disillusionment in his heart. Despite what he knew about her now. Despite his own weakness for her that even her distasteful manipulations couldn't erase.

"I warned you," he'd said softly. Deliberately. "You wanted this."

"I wanted—" But she'd thought better of whatever she'd been about to say, and had pressed her lips together.

"Be careful what you wish for next, *cara,*" he'd advised her silkily. "You might get that, too."

Alessandro moved farther out on the terrace now, frowning down at her. That exchange had been days ago. He'd spent a good hour this morning working out his weakness in his pool, swimming lap after lap and still not managing to shift this thing off him that made him want her like this. That made him hunger for her no matter how little he liked her.

That made him *long* and *yearn* and *wish*, like he was someone else entirely.

Or as if she was.

She sat out in his sweet-smelling meadow on a bright orange blanket, her eyes closed and her head tipped back, soaking in the sunshine like some kind of flower. Like something utterly innocent, clean and pure. His mouth twisted. She wore a short, flirty dress in a pale yellow color that left her golden-skinned arms and legs bare, then tucked in at her delectable waist to highlight the unmistakable elegance of her lean, slender form.

He let his gaze trace the beautiful lines of her face, that perfectly lush mouth and the loose waves of the blond hair that she hadn't pulled back again since that first night. It danced around her in the ocean breeze, the color of country butter with hints of white-blond, as well, and he hated that she could be so pretty, so effortlessly lovely, when he knew the sordid truth about her.

She was engaged to Niccolo Falco, and she'd slept with him, anyway.

He couldn't understand why that alone wasn't the end of this pitched battle inside of him. Why that simple fact didn't end this need for her that still burned him up and kept him from his sleep. It should have been all he needed to dismiss her from his thoughts entirely. He was not the kind of man who enjoyed poaching, unlike his cousin Matteo. He got no pleasure from finding himself in the middle of other people's relationships. Life was complicated enough, he'd always thought, and his own parents' squalid legacy had seemed to confirm it. Why cause himself more trouble?

After all, he had more than his share already. It was his birthright.

He'd spent the bulk of the morning fuming over his voice mail and most of his text and email messages, sending his beleaguered assistant increasingly terse instructions to deal with whatever came up as best he could, and not to bother Alessandro with any of it unless it was an emergency. An objectively dire one. The various pleas and attempts to draw him out from friends and family he deleted without a reply—all except for Santo, who got a terse line indicating that Alessandro was alive, and only because his messages had focused on Alessandro's well-being instead of the family.

His goddamned family.

He wasn't coming home to sort out the cursed business deal his aborted wedding had left in tatters. He didn't want to know that his illegitimate half-brother, Angelo, ignored all his life by their father and understandably furious about it, was making his move at last. He wasn't interested in what the latest Corretti family scandal was now that he'd removed himself. He didn't want to hear his mother's pathetic excuses for the way she'd savaged his sister, Rosa, in earshot of most of Palermo society, dropping the truth of her parentage on her like a loud, drunken guillotine. He didn't care where his runaway bride had gone and he certainly didn't want to join in the speculation about whether or not his cousin Matteo had gone with her.

He wanted to be numb. He wanted to encase himself in ice and steel and feel nothing, ever again. No useless sense of duty. No pathetic compulsion to play the rescuer, the hero, for his endlessly needy family members, none of whom ever quite appreciated it. No useless longing for a woman who neither deserved it nor wanted it.

No wondering what it was in him that was so twisted, so ruined and corrupt and despicable, that the bride he'd carefully arranged and contracted abandoned him at the altar and the beautiful stranger he'd fallen for so disastrously at a glance wanted nothing more than to use him for her own ends.

He wanted to be numb.

But if he couldn't be numb, he decided then, staring down at her luxuriating in all of that sunlight, he might as well explore that darkness inside of him that he'd fought his whole life.

Elena wanted to play her games with him. Dangerous games, because she thought she was dealing with another brutish thug like her fiancé. Maybe he should give her what she wanted. Maybe he should bring out the whole of his arsenal in return.

Maybe it was finally time to be who he was: a Corretti, callous and selfish, destined for nothing but depravity from the moment of his birth.

Just like all the rest of them. Just like the father he'd always despised.

"I want to be inside you," Alessandro said casually. He was standing at the windows, his back to her. "Now."

Elena froze in her seat. She set her fork down carefully.

She'd grown used to these long, fraught meals they shared each night, prodding each other for weaknesses. She'd come to enjoy the strange exhilaration she got from matching wits with him, so different from meals with Niccolo—who had done the talking while she'd sat there adoringly, grateful for her good luck.

She'd grown used to the dark looks he sent her way whenever he saw her, cold condemnation and a banked fury, a far cry from the flat coldness she'd once seen in Niccolo's eyes, moments before he'd showed her who he really was. She'd told herself she was used to this by now. To Alessandro himself. To all this forced exposure to the man who had chased her through dreams for six long months.

"I gave in to that urge once already," she murmured. "And look what's happened."

She hadn't thought to worry about sex.

She hadn't imagined it would be an issue, after that first day. He'd looked at her as if he'd rather die than touch her again, and she'd told herself she was glad of it.

Of course she was.

"I might be pregnant," she reminded him now, though she tried to think of it as little as possible. It was too much to take in. She kept that faintly amused note in her voice. "And we are trapped here, strangers who think the worst of each other. I'll pass on a reprise, thank you."

"This table will do well enough," he continued as if she hadn't spoken, turning so she could see his starkly sensual expression. And that passion in his dark green eyes. Elena's heart gave a hard kick to her ribs, and she felt much too warm, suddenly. "All you need to do is bend over."

The image exploded through her, too vivid, too real. It didn't take much effort at all to imagine him behind her, deep inside her—

"You've obviously had too much to drink," she said. She pressed her napkin to her mouth, more to check that she wasn't trembling than to wipe anything away. She had to stay calm, focused. She had to remember why she was here, why she was doing this.

"Does it make you feel better to think so?" He smiled, and the heat of it catapulted her back to that night in Rome. That dance. The way he'd looked at her, smiled at her, as if she was precious to him. "I haven't. But I want you either way."

She forced a cool smile, and tried to force the past from her head. "You can't have me."

"Why not?" He looked amused, his face carved in those fiercely sensual, powerfully masculine lines, his dark eyes gleaming. Elena fought to restrain her shivery reaction, to ignore that melting, pulling sensation low in her belly. "You've already betrayed your fiancé. What does it matter now how many times you do it?"

She was shocked by how easily he could hurt her, when he should never have had that kind of power in the first place. She should have been pleased that he hated her so openly, that he disdained her so completely. She'd gone out of her way to make sure he did. Instead, it hurt. *It hurt.*

But she couldn't show him that. She could only show him what he wanted to see—what he already saw. A cold, hard woman. Brazen and base.

"I don't like to repeat myself," she said, holding his gaze. "It's boring."

She expected the lash of his temper, but Alessandro laughed. It made the green in his eyes brighten, and worse, made everything inside of her seem to squeeze tight. Breath, belly, core. Even her traitorous heart.

"But you're the one in control, are you not?" he asked, too arrogant, too confident, to believe what he was saying. "Your wish is my command. If you're bored, you need only demand that I relieve it and I will." His smile took on that wolfish edge. "I'm very inventive."

She had a sinking sensation then, as if she'd somehow strayed into quicksand and was moments away from being sucked under. *Think*, she ordered herself in a panic. *Turn this around!*

"And that's all it takes?" She arched her brows high in disbelief. "I need only click my fingers and you'll serve my every whim?"

"Of course." The amusement on his ruthless face did nothing to ease the fierceness of it. And the lie on his lips was laced with laughter. "I am powerless in the face of your machinations, Elena."

Her pulse was wild in her veins, and she felt like prey—like he was stalking her when he hadn't moved. He only stood there, his hands thrust deep in his pockets, and she felt as if she was running hard and scared with his hot breath *right there* on the back of her neck—

"Somehow," she managed to say, her voice cool and dry rather than panicked, though it cost her, "I have trouble seeing you as *quite* that submissive."

"But this is what you want," he replied in that soft, taunting way, his dark eyes alight. "Isn't that why we're here at all? You demanded it. I obeyed."

Elena had to leave. Now. She had to shut this down before she betrayed herself, before she gave in to the need blazing through her. She would lock herself inside her room, ignore the emptiness and yearning inside of her, and pretend she was locking him out rather than keeping herself in. All she had to do was walk away from him.

She stood in a rush, aware she gave herself away with the speed of it, the total lack of grace. His hard mouth moved into that devastating curve that seemed to curl into the very core of her, making her soften. Ache. She couldn't trust herself to stay, to try to act her way through this. She wanted to run for the door, but she made herself walk instead. As if she was making a simple choice to leave. As if she didn't already feel pursued when he still hadn't moved a muscle.

"I'm not going to chase you through the house, Elena." His voice slid over her, dark and insinuating. Finding its way into her deepest, blackest, most secret corners, far away from any light. Deep into the places she pretended weren't there. "Unless you ask nicely.

Is that what you need? Permission to scream *no* at the top of your lungs and know I'll take you, anyway? No responsibility, no regrets?"

The shudder that worked through her then was fierce and deep, involuntary, and she couldn't pretend it had anything to do with revulsion. She felt weak. Weak and desperate. She had to stop walking, had to reach out and hold on to the wall near the wide, arching doorway. She had to fight to keep from revealing how tempted she was, how twisted that made her. She had to keep from confirming what he already seemed to know.

"I don't—" she began desperately, but he sighed impatiently, cutting her off.

"No more lies. Not about this."

Alessandro was leaning back against one of the windows when she turned to look at him again, but nothing about him was languid. She could see his coiled strength, his seething power. He was dressed all in white tonight, and should have looked relaxed. Casual. But he looked more to her like a warrior king, surveying the field of battle and entirely too confident of his own impending victory.

He smiled again, and she felt it bloom inside of her, almost like pain. That low, impossible almost-pain that never entirely left her and that pulsed now, bright and demanding and hungry. Between her legs. In the fullness of her breasts. Even behind her eyes.

"I didn't realize you wanted to play games," she said stiffly, because she had to say something, and she was rapidly forgetting all the reasons why she couldn't simply throw herself at him and worry about it later.

"Of course you did." Laughter lurked in his voice again, gleamed in those dark, knowing eyes. "You want to play them, too."

"I don't." But what if she did? She flushed red hot, imagining.

You are truly shameless, a cold voice hissed inside her, condemning her anew.

Alessandro only crooked his index finger at her then, ordering her to come to him. To admit the things she wanted—to surrender herself to them. To him.

And she wanted that almost more than she could bear.

"No," she said too loudly, and she knew she was talking to herself. To remind herself of who she was, before she did something else she'd bitterly regret.

He wasn't safe, no matter how much that insane part of her insisted otherwise. He wasn't. And she was too afraid that giving in to him, to this, would make her believe she could trust him with the truth. She couldn't.

No matter how hard that was to remember.

"Stop pretending, Elena," he said then, that darker edge in his voice curling around her, drawing her in, calling her out that easily. "You're halfway to desperate. Up all night, tormented and needy. Longing for more but too afraid to ask for it."

That wolf's smile, challenging her. Daring her. Seeing all the things in her she wanted desperately to keep hidden away in the dark. Making her realize that she'd underestimated him, completely. And that he knew that, too.

"I said no," she managed to get out, but her voice was too thick, and it shook, and his smile only deepened.

"I won't even make you beg." He didn't have to do anything but look at her, predatory and sure, and she wanted everything she couldn't have, everything she couldn't risk. She wanted him more than her next breath. "All you have to do is own it. This. Ask and you will receive, *cara*."

It should have been easy to ignore Alessandro. To shrug off the darkly stirring things he said to her, the fantasies he brought to life within her with so little effort. It should have been simple to concentrate on these weeks of reprieve, and what it meant not to have to look over her shoulder after all these months, not to have to run.

Elena didn't understand why she couldn't seem to do it.

"It's only a matter of time," he'd said in his devastating way that night, when she'd finally turned to go. "Inevitable."

"Nothing is inevitable," she'd bit out over her shoulder, fully aware that he'd been throwing that word back in her face. Remembering exactly when she'd whispered it to him, what she'd felt when she did.

He'd laughed at her. "Keep telling yourself that."

So she did—fervently and repeatedly—but it didn't seem to work.

The nights were long and precarious. Each night she lay awake for hours, trying desperately to think of anything but him, and losing herself in need-infused fantasies instead. Or worse, reliving what had already happened.

Every touch. Every sigh. Every telling whisper.

Even if she managed to fall asleep, there was no relief. She would dream only of him and then wake, heart pounding and mouth dry, her body screaming for his touch. Memories of his possession hot and red in her head, branded into her.

The days were no better. No matter what she did, or where she went in his rambling house or the surrounding grounds, he found her. He was always there. Always watching her with those dark, hungry eyes of his, that wicked smile on his cynical mouth. Always, she understood, a word from her away from catapulting them both straight back into that glorious, terrifying fire that was never quite banked between them.

And all the while, she had to play her role. Cool, sometimes amused, forever teetering on the edge of boredom. The kind of hard, amoral woman Alessandro thought she was. And maybe, she was forced to acknowledge, he wasn't far off.

She could be pregnant—*pregnant*—and all she thought about was the way he'd touched her. While he—the man who might even now be the father of her child—believed she'd sought him out deliberately for sordid reasons of her own, and kept angling to touch her again, anyway. It was appalling. Heartbreaking. Sickening, even. Yet she had no choice but to keep the charade going.

She tried to give him exactly what he expected.

Give him what he wanted, she reasoned, and—assuming she wasn't pregnant, as she had to or she'd go mad—when their time was up he'd send her on her way without another thought, Rome nothing but a distant and dismissed memory. That meant that she would be safe from him and the dark menace of the Corretti family. She was gambling that it also meant he wouldn't bother to use her as any kind of leverage or bartering piece with Niccolo.

But the sick part of her...yearned. No matter what terrible thing came out of her mouth. No matter how much she wished otherwise. It had been hard enough to dance with him, to look at him on that dance floor and *know* him like that. To open up a part of her she'd never known was there, that only he called into being. To feel so safe, so cherished, so perfectly fitted to a complete stranger.

It was worse now. She knew what it was like to have him. She didn't have to *imagine*, she could *remember*. One taste of him wasn't enough. And despite what a mess this all was, despite how much messier it could get if she wasn't careful—she wanted more.

She hated herself for that. It only underscored everything that was wrong with her. Niccolo had been bad enough—but at least he'd fooled her. At least she'd honestly believed he was the man he pretended he was. There was no excuse at all for anything that happened with Alessandro. She'd known better even back in Rome.

She knew better now. But she still couldn't seem to stop.

"Tell me about yourself," he said one night at another long and perilous dinner, his dark voice amused as it so often was. "The story of Elena. We'll endeavor to ignore the sexual tension in the room and you can tell me lies about your idyllic childhood."

"My childhood really was idyllic," she replied, moving her perfectly grilled fish around on her plate.

There was still that part of her that wanted her to tell him everything, to trust him. That part of her that viewed his dark strength as a shelter. He made a sound of disbelief, snapping her out of that same old internal battle.

"It was," she said. "I was loved. I was happy."

He stared at her as if he couldn't make sense of her words, and something twisted inside of her. If he was this thrown by the idea of a happy childhood, it spoke volumes about his own, didn't it? *Don't make him into some kind of misunderstood hero*, she cautioned herself. *He's not one.*

And yet her voice was softer when she continued.

"My parents are good people," she said. It killed her that she had let them down so badly. That she might let them down still further. That she couldn't answer her mother's carefully uncritical emails asking when she'd come home the way she should. It made her want to cry, as usual, and she nearly did. "It was a good life."

"Yet not quite good enough," he said cynically. "You took to Niccolo Falco's version of the high life with alacrity."

"You have no idea what you're talking about," Elena replied, trying to keep the bite from her voice. Though she knew she couldn't defend herself. Not the way she wanted. And certainly not with the truth.

"Money, cars, houses and jewels," he taunted her, as he had long ago. "They make the transition to the ballrooms of Rome feel a great deal smoother, I imagine." His cynical mouth quirked in one corner. "All you have to do is sell your soul, isn't that right?"

"I'm tired of talking about Niccolo," she said, because she couldn't argue with him without giving herself away, and the fact that she still wanted to explain this to him, that she still so desperately wanted him to know who she really was, horrified her. She eyed him. "What about you?"

"My childhood was significantly less idyllic."

He might as well have been an unyielding, forbidding wall as he gazed back at her. And yet she felt that twist inside of her again.

That poor child, she thought, unable to keep herself from it. *Growing up with those people.*

His eyes narrowed as if he could sense her softening.

"Have we covered enough ground?" he asked, the hint of impatience in his voice, his gaze. "Are you ready to stop playing this game?" His eyes were so dark, so knowing. "I beg of you," he whispered. But he wasn't really begging. He wasn't a man who begged. "Say the word."

But she couldn't let herself do that. She might trust him on some primitive level that defied all reason, that she didn't even understand—but she didn't trust herself. It was much too risky. She shook her head slowly, not looking away from him.

"Don't tell me this is your version of misplaced loyalty," he said, his dark gaze moving over her face. "Once was business, but twice is a betrayal of your beloved Niccolo?"

"Business?" she asked in confusion, but then she remembered. She sighed. "Yes, because I'm spying on you. Over decadent gourmet meals. So far the only thing I've discovered, Alessandro, is that you employ a fantastic chef."

He shook his head, as if she'd disappointed him. "He doesn't deserve your loyalty. He never did."

"Enough about Niccolo," she said, pretending she didn't feel his disappointment like a blow. Pretending she wasn't clamoring to share everything with this man who was wise enough to hate Niccolo. She forced a smile, aware that it was brittle. "Why don't we talk about your fiancée, for a change?"

"What about her?" he asked, as if he'd forgot he ever had a fiancée in the first place. He laughed. "She's hardly worth mentioning. In truth, she never was."

CHAPTER FIVE

"WHAT A LOVELY sentiment," Elena said dryly. "No wonder she left you."

Something desolate moved over his face then, though he hid it almost the very second she saw it. The lump in her throat stayed where it was.

I hate this, she thought furiously. *I hate* me *like this.*

"Alessia Battaglia had exactly one promise to keep," Alessandro said, no sign of any desolation whatsoever in his hard voice, as if she'd imagined it. "Only one. And she not only failed to keep it, she did so in the most public way possible—designed, I can only assume, to cause me the maximum amount of embarrassment professionally and personally. Which she achieved." His lips twitched. "What is worth mentioning about that?"

"Sometimes people fall out of love," she offered. She was such a fool. She wanted that bleakness she'd seen in his eyes to mean something. His dark green gaze was contemplative as he studied her, and it took everything she had not to look away.

"It was a business arrangement, Elena. Love had nothing to do with it."

An odd sensation worked its way through her then, blooming up from the darkest part of her and uncurling, and it took her long moments to understand that it was a fierce, unwarranted satisfaction. As if the fact he had not loved his fiancée, did not care that she'd left him as much as the fact he'd been left, was not more evidence that he was the worst kind of man—but instead something to celebrate. She despaired of herself.

"And you're surprised she changed her mind?" she asked. That strange feeling hummed in her, making it hard to sit still, to keep her voice so smooth. "Why would anyone subject themselves to an arranged marriage in this day and age? That sounds like the perfect recipe for a lifetime of misery."

"As opposed to what?" He laughed. "The great benefits romance brings to the equation? The jealousy, the emotional manipulation, the very real possibility that at any moment, as you say, people could fall out of it? What makes you think that's the kind of security rational people should build a life on?"

"Because if it's not entirely rational, at least it's

honest," she blurted out before she could think better of it. "It's real."

"So is a contract." His voice was dry. Amused. "Which has the added benefit of being tangible. Inarguably rational. And enforceable by law."

"Maybe you were no more than collateral damage." Elena didn't know why she couldn't stop. Why did she care why this man's fiancée had abandoned him? He was Alessandro Corretti. Surely that was reason enough for anyone. "Maybe it wasn't about you at all."

"I was the only one standing at the altar," he said, tilting his head slightly as he gazed at her. "Do you imagine she objected to the priest her father chose? Palermo's great basilica itself? Hundreds of her closest friends and family members?"

"Maybe—" Elena began.

"I don't want to speculate about Alessia Battaglia's tangled, self-serving motives," he said impatiently. "All that matters are her actions. If you want to psychoanalyze a doomed engagement, why not focus on your own?"

"I don't want to talk about Niccolo again." Or that doom he mentioned. Especially not that.

"Then let's talk about you." He lounged there so casually, but Elena knew better. He was still picking at her resistance, over platters of grilled fish and bottles of wine. Over flickering candles and glistening crystal glasses. Over her own objections. "Since you won't let me do what I want to do."

She could almost hear the music they'd danced to, lilting somewhere inside of her. Back when he had looked at her as if she was miraculous, not a battle to be won. Back when he had held her close for such a little while and made her name into a song.

"Fine," she said. Anything to stop the memories, the emotions, that threatened to break her. The lump in her throat returned, and she had to breathe past it. "What do you want to know?"

"The man is a toad." Flat. Certain. Daring her to argue with his characterization. She didn't. "Less than a toad. Yet you agreed to marry him, and for all your faults of character, you don't strike me as the kind of woman you would have to be to overlook such things." Alessandro shifted in his chair, looking even more relaxed, but Elena knew better. She could sense what roared there beneath his skin, powerful and predatory. She could feel it. "Why did you?"

"Because I love—" She caught herself. Barely. She'd almost said *loved*. "I love him." She watched his eyes flash, and enjoyed the fact he didn't like hearing that any more than she liked saying it. "And not because he drove a pretty car or promised me a villa somewhere." She held his gaze, and told the truth. "He was sweet."

"Sweet." Alessandro looked appalled.

"He told me that once he'd seen me, his life could never be the same," she said, letting herself remember when Niccolo had been no more than a handsome, smiling stranger on an otherwise wholly familiar street. "He brought me flowers he picked himself from the hills above the village. He begged me to let him take me to dinner, or even simply take a walk with him near the water. It was the easiest thing in the world to fall for him. He was— He's the most romantic man I've ever met."

"It sounds like a con."

It wasn't as if she didn't agree, but she couldn't show him that. Or admit how ashamed she was of herself for falling for it, head over heels, so easily. Like the little fish she supposed she had been, reeled right into Niccolo's net.

She sniffed. "Says the man who thinks a chilly business contract is a solid basis for a marriage."

"But I am not a toad," he pointed out, dark amusement lurking in his gaze, in the corner of his mouth. "And she did not agree to marry me because I was *sweet*. She agreed to marry me because her father wished it, and because the life I would have given her was generous and comfortable." Again, a lift of those sardonic brows. "That is called practicality. Our situations are not at all similar."

"True." She aimed her smile at him. "But I don't expect Niccolo will leave me at the altar, either."

He stared at her for a long moment, that dark gaze baleful. She shivered, the intensity emanating from him sliding over her skin like a kind of breeze, kicking up goose bumps, though she tried to hide it. Then, not taking his eyes from hers, he threw his napkin on the table and rose.

Liquid and graceful. Powerful and male.

Elena ordered herself to run. But she couldn't seem to move.

Alessandro rounded the table, and then he was behind her, and she thought the heat that exploded through her then might kill her. It hurt when she breathed. It hurt when she held it instead. His hands came down to rest on her shoulders, light and something like innocuous, so nearly polite, and yet she was sure that he could feel the heat of her skin. The bright hot flame she became whenever he touched her.

Remember— an urgent voice cried, deep inside her. *Remember*—

But he was touching her again, he was finally touching her, and she couldn't hold on to a single thought but that.

"Fall for me, then," he said, bending down to speak softly into her ear, his breath tickling her even as it triggered that volcanic need she'd tried too hard to deny. "I'll pick you flowers from the meadow if that's all it takes."

"Stop it," she said, but her voice was so insubstantial. Little more than a whisper, and she knew it told him exactly how affected she was. How little resistance she had left.

"I'll lay you down beneath the moon," he continued as if she hadn't spoken, one clever hand moving beneath her hair to caress the sensitive skin at her nape, and she couldn't contain her shiver then—couldn't hide it from him. "And I'll demonstrate the only kind of love that isn't a sentimental story. The only kind that's real."

He meant sex. She knew he meant sex. And still, *that word*.

That word with his hands on her. *That word* in his low voice, wreaking its havoc as it sunk its claws into her. As it left deep marks that made a mockery of every lie she'd told herself since he'd found her on that boat. Every lie she'd told herself so desperately since that fateful night in Rome.

"I promise you, Elena," he said then, quoting Niccolo, wielding those same words like his own weapon—and a far more deadly one. "Your life will never be the same."

Her heart slammed against her ribs, so hard she worried they might crack. Once. Then again. Elena was lost. Held securely in his hands and unable to think of a single reason why she should extricate herself. Why she should do anything at all but let herself fall into this magnificent fire and burn herself away until there was nothing left of her but smoke. And him.

His hands dropped to her chair to pull her back from the table, and by the time she stood on her trembling legs, by the time she turned to look at his beautiful face made no less arrogant by the heat stamped across it, she remembered. If not herself, not entirely, than some tiny little spark of self-preservation that reminded her what was at stake. What there was left to lose.

His clever eyes moved over her face, and he frowned, reaching out again to take her upper arms in his hands. His thumbs moved over the skin the sleeveless empire-cut top she wore left bare, sending his personal brand of electricity arrowing straight into her core.

Where she ached. And melted. And ached anew.

"Don't," he said, urgency making his voice harsh. "Don't walk away again."

"I have to," she replied, but she couldn't look away from him. She couldn't move.

"There's no one on this island but you and me and the people I pay exorbitantly to keep my secrets," he said, all temptation and demand, and she could feel him, feel *this*, feel the dizzying intensity in every cell of her body. In every breath. In the way her heart beat and her pulse pounded. "No one to see what you do. No one to know. No one to contradict you if you lie about it later."

"I'll know," she said quietly.

And knew immediately, when his expression changed, that she'd made a critical mistake. For a moment she didn't understand, though the air between them seemed to burst into flames. His face lit with a dark, almost savage triumph, and his hard mouth curved.

"Yet we both know where your moral compass points, don't we?"

"Away from you," she said hurriedly, but it was too late.

"Another lie is as good a word as any, Elena," he said then, more wolf in that moment than man. "I accept."

Alessandro pulled her to him with that ruthless command that undid her—that thrilled her no matter how she wished it didn't. And her body simply obeyed. She knew she should resist this. She knew she needed to push him away, to wrench herself out of his arms before—

But she didn't.

She didn't even try.

He took her mouth, masterful and merciless at once, inevitable, and Elena melted against him, went up on her toes, and met him.

Finally.

His mouth was on her again, at last, and it wasn't enough. Her taste flooded him, driving him wild. Her tongue was an exquisite torture against his, her head tilting at the slightest touch of his hand for that perfect, slick fit he craved. He pulled her even closer, bending her back over his arm, kissing her as if both their lives depended on it.

Mine, he thought, with a ferocity that shook through him and only made him want her that much more.

She was pliant and beautiful, graceful in his arms, her luscious body plastered against him. He could feel her breasts against his chest, her hips pressed to his, and he was fervently grateful she was the sort of woman who wore shoes with wicked heels so gracefully. It made it that much easier to haul the delectable place where her legs met against the hardest part of him, right where he wanted her.

God, how he wanted her.

He lost his head. He forgot what he'd planned, what he'd intended here—he tasted her and the whole world fell away, narrowed down to one specific goal. To thrust himself inside her, again and again. To make them both shatter into a thousand pieces.

To take them both home.

He reached down and pulled her black top up over those fantastic breasts she never covered with any kind of bra, muttering words he hardly understood in Sicilian as well as Italian. He ran his fingers over her taut nipples, watched her bite her lip against the pleasure of it, her head falling back to give him better access.

But it wasn't enough, so he backed her up against the table and set her there, leaning down to lick his way from one delicious crest to the other. To lose himself in the softness of her warm skin, the scent of it, and those small, high cries she made when he took a nipple deep into his mouth.

She was gripping the edge of the table, her breath coming in hard, quick bursts, and she was so beautiful he thought he might die if he couldn't bury himself in her. If he couldn't feel her tremble all around him, screaming out his name. If he couldn't drive so deep into her he'd forget all about who he'd once imagined she was. Who she should have been.

Who she wasn't, damn her.

He remembered the stark, sensual picture he'd drawn for her at that dinner weeks back and smiled then, against the delicate skin beneath one of her breasts. He straightened, tugged her to her feet and found himself distracted by the glaze of passion in her bright summer eyes, the color high on her cheeks. He held her face between his hands, his thumbs sweeping from her temples to those elegant cheekbones that drove him mad, and plundered her mouth.

Taking, tasting. Exulting in this, in her. Making her his the only way he could.

He tore his mouth from hers, then spun her around. He felt her tremble against him as he leaned her forward, spreading her before him over the table, using one hand to push a forgotten serving dish, piled high with the remains of fluffy, fragrant rice, out of her way.

"Alessandro…" she whispered as she bent there, offering him the perfect, delectable view. A prayer. A vow. So much more than simply his name.

He smoothed his hands down her back, the sensual shape of her making him harder, making him desperate. But he didn't rush. He reached around beneath her to flatten his hands against the delectable curve of her belly.

He held his hands there for a moment, savoring the fine, low tremor that shuddered through her. Letting her absorb the heat of his hands. And then he moved lower, pulling open the button fly of her trousers with one hand as the other slid inside to cup her scalding heat in his palm.

She was panting now, leaning her forehead against the table, and he held her femininity in his hand, hot and damp and swollen with desire. And then he squeezed.

Elena bucked against him, against the table, and he did it again. Then again.

Slowly, deliberately, he built up a rhythm. Teasing her. Seducing her. Pressing against her urgent center with every stroke. Her breath grew ragged, her heat bloomed into his hand, and only then—only when she was mindless before him, stretched out breathless and boneless and his to command—did he pull his hand away.

Leaving her trembling right there on the edge.

She sobbed something incoherent into the arm she had thrown up near her head and then let out a moan as Alessandro tugged on her trousers, peeling them over her hips and shoving them down her legs to her knees. He left her panties where they were, an electric blue thong that beautifully framed then disappeared between the perfect twin curves of her pert bottom.

She was restless, shifting her weight from one foot in its high wedged sandal to the other, her hips swaying in an age-old invitation that speared into him like a new heat, mesmerizing him for a moment. Her shoes lifted her to him, making her arch her back slightly as she sprawled there before him, mindless and moaning. His in every way.

He loved it. He thought he could die in this moment a happy man at last, this woman his own, perfectly crafted feast—and he intended to eat every bite. He traced over her thong with a lazy finger, then ran his hands over her bottom, vowing that one day he would learn every millimeter of her with his mouth. Every hollow. Every mark. With his teeth. His tongue.

But not now. His need was like a wild storm in him, pounding in his blood, making his chest tight and his vision narrow.

He freed himself from his trousers and quickly rolled on the protection he'd carried in his pocket, then bent over her, shoving her thong down and out of his way. She was still trembling, still breathing hard and fast, and her eyes were shut tight. He braced himself on one arm, his hand flat against the table near her shoulder.

"Alessandro," she said again, her voice strangled, but she lifted her hips when he slid a hand beneath her, pressing her face against the table as if it was a pillow.

He reached down and pressed hard against her center even as he shifted his position and drove straight into her.

She came apart beneath him, sobbing and wild.

He had to grit his teeth as she shuddered, as her

fingers pressed into the table's hard surface as if she could find some hold. He let her ride it out, waiting hot and hard and deep inside of her, her perfect bottom snug against him, almost more enticement than he could bear.

When she started to come back to him, he began to move.

He wasn't gentle. She made that small, highly aroused noise in the back of her throat, the sweetest sound he'd ever heard, and met him, thrust for thrust. She was sinuous and lithe, arched there before him with her black top flowing all around her as she moved with him, like some kind of erotic dance.

It was almost too much for him. He reached out and held the nape of her neck in his hand, making her shudder, then keeping her still.

And then he simply took her.

He ravaged. He savored. *He took.*

And all the while she cried out her pleasure, her hips wild against his, her eyes shut tight and her cheeks stained red with all of that desperate, delicious heat.

It was perfect. She was perfect.

"You are mine," he ground out from between his teeth, his hips hard against hers, riding her, devouring her. *"Mine."*

When he couldn't hold on any longer he slid a hand beneath her once more, finding the heart of her hunger and rubbing hard against it, making her jerk against him.

"Again," he ordered her, his voice so deep, so guttural, he hardly recognized it. And he didn't care, his own climax roaring toward him. "Now."

She obeyed him with a beautiful scream, her feet leaving the ground as she shattered into a flare of white hot heat around him, catapulting over that edge once more.

And finally, *finally,* he followed.

Alessandro didn't know how long it was before he caught his breath. Before he was himself again, and not just a handful of scattered fragments thrown to every corner of this island. Of the globe.

Elena still lay beneath him, her cheek pressed against the tabletop, and he could feel every breath she took. He angled himself back and off her, regretting that he had to pull out of her soft heat.

She didn't move, or open her eyes. Alessandro rid himself of the protection he'd used, fastened his trousers, and still she lay there. Making a perfectly debauched, impossibly lovely picture. Her trousers and thong were a tangle at her knees, her sweet bottom and the feminine secrets beneath on display as she bent there over his table so obediently, her mouth slightly ajar as she breathed and her slender arms thrown out before her as if in total surrender.

Desire coiled within him again, and he rubbed his hands over his face as if that might make sense of this hunger. Nothing eased it. Not even the one thing that should have.

He wondered, then, if it would ever leave him. If he would ever be free of it. Of her.

Is that what you want? a voice queried from a place inside of him he preferred to ignore, and he shoved it away.

"Elena."

She stirred then, her eyes fluttering open, and Alessandro watched as she slowly peeled herself up from the table, then reached down to pull her panties and her trousers into place, all without looking his way. All a bit shaky, a bit too careful, as if she wasn't sure her legs would hold beneath her. Her hair was a wanton tangle around her face but she ignored it, not even pushing it out of her way as she buttoned up her denim trousers.

So he did it for her, tucking a silken blond sheaf behind one ear.

"Are you all right?"

Her gaze flicked to his, then away.

"Yes," she said. Her voice was rough and she coughed. "Of course."

But there was a defenseless cast to her jaw as she said it, and he reached over to tilt up her chin, forcing her to look at him. Her blue eyes were stormy, and there was something somehow bruised about the way she stared back at him. He felt cold.

"Are you?" he asked again, his tone serious. Gruff.

She knocked his hand away. He let her.

"Please don't patronize me." She looked around as if in search of something, but only hugged herself instead. As if, he thought, she was very small. The cold in him grew wider, deeper. "I said I was fine."

He studied her, battling the strangest urge to pull her into his arms, to hold her against him. To warm them both. It was ridiculous.

And then he did it anyway, not understanding himself at all.

She fit beneath his chin and securely against his chest, and he couldn't have said what he felt then. It didn't make sense. He didn't recognize it—or himself. And yet he held her, he listened to her breathe, and he hated it when she pulled away from him.

"Stop this," she said in a low voice, her gaze dark and troubled. "I don't need your backhanded form of comfort."

He didn't understand any of this. Why was he having this conversation in the first place? He didn't tolerate scenes like this. He avoided even the faintest hint of what he saw swimming there in all of that summer blue. So why was he still standing here?

"Elena," he began.

She blew out a breath. "I asked you to stop," she whispered.

Alessandro felt profoundly off balance. Uneven down into his soul. He scowled.

"So I can take you any way I please," he said in a less pleasant voice than he might have, had he been able to make this strange feeling disappear. Had any of this made sense to him. "I can bend you over a table and make you scream and shake, and you'll submit to that happily. Greedily."

Her face paled, but that didn't stop him. And whatever was happening inside of him shifted, turned furious. At himself, at her—he couldn't tell the difference. He just needed this feeling to stop. Now.

"There is nothing I couldn't make you beg me to do to you, is there?" He folded his arms across his chest. "Nothing at all."

"Does this make you feel better?" she asked, lifting her head, her eyes flashing.

"I'm not the one who has convenient pretensions of modesty, Elena," he bit out. "But only when it suits."

He watched her shake that off, a quick jerk of her smooth shoulders, and wondered that it even hurt her.

"I know you don't respect me, Alessandro," she said,

and her voice wasn't angry. It was something else. Something that worked in him like shame, oily and thick. "I know exactly what you think of me. You've told me repeatedly. You don't have to act it out again now."

"You don't respect yourself!" he threw at her. How did she dare?

"But you should." She shook her head, then he saw to his horror that her eyes were full. Though she didn't cry. She only looked at him with tears bright in her gaze and he felt small. Mean. "Shouldn't you? What kind of man does the things you do with me, revels in them, and yet has no respect for me at all?"

"Elena," he began, but there was too much inside of him. It was too big and too dangerously unwieldy, and it had something to do with that way she looked at him. As if she thought he was a better man. That he ought at least to try. And that vulnerability in the way she held herself, as if she knew what he'd long suspected—that, deep down, he wasn't. And never had been.

"You call me a whore and then you call me yours," she said quietly. "Am I the one who doesn't respect myself or is that you?"

He felt buffeted by wild, treacherous storms—but yet he stood still, and there was only that way she gazed at him, as if she saw through all of his darkness and saw what lay there on the other side of it. Something he refused to name.

Something that could not exist. He wouldn't allow it.

"It's like you're two different women," he told her when he was sure he could keep his balance. When he'd beat back the storms as best he could. "One I know all too well. One who would marry a man like Niccolo Falco and defend that choice, call it romantic."

She looked away from him then. In shame? In some kind of triumph that he cared this much, so much more than he should, than he even admitted to himself?

How could he still not know?

"But the other, Elena." He dropped his voice, and saw her eyes close against it, as if it tempted her beyond endurance, or hurt her. As if he did. "The other…"

Was the woman he'd imagined she was when he'd met her. The woman he'd wanted so desperately he'd ignored her association with Niccolo to dance with her, to hold her. The woman he'd called his before he knew her name. The woman he sometimes saw in her still—like now….

That woman doesn't exist, he reminded himself harshly. She hadn't then and she never would.

"People are complicated," she said after a moment, a bleakness making her blue gaze gray when she looked at him again. "You can't shove them into little boxes. And you can't really know them unless they let you."

"Or they show you," he agreed. "As you have."

She swallowed, and then her head bowed forward, only slightly, but Alessandro saw it. He knew defeat when it stood before him. That should mean he'd won, that he was victorious in this—whatever this was. It should mean he felt triumph at the very least. And instead what he felt was empty.

"The show's over, Alessandro," she whispered, and he couldn't make sense of what he saw on her face then.

Perhaps because he couldn't, he didn't stop her when she turned and walked away from him, again, leaving him there alone in the quiet room, the echoes of the passion they'd shared seeming to cling to the walls like rich, wild tapestries.

And still he tried to work out what he'd seen on her elegant features before she'd left. Temper, certainly. The lingering trace of that powerful desire that, it seemed, never truly left either one of them. A kind of weary resignation.

And sadness.

It was like a punch to the gut.

Elena was sad. And he'd made her that way.

She had looked at him like he was a monster. Worse, as if she knew he'd chosen to become exactly that. As if she knew he'd vowed he would never become this kind of man—a man of cruelty and dark impulse like his father—no matter the provocation, and then had gone ahead and done it, anyway.

As if she knew.

He wasn't sure he could live with it. He wasn't sure he could bear being this much of a disappointment to himself, this much of a bastard.

But he didn't know how to stop.

CHAPTER SIX

"I WANT YOU in my bed," he said curtly later that same night, appearing in the doorway of her bedchamber.

Elena was curled up in the blue-and-white armchair near one of the sweeping, open windows, staring out at the dark sea and the silver pathway that rippled there, stretching toward the swollen orange moon hanging low on the horizon. She'd been thinking about resistance. About surrender.

About how to use this uncontrollable passion for her own ends before it swallowed her whole.

"I knew I meant to lock that door," she murmured, dropping her mask into place as she turned to look at him.

"Tonight," Alessandro told her in that same clipped, commanding tone, the slight narrowing of his fierce eyes the only indication he'd heard her. "And for good.

This particular game is over and I think we both know you lost."

He'd showered. She could smell the faint scent of his soap, fresh and clean. His thick hair lay in damp waves on his head, and he no longer looked the way he had when she'd left him in the dining room. Bereft, she might have said, if he were a smaller creature, a lesser man.

He expected her to resist him. Still. Again. Elena could see it in the way he held himself, the fine lines of his powerful body taut. She could see it in the way his dark green gaze was hooded, yet tracked her every breath.

So what if you lose a little bit more of yourself? she asked herself briskly, shoving aside what felt like a kind of despair, concentrating instead on that ravenous hunger for him she couldn't seem to escape. That was what she had to exploit. The possibility of a pregnancy had brought her this far—passion would do the rest. It had to. *There are worse things to lose—and far worse fates.*

"All right," she said.

The moment stretched out. He cocked his head slightly to one side, eyes narrow and jaw hard. "What did you say?"

"I'm agreeing with you, Alessandro." She swung her feet off the chair, pressing her bare toes into the polished wood floor beneath her. Like that would keep her grounded. Like anything could. "You win."

There was a tense, shimmering silence. Elena kept her gaze trained down at her bare feet, on the toes she'd painted a bright pink in some attack of hopefulness when she'd still worked on his yacht—but then, she didn't have to look at him to feel the way he was glaring at her. The fire and the force of him like a wild heat against her skin. A dark magic inside of her, changing her. Ruining her.

Only if I let it, she assured herself. She might lose a bit of herself, but it was worth it, wasn't it? She was safe here, and she needed to stay that way. And he would lose interest in her all the quicker once she ceased to be a challenge, because that was how men like him operated—so this would ensure that when their forty days were up, he would wash his hands of her. Discard her, happily, without bothering to inform on her to Niccolo. She would be free, and Niccolo would have lost her trail completely.

This was insurance, plain and simple.

"And what," he asked, his low voice threaded with seductive, sensual menace, "do I win, Elena? Be specific."

She lifted her head. His expression was deeply cynical, his stance tense, and yet that same passion burned in him, bright and hot, as obvious to her as if it was tattooed across his face.

"Whatever you like," she told him.

She raised her brows as he only stood there in the doorway and did no more than continue to study her, as if she was a code he intended to break. A trickle of apprehension worked its way down her spine— because she couldn't let him do that. He could have her, but not all of her. And never the truth.

"Isn't this what you want?" she asked, taunting him. Distracting him. She smiled, cool and challenging. "My complete and total surrender, entirely on your terms? Well, here it is. This is what it looks like. You should be pleased, surely."

"Is that meant to shame me?" he countered, a dark gleam in his eyes then, and Elena had to fight back an involuntary shiver. "I think you'll find I'm far past that. Nothing can. Certainly not you."

"Then you have nothing to fear." She stood, smoothing her hands down the front of the silk-and-lace chemise she wore, in a soft champagne shade that she knew made her eyes that much bluer. "I found this on the end of the bed, like all the rest of the clothes I've found waiting for me since I got here. It's as if you make them all yourself in some secret workshop in the night."

"Not me." There was a sardonic curve to his mouth, but his dark eyes burned as he watched her walk toward him. Possessive. Hungry. "My cousin Luca runs a fashion house. We may not be close, but the clothes speak for themselves."

Elena didn't say anything. She wasn't sure she could, now that she was really going through with this. It was one thing to decide to surrender herself to this man, at least in bed. It was something else again to *do* it.

It might very well shred her into tiny little pieces she wasn't sure she'd ever manage to put back together. But she knew this was the only way.

And she couldn't deny the fact that it excited her. That he did. That the idea of sharing his bed made her shiver with need, no matter what price she'd end up paying.

She walked toward him, holding his gaze. Letting her hips sway beneath the silken embrace of the fabric that clung to her. Letting him watch, wait. She could see the stamp of hunger across his face. She could see the blaze of it in his eyes.

And felt more powerful in this moment than she had in a very long time. Since she'd looked up from her life to find a shockingly beautiful man watching her as if she was a goddess come down to earth. She felt it hum in her like an electrical current.

She stopped when she was no more than a breath away and stood there. She waited. He tensed, but he didn't move. His hands were thrust deep into the pockets of his loose black trousers as if he was perfectly at ease, but she knew better.

"Do you think this will work, Elena?" he asked, his voice hoarse. "This suspicious capitulation, this attempt at seduction, coming so soon on the heels of your deep concerns about respect?"

"You should ask yourself," she said, her tone light, though her gaze was hard on his, "why even when I do what you say you want, you accuse me of something. Anything."

"Because it won't," he said, answering his own question. His mouth twisted. "Not the way you imagine. I don't care how you come to me. I don't care how I have you. I don't care at all, so long as I do. Are you prepared for that?"

"I told you," she said softly. "You win." She held out her arms like some kind of supplicant, but she smiled like a queen. "To the victor go the spoils—isn't that what they say?"

"They do."

He reached over and traced a deceptively lazy trail from the wildly fluttering pulse in her throat to the hollow between her breasts. All of his ruthlessness, all of his simmering power, in that one fingertip.

"You should be afraid of me," he told her then, and his voice moved in her, threat and promise, sex and demand, and something even darker in his eyes. "Why aren't you?"

"I'm terrified," she whispered, but she wasn't. And she could see he knew it.

"I wish I knew which one of us is the greater fool," he replied in the same harsh whisper, and it made her throat constrict.

"Someone once told me you should be careful what you wish for, Alessandro," she said, because it was better to taunt him. It was better to push. Safer. "You just might get it, and then what will you do?"

Her heart beat like a hammer in her chest, in her breasts, between her legs, and she could swear he heard it, too, because his hard mouth curved, not a trace of cynicism to be seen. Only desire.

And that was all the warning she got.

He hauled her up into the air, then threw her over one shoulder like she weighed nothing at all. Like the warrior king she'd imagined him. Claiming her that easily—that completely.

She gasped—but his hand came down on her bottom, his big, hard palm holding her fast and warning her, and she gulped her own words down.

His shoulder was wide and hard against her belly as he moved through the house; his hand was a hot brand of fire against the exposed skin of her behind, the backs of her thighs. She caught a glimpse of herself as they passed a mirror, hanging down his strong back, her hair wild and her face flushed, and it made her breath go shallow. She couldn't stop trembling, and it still wasn't fear.

Surrender, she told herself. *It's the only way to save everything else that matters.* But what scared her wasn't the act of surrendering to him. It was that it was so easy. That it felt so good.

Alessandro tossed her down in the center of his bed, and she had only a quick impression of bold colors, dark woods and arching windows wide open to let the night inside. Then her gaze fixed on him, and stayed put. He stood by the side of the wide bed for a moment, looking down at her as she sprawled there, and she couldn't quite read the intense look in his eyes, on his hard face.

But she trembled. And wanted. And melted into liquid fire.

He didn't ask. He didn't ply her with more of those lethal, sensual promises of his, those half terrifying and half intriguing things he'd said he would do to her, with her, if only she'd ask.

He simply took.

And she gloried in that, too.

This is exactly what you wanted, Elena reminded herself a week or so later as she stood in that gorgeous shower room built outside to take in the sunlight and the crisp sea air.

She tilted her face up into the spray, and let the heat work its way into her as she considered her success. Her delicious, dangerous surrender.

There was no part of her body Alessandro hadn't claimed. No millimeter of skin he hadn't investigated with his fingers, his mouth, his wicked tongue. He took her with a ferocity and a kind of desperation she understood too well, because it was in her, too, this terrible hunger. It was never satisfied. It never dimmed.

No matter how many times he tore her apart, no matter how often she screamed his name and then held him close as he collapsed against her, it was still there. Moving within her. Ripping her open. Making her fear it would be impossible to ever really leave this man, that this kind of hunger would mark her, scar her....

But she'd returned the favor. She'd thrown herself headfirst into that fire, and who cared what burned? She'd pushed him down on that same dinner table and climbed on top of him, using her mouth and hands to make him groan. She'd learned what made him burst into flame, what made him roll her over and take control, what made him laugh in the dark as they explored each other. She'd teased him, taken him, taunted him—and then slept wrapped up against him, held close against that powerful chest of his, lulled into sleep by the steady beat of his heart.

This is what success feels like, she told herself now. *You should be happy.* But instead, she pictured them dancing, around and around in that ballroom, all of that wonder and delight between them. It glowed in her still, even here. Even now.

What they could have been. What they should have been.

She shouldn't let herself dream about such things, because it only hurt her. She shouldn't let herself imagine what it would be like if none of what had happened on this island had that darker undertone, if this wasn't one more game they played. If it really meant something when he kissed her face and smiled at her, when she held him close and whispered his name.

If it meant what she'd seen back then, glimmering between them, just out of reach—

Snap out of the daydream, she ordered herself now, annoyed at herself and that gnawing ache in her chest that made her feel so hollow. *You're here to be the whore he thinks you are. Nothing more.*

It turned out, she was good at that.

She shut off the water and reached for her towel, and he was there when she opened her eyes. Her stomach still clenched. Her heart still jumped. He was still so impossibly beautiful, fierce and male, standing in the open door between his suite and the open shower area, his arms crossed over his bare chest.

"How long have you been there?" she asked. She had to fight to make her voice smooth, and she didn't know why. It should have been easy after all this practice. It should have been second nature by now.

"Not long."

"Weren't you going for a run?"

"I was." He smiled. "I did."

"I must have spent more time in the shower than I realized."

She wanted to sound light. Easy. She couldn't understand why that raw, hollow place inside of her still bled into everything. As if it mattered how close this all was to what it should have been, yet wasn't.

And won't ever be, she reminded herself.

"Do you think you're pregnant?" he'd asked one afternoon, the sun pouring in through the windows, bathing them both in white light as they moved together on his bed. He'd run his hands over her belly, his gentle touch at distinct odds with his gruff voice. It had been too much. There'd been that look in his eyes, so close to a kind of yearning. It had torn her up inside.

She'd been straddling him, and she'd twisted her hips to take him deep inside of her. Sex was better than emotion. Easier. He'd hissed out a breath, his dark eyes narrowing.

"We'll find out soon enough," she'd said, reminding him who they were, moving against him to make her point. "And then we can stop pretending there's anything more to this than sex."

He'd reached up to pull her mouth down to his, and he'd whispered something against her lips. It had only been later, when they'd collapsed again, breathless and destroyed, that she'd realized what he'd said. *Damn you.*

She walked toward him now, wrapping the towel around her, and he stepped back to let her pass. She made her way into his bedroom and over toward the massive bed that dominated the far wall, angled for the best view out of the many windows.

None of this was what she'd thought it would be. He wasn't the man she'd believed he was. He was nothing like Niccolo, and she didn't know how to process that. She'd expected the fire to dissipate the more she indulged herself in him, showing her what horrors lay beneath. But Alessandro wasn't made of Niccolo's brand of bright surface charm to hide the bully within, or if he was, he was better at concealing it. He was gruff and hard, ruthless and demanding—but he was also surprisingly thoughtful. Caring in ways that made it hard for her to breathe, much less throw out the next, necessary barb. As likely to take the hairbrush from her hand and brush her hair, making her tremble with something far different from lust when he met her eyes in the mirror, as he was to throw her up against the nearest wall and let the raging fire consume them.

He's like Niccolo. He's worse than Niccolo. She chanted it at herself. *You might not be able to see it, but it's there. It has to be there.*

Because if he wasn't like Niccolo, if she'd been that terribly wrong about him, then she had no reason not to trust him the way she wished she could. She might feel oddly safe with him, still. He might thrill her in ways she was afraid to admit to herself. But she'd been running for too long, and there was as much to lose now as there had been when she'd started.

More, perhaps, if she counted her foolish heart, and the way it beat for him.

"What's the matter?" he asked from behind her, that combination of perception and kindness in his tone that was uniquely his. It undid her.

But she couldn't cry. She couldn't betray herself like this, when she'd come so far and given up so much.

Elena turned to face him. She met his dark gaze, saw the concern there that she couldn't acknowledge, that she couldn't let herself accept. Alessandro's mouth crooked in one corner, and that was all it took for her to melt. To want. To topple over into that stark, demanding need.

"Come here," she said, her voice husky with the things she couldn't say, the truths she couldn't tell.

And he obeyed, this fierce predator of a man, his dark eyes bright and fixed on her with that same hunger. She waited until he was close and then she dropped the towel, and he laughed.

"You'll be the death of me," he said in that low voice that made her skin prickle, and then his hands were on her skin, lifting her and pushing her back onto the bed, coming down on top of her with that delicious weight of his, smooth muscle and dangerous man.

"I'll sing the elegy at your funeral," she promised him, and his smile deepened in a way that made her ache everywhere, hot and greedy for him.

"I won't die alone." He buried his hands in her wet hair, pulling her mouth to within a breath of his. "I promise you that."

Their gazes tangled, held, as she reached between them and pulled him free from his running shorts. As she reached for the side table, then rolled protection down over the hard, smooth length of him. As she guided him to her entrance.

"Elena," he whispered. "I—"

But words were even more dangerous than he was. She couldn't have it. She couldn't risk it. She moved her hips against him, inviting him in. Making him groan. Keeping him quiet.

Being the whore he thought she was, or she thought she was, or this situation had made her. She told herself it didn't matter anymore. She only knew she had to see it through.

He pushed inside of her, and they both sighed. That perfect, impossible fit. That slick, wild fire. That coil of desire, tight and hot, that only seemed stronger every time.

This was killing them, she thought then, her gaze locked to his, lost in his, truths shimmering between them that she refused to voice. He knew things he shouldn't know, the way he always had, and they might as well be dancing still, around and around, as familiar and as lost to each other as ever.

But he moved in her then, commanding and powerful and hers—hers despite everything as he had been from that first glance, that very first touch of their hands—and she forgot again, the way she always did.

For a little while.

Alessandro stalked out of the house.

He moved across the terrace toward the pool, where Elena sat on one of the loungers, whiling away another summer morning. She looked perfectly at ease, while he was still boiling over with all the frustration he'd unloaded on his assistant over the past few hours. He made a mental note to increase the man's annual bonus.

"One more week, Giovanni," he'd snapped when yet another Corretti family crisis had been trotted out as if it was a critical business issue that required his immediate attention. Because Alessandro was expected to care, to be responsible. To handle everyone else's mess. "I'm on holiday. Tell them to sort it out themselves, or wait."

"But, sir…" His assistant had cleared his throat. "They grow more insistent by the hour!"

"Then I suggest you earn your outrageous salary," Alessandro had growled, ending the call. But it hadn't done much for the restless agitation that still coursed through him, making him feel edgy.

He slowed as he drew closer to Elena, tucked up in the shade of an umbrella, paging through foreign magazines with every outward appearance of lazy contentment. For some reason, that flipped a kind of switch in him.

One more week to forty days. One more week until he and Elena were finished—or bound together in a way he'd tried not to think about too closely. One more week, and he wasn't ready.

He didn't want the life he'd left behind when he'd fled Sicily a month ago. He didn't want to slip back into that same old role that had brought him nothing but grief for the whole of his adult life. He didn't want to dance to the tune of a dead man, or fight these losing battles against his family's bad reputation. He was as tired of it as he'd been the day he'd left.

Just as he was fed up with Elena's stubborn determination to keep him at arm's length.

He knew what she was doing, with her mysterious smiles and the sex she doled out as if she was nothing more than a sensual buffet and he a mindless glutton. She was giving him what she thought he wanted. Soothing the savage beast.

But he knew there was more to her, and he wanted it. He was so damned tired of half measures, of *almost*. He wanted everything she had. Every last secret. He wanted to know her better than he knew himself.

He wanted *her*.

Alessandro was sick and tired of settling for less.

"It's been thirty-three days, Elena," he said when he reached her side. He waited until she looked up from her magazine, and then smiled. "Does that mean we already have our answer?"

"Good morning to you, too," she said in her usual way, arch and arid, but this time he sensed her temper beneath it. And he couldn't have said why he wanted to see it so much, so badly. "And no. There are a few days left before I'd jump to any conclusions."

For a moment, they only gazed at each other, and he could feel what flowed between them. That wild electricity, as always, but there was something else beneath it. Something real. He was sure of it.

She shifted position, and smiled in a way she knew by now was guaranteed to poke at his hunger. Her fingers plucked at the ragged hem of the denim shorts she wore beneath an open-necked, nearly sheer shirt that flowed all around her in bright reds and deep blues, hinting at the delectable curves beneath. Her smooth legs went on forever, sun-kissed and shaped so beautifully. She patted the lounger beside her, and it caused him physical pain not to put his hands on her. Not to wrap those legs around his waist, throw them over his shoulders, revel in all the ways he wanted her.

But it wasn't enough, and he didn't care that she wanted it that way. That she was using their explosive chemistry to hide in. He couldn't allow it any longer.

"I wonder what would happen if we kept our clothes on," he said then, quietly, and her eyes widened. "What then, Elena? What do you think we'd discover?"

"That we are perfect strangers," she replied coolly, but her clear eyes darkened. "Who never should have met in the first place."

"I'm not convinced." He held her gaze, saw the hint of panic in hers. "What are you hiding?"

He was sure he saw her flinch, then control it. Almost too fast to track.

"What could I possibly be hiding?" she retorted. "You've taken everything. You know everything. There's nothing left."

"I've taken your body, yes," he agreed. "I know it very well, just as you intended. But what about the rest of you?"

He watched her struggle, one emotion after the next moving across her face, and he knew he was right. She shook her head, her blue eyes cloudy.

"What do you care?" she asked quietly. "You have what you want."

"I want everything," he said, raw and intense, and smiled when she jerked back against the lounger.

And everything might not be enough, a voice whispered deep inside of him. He might have been a ruined thing, twisted and dark all the way through, but he needed this. He needed her. He didn't care why. He only knew he did.

He watched her pull in a breath, then another, and she curled her hands into tight fists on her thighs. He forced himself to wait. She looked away for a long, tense moment, and when her eyes met his again, he saw her. *Her.*

At last.

"I knew it," he said with deep satisfaction. "I knew you were right there, simmering beneath the surface."

"What do you want, Alessandro?" she asked, and her voice was neither cool nor amused, for the first time in a very long while. "We only have a few days left here. Why ruin them with this?"

"I want the woman I met in Rome," he told her. "I don't want a damned sex toy."

She let out a short, derisive laugh. "Of course you do. Men like you always do."

He felt that same familiar darkness in him expanding, rising, sweeping through him, reminding him how ruined and twisted he was and always had been, since the day he was born. *Men like you.* Would he never escape his name? Was he doomed to be exactly like his father, no matter how hard he'd struggled against it?

"I don't care if you hate me, Elena," he gritted out. "But whatever else this is, whatever happens, I want it to be real."

Because one thing in his life had to be. Just one thing.

"'Real,'" she repeated in a flat tone. "You. That's almost funny. What do you know about *real*?" Her face heated as she spoke, her temper flooding in like a rising tide and as beautiful to him, however perverse that was. "You almost married a woman for what? A business expense?"

"Duty," Alessandro corrected her, and she laughed. *She laughed.*

"The reality, Alessandro, is that you are not a good man," she said with an awful, deliberate finality, staring straight at him, deliberate and pointed. "How could you be? You're a Corretti."

Condemnation and curse, all wrapped up in his name. His damned name. She said it as if it was the vilest word imaginable. As if the very saying of it blackened her tongue. He felt something crack open inside of him.

Because, of course, he wasn't simply a Corretti. He was the one his family was happy to sacrifice to serve their own ends. He was the one who was expected to do his duty, because he always had. His own parents had used him as a pawn. His grandfather had manipulated him. His "business expense" had walked out on him. Then Elena had crashed into his life like a lightning bolt, illuminating all of his darkest corners in that single, searing, impossible dance, but she hated him—he'd made sure of it. He had never been anything but a dark, ruined thing, masquerading as a man.

"Your conscience will be your undoing, boy," Carlo had jeered at him more than once. "It makes you weak."

As long as it didn't make him Carlo, he thought now, bitterly. Perhaps that was the most he could hope for.

Elena had no clue what she was dealing with. No possible clue what he held in check. "You don't have the slightest idea who I am."

"The entire world knows who you are," she retorted, glaring at him as if he'd never been anything but a monster, and he couldn't stand it. Not any longer. Not from her. "You're—"

"I am so tired of paying for the sins of others," he gritted out. He slashed a hand through the air when she opened her mouth and she shut it again, sinking back against the lounger, her hands in fists at her sides. "I've spent my life doing nothing but the right thing, and it still doesn't matter. Yes, I was going to marry that girl." He raked a hand through his hair. "Because it was my grandfather's dying wish and I am many things, Elena, none of them as polluted or as vile as you seem to believe, but I could not defy my own grandfather."

"Your grandfather—" she began, her eyes flashing, and he knew what she was about to say. The stories she was about to tell. His twisted family history in all its corrupt glory.

"Was no saint," he interrupted her. "I know. But he was my *grandfather,* Elena, and whatever else I might think of the way he lived his life, I have him to thank for mine. How do you repay that kind of debt?"

"Selling yourself off to the highest bidder is an interesting answer to that question."

"You're one to talk," he retorted, and she sucked in a breath, her face going white, then flushing deep red.

He hated himself for that, but that was nothing new, so he kept going—as if he could explain himself to her. As if she might understand him, somehow. How sad was that? How delusional? But he couldn't seem to stop.

"The docklands project that the wedding was supposed to secure would have done what years of struggle on my part couldn't—assure the Corretti family's legacy into the future, legitimately. Bring all the warring factions of the family together." He searched her face. "How could I refuse to do something so important? Why would I? I was prepared to do my duty to my family, and I can't say I wouldn't do it again."

But she was shaking her head, and she even let out another laugh that seemed to pierce him through the chest, leaving only an icy chill in its wake.

"I've heard all of this before," she said, shrugging. "The struggle to be a good man, the weight of the family name, the call to duty. It's like a song and I know all the words." Her gaze slammed into his, and he was amazed to find it felt as if she'd used a fist instead. "But when Niccolo said it, I believed him."

CHAPTER SEVEN

NICCOLO FALCO. AGAIN. Always.

"Your beloved Niccolo is a liar and a crook," Alessandro said through his teeth. "He wouldn't know the right thing to do if it attacked him on the streets of Naples, and he certainly wouldn't do it. Don't kid yourself."

She got to her feet then, stiff and jerky, as if she thought she might break apart where she stood. "I would never lower myself to a Corretti scum like you," she'd hissed at him on that dance floor, and he'd believed her then.

He didn't know why he wanted so badly not to believe her now.

"Is this what you meant by *real,* Alessandro?" she asked in a harsh whisper, her bright eyes ablaze. "Are you satisfied?"

"It would be so much easier to simply give in," he

threw at her, his voice unsteady. As if he'd lost control of himself, which was unacceptable, but he couldn't stop. "To simply be the man everyone thinks I am, anyway, no matter what I do. Even you, who shouldn't dare to throw a single stone my way for fear of what I could throw back at you. *Even you.*"

She sucked in a breath, as if he really had thrown something at her.

"Because there could be no one lower in all of Italy." Something in the way she said it ripped at him, or maybe that was the way she looked at him, as if he'd finally managed to crush her—and he detested himself anew. "Not one person lower than me. Yet you can't keep your hands off me, can you?"

"You know exactly what kind of man Niccolo is," he said then, because he couldn't handle what her voice did to him. What that look in her eyes made him feel. "You're here at his bidding, to do whatever dirty work he requires. And it's certainly been dirty, hasn't it? But you sneer at *my* name?"

"I am here," she threw back at him, her voice still so ragged and her eyes so dark, too dark, "until we discover whether or not our recklessness results in a pregnancy neither one of us wants. We risked bringing a brand-new life into all of this bitterness and hate. That's the kind of people we are, Alessandro."

"Why don't you teach me," he said then, his gaze

on hers, hot and hurt and too many other things he couldn't define and wasn't sure he wanted to know, though he could feel them all battering at him.

"Teach you what? Manners? I think we're past that."

"You're the expert on *men like me*," he said, fascinated despite himself when she blanched at the way he said that. "You know all about it, apparently. Teach me what that means. Show me. Help me be as bad as you think I am already."

Something shifted in the air between them. In her gaze. The way her blue eyes shone with unshed misery, and the way she suddenly looked so small then, so vulnerable. So shattered.

And all he felt was…raw. Raw and ruined, all the way through to his bones.

Or maybe that was the way she looked at him.

"Let me guess what makes me the perfect teacher," she said, her voice cracking.

"You tell me, Elena," he said, his own voice a low, dark growl. "You're the one in bed with the enemy."

And she swayed then, as if he'd punched her hard in the gut. He felt as if he had, a kind of hot, bitter shame pouring over him, almost drowning him. But she steadied herself, and one hand crept over her heart, as if, he realized dimly, it ached. As if it ached straight up through her ribs, enough for her to press against it from above.

"I can't do this anymore."

Her voice was thick and unsteady, and he had the impression she didn't see him at all, though she stared right at him. Her eyes were wide and slicked with pain, and he watched in a kind of helpless horror as they finally overflowed.

"I don't…" She shook, and she wept, and it tore him apart. And then her uneven whisper smashed all the pieces. "I don't know what I'm doing here."

Alessandro reached for her then because he didn't know what else to do. Elena threw her free hand out to stop him, to warn him. Maybe even to hit him, he thought—and he'd deserve it if she did. He did yet another thing he couldn't understand, reaching out and lacing his fingers through hers, the way he had on that dance floor long ago. She shuddered, then drew in a harsh breath.

But she didn't pull away, and something in him, hard and desperate, eased.

"I can't breathe anymore," she whispered, those tears tracking down her soft cheeks. He felt the tremor in her hand, saw it shiver over her skin. "I can't breathe—"

He pulled her to him, cradling her against his chest as if she was made of glass, the need to hold her roaring in him, loud and imperative and impossible to ignore. She bowed her head into him and he felt the hand she'd held against her own heart ball into a fist against the wall of his chest.

He ran his free hand down the length of her spine and then back up. Again and again. He found himself murmuring words he didn't entirely comprehend, half-remembered words from the long-ago nannies who had soothed his nightmares and bandaged his scrapes as a boy. He bent his head down close to hers and rested his cheek on top of her head.

She shook against him, silent sobs rolling hard through her slender body, and he held her. He didn't think about how little sense this made. He didn't think about what this told him about himself, or how terrified he should be of this woman and the things she made him feel. And do. He simply held her.

And when she stopped crying and stirred against him, it was much, much harder than it should have been to let her pull away. She stepped out of his arms and dropped his hand, then scrubbed her palms over her face. And then she looked up at him, tearstained and wary with a certain resolve in her brilliant blue eyes, and something flipped over in his chest.

"I'm not a whore," she said, something naked and urgent moving over her face and through her remarkable eyes as they met his. "I'm not engaged to Niccolo. I ran out on him six months ago after he hit me, and I've been hiding from him ever since."

He only stared at her. The world, this island, his house, even he seemed to explode, devastating and silent, leaving nothing but Elena and the way she looked at him, the faint dampness against his chest where she'd sobbed against him and what she'd said. What it meant.

She was not engaged. She was not a whore. She wasn't a spy.

It beat in him, louder and louder, drowning out his own heartbeat.

"I'm risking everything I care about to tell you this," she continued, and he heard the catch in her voice, the tightness. *The fear,* he thought. *She's afraid. Of me.* "The only things I have left. So please…" She choked back a sob and it made him ache. It made him loathe himself anew. "Please, Alessandro. Prove you're who you say you are."

"A Corretti?" He hardly recognized his own voice, scratchy and rough, pulled from somewhere so deep in him he hadn't known he meant to speak.

She crossed her arms, more to hold herself than to hold him off, he thought. She took a deep breath. Then her chin lifted and her blue eyes were brave and somber as they held his, and he felt everything inside of him shift. Then roll.

"Be the man who does the right thing," she said, her voice quiet. And still it rang in him, through him, like a bell. Like a benediction he couldn't possibly deserve. "Who does his duty and would again. If that's who you are, please. Be you."

"Come," Alessandro said in a hushed voice Elena had never heard before.

She was so dazed, so hollowed out by what had happened, what she'd done, that she simply followed where he led. He ushered her out onto a small nook of a terrace that jutted out over the water, settling her into the wide, swinging chair that hung there, swaying slightly in the soft breeze.

"Wait here," he told her, and then walked away.

She couldn't have moved if she'd wanted to, she realized. She drew her knees up onto the bright white seat and leaned back. The chair swung, gently. Rocking her. Soothing her the way his hand had, warm and reassuring along her back as she'd cried. Down below, the rocky cliff fell steeply into the jagged rocks, and the sea sparkled and danced in the afternoon sun, as if everything was perfectly fine. As if none of this mattered, not really.

But Elena knew better.

She'd betrayed her family and her village and every last thing she'd clung to across all of these months, and yet somehow she couldn't seem to do anything but breathe in the crisp air, the scent of sweet flowers and cut grass in the breeze.

Almost as if she really believed she was safe. Almost as if she thought *he* was, the way she always had. When she suspected the truth was that she was simply broken beyond repair.

Alessandro returned with a damp cloth in his hand and when he squatted down before her his hard face was so serious that it made her chest feel tight. She leaned forward and let him wash the tears from her face. He was extraordinarily gentle, and it swelled in her like pain.

He pulled the cloth away and didn't move for a moment. He only looked up at her, searching her face. She had no idea what he saw.

"Tell me," he said.

It was an order as much as it was a request, and she knew she shouldn't. Her mind raced, turning over possibilities like *tavola reale* game pieces, looking for some way out of this, some way to fix what she'd done, what she'd said, what she'd confessed....

But it was too late for that.

This was the price of her foolishness, her selfishness. First Niccolo had tricked her, and then this man had hurt her feelings, and she was too weak to withstand either. Now that her tears were dry, now that she could breathe, she could see it all with perfect, horrifying clarity. She hadn't kept her village or her family's legacy safe the first time, and given the opportunity to fix that, she'd failed.

Because he thought too little of her, and she couldn't stand it.

She was more than broken, she thought then. She was a disgrace.

"Tell me what happened to you," he said then, carefully, again so very gentle that her throat constricted. "Tell me what he did."

He rose and then settled himself on the other end of the swinging chair, one leg drawn up and the other anchoring them to the floor. His hard mouth was in a firm line as he gazed at her, his dark green eyes grave. For a moment she was thrown back to that ballroom in Rome, when she'd looked up to see a stranger looking at her, exactly like this. As if the whole world hinged on what might happen next.

Which she supposed it had then. Why not again?

"I'm from a long line of very simple fishermen," she said, pushing past the lump in her throat, concentrating on her hands instead of him. "But my great-grandfather eloped with the daughter of a rich man from Fondi. Her parents begged her to reconsider, but she refused, and they decided it was better their daughter live as a rich fisherman's wife than a poor one's.

They gave my great-grandfather her dowry. It was substantial."

She pulled up her knees, then wrapped her arms around her legs, fully aware that this was as close to the fetal position as she could get while sitting up. And she fought off her sense of disloyalty, the fact that she should be protecting this legacy, not handing it over to man who was perfectly capable of destroying it. On a whim.

But she didn't know what else to do.

"He was a proud man and he didn't want their money," she continued, swallowing back the self-recrimination. "But my great-grandmother convinced him to put it toward a big stretch of land along the coast, so her family need not be as dependent on the whims of the sea as the rest of the village. And the land has been handed down ever since, from eldest son to eldest son."

She looked past him then, out toward the water, as if she could squint hard and see all the way across the waves to the remote little village she was from, tucked up in its rocky hills so far away. She could imagine every rock, every blade of grass, every tree, as if she was standing there now. She knew every house that clung to the hillside, every boat in the harbor. And most of the faces, too.

"It must," Alessandro said quietly, "be worth a great deal more now than it was then."

Elena should have thanked him, she thought, her eyes snapping back to his, for reminding her where she was. And who he was. She wasn't sharing this story with him—she was gambling everything on the slim possibility he was a better man than she thought he was. She nodded.

"It is," she said. "And my parents had only me."

"So the land is yours?" he asked, his brows lifting.

"My father is a traditional man," Elena said, looking down the sweep of her legs, staring at her feet against the bright white cushions. Anywhere but at Alessandro. "When he dies, if I'm not married, the land will be held in trust. Once I marry it will transfer to my husband. If I'm already married when he dies, my husband will get the land on our wedding day."

"Ah," Alessandro said, a cynical twist to his lips when she looked at him again. "You must have been Niccolo's dream come true."

"Last summer my father was diagnosed with a brain tumor," she told him, pushing forward because she couldn't stop now. "There was no possible way to operate." So matter-of-fact, so clinical. When it had cast her whole world into shadow. It still did. "The doctors said he had a year to live, if he was lucky."

"A year?" His dark green gaze felt like a touch.

The long arm he'd stretched out along the back of the seat moved slightly, as if he meant to reach for her but thought better of it. That shouldn't have warmed her. "It's nearly July."

She hugged herself tighter, guilt and shame and that terrible grief flattening her, making it hard to breathe.

"About a month after we got the news, I was walking home one evening when a handsome stranger approached me, right there in the street," she said softly.

Alessandro's lips thinned, and he muttered something guttural and fierce in Sicilian. He looked furious again, dark and powerful, like some kind of vengeful god only pretending to sit there so civilly. Only waiting.

"Do you want to hear this?" she asked then, lifting a hand to rub at the pressure behind her temple and only then realizing that she was shaking. "All of it?"

"I told you," he said, a kind of ferocity in his voice, all that ruthlessness and demand gleaming in his dark green eyes. He touched her then, reaching over to tuck a wayward strand of her hair behind her ear, that hard mouth curving when goose bumps rose along her neck, her shoulder. "I want everything."

And Elena understood then that she was open and vulnerable to this man in ways she'd never been before. This really was everything. This was all she had left inside of her, all she'd had left to hold, laid out before him because she'd finally given in. She'd finally let go. This was everything lost, her whole world ruined, and nothing left to hope for but the possibility of his mercy.

This was surrender. Everything else had been games.

"I didn't think I was particularly naive," she said then, because he was looking at her in that too-incisive way of his, and she was afraid of what he might see. And of what he might do when she was finished. "I'd been to university. I have a law degree. I was starting to take on all the duties and responsibilities of the family business. The land. The money. The constant development proposals." She shook her head, scowling at her own memories. Her own stupidity. "I wasn't just some silly village girl."

And that was the crux of it. She felt new tears prick at the backs of her eyes, and hurriedly blinked them back. She'd thought she was better than where she came from. She'd thought very highly of herself indeed. She'd been certain she *deserved* the handsome, wealthy stranger who had appeared like magic to sweep her off her feet.

Such vanity.

She only realized she'd said it out loud when Alessandro said something else in his brash Sicilian, so little of which she understood even after her time there.

He shifted in his seat, making it swing with him as he did.

"I told you before," he said. "It was a con."

"I believed him," Elena said simply, shame and regret in her voice, moving in her veins like sludge. She felt it all over her face, and had to stop looking at him before she saw it on his, too. "I believed every single thing he told me. All of his big dreams. All of his plans. That he and I were a team." Her voice cracked, but she kept going. "That he loved me. I believed every word."

"Elena," he said in a voice she'd never heard him use before. She had to close her eyes briefly against it. As if her name was an endearment she couldn't believe a man so hard even knew. "You were supposed to believe him. He set you up."

She didn't know why she wanted to weep then, again.

"I knew you were lying to me in Rome," she said fiercely, hugging her knees tight, keeping her eyes trained on the sea, determined to hold the tears back. "About everything. You had to be lying, because Niccolo couldn't possibly be the man you described, and because, of course, you were a Corretti."

"Of course." His tone made her wince. She didn't dare look at his expression.

"I went looking for things to prove you were a liar.

One night while Niccolo slept, I got up and decided to search the laptop he took everywhere with him."

She heard Alessandro's release of breath, short and sharp, but she still couldn't look at him. Especially not now.

"He caught me, of course, but not until after I read far too many emails that explained in detail his plans for my family's land." She frowned, as horrified now as she had been then. "He wanted to build a luxury hotel, which would transform my forgotten village into a major tourist destination. We're fishermen, first and foremost. We don't even have a decent beach. We like to visit Amalfi, but we don't want to compete with it."

She shook her head, remembering that night in such stark detail. She'd only thrown on a shirt of Niccolo's and a pair of socks, and had snuck down to the kitchen to snoop on his computer while he snored. It had been cold in his villa, and she remembered shivering as she sat on one of the stools, her legs growing chillier the longer she sat there.

And she remembered the way her stomach had lurched when she'd looked up to see him in the doorway.

He hadn't asked her what she was doing. He'd only stared at her, his black eyes flat and mean, and for a terrifying moment Elena hadn't recognized him.

She'd told herself she was only being fanciful. It had

been well after midnight and she hadn't heard him approach. But he was still her Niccolo, she'd assured herself. He was in love with her, he was going to marry her, and while they were probably going to fight about his privacy and all these emails she couldn't understand, it would all be fine.

She'd been so sure.

"I asked him what it meant, because I was certain there had to be a reasonable explanation." She let out a hollow laugh. "He knew we wanted to conserve the land, protect the village. He'd spent hours talking to my father about it. He'd promised."

"I imagine he did not have a satisfying explanation," Alessandro said darkly.

"He slapped me." Such a funny, improbable word to describe it. The shock of the impact first, then the burst of pain. Then she'd hit the cold stone floor, and that had hurt even more.

Alessandro went frighteningly still.

Elena's heart raced, and she felt sick. Her knuckles were white where she gripped her own legs, and she still wanted to curl up further, disappear. But it didn't matter if he believed her, she told herself staunchly. Her own parents hadn't believed her. It only mattered that she told this truth, no matter what he thought of it.

"He slapped me so hard he knocked me down. Off my stool. To the floor." She made herself look at Alessandro then, burning there in his quiet fury, his dark green eyes brilliant with rage.

Directed at Niccolo, she understood. Not at her. And maybe that was why she told him something she'd never told anyone else. Something she'd never said out loud before.

"He called me a whore," she told him quietly. "Your whore, in fact."

Alessandro swore, and his hand twitched along the back of the swing as if he wanted to reach through her memories, through her story, and respond to Niccolo in kind.

"When was this?" he asked, his voice hoarse.

"A few days after the ball," she said. "After…"

"Yes," he said in a low voice with too many deep currents. "After."

She let go of her iron grip on her legs before her hands went numb, and used them, shaky and cold, to scrape her hair back from her face.

"He said it was bad enough he had to marry me to get the land, but now he had to do it after I'd made him a laughingstock with his sworn enemy?" She didn't see the sea in front of her then. She only saw Niccolo's face, twisted in a rage. She saw the way he'd stood over her, so cruel, so cold, while she lay there too stunned to cry. "He told me that if I knew what was good for me, I'd shut my mouth and be thankful the land was worth more than I was. And then he walked out of the villa and left me there on the floor."

"Elena."

But she had to finish. She had to get it out or she never would, and she didn't want to think about why it was suddenly so important to her that the man she'd never thought she'd see again know every last detail. Every last way she'd made such a fool of herself.

"I left, of course," she said, ignoring the wobble in her voice and the constriction in her throat. And all of his heat and power beside her. "But I didn't really mean it. I thought there was some kind of misunderstanding. He couldn't have meant to hit me, to say those things to me. Maybe he'd been drinking. I went home to my parents, as I always did." She swallowed, hard. "And they hugged me, and told me that they loved me, and then they told me they blamed themselves that I'd turned out so spoiled, so highstrung. So selfish."

She shook her head when he started to speak and he stilled, frowning.

"They were so *kind*. Niccolo was going to be my husband, they told me, and marriages took work. Commitment. I was going to have to grow up and stop telling terrible stories when I didn't get my way." She laughed again, and it sounded broken to her own ears. "Niccolo was a good man, they said, and I believed them. I *wanted* to believe them. It was easier to believe that I'd made up the whole thing than that he was the person I'd seen that night."

Alessandro shifted, and put his arm around her, then gathered her close to his side. Holding her again. Holding her close, as if he could fight off all her demons that easily. She wondered if he could, if he even wanted to bother, and her eyes slicked over with a glaze of heat.

"He laughed when I rang him," she whispered. "He told me that I was a stupid bitch. A whore. He told me I had twenty-four hours to get back to the villa and if I didn't he'd come get me himself, and I would really, truly regret it. That he didn't care if he had to marry me in a wheelchair."

Alessandro's arm tightened around her, and she allowed herself the comfort of his heat, his strength, even though she knew it was fleeting at best. That it wasn't hers, no matter how much it felt as if it was. That he was far more dangerous to her now, armed with all of the knowledge she'd given him, even if he really was the man he claimed he was.

Neither one of them spoke for a long while. His hand moved over her hair, stroking her as if she was something precious to him. She accepted that she wished she was. That she always had. That she'd wanted too much from him from the start, and had been paying for it ever since.

"And that time," she said when she could speak again, giving him everything he'd asked for, everything she'd been hiding, *everything,* "I believed him."

Alessandro stood on the balcony outside his bedroom long after midnight, staring out into the dark.

He couldn't sleep. He could hardly think straight. Once again, she'd shoved his world off its axis, and he was still reeling.

"Why didn't you tell me sooner?" he'd asked her as the light began to change, still holding her on the swinging chair, pulling her closer as the wind picked up.

"You would never have believed me."

"Perhaps," he'd said, but she'd only smiled. "Perhaps, in time, I might have."

But she'd been right. He would have thought it was another game. He would have laughed at her. Hated her all the more. He would have treated her exactly the same—worse, even. He couldn't pretend otherwise.

He balled his hands into fists against the rail now, scowling.

He should have known. He had been too busy concentrating on the darkness in him, too busy nursing his wounded pride. The truth had always been there, staring him in the face. In every kiss, every touch. In the way she'd given herself to him so unreservedly.

In what he'd known about her the moment he'd seen her in Rome.

He should have tried to reach her then. Instead, he'd stormed off that dance floor and left her to be brutalized. He'd put her through hell all on his own. And he couldn't blame his family for that. That had been all him.

He was no different from them at all. He couldn't imagine how he'd ever believed otherwise.

He sensed her behind him a moment before she stepped to the rail beside him, hugging herself against the cool night air.

"I didn't mean to wake you," he said.

She smiled, but she didn't look at him. "You didn't."

He watched her, feeling something work through him, something powerful and new and all about that tilt to her jaw, that perfect curve of her hip, the way she squared her shoulders as she stood there. Her lovely strength. Her courage.

He didn't have the slightest idea what to do with any of it. Or with her.

Alessandro couldn't help but touch her then, his hands curving over her bare shoulders and turning her to face him. She was as beautiful in the shadows as she was in the light, though the wariness in her gaze made his chest ache. He wanted to protect her, to keep her safe. From Niccolo. From the world.

Even from himself.

He stroked his fingers down her lovely face, and felt the way she shivered, heard the way she sighed. He thought of that first touch, so long ago now, that glorious heat. He thought of that marvelous glow between them. That easy, instant perfection.

And all of it was true.

Everything he'd felt. Everything he'd imagined. Everything he'd wanted then, and thought impossible.

"What happens now?" she asked softly, her eyes searching his.

He smiled then, over the rawness inside of him, the dangerous, insidious hope.

"Now?" he asked, his voice gruff. As uneven as he felt. "I apologize."

And then he kissed her, gently, and she melted into him. Like the first time all over again. Better.

Real.

Elena woke in his wide bed, safe and warm.

She lay on her side and gazed out at the morning light, the blue sky, and the previous afternoon came back to her slowly, drip by drip. Then the night. The way he'd picked her up so gently and carried her back to bed. The way he'd moved over her, worshipping every part of her, taking his time and driving her into a sweet, wild oblivion, before curling around her and holding her close as they fell asleep together.

It had been so different, Elena thought now. She smiled to herself. It had felt like—

But she pushed that thought away, afraid to look at it too closely. Her stomach began to ache, and she cursed herself. Things were precarious enough already. There were any number of ways Alessandro could use what she'd told him against her. No need to tangle her emotions any further. No need to make it that much worse.

No need to walk straight into another disaster as blindly as she had the first.

She climbed from the bed and started for the bathroom, aware with each step that she didn't feel well— as if her body was finally taking all of the past weeks' excesses out on her. As if it was punishing her. She had a slight headache. Her stomach hurt. Even her breasts ached. And she felt heavy, all the way through. Almost as if—

She stopped in her tracks and, for a moment, was nothing at all but numb. Then she walked into the bathroom, confirmed her suspicion and had only just come back out again and pulled on the first thing she could find—the long-sleeved shirt he'd been wearing the night before, as it happened—when Alessandro walked through the bedroom door.

He had his mobile phone clamped to his ear, a fierce scowl on his beautiful face, and Elena simply stood there, helplessly, and stared. Everything had changed. Again. She didn't have any idea how this would go, or what might happen next.

And he still made her heart beat faster when he walked into a room. He still made her knees feel weak. All this time, and she hadn't grown used to him at all. All of these weeks, and if anything, she was even more susceptible to him than she had been at the start.

She didn't dare think about what that meant, either. She was terribly afraid she already knew.

"I don't care," he growled into the phone. He raked an impatient hand through his hair. "I'm running out of ways to tell you that, Mother, and I ran out of patience ten minutes ago. None of this has anything to do with me."

He hung up, then tossed the phone on the bed. His dark green eyes narrowed when they found hers. He stilled, that restlessness she could see written all over him fading.

"Has something happened?" Elena asked, and she could hear the nerves in her voice. The panic. His gaze sharpened, telling her he did, too.

"Just one more scandal linked to the Corretti name, though this time, happily, not mine," he said. "Or not entirely mine, though it gives rise to all sorts of speculation I should probably care about." His focus was on Elena, his dark green eyes speculative as they swept over her face. "Alessia Battaglia is pregnant."

Elena swallowed. "Oh," she said.

She wished she wasn't wearing only his shirt. It was like déjà vu. The last time she'd worn a man's shirt— But she couldn't let herself think that way. It would only make this harder.

"Well," she said lamely. She had to clear her throat. "I…am not."

For a long moment, there was only the sound of her heartbeat, loud in her ears. And the way he looked at her across the expanse of his bed, that fierce and arrogant face of his unreadable.

"You're sure?" he asked.

Her throat was dry. "I am."

She didn't know what she expected. But it wasn't the way his face changed, the way his eyes darkened—a brief, searing flash. It wasn't the way that pierced her, straight to the bone.

Regret.

That was what she saw on his face, in his dark gaze. For a dizzying moment, she couldn't breathe.

Because she felt it, too, like a newer, deeper ache. As if they'd lost something today. As if they should grieve this instead of celebrate it, and that didn't make any kind of sense at all.

"All right," he said then. "That's good news, isn't it?"

She nodded, because she didn't trust her voice.

"We must be lucky," he said quietly. But his smile was like a ghost, and it hurt her.

It all hurt.

And she knew why, she thought then, in dawning understanding and a surge of fear. This hadn't been about the games they played, or any of the things she'd been telling herself so fiercely for so long. The lust and the hurt and the wild, uncontrollable passion had been no more than window dressing, and she'd been desperately ignoring what lay beyond all of that since the moment she'd laid eyes on this man in Rome.

Because it shouldn't have happened like that. It shouldn't have happened at all. Love at first sight was nonsense; it belonged in poems, songs. Sentimental films. Real people made choices, they didn't take one look at a stranger on a dance floor and feel the world shift around them, a key turning in a lock.

Elena had been telling herself that for months, and here she was anyway, not carrying his child and as absurdly upset about it as if they'd been trying to get pregnant instead of simply unpardonably reckless.

She was in love with him, God help her. *She was in love with him.*

It rang in her, long and low and deep. And it wasn't new. It had been there from that very first glance. It had happened that fast, that irrevocably, and she simply hadn't wanted to accept that it could be true. But it was.

And now she simply had to figure out how to survive the end of her time with him, the end of these months that had changed her life forever, without giving him that last, worst weapon to use against her.

"Yes," she agreed, aware he was watching her with those clever eyes of his and she knew he saw too much, the way he always did. "Very lucky."

CHAPTER EIGHT

THE FORTIETH DAY dawned with no less than three emails from his assistant detailing the precise time the helicopter would arrive to transport him back to Sicily, and Alessandro still wasn't ready.

He'd run out of excuses. He had to return home or risk damaging Corretti Media in a way he might not be able to fix, and despite his attempts to cut off the part of him that cared about that, he knew he couldn't let it happen. He was the CEO, and he was needed. And he had to deal with his family before they all imploded, something his mother's daily, increasingly hysterical voice-mail messages suggested was imminent.

He had to go back to his life. His attempt to leave it behind had only ever been a temporary measure, a reaction to that cursed wedding. It wasn't him. Duty, responsibility—they beat in him still, and grew louder by the day.

But he couldn't leave Elena. Not now that he'd discovered she was the woman he'd believed she was from the start. Not now that everything had changed.

He didn't know what she wanted, however, and the uncertainty was like a fist in his gut. It had been hard enough to convince her to remain on the island once she'd discovered she wasn't pregnant.

"There's no reason to stay here any longer." She'd attempted that calm, cool smile he hated and he'd taken pleasure in the fact she couldn't quite pull it off, sitting there so primly in the sitting area of his bedchamber, dressed only in one of his shirts and all of the smooth, bare flesh of her legs on display. "Our arrangement was based entirely around waiting to find out—"

"That arrangement was based on the premise that you were still engaged to Niccolo Falco," he'd said, cutting her off. "Working for him, in fact. A spy." He'd smiled. "You are none of those things, *cara*."

"Most importantly, I'm not pregnant," she'd argued, with a stubborn tilt to her chin. "What you thought about me until yesterday is irrelevant, really."

"Do you think he's still searching for you?" he'd asked calmly when he'd wanted nothing more than to put his mouth on her—to remind her how they were anything but irrelevant. And despite that black punch of murderous rage that slammed into him at the thought of Niccolo.

"I know he is," she'd said with a shrug. "He sends me an email every week or so, to make sure I never forget it." She'd smiled then, but it was far too bitter. "It was a good thing I stopped waitressing and took the yacht job. He was in Cefalù only a few days behind me."

He'd had to force his violent fury down, shove it under wraps, before he'd been able to say another word—and even then, the dark pulse of his temper was in every clipped syllable.

"Do you really believe I will simply let you go like this?" he'd asked. "Wash my hands of you and go about my business while that bastard runs you into the ground? What makes you think that's a possibility?"

Something he hadn't been able to identify chased over her face then, but had echoed in him all the same.

"It's not your decision," she'd said after a moment. "It's mine."

They'd stared at each other for a long while.

"You must know I can keep you here," he'd said quietly. "No one comes or goes from this place without my permission."

"You won't do something like that," she'd replied with conviction, her eyes meeting his. Holding. "You're better than that."

And, damn her, he'd wanted to be.

He'd reached over to take her hands in his, threading his fingers through hers, then pulling their joined hands up to his mouth. She'd sighed, her eyes filling with all of that heat and passion that had delivered them here in the first place. And he'd willed her to relent. To bend. To yield.

To want to hold on to him the way he needed to hold on to her.

"You're the one who wanted forty days," he'd said, searching her face, trying to see what he needed to see written there. "There's almost a whole week left."

She'd shaken her head. "Playtime is over, Alessandro."

"Forty days," he'd repeated, because he hadn't known what else to say, how else to convince her. She couldn't leave. This wasn't over—it had only just begun.

"Alessandro…"

"Elena. Please." He hadn't recognized his own voice, much less what coursed through him as he'd said it. "Stay."

He'd begged. There was no other word for it.

But she'd looked up at him then and he hadn't cared at all that he'd bent in a way he'd previously believed impossible. He'd only cared that it worked.

"I'll give you forty days," she'd said when he'd

begun to lose hope, her eyes changing from blue to gray. "But that's it. This can't go on any longer than that."

He'd only moved closer to her, and then he'd taken her mouth with his, answering her as best he could.

It had all gone by too quickly, he thought now, glaring out his window at the sea as if it had betrayed him. As if nature and time had conspired against him. He sensed her come into the master suite before he heard her, that familiar spark of lightning down his spine and straight into his sex—and that fist in his gut seemed to burrow deeper.

"Are you ready?" he asked without turning around. He had to fight to keep his voice level, to keep his temper under control, and it was much harder than it should have been. How could he lose her when he'd just found her? "The helicopter will be here any moment."

"Of course," Elena said, back to that smooth voice he loathed. "I packed everything that's mine."

"And my staff packed everything else," he said evenly. "What use do you imagine I have for the clothes you wore while you were here?"

She didn't answer. He shoved his hands into his pockets so she wouldn't see that he'd balled them into fists. He knew she was still standing there—he could feel her—but the silence stretched out between them, sharp and treacherous. He didn't know what to do, or say.

He only knew he couldn't stand this.

Alessandro heard the unmistakable sound of his helicopter then, roaring toward the meadow for its landing. Coming down fast to hasten this unacceptable ending.

Too late, he thought. *It's always too late.*

He turned then, abruptly, and caught the look on her face. Resolute. Miserable. Brave and determined. He concentrated on *miserable*.

"Stay with me," he bit out. An order this time, with no silk or seduction or even begging to sweeten it.

"Stay?" she echoed, as if she didn't understand the word. "Here?" She shook her head, sketched that airy smile. "You can't keep hiding away here, Alessandro. It's time to go home."

She was dressed for the outside world. No flowing dress, no tiny shorts, no skimpy bikini. She wore those white denim trousers that made him uncomfortably hard, another pair of wicked heels and a peach-colored top that flirted with her curves beneath a cream-colored scarf looped lazily around her neck. Her hair was slicked back into a sleek ponytail, and she had sunglasses perched on her head, ready to slide over her eyes. She looked casually fashionable, impenetrably lovely, and he knew it was armor.

He hated it.

"Come to Palermo with me," he threw out without thinking, but it didn't matter. He didn't care how complicated that could become. He didn't care if it started a damned war with the Falco family. He'd fight it with his own bare hands if he had to. He didn't care about anything but her.

And if an alarm sounded deep inside of him then, he ignored it.

"You know that's impossible," she said fiercely. As if he'd finally struck a nerve. "You know I have to go."

Alessandro remembered that night, so long ago now, when he'd told her he would chase her through the house if she wanted him to do it. That he would let her abdicate any responsibility for what happened between them, let it all be on him, if that was what it took. Was that what she needed?

But he couldn't do it.

"I won't hold you against your will. I won't even beg." His voice was low, but all of their history was in it. That dance. This island. All the truths they'd finally laid bare. "Come with me anyway."

"This isn't fair," she whispered, and he shouldn't have taken it as a kind of harsh victory that she sounded as agonized as he felt. As torn apart. "We agreed."

"Just this once," he said fiercely, "just this one time,

admit what's happening here. What's always been happening here. For God's sake, Elena—come with me because you can't bear to leave me."

Whole worlds moved through her gaze then, and left the overbright sheen of tears in their wake. And it wasn't enough, that he knew she wanted him, too, that he knew exactly how stark her need was. That he could feel it inside of him, lighting up his own. That he knew he could exploit it, with a single touch.

He needed her to admit it. To say it. He needed all of this to matter to her. And the fact that he was uncomfortable with the intensity of that need—that it edged into territory he refused to explore—didn't make it any less necessary.

A moment dragged by, too sharp and too hard. Then another.

"I'm not a good person," she said finally. Her hands opened and closed fitfully, restlessly, at her sides. "And neither are you. A good person would never have allowed what happened between us in Rome to happen at all. I was *engaged.* And you knew I was with Niccolo when you approached me." Her gaze slammed into his. "All we do is make mistakes, Alessandro. Maybe that's all this is. Maybe that's what we should admit."

He started toward her, watching her face as he drew closer. He had never been so uncertain of anything or anyone in his life, and yet so oddly sure of her at the same time. So sure of *this*. He didn't understand it. But like everything with Elena, from that very first glance, it simply was. Undefinable. Undeniable. But always and ever *his*.

"I know that you don't trust me," he said when he reached her, looking down into her troubled blue gaze. "I know what the name Corretti means to you. I know you think all manner of terrible things about me, and I know you're waiting for the next blow." He reached over to trace the vulnerable curve of her mouth with his thumb, making her tremble. "Come to Palermo. Have faith."

He read the storms in her eyes, across her pretty face. And he forced himself to do nothing at all but wait it out. Wait her out.

"I don't believe in faith anymore." A great cloud washed over her, across her face and through those beautiful eyes, and left them shadowed. She pulled in a deep, long breath, then let it out. "But I'll do it," she said finally, as if the words were wrenched from her. "I'll come with you."

Satisfaction and intense relief ripped through him, making him feel bigger. Wilder. Edgy with a ferocious kind of triumph.

But he wasn't finished.

"Tell me why."

Her eyes darkened, and she started to shake her head, started to retreat from him. He slid his hand along her jaw, and held her like that, forcing her to look at him. Keeping her right there in plain sight. Her lips parted slightly, and her breath came hard, as if she was running away the way she no doubt wished she was.

"Tell me," he said quietly. "I need to hear you say it."

She gazed back at him. He could feel her pulse against his hand, could see it wild and panicked in her throat. "Because…" she began, and had to stop, as if her throat closed in on her. Her eyes were filled with heat and damp. She swayed on her feet as if there was a great wind howling around them, and it threatened to knock her flat.

But she didn't fall.

He brushed the knuckles of his other hand over her soft cheek, her distractingly elegant cheekbone.

"Say it," he whispered.

"Because I can't leave you," she said finally, in a broken, electrifying rush. He felt it from the top of his head to the bottom of his feet, as if he'd been struck by lightning, by her, all over again. As if she'd shone that bright light into all of that darkness within him, chasing it away at last. "Not yet."

The helicopter ride was bumpy and noisy, despite the bulky headphones she'd been given to wear, but Elena was happy enough to stay silent while Alessandro and the assistant who'd flown out to meet him discussed Corretti Media business concerns. She soaked in the beckoning Mediterranean blue far below, and pretended the only thing in her head was the sea. The golden sun. The lovely view.

But it didn't work. The enormity of what she'd done was like iron in her chest, making it harder and harder to breathe. It had been one thing to hand over her body, another still to offer up her story to his mercy, such as it was. But she was very much afraid that, today, Alessandro had demanded she give him her soul.

And she'd done it.

She couldn't believe she'd actually done it.

Too soon, the helicopter was making its way through the Palermo skyline, and then setting down on the roof of the landmark Corretti Media tower. Elena climbed out slowly, staying behind Alessandro and the assistant who hadn't stopped talking in all this time, trying to pretend she was not in the least bit overwhelmed. That she gave away her soul like it was little more than a trinket every day of the week. That she was in control of this.

"Signorina Calderon and I are going to eat something," Alessandro said then, breaking into his assistant's stream of chatter in a steely tone she'd never heard before. It brought Elena back to the present with a jolt.

"But, sir," his assistant said in a rush. "Since you've been gone, your family..." His voice trailed off as Alessandro glared at him, but he visibly rallied. "The Battaglia situation is only getting more heated, and time is nearly up for the new docklands proposal—"

"I will come into the office later, Giovanni," Alessandro said with wintry finality.

Elena's stomach twisted. He was cold, harsh, commanding—but with none of that dark fire she knew so well beneath it. This must be Alessandro, the much-feared and much-respected CEO. Alessandro, the eldest Corretti heir. No wonder people spoke of him in such awed, cowed tones. He was terrifying.

"My apologies," his assistant said smoothly, inclining his head. "Of course, that is perfect. We will expect you after lunch."

"If you want me to sign those papers," Alessandro continued in an impatient tone, stalking across the rooftop toward the entrance to the building, "I suggest you do it in the elevator. Quietly."

Elena walked faster as Alessandro's assistant got on his mobile, ordering the car brought around and demanding that someone make sure that Alessandro's favorite table was waiting for him. She reminded herself to breathe as she stepped into the shiny, gold-plated elevator where Alessandro waited, looking for all the world like a surly, caged animal. Dangerous and unpredictable.

The elevator started its descent. Alessandro signed the papers his assistant handed him on a hardbacked folder, one after the next. Without bothering to read them, Elena thought in some surprise—but then he scowled down at one of them.

"These terms are unacceptable. As both you and Di Rossi are well aware."

"He insisted that you had caved," his assistant said mildly, as if he heard that tone from Alessandro every day.

"Send it back," Alessandro ordered. "If he has a problem with it, tell him he can take it up with me personally."

His assistant's brows rose. That was obviously a threat.

The elevator stopped smoothly, discharging Alessandro's assistant on one of the higher floors, and then the doors swished shut and they were alone again. Elena told herself there was no reason at all to be so nervous. Alessandro lounged against the far wall of the car, looking deceptively languid in what was clearly a bespoke suit, the way it marveled over every fine line of his physique. The bright golden walls seemed to shrink into her as the car kept moving. His dark green eyes found hers, and Elena's heart picked up speed.

"Second thoughts?" he asked softly. A challenge.

"You're a very formidable man," she said. "Do you enjoy it?"

He only watched her, that arrogant face a study in careless, encompassing masculine power. His dark brows rose in query.

"Wielding that kind of authority like that," she said. "Making that poor man jump through your hoops without even the faintest pretense of politeness."

Dark green eyes lit with amusement. "Are you calling me rude, Elena? Or just a bad boss?"

"If that's how you treat your employees, I shudder to think how you treat your enemies." She smiled coolly. "Oh, but wait. I already know."

Alessandro's mouth crooked. "Point taken," he said gruffly, surprising her. "I apologize."

"Your assistant is very likely weeping in the toilet," she continued, her tone dry, burying her confusion. Alessandro? Apologizing? "Don't feel you have to apologize to *me*."

"For the record," he said, laughter in his voice, "'that poor man' comforts himself with a new Maserati every fiscal year. He's certainly not weeping as he cashes his paycheck."

"If you say so."

"Come here." His voice dropped, became something else. Something that wound through her like honey, golden and slow, making it hard to remember that he even had an assistant, or why on earth she cared.

"You're at your place of business," she said primly, but she went to him, anyway. "Smiting down every assistant in your path, apparently. All in a day's work, no doubt."

He slid a hand around to the back of her neck and then tugged her off balance so she sprawled against his chest.

This was familiar, finally. His scent, his heat. That gleam in his eyes. Her immediate reaction, molten and hot. And only as it washed through her did she understand how much she'd needed the reminder. That it didn't matter how formidable he might seem here. How distant. That this was still theirs, this electric current. This need.

It was why she was here.

"Ah, Elena," he murmured, simply holding her there against the wall of his chest, his thumb moving against her nape, his expression so intent it made her knees feel like water. "What am I going to do with you?"

"Do you mean in general or in this elevator?" she asked, aware of the breathlessness in her voice, the pounding desire that she had no doubt he could see all over her, the way he always did.

His mouth curved. "I already know what I'm going to do to you in this elevator," he told her, his other hand wrapping around her hip and pulling her against him, letting her feel how much he wanted her. His voice lowered to that sexy growl that lit her up, heating her blood, making her melt. "It might be acrobatic, but I think you can handle it."

Elena heard the *ping* that announced they'd arrived at the ground floor, but Alessandro didn't move. Her hands were pressed against the fascinating muscles of his perfect torso as she arched into him. It wasn't enough, and she didn't care where she was. This was his company—let him care. She lifted herself up on her toes and moved her mouth so close to his that if she licked her lips, she'd taste him.

"Go ahead, then," she whispered, daring him. "Show me some acrobatics."

On some level she was vaguely aware of the elevator doors sliding open, but all that mattered was Alessandro. That dark, consuming green gaze. That familiar fire, still so devastating and far too hot. As if he blacked out everything else.

He laughed, sex and heat and delicious challenge, and she shivered in anticipation, because she knew that sound, she knew its sensual promise—

And everything exploded.

Flashing lights, shouting. The press of too many bodies, the harsh slap of all that noise—

It took her too long to make sense of it—to understand that a scrum of paparazzi crowded into the open elevator door, cameras snapping and tape rolling, while Elena was still plastered against Alessandro's chest, clinging to him, announcing their relationship in stark, unmistakable terms.

But then she understood, and that was worse.

It was the end of the world as she knew it, right there and then.

Elena couldn't stop pacing.

Alessandro's penthouse spread out over the top of the Corretti Media tower, three stories in all. It was magnificent. Glass, steel and granite, yet decorated with a deep appreciation of color and comfort. Lush Persian carpets stretched in front of fireplaces and brightened halls. Stunning, impressive art hung on the high walls, all bold colors and graceful lines. He favored deep chairs, dark woods, and all of it somehow elegant and male. Uniquely him.

And she couldn't enjoy any part of it. She could hardly see it through her panic.

"Of course he'll see the pictures," she said, not for the first time, worrying her lower lip with her fingers as she stared out the great windows. "You can count on it."

Alessandro was sprawled on one of his couches, a tablet computer in his hand. He shot a dark, unreadable look in her direction, but he didn't answer. But then, Elena was really only talking to herself.

He'd dealt with the paparazzi as best he could. He'd stepped in front of her, concealing her from view. He'd alerted his security, then whisked her up to his penthouse and hidden her away from any more cameras.

"Jackals," he'd snarled when the elevator doors finally closed again, leaving them in peace once more. "Nothing but scavengers."

But it was too late. The damage was already done.

Elena's head had spun wildly. She'd let him lead her out of the elevator bank and into his opulent home, and as soon as he'd closed that heavy penthouse door behind them she'd grabbed hold of the nearest wall and sunk down to the floor. Six months of fear and adrenaline and grief had coalesced inside of her and then simply…broken open. Flooding her.

"Don't you understand?" she'd cried. "Niccolo will see those pictures! He'll know exactly where I am! It will take him, what? A matter of *hours* to get to Palermo?"

Alessandro had gazed down at her, an enigmatic expression on his hard face.

"He won't go through me to get at you," he'd said. "He's a coward."

"I'm thrilled for you that you don't have to take him seriously," she'd thrown at him. "But I do. Believe me, Alessandro. *I do.*"

"Elena."

She'd hated the way he said her name then, the way it coiled in her, urging her to trust he'd somehow make this go away. To *have faith.*

"You can't make this disappear simply because you command it," she'd told him, caught between weariness and despair. "You have no idea how devious he is, or how determined."

"If you must insult me," Alessandro had said then, "please spare my security detail. Aside from today's disaster, they're very good at their jobs."

"For how long?" she'd demanded. "A week or two? Another forty days? When will you tire of this—of me?" She'd stared up at him, daring him to contradict her. Daring him to argue. "Because when that day comes, as we both know it will, Niccolo will be waiting. If I have faith in anything, it's that."

Alessandro's expression had shuttered, but he'd only held her gaze for a strained moment before turning on his heel, murmuring something about unavoidable paperwork and walking out. Leaving her there on his floor to drive herself out of her head with worry and the cold, hard fear that had spurred her on all this time.

The fear she'd set aside when she'd been on Alessandro's island. When she'd been safe.

She had to leave, she thought now, frowning out the towering windows at the coming dark. She had to run while she still could. That was the obvious conclusion she'd been circling around and around, not wanting to admit it was the only thing that made sense.

Because he'd been right. She didn't want to leave him. She loved him. It was that simple and that complicated. It always had been.

She turned to look at him then. He was so impossibly, powerfully beautiful. He'd stunned her from the start. And now she knew how that proud jaw tasted. She could lose herself for hours in his hard, cynical mouth. She knew what he could do with those elegant hands of his, with every part of his lean, hard frame. She knew that he felt deeply, and darkly, and that there were mysteries in him she desperately wanted to solve. She knew he'd comforted her, soothing something in her she'd thought ripped forever raw. She knew what it was like when he laughed, when he teased her, when he told her stories. She wanted all of this to be real, for him to be the man she so desperately wanted to believe he was.

She wanted to have faith. She wanted to stay.

God, how she wanted to stay.

He'd thrown off his jacket when he'd returned to the penthouse, lost his tie and loosened the top buttons of his shirt. He looked like what he was. The infinitely dangerous, ruthless and clever CEO of Corretti Media. A man of great wealth and even greater reach. The man who'd taken her body, her painful history, her heart and even her soul. And would take much more than that, she had no doubt. If she let him. If she stayed.

But he didn't love her. She didn't kid herself that he ever would. He spoke only of *want*.

This was sex. Need. A shockingly intense connection mixed with explosive chemistry. Clear all of that away and Elena was as on her own as the day she'd realized even her parents' home wasn't safe for her, and had gone on the run. The past forty days had been nothing but consuming lust, blinding fireworks, and all of it a distraction from that ugly little truth.

He looked up then, his dark green eyes searing and too incisive.

"They've been posted," he said without inflection.

That was it, then. The paparazzi pictures were online. The clock had started ticking. She had to assume Niccolo was on his way even now. Which meant she was standing here on borrowed time.

"I have to go," she said, quick and fierce, before she

could talk herself out of it. Before he could. "I have to leave immediately."

"And may I ask where you plan to go?" That cool CEO's voice. It felt like nails against her skin. "Do you have a plan or are you simply…running away? Again?"

"It doesn't matter where I go," she said, trying so hard to keep all of her feelings out of this. They could only hurt her—and so could Niccolo. It was better to think of him, and run. "So long as it's far from here."

Alessandro tossed his tablet to one side. He gazed at her for a long while, as if he'd never seen her before. As if he saw too much.

Elena repressed an involuntary shiver, and found she couldn't breathe.

"I think you should marry me," he said.

CHAPTER NINE

HER HEART STOPPED in her chest.

Elena stared at him. She couldn't move. She certainly couldn't speak.

Alessandro shrugged, as if what he'd said was as casual as an invitation to coffee, though his dark green eyes were shrewd. They didn't leave her face.

"It's the only way to beat Niccolo at his own game," he said. So matter-of-fact. So calm, so controlled. As if this was nothing but one more contract that required his signature, and not one he needed to read all that closely. "Running from him hasn't worked. How else can this end?"

"It will end when my father dies," she said, though her tongue felt as numb as the rest of her. She was dimly surprised it worked at all. "I'm the executor of the trust. Obviously, he won't be able to manipulate me the way he's manipulated my father."

"He told you he would put you in a wheelchair if necessary," Alessandro reminded her with an edge in his voice and too much dark in his eyes. "He's not going to stop. In fact, he's likely to club you over the head and marry you while you're in a coma."

Elena couldn't think. The room had started revolving around her, whirling in lopsided, drunken circles. She was afraid she might fall over. She ignored the kick of hard, fierce joy inside her, because this wasn't real. It couldn't be real. And if it was? Then it was simply one more game. It wasn't something she should be joyful about.

But it only kicked harder.

"I don't think the solution is to marry you instead," she managed to say.

"Yes, of course," he said then with definite edge that time. "Because you are opposed to marrying for practical reasons, if memory serves. Or is it that you'd prefer to be dragged to the altar by your hair, to the delightful wedding music of Niccolo's abusive threats?"

"This isn't practical" was all she could think of to say.

"He won't touch you if you're my wife," Alessandro replied, steel and fire in his gaze. "The impetus to do so would disappear the moment we said our vows. If you're married, the land is no longer in any dispute. It becomes mine, and your problem is solved."

"On our wedding day," Elena heard herself say from somewhere far away. She couldn't make sense of the words. Or anything else.

His dark eyes gleamed. Something male and primitive moved over his face, then was gone. *Hidden,* something inside of her whispered, but what could he have to hide? He shrugged again, then reached beside him for the tablet, dismissing her.

As if none of this mattered to him, either way. As if this was a minor favor he'd thought he might do her, nothing more.

"Do you really think I'll let you go like this?" he'd asked a week ago on the island, so fiercely. "Wash my hands of you?"

She'd wanted to believe that he wouldn't—that he couldn't. She still did.

"Your choice, Elena."

He wasn't even looking at her. As if this conversation, his proposal of marriage, hardly maintained his interest. But she didn't believe that, either. He was not a man who begged, and yet he had. Surely that meant something. Didn't it have to mean something?

"I know you have strong feelings about the Corretti name," he said in the same offhanded way, "but all you have to do is take it and this insanity ends. It's simple."

It wasn't simple, she thought in a wash of something like anguish. It was anything but simple.

But even as she opened her mouth to refuse him—to do the sane thing and leave him, leave Sicily, save herself the only way she knew how—Elena knew she wouldn't do it. She would take him any way she could have him, even marry him under these questionable circumstances, knowing he would never feel the way she felt.

Nothing had changed. She was the same selfish, foolish girl she'd ever been. She wanted yet another man to love her when she knew that no matter what she'd thought she glimpsed in him now and again, this was nothing more than a game to him, and she no more than another piece on a chessboard he controlled. Eventually, he would grow tired of her. He would leave her.

And yet some part of her was still vain enough to think he might change his mind, that *she* might change it. Still silly enough to risk everything on that slim, unlikely chance.

She hadn't learned a thing in all this time.

"By all means," he said then, languidly scrolling down a page on his tablet, "take your time agonizing over the only reasonable choice available to you. I'm happy to wait."

Could she do it? Could she surrender the most important thing of all—the one thing even Niccolo had never got his hands on? The entire future of her village. Her family's heritage. The land. All because she so desperately hoped that Alessandro was different. That he really would do the right thing.

Because she loved him.

Idiot. The voice in her head was scathing.

Elena jerked herself around and stared out his impressive windows at the lights of the city spread out before her, but what she saw were her parents' faces. Her poor parents. They deserved so much better than this. Than her.

"What a romantic proposal." She shut her eyes. She hated herself. But she couldn't seem to stop the inevitable. She was as incapable of saving herself now as she'd been on that dance floor. And as guilty. "How can I possibly refuse?"

Late that night, Alessandro stood in the door of his bedroom and watched Elena sleep. She was curled up in his bed, and the sight of her there made the savage creature in him want to shout out his triumph to the moon. He almost did. He felt starkly possessive. Wildly victorious.

He could wake her, he knew. She would turn to him eagerly—soft and warm from sleep, and take him inside of her without a word. She would sigh slightly, sweetly, and wrap herself around him, then bury her face in his neck as he moved in her.

She'd done it so many times before.

But tonight was different. Tonight she'd agreed to become his wife.

His wife.

He hadn't known he'd meant to offer marriage until he had. And once he had, he'd understood that there was no other acceptable outcome to this situation. No alternative. She needed to be his, without reservation or impediment. It had to be legal. It had to last. He didn't care what trouble that might cause.

There were words for what was happening to him, Alessandro knew, but he wasn't ready to think about that. Not until he'd secured her, made her his. He turned away from the bed and forced himself to head down the stairs.

Down in his home office, he sat at his wide, imposing desk and frowned down at all of the work Giovanni had prepared for his review. But he didn't flip open the top report and start reading. He found himself staring at the photo that sat on the corner of his desk instead.

It was a family shot he'd meant to get rid of ever since his grandmother had given it to him years ago. All of the Correttis were gathered around his grandmother, Teresa, at her birthday celebration eight years ago. Canny old Salvatore was smirking at the camera, holding one of Teresa's hands in his, looking just as Alessandro remembered him—as if death would never dare take him.

Alessandro's father and uncle, alive and at war with each other, stood with their wives and children on either side of Teresa, who had long been the single unifying force in the family. Her birthday, at her insistence, was the one day of the year the Correttis came together, breathed the same air, refrained from spilling blood or hideous secrets and pretended they were a real family.

Alessandro sighed, and reached over to pick up the photograph. His uncle and four cousins looked like some kind of near mirror image of his own side of the family, faces frozen into varying degrees of mutiny and forced smiles, all stiffly acquiescing to the annual charade. They were all the same, in the end. All of them locked into this family, their seedy history, this bitter, futile fight. Sometimes he found himself envious of Angelo, the only family member missing from the picture, because at least he'd been spared the worst of it.

His sister, Rosa—because he couldn't think of her any other way, he didn't care who her father was— smiled genuinely. Alessandro and Santo stood close together, looking as if they were biting back laughter, though Alessandro could no longer remember what about. His father glared, as haughty and arrogant as he'd been to his grave. And his mother looked as she always did: ageless and angry. Always so very, very angry.

"You should never have stayed away so long," she'd seethed at him earlier today. "It looks like weakness. As if you've been off licking your wounds while your cousin has stolen your bride and made our side of the family the butt of every joke in Palermo!"

"Let him," Alessandro had retorted.

"Surely you don't plan to let the insult stand?" Carmela Corretti had gasped. "Our family's honor demands—"

"Honor?" Alessandro had interrupted her icily. "Not the word I'd choose, Mother. And certainly not if I were you."

She'd sucked in a breath, as if he'd wounded her.

But Alessandro knew the woman who'd raised him. He knew her with every hollow, bitter, blackened part of his Corretti soul. She was immune to hurt. And she always returned a slap with cannon fire.

"You're just like your father," she'd said viciously. And it had speared straight through him, hitting its mark. "All of that polish and pretense on the surface, and rotten to the core within. And we know where that leads, don't we?"

He was so tired of this, he thought now. Of this feud that rolled on and on and did nothing but tear them all apart. Of the vitriol that passed for family communication, the inevitability of the next fight. Would they all end up like his father and uncle, burned on their mysterious funeral pyre, while the whole world looked on sagely and observed that they'd brought it upon themselves? Violent lives, desperate acts—it all led to a terrible end. The cycle went on and on and on.

And was Alessandro really any different? Carlo Corretti had never met a person he wouldn't exploit for his own purposes. He'd never been honest when he could cheat, had never used persuasion when violence worked instead, and he'd never cared in the least that his hands were covered in blood.

"Right and wrong are what I say they are," he'd told Alessandro once, after ten-year-old Alessandro had walked in on him with one of his mistresses. There hadn't been the slightest hint of conscience in his gaze as he'd sprawled there in the bed he shared with Carmela. Right there in the family home. "Are you going to tell me any different, boy?"

Alessandro had hated him. God, how he'd hated him.

He looked up as if he could see Elena through the floors that separated them. She deserved better than this, and he knew it. She wasn't the Battaglia girl, auctioned off by her father to the highest bidder and fully aware of what joining the Corretti family meant—even if, as it turned out, she'd preferred a different Corretti. Elena had already escaped Niccolo Falco and whatever grim fate he'd had in store for her.

If he was any kind of man, if he was truly not like his viciously conniving father, he would set her free immediately.

Instead, he'd manipulated her, and he'd done it deliberately. She didn't have to marry him to be safe; he had teams of lawyers who could help her and her village. Who could deal with the likes of Niccolo Falco in the course of a single morning.

His mother was right. He was following in his father's footsteps. He couldn't pretend any differently. But in the end, even that didn't matter. He wanted her too much, too badly, to do what he knew was right.

He would do his penance instead, as small as it was in the grand scheme of things. He would keep his hands off her until he married her. He would torture himself, and pretend that made this all right. That it made him something other than what he was: his father's son.

Alessandro simply didn't have it in him to let her go.

Four days later, by a special license she hadn't asked how he'd managed to obtain, Elena married Alessandro Corretti in a small civil ceremony.

It was 10:35 in the morning, in a small village outside of Palermo that Elena had never heard of before. But then, she didn't know the name of the man who married them, either, though he had introduced himself as the local mayor. Nor did she know either of the two witnesses who stood with them, both happy to take handfuls of Alessandro's euros for so little of their time.

It took all of twenty minutes.

In the private antechamber even more of Alessandro's money had secured for them, Elena stared at herself in the room's small mirror and ran her fingers down the front of the dress she wore. It was a rich, deep cream. It had delicate sleeves and fell from a pretty scooped neck into a flattering A-line that ended at her knees. Her hair was twisted back into a sophisticated chignon, and she wore a single strand of stunning pearls around her throat to match the diamond-and-pearl clusters at her ears. She looked elegant and chic. Polished. Smart.

She looked nothing at all like herself.

And why should you? a caustic voice inside her demanded. Elena Calderon was no more. She was Alessandro's wife now. *Signora Elena Corretti.*

She swallowed against the tide of emotion she didn't dare examine here, and chanced a look in Alessandro's direction. He was her husband. *Her husband.*

But he didn't love her.

Better to deal with the repercussions of that sooner rather than later, she thought, bracing herself. Better to ensure she didn't fall prey to her own imagination, her own precarious hopes. And what better place to make everything between them perfectly clear than the lounge of a town hall in a sleepy village, fitted with two ugly chairs and a desperate-looking sofa arranged around a cracked wood floor?

Congratulations on your hasty and secretive wedding, Signora Corretti, she mocked herself. *No expense or luxury was spared for your happy day!*

Alessandro stood near the closed door, on his mobile. The phone had beeped some thirty seconds after they'd signed the register. He'd announced he needed to take the call, and had waved her back into the antechamber she'd used before the ceremony.

She was almost positive she'd seen pity on the mayor's face before Alessandro had closed the door behind them.

"When do you think we should divorce?" she asked briskly when he ended his call, looking out through the small windows at the Sicilian countryside. Proud mountains with vineyards etched into the lower slopes. Red-roofed houses clinging to green hillsides. Olive groves and ancient ruins. All of it piercingly, hauntingly lovely. There was no reason at all it should have made her chest ache. "Did you have a particular time frame in mind?"

When he didn't respond, Elena turned away from the window—

And found him staring at her in amazement.

"We have been married for ten minutes, Elena," he said in a voice that made her skin pull tight. "Possibly fifteen. This conversation seems a trifle premature."

"This was the only reasonable choice I had, as you pointed out, and a convenient way to fix the Niccolo problem." She was suddenly too aware of the rings he'd slid onto her finger—a trio of flawless diamonds set in platinum on the drive over, and a diamond-studded platinum band during the ceremony, such as it was. It occurred to her that she was, in fact, deeply furious with him. She'd wanted this to mean something. She'd wanted it to matter. She was an idiot. "Nothing more than that. What does it matter if we discuss it now?"

He went incandescent. She actually saw him catch fire. His dark eyes were ferocious, his mouth flattened, and she was certain she could hear his skin sizzle with the burn of his temper from across the tiny room.

And it didn't scare her. She welcomed it. It was a happy alternative to the icy cold CEO who'd taken Alessandro's place since they'd returned to Sicily. Since the paparazzi had found them and plastered their faces across every gossip magazine and website in Europe. Since he'd shocked her with his proposal. He'd been distant. Controlled. He hadn't laid a finger on her, and there'd been nothing but winter in his dark green eyes.

She preferred this Alessandro. She knew this Alessandro.

No matter how tight and close it felt suddenly, in such a small room, with him blocking the only exit.

"I suggest you drop this subject," he advised her, hoarse with the force of his temper. There was that glitter of high passion, furious desire, in his too-dark eyes, and she exulted in it. She needed it.

"Oh," she said brightly, unable to help herself. "Were you thinking an annulment would work better?"

He laughed. It was a hard, male sound, primitive and stirring. It coursed through her, made her shiver with the heat of it. Made her ache. And the look he turned on her then melted her bones.

"I did warn you," he said.

He reached behind him and locked the door, and Elena felt it like a bullet. Hard and true, straight into her core. He crossed the room in a single stride, hauled her to him and then pulled her down with him as he sat on the sad, old sofa. Then he simply lifted her over his lap.

He hiked her dress up over her hips, ripped her

panties out of his way with a casual ferocity that made her deliciously weak, then stroked two long fingers into the melting furnace of her core. Elena gasped his name. He laughed again at the evidence of how much she wanted him, all of her molten desire in his hand. She braced her hands on the smooth lapels of his wedding suit, another stunning work of art in black, and not half as beautiful as that mad hunger that changed his face, made him that much starker. Fiercer.

Hers.

Alessandro didn't look away from her as he reached between them and freed himself. He didn't look away as he ripped open a foil packet with his teeth and rolled protection on with one hand. And he didn't look away as he thrust hard into her, pulling her knees astride him, gripping her bottom in his hard hands to move her as he liked.

"An annulment is out of the question," he told her, his voice like fire, roaring through her. "And in case you're confused, this is called consummation."

Elena's head fell back as she met his thrusts, rode him, met his passion with every roll of her hips. She felt taken and glorious and his.

Completely his.

He changed the angle of her hips, moving her against him in a wicked rhythm, and she felt herself start to slip toward that edge. That easily. That quickly.

Still fully dressed. Still wearing her wedding shoes and the pearls he'd presented her this morning. Still madly in love with this hard, dangerous man who was deep inside of her and knew exactly how to make her blind with desire. This man who was somehow her husband.

Whatever that meant. However long it lasted. Right then, she didn't care.

"You are mine, Elena," he whispered fiercely, his voice dark and sinful, lighting her up like a new blaze. "You are my wife."

It was that word that hurled her over, sent her flying apart in his arms, forced to muffle her cries with her own hand as he muttered something hot and dark and then followed right behind her.

When she came back to herself, he was watching her face, and she wondered in a surge of panic what he might have seen there. What she might have revealed.

"Don't talk to me about divorce," he said in a low voice, his dark green eyes hot. "Not today."

He shifted forward, setting her on her feet before him. She felt unsteady. Utterly wrecked, yet a glance in the mirror showed he hadn't disturbed a single hair on her perfectly coiffed head. She smoothed her dress back down into place, her hands trembling slightly. Alessandro tucked himself back into his trousers and then reached down to scoop up the lace panties he'd torn off her.

Because he'd been too desperate, too determined to get inside her, to wait another instant. She didn't know why that should make her feel more cherished, more precious to him, than all twenty strange minutes of their wedding ceremony.

She held out her hand to take the panties back. His hard mouth curved, his dark eyes a sensual challenge and something far more intense, and then he tucked them in his pocket.

"A memento of our wedding day," he said, mocking her, she was sure. "I'll treasure it."

She smiled back at him, cool and sharp.

"An annulment it is, then," she said. "This has been such a useful, rational discussion, Alessandro. Thank you."

He laughed again then, almost beneath his breath, and then he was on his feet and striding for the door, as if he didn't trust himself to stay locked in this room with her a moment longer. She allowed herself a small, satisfied smile.

"We can argue about this in the car," he said over his shoulder. "I have a one o'clock meeting I can't miss."

Because, of course, the CEO of Corretti Media didn't stop doing business on his wedding day, not when the wedding meant so little to him. Her smile vanished. It was a brutal reminder of reality. Of her place. It didn't matter how hot they burned. It didn't matter how desperate he'd been. Elena clenched her hands into fists and felt the bite of the unfamiliar bands around her finger like one more slap.

And then followed him, anyway.

His mobile beeped again as they walked. He answered it, slowing down as he talked. Elena heard the words *docklands, cousin* and *Battaglia*. Alessandro pushed open the glass doors at the entrance of the village hall, and nodded her through, almost as if he had a chivalrous bone in that powerful body of his.

"Wait for me in the car," he said, and then turned back toward the interior of the hall. Dismissing her.

The door swished shut behind her as she stepped through it, and Elena pulled in a long, deep breath. The morning was still as bright and cheerful as it had been when she'd walked inside. A lovely July day in the rolling hills of Sicily. The perfect day for a wedding.

She had to figure out how to handle this, to enjoy it while it lasted, or she'd never survive it. And she had to do it fast.

Elena kept her eyes on the stairs below her as she climbed down the hall's steps, her legs still so shaky and the heels she wore no help at all, so she had to hold tight to the bannister as she went. Cracking her head open on the pavement would hardly improve matters.

She made it to the bottom step in one piece, and started to walk around the man who stood there, his back to the hall. Alessandro's sleek black sports car was parked near the fountain in the center of the pretty village square, the convertible top pulled back, reminding her of how silly she'd been on the drive over—glancing at the way the ring sparkled on her hand, allowing herself to yearn for impossibilities.

"Excuse me," she murmured absently as she navigated her way around the man, glancing at him to smile politely—

But it was Niccolo.

All of the blood drained out of her head. Her stomach contracted in a sickening lurch, and she was sure her heart dropped out of her body and lay at her feet on the pavement.

"Niccolo…" she whispered in disbelief.

Niccolo, like all of the nightmares that had kept her awake these past months. Niccolo, his arms folded over his chest and his black eyes burning mean and cold as he soaked in her reaction.

Niccolo, who she'd thought she loved until Alessandro had walked into her life and showed her how pale that love was, how small. Niccolo, who she'd trusted. Who she'd laughed with, thinking they were laughing together. Who she'd dreamed with, thinking they were planning a shared future. Niccolo, who had hunted her across all these months and the span of Italy, and was looking at her now as if that slap in his villa was only the very beginning of what he'd like to do to her.

She couldn't believe this was happening. Today. Here. Now.

"Elena," he said, his voice almost friendly, but she could see that nasty gleam in his eyes. She could see exactly who he was. "At last."

CHAPTER TEN

ELENA NEEDED TO say something, *do* something.

Scream for help, at the very least. Kick off her shoes and run. She needed to get as far away from Niccolo as possible, to distance herself from that vicious retribution she saw shining in his black eyes and all across his boyishly handsome face.

But she couldn't seem to move a single muscle.

His lip curled. "Did you really think you could outrun me forever?"

She threw a panicked glance back up the stairs. Alessandro was still there, on the far side of the glass door, but he had his back turned to the square. To what was happening. To her.

Elena didn't know why she'd believed he could save her from this, even for an instant. Hadn't she always known she would have to handle it herself?

Niccolo looked up at Alessandro, then back at her, and his expression grew uglier.

"You've never been anything but a useless little whore, Elena," he said, his black eyes bright with malevolence. "I took you out of that fishing boat you grew up in. I made something out of you. And this is how you repay me?"

Elena straightened. Pulled in a breath. He was shorter than she remembered. Thicker and more florid. The observation gave her a burst of strength, because it meant things had changed—*she* had changed.

"You didn't do any of that for my benefit," she said, finding steel inside her, somewhere. "You did it because you wanted the land. And then you hit me."

"You owed me that land," he snarled at her. "I dressed you up, took the stink of fish out of your skin. And then you let a Corretti steal it."

"He didn't steal anything," she told him, keeping her gaze steady on his. "And he hasn't hit me, either."

"Just how long were you sleeping with him?" Niccolo demanded. "I know you lied to me. There's no way that night was the first time you met him. How long were you stringing me along?"

"You *hit* me, Niccolo," she said fiercely. "You threatened me. You lied to my family. You—"

"I let you off easy," he interrupted her, and the names he called her then, one after the next, were vile. They made her feel sick—and sicker still that she had ever loved this man, that she'd touched him, that she'd failed to see what he really was. "What I want to know is how Corretti feels every time he takes a piece of my leavings."

His hand flashed out and he grabbed her arm in a painful grip, but she didn't make a sound. She didn't even flinch. She refused to give him the satisfaction of thinking he'd hurt her again.

"Does he know, Elena?" he snarled. "Does he know I've already been there?" He smirked, smug and mean. "He's not the kind of man who likes to share."

Something in her changed then. She felt it shift. Elena didn't care that his fingers around her arm hurt. She didn't care that the look on his face would have frightened her once.

She didn't have to be afraid of him any longer. She didn't have to run. Alessandro had given her that much. As she looked up at Niccolo now, Elena finally accepted that even if Niccolo had been who he'd pretended to be, it still would have been over between them.

It had been over the moment she'd met Alessandro.

Even if she'd never seen him again after that night in Rome, she would have known the truth: that she'd loved a stranger for the duration of a dance far more than she'd loved her fiancé. It would have ended her engagement one way or another. Maybe, she thought then, she'd actually been lucky that dance had forced Niccolo to reveal himself. It would have been much, much harder to leave the man she'd thought he was.

"But then," Niccolo was saying, "he doesn't care about you, does he? He wants the land. Do you think he would trouble himself to marry you otherwise?"

He shook her, and that hurt, too, but she didn't try to pull away. She didn't defend Alessandro's motives or worry that she didn't know what they were. She didn't cry or protest. She stared at him, memorizing this, so she would never forget what it felt like the moment she'd not only stopped being afraid of Niccolo Falco, but stopped feeling guilty about how this had all happened in the first place.

Inevitable, something whispered inside of her. *This was all inevitable.*

"I never would have married you," she said then, her voice smooth and strong. "Alessandro only expedited things. You would have shown your true face sooner or later. And I would have left you the moment I saw it."

"Look at where you are," Niccolo ground out, his fingers digging into her arm. "This tiny town, all alone. Have you really convinced yourself that a man like Alessandro Corretti, who invited half of Europe to his last wedding, cares about a nobody like you?" He laughed. "Wake up, Elena. The only difference between Alessandro Corretti and me is that he has enough money to be a better liar."

Elena would have to think about that, she knew. She would have to investigate the damage he'd caused with that hard, low blow. But not now. Not here.

"You don't need to concern yourself with that land," she said, ignoring the rest of it. She let him see how little she feared him, let him see she wasn't shaking or cowering. "It will never be yours. You lost it the moment you thought you could hit me."

His face flushed even redder, even angrier than before. He yanked her closer to him, shoving his face into hers, trying to intimidate her with his size and strength. He was a petty man, a vicious one. But she still wasn't afraid.

"I'm not scared of you anymore, Niccolo," she said very distinctly, tilting her head back to look him full in the face. Not hiding. Not running. Not afraid. "And that means you need to let go of my arm. Now."

Whatever he saw in her face then made him drop her arm as if she'd turned into a demon right there in front of him. And Elena smiled, a real and genuine smile, because she was free of him.

After all this time, she was finally free of him.

"Step away from my wife, Falco."

Alessandro's icily furious voice cracked like a whip, startling Elena. Better, it made Niccolo move back.

Alessandro was beside her then, his hand stroking down her back, as if he was reassuring himself that she still stood in one piece.

Or, the cynical part of her whispered, *marking his territory.*

"Give us a minute."

It took Elena a moment to realize that Alessandro was speaking to her as he stared at Niccolo, murder in his dark green gaze. She frowned up at him.

But the Alessandro she knew was gone. There was nothing but darkness and vengeance on his fierce face. The promise of violence, of blood. Like a black hole where the man she loved should have been. It made every hair on the back of her neck prickle in warning. It made her pulse pick up speed.

It made her want to cry, as if they'd lost something.

"Alessandro, please," she said softly. "He's not worth it."

Niccolo sneered. Alessandro only seemed to grow bigger, taller. Darker. More terrifying. And she'd never seen his face so cold, those dark green eyes so remote.

"Alessandro," she said again.

But he still didn't look at her.

"Get in the car," he ordered her in a voice she'd never heard before. As if the man she knew was gone and in his place was this frigid and furious stranger, capable of anything. As if Niccolo was right, and she didn't know him at all. As if she never had. "Do it now."

And she didn't know how to reach him, or if she could. She didn't understand what was happening here, only that she shouldn't let him do the things she saw promised on his hard face, in those deadly eyes....

But he didn't love her. She was a temporary wife, at best.

And for all she knew, he'd married her for the land and this was simply another truth she'd been too blind to see. His true face, after all.

It ripped her up inside, but she obeyed him.

Alessandro wanted to kill Niccolo Falco. Very, very slowly.

"My congratulations," the little pissant sneered, puffing out his chest and stepping suicidally close. "You keep her on a tight leash."

His father would have simply kicked in one of Niccolo's kneecaps, the better to drag him off and beat the life out of him in a more private place. Alessandro had seen Carlo do exactly that when he was fourteen.

"Men deal with problems like men, boy," Carlo had told him, clearly disappointed that Alessandro hadn't reacted better. "Take that scared look off your face. You're a Corretti. Act like one."

And Alessandro had never felt more like a Corretti,

with all of the blood and graft and misery that implied, than he did right now.

Retribution. Revenge. Finally, he understood both.

"Be very careful," Alessandro said through his teeth, trying to push back the red haze that obscured his vision. "You're talking about my wife."

Niccolo's neck was flushed. His black eyes were slits of rage, and his thick hands were in fists. Alessandro knew he'd used one of those meaty hands on Elena, once before and once today, and had to battle back the urge to break the both of them.

He had no doubt at all that he could. He hadn't fought in over forty days now—but he wasn't drunk this time.

"I had her first," Niccolo threw at him, a sly look in his eyes. "In every possible—"

"I won't warn you again."

It would be so easy. To simply end this man, as he richly deserved. He was nothing but a parasite, a lowlife. Alessandro didn't even have to get his hands dirty, the way his father had so enjoyed. He knew which former associates of his father's he could call to "handle" this. It was part and parcel of his blackened family legacy. It would take a single phone call.

This was who he was. Just as his mother had told him. Just as Elena had accused him. Just as he had always feared.

But this would be justice, that seductive darkness whispered. *Simple. Earned.*

Alessandro had to force air into his lungs. All the choices his father and uncle and grandfather had made, all the blood that stained their hands as they'd built this family up from nothing and punished whoever dared stand in their way—he'd always looked down on them for it.

He'd never understood how easy it might be to step across that line. He'd never understood the temptation. Or that it could seem not only right to exterminate a cockroach like Niccolo Falco, but inarguably just.

Necessary.

That darkness in him didn't even seem particularly dark to him today as he stared at the bastard who'd terrorized Elena. It seemed like a choice. The right choice.

But.

But Elena had cried in his arms, and then she'd trusted him when he didn't deserve it at all. When he'd given her no reason to trust him. She'd married him. He couldn't understand why she'd done it. He wasn't sure he ever would.

But it burned in him. It lived in him, bright like hope.

"Be the man who does the right thing," she'd said once. And her eyes were the perfect blue of all his favorite summers, and she'd looked at him as if he could never be a man like his father.

As if she had some kind of faith in him, after all.

"Why take her at all?" Niccolo demanded, stepping even closer, tempting fate. "Because she was mine?"

Alessandro smiled at him, cold and vicious. "Because I can."

Niccolo snorted. "You're nothing but a thug in fancy clothes, aren't you?"

Alessandro was done then. With Niccolo, with all of this. With who he'd nearly become. With that dark spiral he'd almost lost himself in today, that he could still feel inside of him.

But Elena was like light, and he wanted her more.

"Don't let me see you again, Falco. Don't even cross into my line of sight. You won't like what happens." He leaned closer then, pleased in a purely primitive way that he was bigger. Taller. That there was that flicker of fear in the other man's eyes. "And stay the hell away from my wife. That goes for you and your entire pathetic family. You do not want to go to war with me, I promise you."

Niccolo recoiled, the angry flush on his face and neck bleeding into something darker. Nastier.

"Don't worry," he said, ugly and flat. "Once I'm finished with a whore—"

Alessandro shut him up. With his fist.

He felt the crunch of bone that told him he'd broken Niccolo's nose, heard the other man's bellow of pain as he crumpled to the ground. Where he lay in a cowardly heap, clutching at his face.

And Alessandro wasn't his father, he would never be his father, but he was still Corretti enough to enjoy it.

"Next time," he promised, "I won't be so kind."

And then he walked away and left Niccolo Falco bleeding into the ground.

But alive.

"I'm sorry I let him touch you," Alessandro said gruffly when he swung into the car. Elena sat there so primly in the passenger seat, looking perfect. Untouchable. Her face smooth and her eyes hidden away behind dark glasses. "It won't happen again."

"He didn't hurt me," she said. Far too politely. When he only frowned at her, searching her face for some sign, she shifted slightly in her seat. "Don't you have a meeting?"

He reminded himself that he had her torn panties in his pocket. That if he reached over and touched her, he could have her moaning out his name in moments. But he started the car instead, and pulled out onto the small country road that led away from the village and back toward Palermo.

He'd told her Niccolo wouldn't come for her, and

he had. She had every right to be afraid, even angry. To blame him.

He could handle that. He could handle anything—because she'd married him, and they had nothing now but time. The rest of their lives, rolling out before them. There was nowhere to hide. Not for long.

They drove in silence, the warm summer day rushing all around them, sunshine and wind dancing in and around the car. The hills were green and pretty and off in the distance the sea beckoned. She was his wife, and he wasn't his father.

It might not be perfect, Alessandro thought. It might take some work yet. But it was good.

"Why did you hit him?" she asked as they started to make their way into the city sprawl, and the wind no longer prohibited conversation.

"I should have killed him," Alessandro replied shortly. "I wanted to kill him."

But he hadn't.

He hadn't.

"I didn't say he didn't deserve it," she replied in that cool way that he still hated, even now. "I only wondered what horrible thing he might have said to tip you over that edge."

Alessandro eyed her as he stopped at a traffic light. He considered telling her about real edges, and what lay on the other side of them, but refrained. There would be time enough to introduce her to all the poison and pain that was his birthright, to tell her what had happened back there and what he'd finally rejected once and for all.

"He called you a whore."

"Ah," she said. She sat there so elegantly. So calmly. Her hands folded in her lap, her legs neatly crossed. She smiled, and it scraped at him. "So it's only okay when you do it?"

Alessandro pulled in a breath through his teeth.

"Damn it, Elena," he began, but she turned to face the front again, and nodded toward the road with every appearance of serenity.

"The light's changed."

He swore in Sicilian as well as Italian, and then he drove with more fury than skill through the city, screeching to a halt at the valet in front of the Corretti Media tower.

Elena let herself out of the car before he had the chance to come around and get her, starting toward the building's entrance as if she didn't care one way or the other if he followed her. Gritting his teeth, he did.

She said nothing as they walked through the marble lobby. She only slid her dark glasses onto the top of her head and let him guide her into the elevator when it arrived.

"Is there anything else you plan to throw at me

today?" he asked, tamping down on his temper as the doors slid shut. "Do we need to have another discussion like the one we had about divorce?"

Elena stared straight ahead, her gaze fixed on the far wall and the flashing numbers that announced each floor, though a faint flush spread across her cheeks.

"There's nothing else," she said. He didn't recognize that voice she used, the way she held herself. But he knew she was lying. "I'm sorry. I don't know why I said that."

"Are you sure he didn't hurt you?" he asked quietly.

She looked at him then, and her blue eyes were shadowed. Dark.

"No." There was something there then. Something making her voice catch, her mouth take on that hint of vulnerability that killed him. "I told you."

"Elena," he said. "You have to know—"

But his mobile beeped. She blinked, then looked away, and when she glanced at him again her face was that smooth mask. He couldn't stand it.

"Tell me what's wrong," he urged her. "Tell me what happened."

"You should answer that," she said, much too calmly, when his phone kept beeping. "I'm sure it's important."

He pulled out the phone to look at the screen, and wasn't surprised at the number he saw flashing there.

"It's my family," he started, not knowing how to compress the history of the Corretti feuds into something coherent. Not knowing how he felt about any of it, now that he'd pulled himself back from the abyss that had stalked him all these years. "There are all these divisions, these petty little wars—"

"I read the papers, Alessandro," she said gently. "I know about your family." She nodded at his mobile. "You should take the call."

"I always take the call," he gritted out. "And it never helps. Whenever there's a possibility of ending this nonsense, we make sure to destroy it." He shook his head. "I'm beginning to believe we always will."

She looked at him for a long moment, and he had the sense she was weighing something behind those stormy eyes he couldn't read. She reached over and hit one of the elevator buttons, making his main office floor light up.

"Then you should fix it," she said. She even smiled, and it was almost real. He almost believed she meant it. "Isn't that what you do?"

"No," he said shortly, his gaze searching hers. "Obviously not."

Her eyes were much too dark, and it ate at him. Something flared between them in the small space, a different kind of fire, and he had the awful sense that he'd already lost her. That she had already disappeared.

But she was right here, he reminded himself sternly. She had married him slightly more than an hour ago. She was his.

"What's the right thing?" she asked, her voice too quiet. "Do that, even if it hurts. Your family deserves it."

"And if they don't?"

After all these bitter years. After all the pain, the blood.

He thought he saw compassion in her gaze, or maybe he only wanted that. Maybe he was simply desperate for something he recognized, something to ease the gnawing sensation inside of him.

The elevator doors slid open, and she looked away, out toward the hushed executive level of Corretti Media.

His phone beeped again. Insistent. Annoying. He heard Giovanni's voice from the office floor, the valet no doubt having informed him that Alessandro had returned.

"Your family might not deserve it, Alessandro. But you do."

"Me?" He hardly made a sound. He hardly breathed. "I fear I deserve it least of all."

The moment stretched between them, taut and shimmering with all the things he did not, could not, feel, except for her. He said her name again. His favorite incantation. His only remaining prayer.

"Go," she whispered.

And it wasn't until the elevator door had closed on her, and he was striding toward his responsibilities the way he always did, that he realized what he'd seen flash in her eyes then was a deep, dark sadness.

Elena took an early-afternoon flight out of Palermo's Falcone Borcellino Airport, headed for Naples and the car she'd hired for the drive back to her village. She settled into the economy-class seat she'd bought with the money she'd earned waitressing and on Alessandro's yacht, not the money he—or, more likely, his staff—had left for her in the penthouse in a folder with her name on the front and a selection of credit cards and cash within.

And when the plane took off and soared into the air above Sicily, she didn't let herself look back.

"Because I can," he'd said to Niccolo. That was why he'd danced with her. That was why he'd done all of this. Married her. Just as she'd suspected, it was all a game. Because he could.

She hadn't thought she'd hear him admit it.

And as she'd sat in his car in the sun-drenched village square, twisting all of those diamonds around and around on her finger, Niccolo's harsh words circling in her head, she'd had to face the facts she'd been avoiding for far too long.

She'd been so sure that she, Elena Calderon, *deserved* what Niccolo had represented. That she *should* be the one chosen from all the girls in the village to swan off into a posh life, dripping in gowns and villas.

Alessandro had been right to accuse her of that, but wrong about why—and around him it was even worse. He was the most powerful man she'd ever met. His ruthlessness was equal parts intimidating and exciting. He was beautiful and lethal, and he'd wanted her as desperately as she'd wanted him.

Some part of her obviously believed that she deserved no less than the CEO of one of the most successful media corporations in Europe. That she deserved rings made of diamonds, private islands and a three-story penthouse perched over Palermo like an opulent aerie.

How remarkably conceited she was.

She remembered then, as the plane winged across the blue sea, one of the last nights they'd spent on the island. They'd sat together on the beach, watching the sunset. He'd been behind her, letting her sprawl between his legs and against his chest.

He'd played with her hair and she'd watched the sun

sink toward the horizon. She'd felt so filled with hope. So unreasonably optimistic.

Until she'd recalled the last time she'd felt that way.

It had been the night of that fateful charity ball. She'd finished dressing in the new, beautiful gown Niccolo had chosen for her, and she'd been unable to stop staring at herself in the mirror of their hotel suite. She'd looked so glamorous, so sophisticated. And she'd felt the same sense of well-being, of happiness, roll through her.

This is exactly how my life should be, she'd thought then.

On the beach with Alessandro, she'd shivered.

"What's the matter?" he'd asked, tugging gently on her hair so she'd look back at him. The reds and golds of the setting sun cast him in bronze, once again like a very old god, perfect and deadly.

"Nothing," she'd lied, and she'd wanted it to be nothing. Just an odd coincidence. No reason at all for that sudden hollow pit in her stomach.

He'd smiled, and kissed her, then he'd wrapped his arms around her like a man in love and had tucked her under his chin in that way she adored, and she'd known without a shadow of a doubt that it was no coincidence. That it had been a sign, and she'd do well to heed it.

That when the forty days were up she had to leave him. *She had to.*

And she'd gone ahead and married him, anyway.

But then, she thought now, shifting in her narrow seat, every decision she'd made for more than half a year she'd made out of fear.

Fear of what Niccolo would do to her. Fear of her parents' disappointment. Fear of losing Alessandro— a man who had insulted her upon their first meeting, thought the very worst of her even as he slept with her, and had even married her in undue, secretive haste in a sleepy little village where no one knew him.

Niccolo was a disgusting creep, but he'd had a point.

And the truth was, though she never would have phrased it the way he had, she would always smell of fish and hard, thankless work like the people she came from. No matter what airs she tried to put on, what gowns or jewels she wore, she was a village girl. She had no place with a man like Alessandro.

More than that, he was a Corretti.

Maybe Alessandro really was the man he claimed he was, a man who strove to do what was right no matter what his family name. She thought of that painful conversation in the elevator and she ached—because she wanted so badly to believe him. To believe that the darkness she'd seen in him today was an aberration, not the true face he'd kept from her the way Niccolo had.

Maybe.

But she had to accept that it was just as likely that he was exactly who Niccolo had told her he was. Exactly who she'd believed he was.

It was time to go home. It was time to stop playing at games she hardly understood. It was past time.

Elena needed to face up to what she'd done. She needed to beg for her parents' forgiveness—not for calling off one wedding, not for marrying yet another man who might very well ruin everything, but for not trusting them enough. For not staying and fighting the lies Niccolo had told. For not believing that they could love her enough to overcome their disappointment in her. For running away instead.

It had solved nothing. It had been a selfish, scared act. It had hurt the people who loved her. And it had broken her heart.

The land was out of her hands, she thought now, her eyes easing closed as she accepted that bitter reality. As she acknowledged her own failure. In the end, it was only land. Dirt and stones and trees. It wasn't worth all of this suffering.

Elena had to believe that.

She closed the window shade beside her so she wouldn't give in to the temptation to look back, shut her eyes tight and prayed she'd make it home in time.

CHAPTER ELEVEN

ALESSANDRO SAT ALONE in his office on the executive floor of the Corretti Media tower. His mobile beeped insistently at him, but he ignored it. Just as he ignored the new proposal Giovanni had drafted for him, comprising Alessandro's bid for the cursed docklands regeneration project. All he needed to do was sign it.

And then, of course, persuade Alessia Battaglia's grasping, two-faced father to honor the commitment he'd made back when Alessandro and Alessia had agreed to marry.

But instead he'd cleared his office.

The proposal was one more gauntlet thrown down in this same old war. It cut out his cousins completely, following right along in Carlo's footsteps, adhering to the same script his father and uncle had written in their blood decades back.

Alessandro pushed back from his desk and roamed

restlessly around his great office, a suitable corporate celebration of a man of his wealth, power and position. It was a space meant to intimidate. To assert in no uncertain terms the full weight and heft of Corretti authority.

That goddamned name.

He walked to the windows, and looked out over the city of his birth. Palermo basked before him in the summer sun, corrupt and decaying, beautiful and serene. A mass of contradictions imprinted with the fingerprints of history, this place; streets marked with violence surrounding ancient green squares of breathtaking loveliness. Byzantine churches, leftover city walls, influences ranging from the Phoenicians to the Mafia. And it was inside of him. It was home. Unlike his brother, he had never wanted to live abroad. Sicily sang in his blood. Palermo was the key to who he was.

And who he was, who he had always been, was a Corretti.

But he was no longer sure what that meant.

He could have become his father at any time in all these years. He could have stepped all too easily into Carlo's shoes today. He'd finally felt what that would mean. He'd wanted it. He'd even thought Niccolo Falco deserved it.

But the woman who'd told him that he deserved what was right, whatever that was, deserved better than a violent criminal as her husband. And it made him question not only himself, but this whole notion of who the Correttis were. If it was a curse, this name—or it was merely one more choice they all kept making.

Today Alessandro had chosen not to take the easy way, the corrupt and criminal way. His father's way. He'd spent his life believing he did what was right, that he did his duty.

Now it was time to prove it.

He walked back over to his desk and shoved the proposal out of his way, picking up his mobile to make two calls he should have made years ago. To offer, if not an olive branch, a start. A fresh, clean start.

His duty to his family should be about the living, not the dead. The Corretti name should not be forever synonymous with the actions of those long buried.

Because the past didn't matter. What mattered were the choices they made now. He, his half-brother, Angelo, and his cousin Matteo shouldn't have to follow along in the footsteps of monsters, simply because those monsters were their fathers. And they certainly didn't have to become them.

Surely, he told himself, they could simply…stop this.

His cousin Matteo picked up the phone, and Alessandro braced himself for a necessary, if excruciatingly awkward, conversation.

It was only as dark as they allowed it to be, he thought. And it was long past time for the light.

Elena let herself out of her parents' house high up on the rocky hillside, and pulled the door closed behind her quietly, so as not to disturb her father's rest. It was a gray, foggy morning, the air thick and cool against her skin. She pulled her old jacket tighter around her, and set off down the slanting street.

She felt turned inside out. Rubbed entirely raw. Her parents had done nothing but love her since her return yesterday afternoon. Her mother had wept. Her father had smiled as if she was a blessing from on high. Elena was humbled. Grateful.

And she'd still been unable to sleep, her mind and her body torturing her with memories of Alessandro. Images of Alessandro. All of that heat and light, fire and need.

She'd learned nothing.

The sloping streets and ancient stone stairs that led the way down the hillside were second nature to her. Each house, each alley, each clothesline hanging naked in today's weather, was like its own separate greeting. This was home. It had always been home. She was made to smell of the sea, the salt and the sun and the bounty they provided. There was no shame in that.

Yet today she felt out of place in a way she never had before.

It will come, she assured herself as she came to the bottom of the steep hill that led into the main square. *You've been away for a long time.*

Everything seemed different in the thick mist. Sounds were muffled, and strange echoes seemed to nip at her heels. She narrowly avoided one of the village's biggest gossips, darting around the far side of the great statue that sat in the center of the square, and was so busy looking back over her shoulder to be sure she'd escaped that she ran right into someone.

Elena opened her mouth to apologize, but she knew that rock-hard chest. She knew the strong hands that wrapped around her upper arms and righted her.

It seemed to take a thousand years to lift her gaze to his, to confirm what she already knew.

What her body was already celebrating, with an insistent ache in her heart and core alike.

"What are you doing here?" she gasped out.

Alessandro's wicked brows rose in arrogant amazement.

"You left me."

"I had to come home," she blurted out in a rush, the strangest urge to apologize to him, to offer him comfort, working its way through her. Proving, she thought, her terrible weakness. "And what does it matter to you?"

"You left me," he said again, each word distinct and furious.

Elena ignored the things that clamored in her then, all of that fear and despair that she'd lost him, all of her desperate, foolish love for a man she couldn't have. Not really. Not the way she wanted him.

"Is this about the land?" she asked baldly. "Because you didn't have to come all the way here for that. You don't have to pretend anymore."

His eyes blazed, so lethally hot she took a step back, and then cursed herself for it. Alessandro was a lot of things, but he wasn't Niccolo. She knew he would never hurt her—not like that.

"It turns out," Alessandro bit out, betrayal and accusation in those dark green eyes, "that I am sick and tired of being discarded on my wedding day."

Elena paled, then reddened.

"Not here," she managed to get out.

She ducked into one of the ancient passageways that wound around behind a few of the shops and deposited them on a lonely stretch of the rocky cliffs overlooking the small harbor. And then she faced him.

He stood there, dark and furious, dressed in one of those impossibly sleek suits that made him look terrifying and delicious all at once, a symphony of powerful, wealthy male beauty. It reminded her that she was only a village girl in old clothes and messy hair, no doubt smelling again of fish.

"What exactly are you doing, Elena?" he asked, his voice clipped.

"This is where I belong," she said defiantly. "This is who I am."

He only watched her, his dark green eyes narrow and fierce.

"I brought you something," he said after a moment. He reached into an inside pocket of his suit jacket and she was sure, for a dizzy moment, that he was going to pull out those torn panties and then what would she do? But instead, he handed her a thick envelope.

Elena took it, her fingers acting of their own accord, a miserable, sinking sensation washing through her, from her throat to her heart to her belly.

"Is this—?" Her throat was so dry she could hear the words scrape as she formed them. "Are these divorce papers?"

This was what she wanted, she tried to tell herself. This was a good thing. But she wanted only to curl up somewhere and cry.

His hard mouth curved into something far too angry to be a smile.

"It's a legal document," he said, his eyes never leaving hers. "It relinquishes any claim I might have had to your family's land, and hands it back to you." Elena made a small noise, her fingers clutching almost convulsively at the envelope. "And I suggest you take note of the date. It was signed three days ago."

Meaning, it took her a confused moment to understand, that he had signed the land over to her before their wedding.

"I don't..." she whispered.

"In case there is any lingering confusion," he said in that deadly way of his, "I never wanted the goddamn land. I wanted you."

Which meant he really was the man she'd wanted him to be—but Elena couldn't process that. There was nothing but a roar of thunder inside her, loud and overwhelming.

He didn't love her, she reminded herself then, cutting through all the noise. No matter what kind of man he was.

The envelope shook in her hand. "I don't know what to say."

"What a surprise." His voice was cool, but his eyes burned hot, and she burned with them. "And here I thought your silent defection was so eloquent."

He reached out for her other hand, taking it in his, and Elena watched in stunned silence—as if it was not her hand at all, as if it was connected to someone else—as he reached into a different pocket and slid the rings she'd left in the penthouse back onto her finger.

"I don't want those," she croaked out. His hand closed around hers then, and she felt that electric charge sizzle all the way up her arm.

"They're yours," he bit out, his dark eyes flashing. "Just like the clothes you left behind. If you don't want them, fine. Sell them. Burn them in your back garden. But I won't take them back."

She yanked her hand away, as if her palm was on fire. It felt like it was. It felt like she was.

But Alessandro was a dream and it was time to wake up. She had to stop prostrating herself to impossibilities. She had to stop dreaming about what she thought she ought to have, and concentrate instead on what she did have. And that wasn't him.

"I appreciate this more than I can say," she said in a low voice, stepping back from him and tucking the envelope in the pocket of her jacket.

"All I asked was that you have a little faith," he gritted out. "Was that really so hard, Elena? Did it warrant you running away from me mere hours after our wedding?"

"We have sex," she said evenly, because it was time to accept reality. "That's all it is, Alessandro. That's all it ever was."

"You're still such a liar," he said in a kind of wonder.

"It's not real," she continued, determined to make him see reason. "It's chemical. It fades."

"We do not *just* have sex," he said, moving toward her then. "What we have, Elena, is extraordinary. It was there from the moment we met."

He reached over and slid his palm along her jaw, her cheek, anchoring his fingers in her hair. That same fire roared in her, that easily. That same old connection that had caused all this trouble. And he knew it. His mouth curved.

"You can't—" she began, but he only pressed a finger over her lips and she subsided, her heart pounding.

"And if you want something real," he said in a low, stirring voice that did nothing to conceal his temper and seemed to echo in her bones, her veins, her core, making something like shame twist in her, low and deep, "then you're going to have to treat me like I'm real, too. Not something you have to bend and contort to get around. Just a man, Elena. Nothing more or less than that."

That thudded into her, hard. She wrenched herself back, away from his touch. She fought for breath.

"You're a man, yes," she threw at him. "I know that. But your only form of communication is in bed—"

"Do not," he interrupted her furiously, "*do not* claim I can't *communicate* when your version of a discussion involves sneaking off for a plane ride and two hours' drive."

"You don't understand!" She hardly knew what she was saying. She was panicked. Cornered. "I loved you so much I was willing to do anything. I wrecked my engagement. I betrayed my family. I lost myself— anything to have you. But that's not love, Alessandro." She shook her head wildly. Desperately. "It's an addiction. *It's just sex.*"

"Thank you," he said grimly, "for using the past tense. Keep sticking your knife in, Elena. Twist it, why don't you."

But she couldn't stop. It was as if something else had taken control of her.

"We never should have met," she told him. "We were never *meant* to meet. It was a complete disaster at first sight."

"It was love at first sight," Alessandro snapped at her. "And you know it."

That was like a deep, terrible rip, so far inside her she didn't think she could survive it.

"Don't you dare say that!" she hurled at him. "Don't you dare pretend!"

"I love you!" he thundered, the words ricocheting from the stone walls of the village, the rocky cliffs, the thick fog and the water below.

Or maybe that was only in her head. Maybe that was her heart.

Alessandro found her gaze, held it. Frustration and determination gleamed there in all of that dark green, along with something else.

Sincerity, she thought, from some stunned distance. *He meant it.* She heard a small noise, a kind of gasp, and only dimly realized she'd made it.

"I love you, Elena," he said, his voice serious. Certain. "Since the moment I saw you, I've never been the same."

"You…" But she couldn't seem to speak.

"There were no contracts," he said then, fiercely. "No discussions about assets or settlements. No prenuptial agreement. I simply married you, because I can't be without you. I can't let you leave me." His dark eyes flashed. *"I can't."*

She tried to say his name, formed the syllables of it with her mouth, but no sound came out.

"I have a great darkness in me," he said then, intently. "I can't pretend I don't. But it's not going to win. It can't, if I have you."

She shook her head, as if she could shake this off. As if she could push him back into those neatly labeled boxes she'd set out for him. She had to do it, or she might die where she stood. She didn't question that—she simply knew it.

"We were always destined to burn ourselves out, Alessandro," she said when she could speak. "This was doomed from the start."

He closed the distance between them then, and took her shoulders in his hands. Kind and gentle. Heartbreakingly firm.

"Do you want me to convince you?" he asked roughly, a broken look in his dark eyes. "Is that what this is? Because we both know I can."

"What?" Her ears were ringing, louder by the second. "No, I—"

"Tell me what you *want*, Elena," he said, all of his ferocity and all of the desolation she'd sensed in him right there between them, suddenly. Alive in the damp air. "Do you *want* me to hunt you down, make you accept what's between us? Do you *want* me to leave you alone? You need to choose. You need to *fight*."

He dropped his hands then, stepped back, and the distance between them was unbearable. It made her shake.

"You can't put this all on me," he continued, his voice low but with the ring of a kind of finality that made everything inside of her twist tight in anguish.

"I don't know what I want," she lied, and the look in his eyes then shamed her. Destroyed her. Because he knew she was lying. He always knew.

"I loved you before I knew your name," he said then.

"I love you more now, even when you lie to my face. All you have to do is own this, Elena."

She shuddered. She couldn't do it. She couldn't—

"I do," she said desperately. "I love you."

"I know you do," he replied, a slight curve to that hard mouth, but it wasn't enough. "But that's not the issue, is it? It never has been."

And something in her finally broke then. Pride, fear. Selfishness and vanity. All the things she'd been accused of, all the accusations she'd levied at herself. It all simply cracked into pieces and washed over her.

"I left because I couldn't bear to be so stupid," she told him in a rush. "To make such a terrible mistake again." Her eyes filled with tears, spilled over, wetting her cheeks. "But I married you because I wanted to marry you. I wanted you."

She wiped at her eyes, then focused on him, and he took up the whole world. Commanding and strong. But waiting to hear what she'd say next. What she'd decide. As if she was the one with the power, after all.

"I still do, Alessandro," she whispered. "I want you more than I've ever wanted anything else. I can't fight that. I tried."

"You don't have to fight that," he said, his dark green eyes so fierce on hers she trembled. "You don't have to fight me. Just fight *for* this, Elena. Don't run away. Don't hide."

She made a wordless sort of sound, far past the ability to speak, and he pulled her close and let her cry.

"I'm not your enemy," he murmured into her hair.

"I know," she whispered into his strong, warm chest. "I know you're not."

She shuddered against him, and then he kissed her. Sweet, sure. Hot. Like a promise. Like hope. And when he drew back she saw the future she'd been too afraid to imagine, right there in his dark eyes, that curve of his perfect mouth.

"Come back to Sicily with me," he said. "And stay this time. Stay for good."

Elena nodded, too overwhelmed to speak. And this wasn't surrender, she realized. She wasn't losing a thing. She was gaining Alessandro—she was gaining *them*.

She was trading in something broken, something ruined and outgrown, for a shared set of wings and the whole bright sky to call their own.

"I want you to meet my parents," she whispered. "My father. He's not well, but...I think he'll like you."

"That is exceedingly unlikely," he said quietly. "I'm a Corretti."

And it was Elena's turn to kiss him then, to press her mouth against his and set him free with all of that fire that was always, only theirs. To love him with nothing held back, nothing hidden. To bask in that terrible, impossible, extraordinary love that had slammed into them with no warning, changing them both. Changing everything.

"He'll love you," she told him. She looped her arms around his neck and adored the way he smiled down at her. "Because I love you. That's how it works."

He was shadow and light. Ruthless and kind. Dark green eyes and that wild, hot heat when he looked at her.

And all of him hers, as he had been from the start. From that single glance across a crowded room.

"I will always be a Corretti," Alessandro said. It was a warning. Or, she thought, a promise.

Elena smiled. "So will I."

* * * * *

Read on for an exclusive interview
with Caitlin Crews!

BEHIND THE SCENES OF
SICILY'S CORRETTI DYNASTY
with Caitlin Crews

It's such a huge world to create—an entire Sicilian dynasty. Did you discuss parts of it with the other writers?

Oh, yes! The other writers were such a huge part of the experience for me—thank goodness, as they're all so talented! We talked about a lot of different story points, and even shared scenes when we used one another's characters. I couldn't have written it without them!

How does being part of a continuity differ from when you are writing your own stories?

It's a completely different kind of challenge. When you're writing your own books all the choices you make are organic; they all flow together as you write. In a continuity you have to work inside out, in some respects. You have to back into the characters in order to flesh them out, for example. You have to think a lot about *why* they do the things you're told they do. I'd say it's the writing equivalent of coloring in an already drawn character rather than drawing it yourself from scratch. Either way, you have to make them yours, but the process is a bit different.

What was the biggest challenge? And what did you most enjoy about it?

Learning who my characters really were was the biggest challenge—and then, when I did, I just loved them.

As you wrote your hero and heroine was there anything about them that surprised you?

Many things! I never quite knew what either of them would say, or how dark things would get for them before they found their way back to the light.

What was your favorite part of creating the world of Sicily's most famous dynasty?

I loved Alessandro and Elena, but I also had a lot of fun researching Sicily. What a fantastic place!

If you could have given your heroine one piece of advice before the opening pages of the book, what would it be?

I would have told her to trust her heart. But we never do, do we?

What was your hero's biggest secret?

That would be telling!

What does your hero love most about your heroine?

She's seen the dark side of him and she loves him, anyway—she's not afraid of him.

What does your heroine love most about your hero?

That she can trust him to be who he says he is, and not to betray her.

Which of the Correttis would you most like to meet and why?

They're a bit intense, aren't they? I think I'd like to watch them all from afar, as they're so fascinating and gorgeous. Maybe if they were all gathered at a restaurant? Particularly one in Sicily, where I could glut myself on the wonderful food and watch a few Corretti dramas play out over the course of the meal....

'There are rules tonight, Alessia, and you will play by them.'

'Will I?' she asked. She wasn't sure why she was goading him. Maybe because it was the only way in all the world she could feel like she had some power. Or maybe it was because if she wasn't trying to goad him, she was longing for him. And the longing was just unacceptable.

A smile curved his lips and she couldn't help but wonder if he needed this too. This edge of hostility, the bite of anger between them.

Although why Matteo would need anything to hold her at a distance when he'd already made his feelings quite clear was a mystery to her.

'Yes, my darling wife, you will.' He put his hand on her chin, drawing close to her, his heat making her shiver deep inside. It brought her right back to the hotel.

A Hunger for
the Forbidden

MAISEY YATES

First published in Great Britain 2013
Mills & Boon, an imprint of Harlequin (UK) Limited,
Eton House, 18-24 Paradise Road, Richmond, Surrey TW9 1SR

THE CORRETTIS: SCANDALS
© Harlequin Enterprises II B.V./S.à.r.l. 2013

A Hunger for the Forbidden © Harlequin Books S.A. 2013

Special thanks and acknowledgement are given to Maisey Yates for her contribution to *Sicily's Corretti Dynasty* series

ISBN: 978 0 263 90621 9

53-0813

Harlequin (UK) policy is to use papers that are natural, renewable and recyclable products and made from wood grown in sustainable forests. The logging and manufacturing processes conform to the legal environmental regulations of the country of origin.

Printed and bound
by CPI Group (UK) Ltd, Croydon, CR0 4YY

Maisey Yates was an avid Mills & Boon® Modern™ romance reader before she began to write them. She still can't quite believe she's lucky enough to get to create her very own sexy alpha heroes and feisty heroines. Seeing her name on one of those lovely covers is a dream come true.

Maisey lives with her handsome, wonderful, nappy-changing husband and three small children across the street from her extremely supportive parents and the home she grew up in, in the wilds of Southern Oregon, USA. She enjoys the contrast of living in a place where you might wake up to find a bear on your back porch and then heading into the home office to write stories that take place in exotic urban locales.

To the fabulous editors at the M&B office.
You push me to be better and to take risks.
And you make my job fun. Thank you.

CHAPTER ONE

ALESSIA BATTAGLIA ADJUSTED her veil, the whisper-thin fabric skimming over the delicate skin of her neck. Like a lover's kiss. Soft. Gentle.

She closed her eyes, and she could feel it.

Hot, warm lips on her bare flesh. A firm, masculine hand at her waist.

She opened her eyes again and bent down, adjusting the delicate buckles on her white satin heels.

Her lover's hands on her ankle, removing her high heels. Leaving her naked in front of him, naked before a man for the first time. But there was no time for nerves. There was nothing more than the heat between them. Years of fantasy, years of longing.

Alessia swallowed and took the bouquet of bloodred roses from the chair they were resting on. She looked down at the blossoms, some of them bruised by the way she'd laid them down.

Brushing her fingertips over the crushed velvet petals brought another wave of memory. A wave of sensation.

Her lover's mouth at her breast, her fingers woven through his thick dark hair.

"Alessia?"

Her head snapped up and she saw her wedding co-ordinator standing in the doorway, one hand covering her headset.

"Yes?"

"It's time."

Alessia nodded, and headed toward the doorway, her shoes loud on the marble floor of the basilica. She exited the room that had been set aside for her to get ready in, and entered the vast foyer. It was empty now, all of the guests in the sanctuary, waiting for the ceremony.

She let out a long breath, the sound loud in the empty, high-ceilinged room. Then she started her walk toward the sanctuary, past pillars inlaid with gold and stones. She stopped for a moment, hoping to find some comfort, some peace, in the biblical scenes depicted on the walls.

Her eyes fell to a detailed painting of a garden. Of Eve handing Adam the apple.

"Please. Just one night."

"Only one, cara mia?*"*

"That's all I have to give."

A searing kiss, like nothing she'd ever experienced before. Better than any fantasy.

Her breath caught and she turned away from the painting, continuing on, continuing to the small antechamber outside of the sanctuary.

Her father was there, his suit crisp and pressed. Antonioni Battaglia looked every inch the respectable citizen everyone knew he was not. And the wedding, so formal, so traditional, was another statement of his power. Power that he longed to increase, with the Corretti fortune and status.

That desire was the reason she was here.

"You are very much like your mother."

She wondered if there was any truth to the words, or if it was just the right thing to say. Tenderness was something her father had never seemed capable of.

"Thank you," she said, looking down at her bouquet.

"This is what's right for the family."

She knew it was. Knew that it was the key to ensuring that her brothers and sisters were cared for. And that was, after all, what she'd done since her mother died in childbirth. Pietro, Giana, Marco and Eva were the brightest lights in her existence, and she would do, had done, whatever she could to ensure they had the best life possible.

And still, regret settled on her like a cloak, and memory clouded the present. Memories of her lover. His hands, his body, his passion.

If only her lover, and the man waiting behind the doors to the sanctuary, waiting to marry her, were the same.

"I know," she said, fighting against the desolation inside of her. The emptiness.

The double doors parted, revealing an impossibly long aisle. The music changed, everyone turned to look at her—all twelve hundred guests, who had come to watch the union of the Battaglia family and their much-hated rivals, the Correttis.

She held her head up, trying to breathe. The bodice of her dress threatened to choke her. The lace, which formed a high collar, and sleeves that ended in a point over her hands, was heavy and scratched against her skin. The yards of fabric clung to her, heat making her feel light-headed.

It was a beautiful dress, but it was too fussy for her. Too heavy. But the dress wasn't about her. The wedding wasn't about her.

Her father followed her into the sanctuary but didn't take her arm. He had given her away when he'd signed his agreement with the late Salvatore Corretti. He didn't need to do it again. He didn't move to take a seat, either, rather he prowled around the

back of the pews, up the side of the church, his steps
parallel to hers. That was Antonioni Battaglia all
over. Watching proceedings, ensuring all went well.
Watching her. Making sure she did as she was told.

A drop of sweat rolled down her back and another
flash of memory hit her hard.

*His sweat-slicked skin beneath her fingertips. Her
nails digging into his shoulders. Her thighs wrapped
around lean, masculine hips...*

She blinked and looked up at Alessandro. Her
groom. The man to whom she was about to make
her vows.

God forgive me.

Had she not been holding the roses, she would have
crossed herself.

And then she felt him. As though he had reached
out and put his hands on her.

She looked at the Corretti side, and her heart
stopped for a moment. Matteo.

Her lover. Her groom's enemy.

Matteo was arresting as ever, with the power to
draw the breath from her lungs. Tall and broad, his
physique outlined to perfection by his custom-made
suit. Olive skin and square jaw. Lips that delivered
pleasure in beautiful and torturous ways.

But this man standing in the pews was not the man
who'd shared her bed that night a month ago. He was

different. Rage, dark and bottomless, burned from his eyes, his jaw tight. She had thought, had almost hoped, that he wouldn't care about her being promised to Alessandro. That a night of passion with her would be like a night with any other woman.

Yes, that thought had hurt, but it had been better than this. Better than him looking at her like he hated her.

She could remember those dark eyes meeting hers with a different kind of fire. Lust. Need. A bleak desperation that had echoed inside of her. And she could remember them clouded by desire, his expression pained as she'd touched him, tasted him.

She looked to Alessandro but she could still feel Matteo watching her. And she had to look back. She always had to look at Matteo Corretti. For as long as she could remember, she'd been drawn to him.

And for one night, she'd had him.

Now...now she would never have him again.

Her steps faltered, her high heel turning sideways beneath her. She stumbled, caught herself, her eyes locking with Matteo's again.

Dio, it was hot. Her dress was suffocating her now. The veil too heavy on her head, the lace at her throat threatening to choke her.

She stopped walking, the war within her threatening to tear her to pieces.

* * *

Matteo Corretti thought he would gag on his anger. Watching her walk toward Alessandro, his cousin, his rival in business and now, because of this, his enemy.

Watching Alessia Battaglia make her way to Alessandro, to bind herself to him.

She was Matteo's. His lover. His woman. The most beautiful woman he had ever seen in his life. It wasn't simply the smooth perfection of her golden skin, not just the exquisite cheekbones and full, rose-colored lips. It was something that existed beneath her skin, a vitality and passion that had, by turns, fascinated and confused him.

Her every laugh, every smile, every mundane action, was filled with more life, more joy, than his most memorable moments. It was why, from the first time he'd sneaked a look at her as a boy, he had been transfixed.

Far from the monster he'd been made to believe the Battaglias were, she had been an angel in his eyes.

But he had never touched her. Never breached the unspoken command issued by his father and grandfather. Because she was a Battaglia and he a Corretti, the bad blood between them going back more than fifty years. He had been forbidden from even speaking to her and as a boy he had only violated that order once.

And now, when Salvatore had thought it might benefit him, now she was being traded to Alessandro like cattle. He tightened his hands into fists, anger, anger like he hadn't felt in more than thirteen years, curling in his gut. The kind of rage he normally kept packed in ice was roaring through him. He feared it might explode, and he knew what happened when it did.

He could not be held responsible for what he might do if he had to watch Alessandro touch Alessia. Kiss her.

And then Alessia froze in place, her big, dark eyes darting from Alessandro, and back to him. Those eyes. Those eyes were always in his dreams.

Her hand dropped to her side, and then she released her hold on her bouquet of roses, the sound of them hitting the stone floor loud in the sudden silence of the room.

Then she turned, gripping the front of her heavy lace skirt, and ran back down the aisle. The white fabric billowed around her as she ran. She only looked behind her once. Wide, frightened eyes meeting his.

"Alessia!" He couldn't stop himself. Her name burst from his lips, and his body burst from its position in the pews. And he was running, too. "Alessia!"

The roar of the congregation drowned out his words. But still he ran. People were standing now, filing into the aisle, blocking his path. The faces of the crowd were a blur, he wasn't aware of who he touched, who he moved out of his way, in his pursuit of the bride.

When he finally burst through the exterior doors of the basilica, Alessia was getting into the backseat of the limo that was waiting to carry her and her groom away after the ceremony, trying to get her massive skirt and train into the vehicle with her. When she saw him, everything in her face changed. A hope in her eyes that grabbed him deep in his chest and twisted his heart. Hard.

"Matteo."

"What are you doing, Alessia?"

"I have to go," she said, her eyes focused behind him now, fearful. Fearful of her father, he knew. He was gripped then by a sudden need to erase her fears. To keep her from ever needing to be afraid again.

"Where?" he asked, his voice rough.

"The airport. Meet me."

"Alessia…"

"Matteo, please. I'll wait." She shut the door to the limo and the car pulled out of the parking lot, just as her father exited the church.

"You!" Antonioni turned on him. "What have you done?"

And Alessandro appeared behind him, his eyes blazing with fury. "Yes, cousin, what have you done?"

* * *

Alessia's hands shook as she handed the cash to the woman at the clothing shop. She'd never been permitted to go into a store like this. Her father thought this sort of place, with mass-produced garments, was common. Not for a Battaglia. But the jeans, T-shirt and trainers she'd found suited her purpose because they were common. Because any woman would wear them. Because a Battaglia would not. As if the Battaglias had the money to put on the show they did. Her father borrowed what he had to in order to maintain the fiction that their power was as infinite as it ever was. His position as Minister for the Trade and Housing department might net him a certain amount of power, power that was easily and happily manipulated, but it didn't keep the same flow of money that had come from her grandfather's rather more seedy organization.

The shopgirl looked at her curiously, and Alessia knew why. A shivering bride, sans groom, in a small tourist shop still wearing her gown and veil was a strange sight indeed.

"May I use the changing room?" she asked once her items were paid for.

She felt slightly sick using her father's money to escape, sicker still over the way she'd gotten it. She must have been quite the sight in the bank, in her wedding gown, demanding a cash advance against a card with her father's name on it.

"I'm a Battaglia," she'd said, employing all the self-importance she'd ever heard come from Antonioni. "Of course it's all right for me to access my family money."

Cash was essential, because she knew better than to leave a paper trail. Having a family who had, rather famously, been on the wrong side of the law was helpful in that regard at least. As had her lifelong observation of how utter confidence could get you things you shouldn't be allowed to have. The money in her purse being a prime example.

"Of course," the cashier said.

Alessia scurried into the changing room and started tugging off the gown, the hideous, suffocating gown. The one chosen by her father because it was so traditional. The virgin bride in white.

If he only knew.

She contorted her arm behind her and tugged at the tab of the zip, stepping out of the dress, punching the crinoline down and stepping out of the pile of fabric. She slipped the jeans on and tugged the stretchy black top over her head.

She emerged from the room a moment later, using the rubber bands she'd purchased to restrain her long, thick hair. Then she slipped on the trainers, ruing her lack of socks for a moment, then straightened.

And she breathed. Feeling more like herself again. Like Alessia. "Thank you," she said to the cashier. "Keep the dress. Sell it if you like."

She dashed out of the store and onto the busy streets, finally able to breathe. Finally.

She'd ditched the limo at the bank, offering the driver a generous tip for his part in the getaway. It only took her a moment to flag down a cab.

She slid in the back, clutching her bag to her chest. "Aeroporto di Catania, *per favore.*"

"Naturalmente."

Matteo hadn't lingered at the basilica. Instead, he'd sidestepped his cousin's furious questions and gotten into his sports car, roaring out of the parking lot and heading in the direction of the airport without giving it any thought.

His heart was pounding hard, adrenaline pouring through him.

He felt beyond himself today. Out of control in a way he never allowed.

In a way he rarely allowed, at least. There had been a few breaks in his infamous control, and all of them were tied to Alessia. And they provided a window into just what he could become if the hideous cold that lived in him met with passionate flame.

She was his weakness. A weakness he should never have allowed and one he should certainly never allow again.

Dark eyes clashing with his in a mirror hanging behind the bar. Eyes he would recognize anywhere.

He turned sharply and saw her, the breath pulled from his lungs.

He set his drink down on the bar and walked across the crowded room, away from his colleagues.

"Alessia." He addressed her directly for the first time in thirteen years.

"Matteo." His name sounded so sweet on her lips.

It had been a month since their night together in New York City, a chance encounter, he'd imagined. He wondered now.

A whole month and he could still taste her skin on his tongue, could still feel the soft curves of her breasts resting in his palms. Could still hear her broken sighs of need as they took each other to the height of pleasure.

And he had not wanted another woman since.

They barely made it into his hotel room, they were far too desperate for each other. He slammed the door, locking it with shaking fingers, pressing her body against the wall. Her dress was long, with a generous slit up the side, revealing her toned, tan legs.

He wrapped his fingers around her thigh and tugged her leg up around his hip, settling the hardness of his erection against her softness.

It wasn't enough. It would never be enough.

Matteo stopped at a red light, impatience tearing at him. Need, need like he had only known once before, was like a beast inside him, devouring, roaring.

Finally, she was naked, her bare breasts pressing hard against his chest. He had to have her. His entire body trembling with lust.

"Ready for me, cara mia?*"*

"Always for you."

He slid inside of her body, so tight, much more so than he'd expected, than he'd ever experienced. She cried out softly, the bite of her nails in his flesh not due to pleasure now.

A virgin.

His. Only his.

Except she had not been his. It had been a lie. The next morning, Alessia was gone. And when he'd returned to Sicily, she'd been there.

He'd been invited to a family party but he had not realized that all branches of the Corretti family would be present. Had not realized it was an engagement party. For Alessandro and Alessia. A party to celebrate the end of a feud, the beginning of a partnership between the Battaglias and the Correttis, a change to revitalize the docklands in Palermo and strengthen their family corporation.

"How long have you and Alessia been engaged?" he asked, his eyes trained on her even as he posed the question to Alessandro.

"For a while now. But we wanted to wait to make the big announcement until all the details were finalized."

"I see," he said. "And when is the blessed event?"

"One month. No point in waiting."

Some of the old rage burned through the desire that had settled inside of him. She had been engaged to Alessandro when he'd taken her into his bed. She'd intended, from the beginning, to marry another man the night she'd given herself to him.

And he, he had been forced to watch her hang on his cousin's arm for the past month while his blood boiled in agony as he watched his biggest rival hold on to the one thing he wanted more than his next breath. The one thing he had always wanted, but never allowed himself to have.

He had craved violence watching the two of them together. Had longed to rip Alessandro's hands off her and show him what happened when a man touched what belonged to him.

Even now, the thought sent a rising tide of nausea through him.

What was it Alessia did to him? This wave of possessiveness, this current of passion that threatened to drown him, it was not something that was a part of him. He was a man who lived in his mind, a man who embraced logic and fact, duty and honor.

When he did not, when he gave in to emotion, the danger was far too great. He was a Corretti, cut from the same cloth as his father and grandfather, a fabric woven together with greed, violence and a passion for acquiring more money, more power, than any one man could ever need.

Even with logic, with reason, he could and had justified actions that would horrify most men. He hated to think what might happen if he were unleashed without any hold on his control.

So he shunned passion, in all areas of life.

Except one.

He pulled his car off the road and slammed on his breaks, killing the engine, his knuckles burning from the hard grip he had on the steering wheel, his breath coming in short, harsh bursts.

This was not him. He didn't know himself with Alessia, and he never had.

And nothing good could come from it. He had spent his life trying to change the man he seemed destined to be. Trying to keep control, to move his life in a different direction than the one his father would have pushed him into.

Alessia compromised that. She tested it.

He ran his fingers through his hair, trying to catch his breath.

Then he turned the key over, the engine roaring to life again. And he turned the car around, heading away from the airport, away from the city.

He punched a button on his dashboard and connected himself to his PA.

"Lucia?"

"*Sì?*"

"Hold my calls until further notice."

It had been three hours. No doubt the only reason her father and his men hadn't come tearing through the airport was that they would never have imagined she would do something so audacious as to run away completely.

Alessia shifted in the plastic chair and wiped her cheek again, even though her tears had dried. She had no more tears left to cry. It was all she'd done since she'd arrived.

And she'd done more since it had become clear Matteo wasn't coming.

And then she'd done more when she'd suddenly had to go into the bathroom and throw up in a public stall.

Then she'd stopped, just long enough to go into one of the airport shops and pick up the one thing she'd avoided buying for the past week.

She'd started crying again when the pregnancy test had resulted in two little pink, positive, yes-you're-having-a-baby lines.

Now she was wrung out. Sick. And completely alone.

Well, not completely alone. Not really. She was having a baby, after all.

The thought didn't comfort her so much as magnify the feeling of utter loneliness.

One thing was certain. There was no going back to Alessandro. No going back to her family. She was having the wrong man's baby. A man who clearly didn't want her.

But he did once.

That thought made her furious, defiant. Yes, he had. More than once, which was likely how the pregnancy had happened. Because there had been protection during their times in bed, but they'd also showered together in the early hours of the morning and then...then neither of them had been able to think, or spare the time.

A voice came over the loudspeaker, the last call for her flight out to New York.

She stood up, picked up her purse, the only thing she had with her, the only thing she had to her name, and handed her ticket to the man at the counter.

"Going to New York?" he asked, verifying.

She took a deep breath. "Yes."

CHAPTER TWO

HE'D NEVER EVEN opened the emails she'd been sending him. She knew, because she'd set them up so that they would send her a receipt when the addressee opened her message, but she'd never gotten one.

He didn't answer her calls, either. Not the calls to his office, not the calls to his mobile phone, not the calls to the Palazzolo Corretti, or to his personal estate outside Palermo.

Matteo Corretti was doing an exceptional job of ignoring her, and he had been for weeks now while she'd been holed up in her friend Carolina's apartment. Carolina, the friend who had talked her into a New York bachelorette party in the first place. Which, all things considered, meant she sort of owed Alessia since that bachelorette party was the source of both her problems, and her pregnancy.

No, that wasn't fair. It was her fault. Well, a lot of

it was. The rest was Matteo Corretti's. Master of disguise and phone-call-avoider extraordinaire.

She wished she didn't need him but she didn't know what else to do. She was so tired. So sad, all the time. Her father wouldn't take her calls, either, her siblings, the most precious people in her life were forbidden from speaking to her. That, more than anything, was threatening to burn a hole in her soul. She felt adrift without them around her. They'd kept her going for most of her life, given her a sense of purpose, of strength and responsibility. Without them she just felt like she was floundering.

She'd had one option, of course. To terminate the pregnancy and return home. Beg her father and Alessandro for forgiveness. But she hadn't been able to face that. She'd lost so much in her life already and as confused as she was about the baby, about what it would mean for her, as terrified as she was, she couldn't face losing the tiny life inside of her.

But she would run out of money soon. Then she would be alone and penniless while Matteo Corretti spent more of his fortune on sports cars and high-rise hotels.

She wasn't going to allow it anymore. Not when she'd already decided that if he didn't want to be a part of their baby's life he would have to come tell her to her face. He would have to stand before her and denounce their child, verbally, not simply by ignoring emails and messages. He would have to make that denouncement a physical action.

Yes, she'd made the wrong decision to sleep with him without telling him about Alessandro. But it didn't give him the right to deny their child. Their child had nothing to do with her stupidity. He or she was the only innocent party in the situation.

She looked down at the screen on her phone. She had her Twitter account all set up and ready to help her contact every news outlet in the area.

She took a breath and started typing.

@theobserver @NYTnews @HBpress I'm about to make an important announcement re Matteo Corretti & the wedding scandal. Luxe Hotel on 3rd.

Then she stepped out of the back of the cab and walked up to the front steps of Matteo's world-renowned hotel, where he was rumored to be in residence, though no one would confirm it, and waited.

The sidewalks were crowded, people pushing past other people, walking with their heads down, no one sparing her a glance. Until the news crews started showing up.

First there was one, then another, and another.

Some from outlets she hadn't personally included in her tweet. The small crowd drew stares, and some passersby started lingering to see what was happening.

There was no denying that she was big news. The assumption had been that she'd run off with Matteo but nothing could be further from the truth. And she was about to give the media a big dose of truth.

It didn't take long for them to catch the attention of the people inside the hotel, which had been a key part of her plan.

A sharply dressed man walked out of the front of the hotel, his expression wary. "Is there something I can help you with?"

She turned to him. "I'm just making a quick announcement. If you want to go get Matteo, that might help."

"Mr. Corretti is not in residence."

"That's like saying someone isn't At Home in a Regency novel, isn't it? He's here, but he doesn't want anyone to know it."

The reporters were watching the exchange with rapt attention, and the flash on one of the cameras started going, followed by the others.

"Mr. Corretti is not—"

She whirled around to face him again. "Fine, then if Mr. Corretti is truly not in residence you can stand out here and listen to what I have to say and relay it to your boss when you deliver dinner to the room he is not in residence in."

She turned back to the reporters, and suddenly, the official press release she'd spent hours memorizing last night seemed to shatter in her brain, making it impossible to piece back together, impossible to make sense of it.

She swallowed hard, looking at the skyline, her vision filled with concrete, glass and steel. The noise from the cars was deafening, the motion of the traffic in front of her making her head swim. "I know that the wedding has been much talked about. And that Matteo chasing me out of the church has been the headline. Well, there's more to the story."

Flashes blinded her, tape recorders shoved into her face, questions started to drown out her voice. She felt weak, shaky, and she wondered, not for the first time, if she was completely insane.

Her life in Sicily had been quiet, domestic, one surrounded by her family, one so insular that she'd been dependent upon imagination to make it bearable, a belief of something bigger looming in her future. And as a result, she had a tendency to romanticize the grand gesture in her mind. To think that somehow, no matter how bleak the situation seemed, she could fix it. That, in the end, she would make it perfect and manage to find her happy ending.

She'd done it on the night of her bachelorette party. New York was so different than the tiny village she'd been raised in. So much bigger, faster. Just being there had seemed like a dream and so when she'd been confronted with Matteo it had seemed an easy, logical thing to approach him, to follow the path their mutual attraction had led them down. It was a prime example of her putting more stock in fantasy, in the belief in happy endings, over her common sense.

This was another.

But no matter how well planned this was, she hadn't realized how she would feel, standing there with everyone watching her. She wasn't the kind of woman who was used to having all eyes on her, her aborted wedding being the exception.

"I'm pregnant, and Matteo Corretti is the father of my baby." It slipped out, bald and true, and not at all what she'd been planning to say. At least she didn't think it was.

"Mr. Corretti—" the employee was speaking into his phone now, his complexion pallid "—you need to come out here."

She released a breath she hadn't realized she'd been holding.

"When is the baby due?"

"Are you certain he's the father?"

"When did you discover you were pregnant?"

The questions were coming rapid-fire now, but she didn't need to answer them because this was never about the press. This was about getting his attention. This was about forcing a confrontation that he seemed content to avoid.

"I'll answer more questions when Matteo comes to make his statement."

"Did the two of you leave the wedding together, or are you estranged? Has he denied paternity?" one of the reporters asked.

"I…"

"What the hell is going on?"

Alessia turned and her heart caught in her throat, making it impossible to breathe. Matteo. It felt like an eternity since she'd seen him, since he'd kissed her, put his hands on her skin. An eternity.

She ached with the need to run to him, to hold on to him, use him as an anchor. In her fantasies, he had long been her knight in shining armor, a simplistic vision of a man who had saved her from a hideous fate.

But in the years since, things had changed. Become more complex, more real. He was her lover now. The father of her child. The man she had lied to. The man who had left her sitting alone in an airport, crying and clutching a positive pregnancy test.

For a moment, the longing for those simple, sun-drenched days in Sicily, when he had been nothing more than an idealized savior, was so sharp and sweet she ached.

"Mr. Corretti, is this why you broke up the wedding?"

"I didn't break up anyone's wedding," he said, his tone dark.

"No, I ran out of the wedding," she said.

"And is what why I broke up the wedding?" he asked, addressing the reporter, stormy eyes never once looking at her.

"The baby," the reporter said.

Matteo froze, his face turning to stone. "The baby." Color drained from his face, but he remained stoic, only the change in his complexion a clue as to the shock that he felt.

He didn't know. She felt the impact of that reality like a physical blow. He hadn't even listened to a single message. Hadn't opened any emails, even before she'd started tagging them to let her know when he opened them.

"Is there more than one?" This from another reporter.

"Of course not," Matteo said, his words smooth, his eyes cold like granite. "Only this one."

He came to stand beside her, his gaze still avoiding hers. He put his arm around her waist, the sudden contact like touching an open flame, heat streaking through her veins. How did he manage to affect her this way still? After all he'd done to her? After the way he'd treated her?

"Do you have a statement?"

"Not at this point," he bit out. "But when the details for the wedding are finalized, we will be in touch."

He tightened his hold on her waist and turned them both around, away from the reporters, leading her up the steps and into the hotel. She felt very much like she was being led into the lion's den.

"What are you doing?" she asked, wishing he would move away from her, wishing he would stop touching her.

"Taking you away from the circus you created. I have no desire to discuss this with an audience."

If he wasn't so angry with her, she might think it was a good idea. But Matteo Corretti's rage was like ice-cold water in a black sea. Fathomless, with the great threat of pulling her beneath the waves.

His hold tightened with each step they took toward the hotel, and her stomach started to feel more and more unsettled until, when they passed through the revolving door and into the hotel lobby, she was afraid she might vomit on the high-gloss marble floors.

A charming photo to go with the headlines.

He released her the moment they were fully inside. "What the hell is the meaning of this?" he asked, rounding on her as his staff milled around very carefully not watching.

"Should we go somewhere more private?" she asked. Suddenly she felt like she'd rather brave his rage than put on a show. She was too tired for that. Too vulnerable. Bringing the press in was never about drawing attention to herself, it was about getting information to Matteo that he couldn't ignore. Giving the man no excuse to say he didn't know.

"Says the woman who called a bloody press conference?"

"You didn't answer my calls. Or return my messages. And I'm pretty sure now that you didn't even listen to any of them."

"I have been away," he said.

"Well, that's hardly my fault that you chose this moment to go on sabbatical. And I had no way of knowing."

He was looking at her like she'd grown an extra head. "Take me to your suite," she said.

"I'm not in the mood, Alessia."

"Neither am I!" she shot back. "I want to talk."

"It's just that last time we were in this hotel, talking was very much not on the agenda."

Her face heated, searing prickles dotting her skin.

"No. That's very true. Which is how we find ourselves in this current situation."

"Communication seems to be something we don't do well with," he said. "Our lack of talking last time we were here together certainly caused some issues."

"But I want to talk now," she said, crossing her arms beneath her breasts.

He cocked his head to the side, dark eyes trained on her now with a focus he'd withheld until that moment. "You aren't afraid of me."

"No."

"A mistake, some might say, *cara mia*."

"Is that so?"

"You won't like me when I'm angry."

"You turn green and split your pants?"

"Perhaps taking this somewhere private is the best idea," he said, wrapping his fingers around her arm, just above her elbow, and directing her toward the elevator.

He pushed the up button and they both waited. She felt like she was hovering in a dream, but she dug her fingernails into her palms, and her surroundings didn't melt away. It was real. All of this.

The elevator doors slid open and they both stepped inside. And as soon as they were closed into the lift, he rounded on her.

"You're pregnant?" His words were flat in the quiet of the elevator.

"Yes. I tried to tell you in a less public way, but it's been two months and you've been very hard to get ahold of."

"Not an accident."

"Oh, no, I know. It was far too purposeful to be accidental. You never even opened my emails."

"I blocked your address after you sent the first few."

"Uh," she said, unable to make a more eloquent sound.

"I see it offends you."

"Yes. It does offend me. Didn't it occur to you that I might have something important to tell you?"

"I didn't care," he said.

The elevator stopped at the top floor and the doors slid open. "Is there a point in me going any further, then? Or should I just go back to my friend Carolina's apartment and start a baby registry?"

"You are not leaving."

"But you just said you didn't care."

"I didn't care until I found out you were carrying my child."

She was both struck, and pleased, by his certainty that the child was his. She wouldn't have really blamed him if he'd questioned her at least once.

She'd lied about her engagement to Alessandro. By omission, but still. She knew she wasn't blameless in the whole fiasco.

"What did you think I was trying to contact you for? To beg you to take me back? To beg you for more sex? Because that's what we shared that night, that's all we shared." The lie was an acid burn on her tongue. "I would hardly have burned my pride to the ground for the sake of another orgasm."

"Is that true? You would hardly be the first person to do it."

"If you mean you, I'm sure it cost you to take a Battaglia to your bed. Must have been some epic dry spell."

"And not worth the price in the end, I think."

His words were designed to peel skin from bone, and they did their job. "I would say the same."

"I can see now why you ran from the wedding."

A wave of confusion hit her, and it took her a moment to realize that she hadn't told him the order in which the events had occurred. Wedding abandonment, then pregnancy test, but before she could correct him he pressed on.

"And how conveniently you've played it, too. Alessandro would, of course, know it wasn't his child as you never slept with him. I hope you're pleased with the way all of this unfolded because you have managed to ensure that you are still able to marry a Corretti, in spite of our little mistake. Good insurance for your family since, thanks to your abandonment, the deal between our family and yours has gone to hell."

"You think I planned this? You aren't even serious about marrying me, are you?"

"There is no other choice. You announced your pregnancy to the whole world."

"I had to tell you."

"And if I had chosen not to be a part of the baby's life?"

"I was going to make you tell me that to my face."

He regarded her closely. "Strange to think I ever imagined you to be soft, Alessia."

"I'm a Battaglia. I've never had the luxury of being soft."

"Clearly not." He looked at her, long and hard. "This makes sense, Alessia." His tone was all business now. Maddeningly sure and decisive. "It will put to rest rumors of bad blood, unite the families."

"You didn't seem to care about that before."

"That was before the baby. The baby changes everything."

Because he wanted to make a family? The idea, so silly and hopeful, bloomed inside of her. It was her blessing and curse that she always found the kernel of hope in any situation. It was the thing that got her through. The thing that had helped her survive the loss of her mother, the cold detachment from her father, the time spent caring for her siblings when other girls her age were out dating, having lives, fulfilling dreams.

She'd created her own. Locked them inside of her. Nurtured them.

"I… It does?" she asked, the words a whisper.

"Of course," he said, dark eyes blazing. "My child will be a Corretti. On that, there can be no compromise."

CHAPTER THREE

MATTEO'S OWN WORDS echoed in his head.

My child will be a Corretti. On that there can be no compromise.

It was true. No child of his would be raised a Battaglia. Their family feud was not simply a business matter. The Battaglias had set out to destroy his grandfather, and had they succeeded they would have wiped out the line entirely.

It was the hurt on her face that surprised him, and more than that, his response to it.

Damn Alessia Battaglia and those dark, soulful eyes. Eyes that had led him to ruin on more than one occasion.

"Because you won't allow your child to carry my name?" she asked.

"That's right."

"And what of my role in raising my child?"

"You will, of course, be present."

"And what else? Because more than mere presence is required to raise a child."

"Nannies are also required, in my experience."

"In your experience raising children, or being raised?"

"Being raised. I'm supremely responsible in my sexual encounters so I've never been in this situation before."

"Supremely responsible?" she asked, cheeks flushing a gorgeous shade of rose that reminded him of the blooms in his Sicilian palazzo. "Is that what you call having sex with your cousin's fiancée with no condom?"

Her words, so stark and angry, shocked him. Alessia had always seemed fragile to him. Sweet. But tangling with her today was forcing him to recognize that she was also a woman capable of supreme ruthlessness if the situation required it.

Something he had to reluctantly respect.

"I didn't know you were engaged to be married, as you withheld the information from me. As to the other issue, that has never happened to me before."

"So you say."

"It has not," he said.

"Well, it's not like you were overly conscious of it at the time."

Shame cracked over his insides like a whip. He had thought himself immune to shame at this point. He was wrong. "I knew. After."

"You remembered and you still didn't think to contact me?"

"I did not think it possible." The thought hadn't occurred to him because he'd been too wrapped up in simply trying to avoid her. Alessia was bad for him, a conclusion he'd come to years ago and reaffirmed the day he'd decided not to go after her.

And now he was bound to her. Bound to a woman who dug down far too deep inside of him. Who disturbed his grasp on his control. He could not afford the interruption. Could not afford to take the chance that he might lose his grip.

"Why, because only other people have the kind of sex that makes babies?"

"Do you always say what comes to your mind?"

"No. I never do. I never speak or act impulsively, I only think about it. It's just you that seems to bring it out."

"Aren't I lucky?" Her admission gripped him, held him. That there was something about him that brought about a change in her...that the thing between them didn't only shatter his well-ordered existence but hers, too, was not a comfort. Not in the least.

"Clearly, neither of us are in possession of much luck, Alessia."

"Clearly," she said.

"There is no way I will let my child be a bastard. I've seen what happens to bastards. You can ask my cousin Angelo about that." A cousin who was becoming quite the problem. It was part of why Matteo had come to New York, why he was making his way back into circulation. In his absence, Angelo had gone and bought himself a hefty amount of shares for Corretti Enterprises and at this very moment, he was sitting in Matteo's office, the new head of Corretti Hotels. He'd been about to go back and make the other man pay. Wrench the power right back from him.

Now, it seemed there was a more pressing matter.

"So, you're doing this to save face?"

"For what other reason? Do you want our child to be sneered at? Disgraced? The product of an illicit affair between two of Sicily's great warring families?"

"No."

Matteo tried not to read the emotion in her dark eyes, tried not to let them pull him in. Always, from the moment he'd seen her, he'd been fascinated. A young girl with flowers tangled in her dark hair, running around the garden of her father's home, a smile on her lips. He could remember her dancing in the grass in her bare feet, while her siblings played around her.

And he had been transfixed. Amazed by this girl who, from all he had been told, should have been visibly evil in some way. But she was a light. She held a brightness and joy like he had never seen. Watching it, being close enough to touch it, helped him pretend it was something he could feel, too.

She made him not so afraid of feeling.

She'd had a hold on him from day one. She was a sorceress. There was no other explanation. Her grip on him defied logic, defied every defense he'd built inside of himself.

And no matter how hard he tried, he could read her. Easily. She was hurt. He had hurt her.

"What is it?" he asked.

She looked away. "What do you mean?"

"Why are you hurt?"

"You've just told me how unlucky we both are that I'm pregnant—was I supposed to look happy?"

"Don't tell me you're pleased about this. Unless it was your plan."

"How could I have…planned this? That doesn't make any sense."

He pushed his fingers through his hair and turned away from her. "I know. *Che cavolo*, Alessia, I know that." He turned back to her.

"I just wanted to tell you about the baby."

He felt like he was drowning, like every breath was suffocating him. A baby. She was having his baby. And he was just about the last man on earth who should ever be a father. He should walk away. But he couldn't.

"And this was the only way?"

Her eyes glittered with rage. "You know damn well it was!"

He did. He'd avoided her every attempt at contacting him. Had let his anger fuel the need for distance between them. Had let the very existence of the emotion serve as a reminder. And he had come back frozen again. So he'd thought. Because now Alessia was here again, pushing against that control.

"Why didn't you meet me at the airport?" she asked, her words a whisper.

"Why didn't I meet you?" he asked, his teeth gritted. "You expected me to chase after you like a dog? If you think you can bring me to heel that easily, Alessia, you are a fool."

"And if you think I'm trying to you're an idiot, Matteo Corretti. I don't want you on a leash."

"Well, you damn well have me on one!" he said, shouting for the first time, his tenuous grip on his control slipping. "What am I to do after your public display? Deny my child? Send you off to raise it on your own? Highly unlikely."

"How can we marry each other? We don't love each other. We barely like each other right now!"

"Is that so bad? You were prepared to marry Alessandro, after all. Better the devil you know. And we both know you know me much better than you knew him."

"Stop it," she said, the catch in her voice sending a hot slash of guilt through his chest. Why he was compelled to lash out at her, he wasn't sure.

Except that nothing with Alessia was ever simple. Nothing was ever straightforward. Nothing was ever neat or controlled.

It has to be.

"It's true, though, isn't it, Alessia?" he asked, his entire body tense now. He knew for a fact he was the first man to be with her, and something in him burned to know that he had been the only man. That Alessandro had never touched her as he had. "You were never with him. Not like you were with me."

The idea of his cousin's hands on her… A wave of red hazed his vision, the need for violence gripping his throat, shaking him.

He swallowed hard, battled back the rage, fought against images that were always so close to the surface when Alessia was around. A memory he had to hold on to, no matter how much he might wish for it to disappear.

Blood. Streaked up to his elbows, the skin on his knuckles broken. A beast inside of him unleashed. And Alessia's attackers on the ground, unmoving.

He blinked and banished the memory. It shouldn't linger as it did. It was but one moment of violence in a lifetime of it. And yet, it had been different. It had been an act born of passion, outside of his control, outside of rational thought.

"Tell me," he ground out.

"Do you honestly think I would sleep with Alessandro after what happened?"

"You were going to. You were prepared to marry him. To share his bed."

She nodded wordlessly. "Yes. I was."

"And then you found out about the baby."

"No," she said, her voice a whisper.

"What, then?"

"Then I saw you."

"Guilt?"

"We were in a church."

"Understandable."

"Why didn't you meet me?" she asked again, her words holding a wealth of pain.

"Because," he said, visions of blood washing through his brain again, a reminder of what happened when he let his passions have control, "I got everything I wanted from you that night. Sex. That was all I ever wanted from you, darling."

She drew back as though he'd struck her. "Is that why you've always watched me?"

"I'll admit, I had a bit of an obsession with your body, but you know you had one with mine."

"I liked you," she said, her words hard, shaky. "But you never came near me after—"

"There is no need to dredge up the past," he said, not wanting to hear her speak of that day. He didn't want to hear her side of it. How horrifying it must have been for a fourteen-year-old girl to see such violence. To see what he was capable of.

Yet, she had never looked at him with the shock, the horror, he'd deserved. There was a way she looked at him, as though she saw something in him no one else did. Something good. And he craved that feeling. It was one reason he'd taken her up on her invitation that night at the hotel bar.

Too late, he realized that he was not in control of their encounter that time, either. No, Alessia stole the control. Always.

No more, he told himself again.

Alessia swallowed back tears. This wasn't going how she'd thought it would. Now she wasn't sure what she thought. No, she knew. Part of her, this stupid, girlish, optimistic part of her, had imagined Matteo's eyes would soften, that he would smile. Touch her stomach. Take joy in the fact that they had created a life together.

And then they would live happily ever after.

She was such a fool. But Matteo had long been the knight in shining armor of her fantasies. And so in her mind he could do no wrong.

She'd always felt like she'd known him. Like she'd understood the serious, dark-eyed young man she'd caught watching her when she was in Palermo. Who had crept up to the wall around her house when he was visiting his grandmother and stood there while she'd played in the garden. Always looking like he wanted to join in, like he wanted to play, but wouldn't allow himself to.

And then...and then when she'd needed him most, he'd been there. Saved her from...she hardly even knew what horror he'd saved her from. Thank God she hadn't had to find out exactly what those two men had intended to use her for. Matteo had been there. As always. And he had protected her, shielded her.

That was why, when she'd seen him in New York, it had been easy, natural, to kiss him. To ask him to make love to her.

But after that he hadn't come to save her.

She looked at him now, at those dark eyes, hollow,

his face like stone. And he seemed like a stranger. She wondered how she could have been so wrong all this time.

"I don't want to dredge up the past. But I want to know that the future won't be miserable."

"If you preferred Alessandro, you should have married him while you had him at the altar with a priest standing by. Now you belong to me, the choice has been taken. So you should make the best of it."

"Stop being such an ass!"

Now he looked shocked, which, she felt, was a bit of an accomplishment. "You want me to tell you how happy I am? You want me to lie?"

"No," she said, her stomach tightening painfully. "But stop…stop trying to hurt me."

He swore, an ugly, crude word. "I am sorry, Alessia, it is not my intent."

The apology was about the most shocking event of the afternoon. "I…I know this is unexpected. Trust me, I know."

"When did you find out?" he asked.

"At the airport. So…if you had met me, you would have found out when I did."

"And what did you do after that?"

"I waited for you," she said. "And then I got on a plane and came to New York. I have a friend here, the friend that hosted my little bachelorette party."

"Why did you come to New York?"

"Why not?" She made it sound casual, like it was almost accidental. But it wasn't. It had made her feel close to him, no matter where he might have been in the world, because it was the place she'd finally been with him the way she'd always dreamed of. "Why did you come to New York?"

"Possibly for the same reason you did," he said, his voice rough. It made her stomach twist, but she didn't want to ask him for clarification. Didn't want to hope that it had something to do with her.

She was too raw to take more of Matteo's insults. And she was even more afraid of his tenderness. That would make her crumble completely. She couldn't afford it, not now. Now she had to figure out what she was doing. What she wanted.

Could she really marry Matteo?

It was so close to her dearest fantasy. The one that had kept her awake long nights since she was a teenager. Matteo. Hers. Only hers. Such an innocent fantasy at first, and as she'd gotten older, one that had become filled with heat and passion, a longing for things she'd never experienced outside of her dreams.

"And if…" she said, hardly trusting herself to speak "…if we marry, my family will still benefit from the merger?"

"Your father will get his money. His piece of the Corretti empire, as agreed upon."

"You give it away so easily."

"Because my family still needs the docklands revitalization. And your father holds the key to that."

"And it will benefit Alessandro, too."

"Just as it would have benefitted me had he married you."

Those words, hearing that it would have benefitted him for her to marry someone else, made her feel ill. "So a win all around for the Correttis, then?"

"I suppose it is," he said.

There was a ruthless glint in his eyes now. One she had never seen directed at her before. One she'd only seen on one other occasion.

"What if I say no?" she asked, because she had to know. She wasn't sure why she was exploring her options now. Maybe because she'd already blown everything up. Her father likely hated her.... Her siblings... they must be worried sick. And she wondered if anyone was caring for them properly.

Yes, the youngest, Eva, was fourteen now and the rest of them in their late teens, but still, she was the only person who nurtured them. The only person who ever had.

The life she'd always known, the life she'd clung to for the past twenty-seven years, was changed forever. And now she felt compelled in some ways to see how far she could push it.

"You won't say no," he said.

"I won't?"

"No. Because if you do, the Battaglias are as good as bankrupt. You will be cared for, of course our child will be, too. I'm not the kind of man who would abandon his responsibility in that way. But what of your siblings? Their care will not be my problem."

"And if I marry you?"

"They'll be family. And I take care of family."

A rush of joy and terror filled her in equal parts. Because in some ways, she was getting just what she wanted. Matteo. Forever.

But this wasn't the Matteo she'd woven fantasies around. This was the real Matteo. Dark. Bitter. Emotionless in a way she'd somehow never realized before.

He'd given her passion on their night together, but for the most part, the lights had been off. She wondered now if, while his hands had moved over her body with such skill and heat, his eyes had been blank and cold. Like they were now.

She knew that what she was about to agree to wasn't the fantasy. But it was the best choice for her baby, the best choice for her family.

And more fool her, she wanted him. Still. All of

those factors combined meant there was only ever one answer for her to give.

"Yes, Matteo. I'll marry you."

CHAPTER FOUR

THE HUSH IN the lobby of Matteo's plush Palermo hotel was thick, the lack of sound more pronounced and obvious than any scream could have been.

It was early in the day and employees were milling around, setting up for a wedding and mobilizing to sort out rooms and guests. As Matteo walked through, a wave of them parted, making room for him, making space. Good. He was in no mood to be confronted today. No mood for questions.

Bleached sunlight filtered through the windows, reflecting off a jewel-bright sea. A view most would find relaxing. For him, it did nothing but increase the knot of tension in his stomach. Homecoming, for him, would never be filled with a sense of comfort and belonging. For him, this setting had been the stage for violence, pain and shame that cut so deep it was a miracle he hadn't bled to death with it.

He gritted his teeth and pulled together every last ounce of control he could scrape up, cooling the anger that seemed to be on a low simmer in his blood constantly now.

He had a feeling, though, that the shock was due only in part to his presence, with a much larger part due to the woman who was trailing behind him.

He punched the up button for the elevator and the doors slid open. He looked at Alessia, who simply stood there, her hands clasped in front of her, dark eyes looking at everything but him.

"After you, *cara mia*," he said, putting his hand between the doors, keeping them from closing.

"You don't demand that a wife walk three paces behind you at all times?" she asked, her words soft, defiant.

"A woman is of very little use to me when she's behind me. Bent over in front of me is another matter, as you well know."

Her cheeks turned dark with color, and not all of it was from embarrassment. He'd made her angry, as he'd intended to do. He didn't know what it was about her that pushed him so. That made him say things like that.

That made him show anything beyond the unreadable mask he preferred to present to the world.

She was angry, but she didn't say another word.

She simply stepped into the elevator, her eyes fixed to the digital readout on the wall. The doors slid closed behind them, and still she didn't look at him.

"If you brought me here to abuse me perhaps I should simply go back to my father's house and take my chances with him."

"That's what you call abuse? You didn't seem to find it so abhorrent the night you let me do it."

"But you weren't being a bastard that night. Had you approached me at the bar and used it as a pickup line I would have told you to go to hell."

"Would you have, Alessia?" he asked, anger, heat, firing in his blood. "Somehow I don't think that's true."

"No?"

"No." He turned to her, put his hand, palm flat, on the glossy marble wall behind her, drawing closer, drawing in the scent of her. *Dio.* Like lilac and sun. She was Spring standing before him, new life, new hope.

He pushed away from her, shut down the feeling.

"Shows what you know."

"I know a great deal about you."

"Stop with the you-know-me stuff. Just because we slept together—"

"You have a dimple on your right cheek. It doesn't show every time you smile, only when you're really,

really smiling. You dance by yourself in the sun, you don't like to wear shoes. You've bandaged every scraped knee your brothers and sisters ever had. And whenever you see me, you can't help yourself, you have to stare. I know you, Alessia Battaglia, don't tell me otherwise."

"You knew me, Matteo. You knew a child. I'm not the same person now."

"Then how is it you ended up in my bed the night of your bachelorette party?"

Her eyes met his for the first time all morning, for the first time since his private plane had touched down in Sicily. "Because I wanted to make a choice, Matteo. Every other choice was being made for me. I wanted to…I wanted to at least make the choice about who my first lover should be."

"Haven't you had a lot of time to make that choice?"

"When? With all of my free time? I've spent my life making sure my brothers and sisters were cared for, really cared for, not just given the bare necessities by staff. I spent my life making sure they never bore the full brunt of my father's rage. I've spent my life being the perfect daughter, the hostess for his functions, standing and smiling next to him when he got reelected for a position that he abuses."

"Why?" he asked.

"Because of my siblings. Because no matter that my

father is a tyrant, he is our father. We're Battaglias. I hoped...I've always hoped I could make that mean something good. That I could make sure my brothers and sisters learned to do the right things, learned to want the right things. If I didn't make sure, they would only have my father as a guiding influence and I think we both know Antononi Battaglia shouldn't be anyone's guiding influence."

"And what about you?"

"What about me?"

The elevator doors slid open and they stepped out into the empty hall on the top floor.

"You live your whole life for other people?"

She shook her head. "No. I live my life in the way that lets me sleep at night. Abandoning my brothers and sisters to our father would have hurt me. So it's not like I'm a martyr. I do it because I love them."

"But you ran out on the wedding."

She didn't say anything, she simply started walking down the hall, her heels clicking on the marble floor. He stood and watched her, his eyes drifting over her curves, over that gorgeous, heart-shaped backside, outlined so perfectly by her pencil skirt.

It looked like something from the Corretti clothing line. One thing he might have to thank his damn brother Luca for. But it was the only thing.

Especially since the rumor was that in his absence

the other man was attempting to take Matteo's share in the Corretti family hotels. A complete mess since that bastard Angelo had his hands in it, as well.

A total mess. And one he should have anticipated. He'd dropped out of the dealings with Corretti Enterprises completely since the day of Alessia and Alessandro's aborted wedding. And the vultures had moved in. He should try to stop them, he knew that. And he could, frankly. He had his own fortune, his own power, independent of the Corretti machine, but at the moment, the most pressing issue was tied to the tall, willowy brunette who was currently sauntering in the wrong direction.

"The suite is this way," he said.

She stopped, turned sharply on her heel and started walking back toward him, past him and down the hall.

He nearly laughed at the haughty look on her face. In fact, he found he wanted to, but wasn't capable of it. It stuck in his throat, his control too tight to let it out.

He walked past her, to the door of the suite, and took a key card out of his wallet, tapping it against the reader. "My key opens all of them."

"Careful, *caro*, that sounds like a bad euphemism." She shot him a deadly look before entering the suite.

"So prickly, Alessia."

"I told you you didn't know me."

"Then help me get to know you."

"You first, Matteo."

He straightened. "I'm Matteo Corretti, oldest son of Benito Corretti. I'm sure you know all about him. My criminal father who died in a fire, locked in an endless rivalry with his brother, Carlo. You ought to know about him, too, as you were going to marry Carlo's son. I run the hotel arm of my family corporation, and I deal with my own privately owned line of boutique hotels, one of which you're standing in."

She crossed her arms and cocked her hip out to the side. "I think I read that in your online bio. And it's nothing I don't already know."

"That's all there is to know."

She didn't believe that. Not for a moment. She knew there was more to him than that. Knew it because she'd seen it. Seen his blind rage as he'd done everything in his power to protect her from a fate she didn't even like to imagine.

But he didn't speak of it. So neither did she.

"Tell me about you," he said.

"Alessia Battaglia, Pisces, oldest daughter of Antonioni. My father is a politician who does under-the-table dealings with organized-crime families. It's the thing that keeps him in power. But it doesn't make him rich. It's why he needs the Correttis." She returned his style of disclosure neatly, tartly.

"The Correttis are no longer in the organized-crime business. In that regard, my cousins, my brothers and I have done well, no matter our personal feelings for each other."

"You might not be criminals but you are rich. That's why you're so attractive. In my father's estimation at least."

"Attractive enough to trade us his daughter."

She nodded. She looked tired suddenly. Defeated. He didn't like that. He would rather have her spitting venom at him.

"You could walk away, Alessia," he said. "Even now you could. I cannot keep you here. Your father cannot hold you. You're twenty-seven. You have the freedom to do whatever you like. Hell, you could do it on my dime since I'll be supporting my child regardless of what you do."

He didn't know why he was saying it, why he was giving her the out. But part of him wished she would take it. Wished she would leave him alone, take her beauty, the temptation, the ache that seemed to lodge in his chest whenever she was around, with her. The danger she presented to the walls of protection he'd built around his life.

She didn't say anything. She didn't move. She was

frozen to the spot, her lips parted slightly, her breath shallow, fast.

"Alessia, you have the freedom to walk out that door if you want. Right now."

He took a step toward her, compelled, driven by something he didn't understand. Didn't want to understand. The beast in him was roaring now and he wanted it to shut up. Wanted his control back.

He'd had a handle on it again. Had moved forward from the events of his past. Until Alessia had come back into his life, and at the moment all he wanted was for her to be gone, and for his life to go back to the way it had been.

He cupped her chin, tilted her face up so that her eyes met his. "I am not holding you here. I am not your father and I am not your jailer."

Dark eyes met his, the steel in them shocking. "No, you aren't. But you are the father of my baby. Our baby. I'm not going to walk away, Matteo. If you want an out, you'll have to take it yourself. Don't think that I will. I'm strong enough to face this. To try to make this work."

"It would be better if you would."

"Do you really think that?"

"You think I will be a hands-on father? That I will somehow…be an influence in our child's life?" The very thought made him sick. What could he offer a child but a legacy of violence and abuse? But he couldn't walk away, either. Couldn't leave Alessia on her own. But he feared his touch would only poison a child. His baby would be born innocent, unspoiled by the world, and Matteo was supposed to hold him? With his hands? Hands that were stained with blood.

"You think you won't be?"

"How can you give what you never had?"

"I hardly remember my mother, Matteo, but I did a good job with my brothers and sisters."

"Perhaps I find that an absence of a good parent is not the same as having bad ones. What lessons shall I teach our child, *cara*? The kind my father taught me? How to find a man who owes you money? How to break his kneecaps with efficiency when he doesn't pay up? I think not."

He had thought she would look shocked by that, but she hardly flinched, her eyes never wavering from his. "Again you underestimate me, Matteo. You forget the family I come from."

"You are so soft," he said, speaking his mind, speaking his heart. "Breakable. Like a flower. You and I are not the same."

She nodded slowly. "It's easy to crush a flower. But if it's the right kind of flower, it comes back, every year, after every winter. No matter how many times you destroy the surface, it keeps on living underneath."

Her words sent a shot of pain straight to his chest, her quiet strength twisting something deep inside of him. "Don't pretend you were forced into this," he said softly. "You were given your choice."

"And you were given yours."

He nodded once and turned away from her, walked out of the room ignoring the pounding in his blood, ignoring the tightness in his chest. Trying to banish the image of his hand closing around a blossom and crushing the petals, leaving it completely destroyed.

Alessia looked around the lavish, now empty, suite that she was staying in until…until she didn't know when. Weeks of not being able to get ahold of Matteo, not knowing what she would do if she didn't, and now he was suddenly in her life like a hurricane, uprooting everything, taking control of everything.

She really shouldn't be too surprised about it. That was one thing she did know about Matteo Corretti, beyond that stupid ream of noninformation he'd given her. He was controlled. Totally. Completely.

Twice she'd seen him lose that control. Once, on a sunny day in Sicily while he was staying at his grandparents' rural estate. The day that had cemented him in her mind as her potential salvation.

And their night in New York. There had been no control then, not for either of them.

She pictured him as he'd been then. The way he'd looked at her in the low light of the bar. She closed her eyes and she was back there. The memory still so strong, so painfully sweet.

"What brings you to New York, Alessia?"

"Bachelorette party." It was easy enough to leave out that it was for her. If he didn't know about Alessandro, then she wouldn't tell him.

"Did you order any strippers?"

Her cheeks heated. "No, gosh, why? Are you offering to fill the position?"

"How much have you had to drink?" he asked, a smile on his face. It was so rare for her to see him smile. She couldn't remember if she ever had.

"Not enough."

"I could fix that, but I think I'd like a dance and if you're too drunk you won't be able to keep up."

"Why are you talking to me?" she asked. She'd known there was a chance he could be here. He owned the hotel, after all. Part of her had hoped she'd catch a glimpse of him. A little bit of torture, but torture that would be well worth it.

"What do you mean?"

"You haven't spoken to me since—" something

flashed in his eyes, a strange unease, and she redirected her words "—in a long time."

"Too long," he said, his voice rough.

Her heart fluttered, a surge of hope moving through her. She tried to crush it, tried to stop the jittery feelings moving through her now.

"So, do you have a dance for me?" he asked. "For an old friend?"

"Yes." She couldn't deny him, couldn't deny herself.

She left her friends in the corner of the bar, at their table with all of their fruity drinks, and let Matteo lead her away from them, lead her to the darkened dance floor. A jazz quartet was playing, the music slow and sensual.

He wrapped his arms around her waist and pulled her against his body. Heat shot through her, heat and desire and lust.

His eyes locked with hers as they swayed in time to the music, and she was powerless to resist the desire to lean in and press her lips to his. His tongue touched the tip of hers, a shot of need so sharp, so strong, assaulting her she thought it would buckle her knees then and there.

She parted her lips for him, wrapping her arms around his neck, tangling her fingers in his hair. Years of fantasies added fuel to the moment.

Matteo Corretti was her ultimate fantasy. The man whose name she called out in her sleep. The man she wanted, more than anything. And this was her last chance.

Panic drove her, made her desperate. She deepened the kiss, her movements clumsy. She didn't know how to make out. She'd never really done it before. Another thing that added fuel to the fire.

She'd never lived. She'd spent all of her life at the Battaglia *castello*, taking care of her siblings, making sure her family didn't crumble. Her life existed for the comfort of others, and she needed a moment, a night, to have something different.

To have something for her.

Matteo pulled away from her, his chest rising and falling heavily with each indrawn breath. "We cannot do that here."

She shook her head. "Apparently not." The fire between them was burning too hot, too fast, threatening to rage out of control.

"I have a suite." A smile curved his lips. "I own the hotel."

She laughed, nervous, breathless. She flexed her fingers, where her engagement ring should be. The engagement ring she hadn't put on tonight as she'd gotten ready for the party.

"Please. Just one night," she said.

"Only one, *cara mia*?"

"That's all I have to give."

"I might be able to change your mind," he said, his voice rough. He leaned in and kissed her neck, his teeth scraping her delicate skin, his tongue soothing away the sting.

Yes. She wanted to shout it. *Yes, forever. Matteo, ti amo.*

Instead, she kissed him again, long and deep, pouring everything out, every emotion, every longing that had gone unanswered for so long. Every dream she knew would never be fulfilled. Because Matteo might be hers tonight, but in just a month, she would belong to another man forever.

"Take me to your room."

Alessia shook her head, brought herself back to the present. Everything had been so perfect that night. It was the morning that had broken her heart. The cold light of day spilling over her, illuminating the truth, not allowing her to hide behind fantasy any longer.

She could remember just how he'd looked, the sheets tangled around his masculine body, bright white against his dark skin. Leaving him had broken her.

She'd wanted so badly to kiss him again, but she hadn't wanted to chance waking him.

Somehow that night she'd let her fantasies become real, had let them carry her away from reality, not just in her imagination but for real. And she couldn't regret it, not then, not now.

At least, she hadn't until recently. The way Matteo looked at her now…she hated it. Hated that he saw her as a leash.

But it was too late to turn back now. The dutiful daughter had had her rebellion, and it had destroyed everything in its path.

"You don't go halfway, do you, Alessia?" she asked the empty room.

Unsurprisingly, she got no answer.

CHAPTER FIVE

"YOU CANNOT SIMPLY take what is mine without paying for it, Corretti."

Matteo looked at Antonioni Battaglia and fought a wave of rage. The man had no idea who he was dealing with. Matteo was a Corretti, the capability to commit hideous acts was a part of his DNA. More than that, Matteo had actually done it before. Had embraced the violence. Both with cold precision, and in the heat of rage.

The temptation to do it again was strong. Instead, he leaned forward and adjusted a glass figurine that his grandmother had had commissioned for him. A perfect model of his first hotel. Not one of the Corretti Hotels, the first hotel he'd bought with his own personal fortune.

"And what exactly is that?" Matteo asked, leaning back in his office chair.

"My daughter. You defiled her. She's much less valuable to me now, which means you'd better damn well marry her and make good on the deal I cut with your grandfather, or the Correttis won't be doing any trading out of Sicily."

"My mistake, I thought Alessia's body belonged to her, not you."

"I'm an old-fashioned man."

"Be that as it may, the law prevents you from owning anyone, which means Alessia does not belong to you." He gritted his teeth, thought of Alessia's siblings, of all she'd given up to ensure they would be cared for. "However, at my fiancée's request, I have decided to honor the agreement." He paused for a moment. "What are your other children doing at the moment?"

"I've arranged for the boys to get a job in the family business."

Matteo gritted his teeth. "Is that what they want?"

"You have to take opportunity where it exists."

"And if I created a different opportunity?" He turned the figurine again, keeping his hands busy, keeping himself from violence.

"Why should I do any more business with a Corretti than necessary?"

"Because I hold your potential fortune in the palm of my hands. Not only that, I'll be the father of your first grandchild. Mainly, though, because you'll take what I give you, and no more. So it's by my good grace that you will have anything."

Antonioni's cheeks turned red. It was clear the old man didn't like being told what to do. "Corretti, I don't have to give your family rights to—"

"And I don't have to give you a damn thing. I know you're making deals with Angelo. And you know how I feel about Angelo, which puts you in my bad book right off. I may, however, be willing to overlook it all if you do as I ask. So I suggest you take steps to make me happy. Send your children to college. I'm paying for it."

"That's hardly necessary."

He thought of Alessia, of all she'd sacrificed for them. "Listen to me now, Battaglia, and remember what I say. Memorize it. Make a nice little plaque and hang it above your fireplace if need be: If I say it is necessary, then it is. So long as you do what I say, you'll be kept well in the lifestyle you would like to become accustomed to."

The other man nodded. "It's your dime, Corretti."

"Yes, and your life is now on my dime. Get used to that concept."

Had Alessia's father not said what he had, had he not acted as though her virginity, her body, was his bargaining tool, Matteo might not have taken such joy in letting the other man know his neck was, in effect, under his heel.

But he had. So Matteo did.

"I paid for one wedding," Battaglia said. "I'm not paying for another."

"I think I can handle that, too." Matteo picked up the tiny glass hotel, turning it in front of the light. "You're dismissed."

Battaglia liked that last order least of all, but he complied, leaving Matteo's office without another word.

Matteo tightened his hold on the small, breakable representation of his empire, curling his fingers around it, not stopping until it cracked, driving a shard deep into his palm.

He looked down, watched the blood drip down his wrist. Then he set the figurine back on his desk, examined the broken pieces. Marveled at how easy it was to destroy it with his anger.

He pulled the silk handkerchief out of the pocket of his jacket and wrapped the white fabric around his hand, pressing it hard, until a spot of crimson stained the fabric.

It was so easy to let emotion ruin things. So frighteningly easy.

He gritted his teeth, pushed the wall up around himself again. Control. He would have it, in all things. Alessia Battaglia was not allowed to steal it from him. Not anymore.

Never again.

"I've secured the marriage license, and we will have the wedding at my palazzo." His inheritance after the death of his father. A piece of his childhood he wasn't certain he wanted. But one he possessed nonetheless.

"Not at your family home?"

"I have no use for that place," he said, his tone hard. "Anyway, it has all been arranged."

Alessia stood up from the plush bed, crossing her arms beneath her breasts. "Really? And what shall I wear? How shall I fix my hair? Have you written my vows for me?"

"I don't care. Who gives a damn? And didn't someone already take care of writing vows for weddings hundreds of years ago?"

She blinked, trying to process his rapid-fire response. "I... Don't you have... I mean, don't I need to conform to some sort of image you're projecting or...something?"

"This will be a small affair. We may provide the press with a picture for proof. Or perhaps I'll just send them a photocopy of the marriage license. Anyway, you can wear what you like. I've never seen you not looking beautiful."

The compliment, careless, offhanded, sent a strange sensation through her. "Oh. Well. Thank you."

"It's the truth."

"Well, thank you again."

She wasn't sure what to do, both with him being nice and with him giving her a choice on what to wear to the wedding. Such a simple thing, but it was more than her father had given her when it came to Alessandro.

"As long as it doesn't have lace," she said.

"What?"

"The wedding dress."

"The dress for your last wedding was covered in it."

"Exactly. Hellish, awful contraption. And I didn't choose it. I didn't choose any of that."

"What would you have chosen?"

She shook her head and looked down. "Does it matter?"

"Why not? You can't walk down the aisle naked and we have to get married somewhere, so you might as well make the choice."

"I would wear something simple. Beautiful. And I would be barefoot. And it would be outside."

He lifted his hand and brushed it over his short hair. "Of course. Then we'll have it outside at the palazzo and you may forego shoes." He lowered his hand and she saw a slash of red on his palm.

She frowned and stepped forward. "What did you do?"

"What?" He turned his hand over. "Nothing. Just a cut."

"You look like you got in a fight."

His whole body tensed. "I don't get in fights."

"No, I know. I wasn't being serious." Tension held between them as they both had the same memory. She knew that was what was happening. Knew that he was thinking of the day she'd been attacked.

But she wanted to know what he remembered, how he remembered it, because it was obvious it was something he preferred to ignore. Not that she loved thinking about it except...except as horrible as it had been to have those men touching her, pawing at her, as awful as those memories were, the moment when they'd been wrenched from her, when she'd seen Matteo...the rush of relief, the feeling of absolute peace and certainty that everything would be okay, had been so real, so acute, she could still feel it.

She'd clung to him after. Clung to him and cried. And he'd stroked her cheek with his hand, wiping away her tears. Later she'd realized he'd left a streak of blood on her face, from the blood on his hands. Blood he'd shed, spilled, for her.

He'd been her hero that day, and every day since. She'd spent her whole life saving everyone else, being the stopgap for her siblings, taking her father's wrath if they'd been too noisy. Always the one to receive a slap across the face, rather than allow him near the younger children.

Matteo was the only person who'd ever stood up for her. The only one who'd ever saved her. And so, when life got hard, when it got painful, or scary, she would imagine that he would come again. That he would pull her into impossibly strong arms and fight her demons for her.

He never did. Never again. After that day, he even stopped watching her. But having the hope of it, the fantasy, was part of what had pulled her through the bleakness of her life. Imagination had always been her escape, and he'd added a richer texture to it, given a face to her dreams for the future.

He'd asked if she always spoke her mind, and she'd told him the truth, she didn't. She kept her head down and tried to get through her life, tried to simply do the best she could. But in her mind…her imagination was her escape, and always had been. When she ran barefoot through the garden, she was somewhere else entirely.

When she went to bed at night, she read until sleep

found her, so that she could have new thoughts in her head, rather than simply memories of the day.

So that she could have better dreams.

It was probably a good thing Matteo didn't know the place he occupied in her dreams. It would give him too much power. More than he already had.

"I'm not like my father," he said. "I will never strike my wife."

She looked at him and she realized that never, for one moment, had she believed he would. Her father had kept her mother "in line" with the back of his hand, and he'd done the same with her. But even having grown up with that as a normal occurrence, she'd never once imagined Matteo would do it.

"I know," she said.

"You know?"

"Yes."

"And how is it you know?"

"Because you aren't that kind of person, Matteo."

"Such confidence in me. Especially when you're one of the very few people who has actually seen what I'm capable of."

She had. She'd seen his brute strength applied to those who had dared try to harm her. It had been the most welcome sight in all of her life. "You protected me."

"I went too far."

"They would have gone further," she said.

He took a step away from her, the darkness in his eyes suddenly so deep, so pronounced, it threatened to pull her in. "I have work to do. I'll be at my downtown office. I've arranged to have a credit card issued to you." He reached into his pocket and pulled out a black card, extending his hand to her.

She took it, not ready to fight with him about it.

"If you need anything, whatever you need, it's yours." He turned away and walked out of the room, closing the door behind him.

She'd done the wrong thing again. With Matteo it seemed she could do nothing right. And she so desperately wanted to do right by him.

But it seemed impossible.

She growled, the sound releasing some of her tension. But not enough. "Matteo, why are you always so far out of my reach?"

This was Alessia's second wedding day. Weird, because she'd never technically had a boyfriend. One hot night of sex didn't really make Matteo her boyfriend. *Boyfriend* sounded too tame for a man like Matteo, anyway. Alessia finished zipping up the back of her gown. It was light, with flutter sleeves and a chiffon skirt that swirled around her ankles. It was lavender instead of white. She was a pregnant bride, after all.

There weren't many people in attendance, but she liked that better. Her father, her brothers and sisters, Matteo's grandmother, Teresa, and his mother, Simona.

She took the bouquet of lilacs she'd picked from the garden out of their vase and looked in the mirror. Nothing like what the makeup artist had managed on The Other Wedding Day, but today she at least looked like her.

She opened the guest bedroom door and tried to get a handle on her heart rate.

She was marrying Matteo Corretti today. In a sun-drenched garden. She was having his baby. She repeated that, over and over, trying to make it feel real, trying to hold on to the surge of good feelings it gave her. Because no matter how terrifying it was sometimes, it was also wonderful. A chance at something new. A chance to have a child, give that child the life that had been denied her. The life that had been denied Matteo.

The stone floor was cool beneath her bare feet, the palazzo empty, everyone outside waiting. She'd opted to forego shoes since that was how he said he knew her.

Barefoot in the garden. So, she would meet him as

he remembered her. Barefoot in the garden, with her hair down. Maybe then they could start over. They were getting married today, after all, and in her mind that meant they would have to start trying to work things out. They would at least have to be civil.

She put her hands on the rail of the curved, marble staircase, still repeating her mantra. She walked through the grand foyer, decorated in traditional, ornate furniture that didn't remind her one bit of Matteo, and she opened the door, stepping out into the sun.

The music was already playing. A string quartet. She'd forgotten to say what she wanted for music but this was perfect, simple.

And in spite of what Matteo had said, there was a photographer.

But those details faded into the background when she saw Matteo, standing near the priest, his body rigid, his physique displayed to perfection by a custom-made gray suit.

There was no aisle. No loud click of marble beneath her heels, just grass beneath her feet. And the guests were standing, no chairs. Her father looked like he was ready to grab her if she decided to run. Eva, Giana, Pietro and Marco looked worried, and she didn't blame them. She had been their stability for most of their lives, their surrogate mother. And she hadn't told them she was marrying Alessandro for convenience, which meant her disappearance, subsequent reappearance with a different groom and a publicly announced pregnancy must seem a few steps beyond bizarre to them.

She gave them her best, most confident smile. This was her role. To show them it was all okay, to hold everything together.

But her eyes were drawn back to Matteo. He made her throat dry, made her heart pound.

But when she reached him, he didn't take her hand. He hardly looked at her. Instead, he looked at the priest. The words to the ceremony were traditional, words she knew by heart from attending hundreds of society weddings in her life.

There was nothing personal about them, nothing unique. And Matteo never once met her eyes.

She was afraid she was alone in her resolve to make things work. To make things happy. She swallowed hard. It was always her job to make it okay. To smooth it over. Why wasn't it working?

"You may kiss the bride."

They were the words she'd been anticipating and dreading. She let her eyes drift shut and she waited. She could feel his heat draw near to her, and then, the brush of his lips on hers, so soft, so brief, she thought she might have imagined it.

And then nothing more.

Her breath caught, her heart stopped. She opened her eyes, and Matteo was already turning to face their small audience. Then he drew her near to him, his arm tight around her waist. But there was no intimacy in the gesture. No warmth.

"Thank you for bearing witness," Matteo said, both to her father and his grandmother.

"You've done a good thing for the family, Matteo," his grandmother said, putting a hand over his. And Alessia wondered just how much trouble Matteo had been in with his family for the wedding fiasco.

She knew the media had made assumptions they'd run off together. Too bad nothing could be further from the truth.

Still, her father, his family, must think that was the truth. Because now they were back in Sicily, she was pregnant and they were married.

"Perhaps we should go inside for a drink?" her father suggested.

"A good plan, Battaglia, but we don't talk business at weddings."

Simona begged off, giving Matteo a double kiss on the cheeks and saying she had a party to get to in the city. Matteo didn't seem the least bit fazed by his mother's abandonment. He simply followed her father into the house.

She watched him walk inside, her heart feeling heavy.

Teresa offered her a smile. "I'll see that Matteo's staff finds some refreshments to serve for us. I'll only be a moment." The older woman turned and went into the house, too, leaving Alessia with her siblings.

It was Eva, fourteen and emotional, who flung herself into Alessia's arms. "Where did you go?"

"New York," Alessia said, stroking her sister's hair.

"Why?"

"I had to get away...I couldn't marry Alessandro."

"Then why did you agree to the engagement?" This from Marco, the second oldest at nineteen.

"It's complicated, Marco, as things often are with Father. You know that."

"But you wanted to marry Corretti? This Corretti, I mean," asked sixteen-year-old Pietro.

She nodded, her throat tight. "Of course." She didn't want them to be upset. Didn't want them to worry. She maybe should have thought of that before running off to New York, but she really hadn't been able to consider anyone else. For the first time, she'd been burned out on it and she'd had to take care of herself.

"They're having a baby," Giana said drily. "I assume that means she liked him at least a little bit."

Then she turned back to Alessia. "I'm excited about being an aunt."

"I'm glad," she said, tugging on her sister's braid.

They spent the rest of the afternoon out in the garden, having antipasti, wine for the older children and Teresa, and lemonade for her and younger kids. Her siblings told her stories of their most recent adventures, which ended up with everyone laughing. And for the first time in months, Alessia felt at ease. This was her family, her happiness. The reason she'd agreed to marry Alessandro. And one of the driving reasons behind her decision to marry Matteo.

Although she couldn't deny her own desire where he was concerned. Still, *happy* wasn't exactly the word that she would use to describe herself at the moment. Anxiety-ridden? Check. Sick to her stomach? That a little bit, too.

The sun was starting to sink behind the hills, gray twilight settling on the garden, the solar lights that were strung across the expanse of the grass illuminating the growing darkness.

Their father appeared on the balcony, his arms folded across his chest, his eyes settled on her siblings.

"I guess we have to go," Marco said.

"I know. Come back and stay with us anytime," she said, not even thinking to ask Matteo if it was okay. As soon as she had the thought, she banished it. If she was going to be married to the man, then she wasn't going to ask his permission to breathe in their shared home. It wasn't only his now and he would have to get used to it.

Her father was the unquestionable head of their household, but she was the heart of it. She'd kept it running, made sure the kids got their favorite meals cooked, remembered birthdays and helped with homework. Her role in their lives didn't end with her marriage, and she wasn't equipped to take on a passive role in a household, anyway.

So, on that, Matteo would just have to learn to deal.

She stopped and kissed her brothers and sisters on the head before watching them go up to where their father stood. All of them but Marco. She held him a bit longer in her embrace. "Take care of everyone," she said, a tear escaping and sliding down her cheek.

"Just like you always did," he said softly.

"And I'm still here."

"I know."

He squeezed her hand before walking up to join the rest of the family.

"And I should leave you, as well," Teresa said, standing. "It was lovely to see you again, my dear."

Teresa hadn't batted an eye at the sudden change of groom, had never seemed at all ruffled by the events.

"You care for him," she said, as if she could read Alessia's internal musings.

Alessia nodded. "I do."

"That's what these men need, Alessia. A strong woman to love them. They may fight it, but it is what they need." Teresa spoke with pain in her eyes, a pain that Alessia felt echo inside of her.

Alessia couldn't speak past the lump in her throat. She tried to avoid the *L* word. The one that was stronger than *like*. There was only so much a woman could deal with at once. So instead, she just nodded and watched Teresa walk back up toward the house.

Alessia stayed in the garden and waited. The darkness thickened, the lights burning brighter. And Matteo didn't come.

She moved into the house, walked up the stairs. The palazzo was completely quiet, the lights off. She wrapped her arms around herself, and made her way back to the bedroom Matteo had put her in to get ready.

She went in and sat on the edge of the bed and waited for her husband to come and claim his wedding night.

CHAPTER SIX

MATTEO DIDN'T GET DRUNK as a rule. Unfortunately, he had a tendency to break rules when Alessia Battaglia—or was she Alessia Corretti now?—was involved.

Damn that woman.

Even after his father's death he hadn't gotten drunk. He'd wanted to. Had wanted to incinerate the memories, destroy them as the fire had destroyed the warehouses, destroyed the man who had held so much sway over his life.

But he hadn't. Because he hadn't deserved that kind of comfort. That kind of oblivion. He'd forced himself to face it.

This…this he couldn't face.

He took another shot of whiskey and let it burn all the way down. It didn't burn as much at this point in the evening, which was something of a disappointment. He looked down at the shot glass and frowned. Then he picked it up and threw it against the wall, watching the glass burst.

Now that was satisfying.

He chuckled and lifted the bottle to his lips. *Dio*, in his current state he almost felt happy. Why the hell didn't he drink more?

"Matteo?"

He turned and saw Alessia standing in the doorway. Alessia. He wanted her. More than his next breath. He wanted those long legs wrapped around his waist, wanted to hear her husky voice whispering dirty things in his ear.

He didn't think she'd ever done that, whispered dirty things in his ear, but he could imagine it, and he wanted it. *Dio*, did he want it.

"Come here, wife," he said, pushing away from the bar, his movements unsteady.

"Are you drunk?"

"I should be. If I'm not…if I'm not there's something very wrong with this whiskey."

Her dark eyes were filled with some kind of emotion. Something strong and deep. He couldn't decipher it. He didn't want to.

"Why are you drunk?"

"Because I've been drinking. Alcohol. A lot of it."

"But why?"

"I don't know, could be because today I acquired a wife and I can't say I ever particularly wanted one."

"Thank you. I'm so glad to hear that, after the ceremony."

"You would have changed your mind? You can't. It's all over the papers, in the news all over the world. You're carrying a Corretti. You, a Battaglia. It's news, *cara*. Not since Romeo and Juliet has there been such a scandal."

"I'm not going to stab myself for you just because you've poisoned your damn self, so you can stop making those parallels anytime."

"Come to me, Alessia."

She took a step toward him, her movements unsteady, her lips turned down into a sulky frown. He wanted to kiss the expression off her face.

"You left your hair down," he said, reaching out and taking a dark lock between his thumb and forefinger, rubbing the glossy strands. "You're so beautiful. An angel. That was the first thing I thought when I saw you."

She blinked rapidly. "When?"

"When we were children. I had always been told you Battaglias were monsters. Demons. And I couldn't resist the chance to peek. And there you were, running around your father's garden. You were maybe eleven. You were dirty and your hair was tangled, but

I thought you looked like heaven. You were smiling. You always smile." He frowned, looking at her face again. "You don't smile as much now."

"I haven't had a lot of reasons to smile."

"Have you ever?"

"No. But I've made them. Because someone had to smile. Someone had to teach the children how to smile."

"And it had to be you?"

"There was no one else."

"So you carry the weight of the world, little one?"

"You should know something about that, Matteo."

He chuckled. "Perhaps a little something." He didn't feel so much like he was carrying it now.

He took her arm and tugged her forward, her dark eyes wide. "I want you," he said.

Not waiting for a response, he leaned in and kissed her. Hard. She remained immobile beneath his mouth, her lips stiff, her entire body stiff. He pulled her more firmly against him, let her feel the evidence of his arousal, let her feel all of the frustration and need that had been building inside of him for the past three months.

"Did he kiss you like this?" he asked, pressing a heated kiss to her neck, her collarbone.

She shook her head. "N-no."

"Good. I would have had to kill him."

"Stop saying things like that."

"Why?" he asked. "You and I both know that I could, Alessia. On your behalf, I could. I might not even be able to stop myself." He kissed her again, his heart pounding hard, blood pouring hot and fast through his veins.

"Matteo, stop," she said, pulling away from him.

"Why? Are you afraid of me, too, Alessia?"

She shook her head. "No, but you aren't yourself. I don't like it."

"Maybe I am myself, and in that case, you're wise not to like it."

He released his hold on her. And he realized how tight his grip had been. Regret, the kind he usually kept dammed up inside of himself, released, flooding through him. "Did I hurt you?"

She shook her head. "No."

"Don't lie."

"I wouldn't."

Suddenly, he was hit with a shot of self-realization so strong it nearly buckled his knees. He had done it again. He had let his defenses down with Alessia. Let them? He didn't allow anything, with her it was just total destruction, a sudden, real demolition that he didn't seem to be able to control at all.

"Get out," he said.

"Matteo…"

"Out!" he roared, images flashing before his eyes. Images of violence. Of bones crushing beneath his fists, of not being able to stop. Not being able to stop until he was certain they could never hurt her again.

And it melded with images of his father. His father beating men until they were unconscious. Until they didn't get back up again.

"What did they do?"

"They didn't pay."

"Is that all?"

"Is that all? Matteo, you can't let anyone disrespect you, ever. Otherwise, it gets around. You have to make them an example. Whatever you have to do to protect your power, you do it. And if people have to die to secure it, so be it. Casualties of war, figlio mio.*"*

No. He wasn't like that.

But you were, Matteo. You are.

Then in his mind, it wasn't his father doing the beating. It was him.

"Out!"

Alessia's dark eyes widened and she backed out of the room, a tear tracking down her cheek.

He sank down into a chair, his fingers curled tightly around a bottle of whiskey as the edges of his vision turned fuzzy, darkened.

Che cavolo, what was she doing to him?

* * *

Alessia slammed the bedroom door behind her and tore at the back of her wedding dress, such as it was, sobbing as she released the zipper and let it fall to the floor. She'd wanted Matteo to be the one to take it off her. She hadn't realized how much until now.

Instead, her groom was off getting drunk rather than dealing with her.

"It's more than that," she said out loud. And she knew that it was. He was getting drunk instead of dealing with a whole lot of things.

Well, it was unfair because she couldn't get drunk. She was pregnant with the man's baby, and while he numbed the pain of it all, she just had to stand around and endure it.

There was nothing new to that. She had to smile. Had to keep it all moving.

She sat down on the edge of the bed, then scooted into the middle of it, lying down, curling her knees into her chest. Tonight, there was no fantasy to save her, no way to avoid reality.

Matteo had long been her rescue from the harsh reality and pain of life. And now he was her harsh reality. And he wasn't who she'd believed he was. She'd simplified him, painted him as a savior.

She'd never realized how much he needed to be

saved. The question was, was she up to the challenge? No, the real question was, did she have a choice?

There wasn't a word foul enough to help release the pain that was currently pounding through Matteo's head. So he said them all.

Matteo sat upright in the chair. He looked down at the floor, there was a mostly empty whiskey bottle lying on its side by the armchair. And there was a dark star-shaped whiskey stain on the wall, glass shards gathered beneath.

He remembered...not very much. The wedding. He was married now. He looked down at the ring on his left hand. Yes, he was married now.

He closed his eyes again, trying to lessen the pain in his head, and had a flash of lilac memory. A cloud of purple, long dark hair. He'd held her arm and pulled her against him, his lips hard on hers.

Dio, what had he done? Where had it stopped? He searched his brain desperately for an answer, tried to figure out what he'd done. What she'd done.

He stood quickly, ignoring the dizziness, the ferocious hammering in his temples. He swore again as he took his first step, he legs unsteady beneath him.

What was his problem? Where was his control? He knew better than to drink like that, knew better than to allow any lowered inhibitions.

The first time he'd gotten that drunk had been the night following Alessia's rescue. He hadn't been able to get clean. Hadn't been able to get the images out of his head. Images of what he was capable of.

The stark truth was, it hadn't been the attack that had driven him to drink. It had been what his father had said afterward.

"You are my son."

When Benito Corretti had seen his son, blood-streaked, after the confrontation with Alessia's attackers, he'd assumed that it meant Matteo was finally following in his footsteps. Had taken it as confirmation.

But Matteo hadn't. It had been six years after that night when Benito had said it to him again. And that night, Matteo had embraced the words, and proven the old man right.

He pushed the memories away, his heart pounding too hard to go there.

He knew full well that he was capable of unthinkable things, even without the loss of control. But when control was gone…when it was gone, he truly became a monster. And last night, he'd lost control around Alessia.

He had to find her.

He walked down the hall, his heart pounding a sick tempo in his skull, his entire body filled with lead.

He went down the stairs, the natural light filtering through the windows delivering a just punishment for his hideous actions.

Coffee. He would find coffee first, and then Alessia.

He stopped when he got to the dining room. It turned out he had found both at the same time.

"Good morning," Alessia said, her hands folded in front of her, her voice soft and still too loud.

"Morning," he said, refusing to call it good.

"I assume you need coffee?" she asked, indicating a French press, ready for brewing, and a cup sitting next to it.

"Yes."

"You know how that works, right?" she asked.

"Yes."

"Good."

She didn't make a move to do it for him, she simply sat in her seat, drinking a cup of tea.

He went to his spot at the expansive table, a few seats away from hers, and sat, pushing the plunger down slowly on the French press.

He poured himself a cup, left it black. He took a drink and waited a moment, letting the strong brew do its magic.

"Alessia," he said, his voice rusty, the whiskey burn seeming to linger, "last night...did I hurt you?"

"In what way?" she asked, leaning back in her chair, her dark eyes unflinching.

"Physically."

"No."

The wave of relief that washed over him was profound, strong. "I'm pleased to hear it."

"Emotionally, on the other hand, I'm not sure I faired so well."

"Why is that?"

"Well, let's see, my husband got drunk on our wedding night instead of coming to bed with me. What do you think?"

"I'm sorry if I wounded your pride," he said, "that wasn't my intention." What he'd been after was oblivion, which he should have known wasn't a safe pursuit.

"Wouldn't your pride have been wounded if I'd done the same?"

"I would have ripped the bottle out of your hand. You're pregnant."

There hadn't been a lot of time for him to really pause and think through the implications of that. It had all been about securing the marriage. Staying a step ahead of the press at all times. Making sure Alessia was legally bound to him.

"Hence the herbal tea," she said, raising her cup to him. "And the pregnancy wasn't really my point."

"Alessia…this can't be a normal marriage."

"Why not?" she asked, sitting up straighter.

"Because it simply can't be. I'm a busy man, I travel a lot. I was never going to marry…I never would have married."

"I don't see why we can't have a normal marriage anyway. A lot of men and women travel for business, it doesn't mean they don't get married."

"I don't love you."

Alessia felt like he'd slapped her. His words were so bald, so true and unflinching. And they cut a swath of devastation through her. "I didn't ask you to," she said, because it was the only truth she could bring herself to speak.

"Perhaps not, but a wife expects it from her husband."

"I doubt my father loved my mother, and if he did, it wasn't the kind of love I would like to submit to. What about yours?"

"*Obsession,* perhaps, was a better word. My father loved Lia's mother, I'm sure of that. I'm not certain he loved mine. At least, not enough to stay away from other women. And my mother was—is, for that matter—very good at escaping unpleasant truths by way of drugs and alcohol." His headache mocked him, a reminder that he'd used alcohol for the very same reason last night.

"Perhaps it was their marriages that weren't normal. Perhaps—"

"Alessia, don't. I think you saw last night that I'm not exactly a brilliant candidate for husband or father of the year."

"So try to be. Don't just tell me you can't, Matteo, or that you don't want to. Be better. That's what I'm trying to do. I'm trying to be stronger, to do the right thing."

"Yes, because that's what you do," he said, his tone dry. "You make things better, because it makes you feel better, and as long as you feel good you assume all is right with your world. You trust your moral compass."

"Well, yes, I suppose that's true."

"I don't trust mine. I want things I shouldn't want. I have already taken what I didn't have the right to take."

"If you mean my virginity, I will throw this herbal tea in your face," she said, pregnancy hormones coming to the rescue, bringing an intense surge of anger.

"I'm not so crass, but yes. Your body, you, you aren't for me."

"For Alessandro? That's who I was for?"

"That isn't what I meant."

"The hell it's not, Matteo!" she shouted, not caring if she hurt his head. Him and his head could go to hell. "You're just like him. You think I can't make my own decisions? That I don't know my own mind? My body belongs to me, not to you, not to my father, not to Alessandro. I didn't give myself to you, I took you. I made you tremble beneath my hands, and I could do it again. Don't treat me like some fragile thing. Don't treat me like you have to protect me from myself."

He stayed calm, maddeningly so, his focus on his cup of coffee. "It's not you I'm protecting you from."

"It's you?"

A smile, void of humor, curved his lips. "I don't trust me, Alessia, why should you?"

"Well, let me put you at ease, Matteo. I don't trust anyone. Just because I jumped into bed with you doesn't mean you're the exception. I just think you're hot." She was minimizing it. Minimizing what she felt. And she hated that. But she was powerless to do anything to stop the words from coming out. She wanted to protect herself, to push him back from her vulnerable places. To keep him from hurting her.

Because the loss of Matteo in her fantasies…it was almost too much to bear. As he became her reality, she was losing her escape, and she was angry at him for taking it. For not being the ideal she had made him out to be.

"I'm flattered," he said, taking another drink of his coffee.

"How do you see this marriage going, then?"

"I don't want to hurt you."

"Assume it's too late. Where do we go from here?"

He leaned forward, his dark eyes shuttered. "When exactly are you due?"

"November 22. It was easy for them to figure out since I knew the exact date I conceived."

"I will make sure you get the best care, whatever you need. And we'll make a room for the baby."

"Well, all things considered, I suppose our child should have a room in his own house."

"I'm trying," he bit out. "I'm not made for this. I don't know how to handle it."

"Well, I do. I know exactly how much work babies are. I know exactly what it's like to raise children. I was thirteen when my mother died. Thirteen when my baby sister and the rest of my siblings became my responsibility. Babies are hard work. But you love them, so much. And at the same time, they take everything from you. I know that, I know it so well. And I'm terrified," she said, the last word breaking. It was a horrible confession, but it was true.

She'd essentially raised four children, one of them from infancy, and as much as she adored them, with every piece of herself, she also knew the cost of it. Knew just how much you poured into children. How much you gave, how much they took.

And she was doing it again. Without ever finding a place for herself in the world. Without having the fantasies she'd craved. True love. A man who would take care of her.

You've had some of the fantasies.

Oh, yes, she had. But one night of passion wasn't the sum total of her life's desires.

"All of this," he said. "And still you want this child?"

"Yes, Matteo. I do. Because babies are a lot of work. But the love you feel for them…it's stronger than anything, than any fear. It doesn't mean I'm not afraid, only that I know in the end the love will win."

"Well, we can be terrified together," he said.

"You're terrified?"

"Babies are tiny. They look very easily broken."

"I'll teach you how to hold one."

Their eyes met, heat arching between them, and this time her pregnancy hormones were making her feel something other than anger.

She looked back down at her breakfast. "How's your head?"

"I feel like someone put a woodpecker in my skull."

"It's no less than you deserve."

"I will treat you better than I did last night. That I promise you. I'm not sure what other promises I can make, but that one…that one I will keep."

She thought of him last night. Broken. Passionate. Needy. She wondered how much of that was the real Matteo. How much he kept hidden beneath a facade.

How much he kept from escaping. And she knew just how he felt in some ways. Knew what it was like to hide everything behind a mask. It was just that her mask was smiling, and his hardly made an expression at all.

"Will you be faithful to me?" she asked, the words catching in her throat.

Matteo looked down into his coffee for a moment, then stood, his cup in his hand. "I have some work to see to this morning, and my head is killing me. We can talk more later."

Alessia's heart squeezed tight, nausea rolling through her. "Later?"

"My head, Alessia."

My heart, you jackass. "Great. Well, perhaps we can have a meeting tonight, or something."

"We're busy tonight."

"Oh. Doing what?"

"Celebrating our marriage, quite publicly, at a charity event."

"What?" She felt far too raw to be in public.

"After what happened with Alessandro, we have to present a united front. Your not-quite wedding to him was very public, as was your announcement of your pregnancy. The entire world is very likely scratching their heads over the spectacle we've created, and now it's time to show a little bit of normal."

"But we don't have a normal marriage—I mean, so I've been told."

"As far as the media is concerned we do."

"Why? Afraid of a little scandal? You're a Corretti."

"What do you want our child to grow up and read? Because thanks to the internet, this stuff doesn't die. It's going to linger, scandal following him wherever he goes. You and I both know what that's like. To have all the other kids whisper about your parents. For our part, we aren't criminals, but we've hardly given our child a clean start."

"So we go out and look pretty and sparkly and together, and what? The press just forgets about what happened?"

"No, but perhaps they will continue on in the vein that they've started in."

"What's that?" She'd, frankly, spent a lot of energy avoiding the stories that the media had written about the wedding.

"That we were forbidden lovers, who risked it all to be together."

It wasn't far from the truth, although Matteo hadn't truly known the risk they'd been taking their night together. But she had. And she'd risked it all for the chance to be with him.

Looking at him now, dealing with all the bruises he'd inflicted on her heart, she knew she would make the same choice now. Because at least it had been her choice. Her mistake. Her very first big one. It was like a rite of passage in a way.

"Well, then, I suppose we had better get ready to put on a show. I'm not sure I have the appropriate costume, though."

"I'm sure I can come up with something."

CHAPTER SEVEN

"SOMETHING" TURNED OUT to be an evening gown from the Corretti fashion line. It was gorgeous, and it was very slinky, with silky gold fabric that molded to her curves and showed the emerging baby bump that she almost hadn't noticed until she'd put on the formfitting garment.

Of course, there was no point in hiding her pregnancy. She'd announced it on television, for heaven's sake. But even so, since she hadn't really dealt with it yet, she felt nervous about sharing it with the public like this.

She put her hand on her stomach, smoothing her palm over the small bump. She was going to be a mother. Such a frightening, amazing thing to realize. She'd been tangled up in finding Matteo, and then in the days since—had it really only been days?—she'd been dealing with having him back in her life.

With marrying him. She hadn't had a chance to really think of the baby in concrete terms.

Alessia looked at herself in the mirror one more time, at her stomach, and then back at her face. Her looks had never mattered very much to her. She was comfortable with them, more or less. She was taller than almost every other woman she knew, and a good portion of the men, at an Amazonian six feet, but Matteo was taller.

He managed to make her feel small. Feminine. Beautiful.

That night they were together he'd made her feel especially beautiful. And then last night he'd made her feel especially undesirable. Funny how that worked.

She turned away from the mirror and walked out of the bedroom. Matteo was standing in the hall waiting for her, looking so handsome in his black suit she went a little weak-kneed. He was a man who had a strong effect, that was for sure.

"Don't you clean up nice," she said. "You almost look civilized."

"Appearances can be deceiving," he said.

"The devil wore Armani?"

"Something like that." He held his hand out and she hesitated for a moment before taking it and allowing him to lead her down the curved staircase and into the foyer. He opened the door for her, his actions that of a perfectly solicitous husband.

Matteo's sports car was waiting for them, the keys in the ignition.

Alessia waited until they were on the road before speaking again. "So, what's the charity?"

He shifted gears, his shoulders bunched up, muscles tense. "It's one of mine."

"You have charities?"

"Yes."

"I didn't realize."

"I thought you knew me."

"We're filled with surprises for each other, aren't we? It's a good thing we have a whole lifetime together to look forward to," she said drily.

"Yes," he said, his voice rough, unconvincing.

And she was reminded of their earlier conversation in the dining room. She'd asked him point-blank if he would be faithful, and he'd sidestepped her. She had a feeling he was doing it again.

She gritted her teeth to keep from saying anything more. To keep from asking him anything, or pressing the issue. She had some pride. She did. She was sure she did, and she was going to do everything she could to hold on to her last little bit of it.

"Well, what is your charity for, then?"

"This is an education fund. For the schools here."

"That's…great," she said. "I didn't get to do any higher education."

"Did you want to?"

"I don't know. I don't think so. I mean…I didn't really have anything I wanted to be when I grew up."

"Nothing?"

"There weren't a lot of options on the table. Though I did always think I would like to be a mother." A wife and a mother. That she would like to have someone who loved her, cherished her like the men in her much-loved books cherished their heroines. It was a small dream, one that should have been somewhat manageable.

Instead, she'd gone off and traded it in for a night of wild sex.

And darn it, she still didn't regret it. Mainly.

"Mission accomplished."

"Why, yes, Matteo, I am, as they say, living the dream."

"There's no need to be—"

"There is every need to be," she said. "Don't act like I should thank you for any of this."

"I wasn't going to," he said, his tone biting.

"You were headed there. This is not my dream." But it was close. So close that it hurt worse in some ways than not getting anywhere near it at all. Because this was proving that her dream didn't exist. That it wasn't possible.

"My apologies, *cara*, for not being your dream." His voice was rough, angry, and she wanted to know where he got off being mad after the way he'd been treating her.

"And my apologies for not being yours. I imagine if I had a room number stapled to my forehead and a bag of money in my hand I'd come a little closer."

"Now you're being absurd."

"I don't think so."

Matteo maneuvered his car through the narrow city streets, not bothering with nice things like braking before turning, and pulled up to the front of his hotel.

"It's at your hotel," she said.

"Naturally." He threw the car into Park, then got out, rounding to the passenger side and opening the door for her. "Come, my darling wife, we have a public to impress."

He extended his hand to her and she slowly reached her hand out to accept it. Lighting streaked through her, from her fingertips, spreading to every other part of her, the shock and electricity curling her toes in her pumps.

She stood, her eyes level with his thanks to her shoes. "Thank you."

A member of the hotel staff came to where they

were and had a brief exchange with Matteo before getting into the car and driving it off to the parking lot. Alessia wandered to the steps of the hotel, taking two of them before pausing to wait for her husband.

Matteo turned back to her, his dark eyes glittering in the streetlamps. He moved to the stairs, and she advanced up one more, just to keep her height advantage. But Matteo wasn't having it. He got onto her stair, meeting her eyes straight on.

"There are rules tonight, Alessia, and you will play by them."

"Will I?" she asked. She wasn't sure why she was goading him. Maybe because it was the only way in all the world she could feel like she had some power. Or maybe it was because if she wasn't trying to goad him, she was longing for him. And the longing was just unacceptable.

A smile curved his lips and she couldn't help but wonder if he needed this, too. This edge of hostility, the bite of anger between them.

Although why Matteo would need anything to hold her at a distance when he'd already made his feelings quite clear was a mystery to her.

"Yes, my darling wife, you will." He put his hand on her chin, drawing close to her, his heat making her shiver deep inside. It brought her right back to that night.

To the aching, heart-rending desperation she'd felt when his lips had finally touched hers. To the moment they'd closed his hotel room door and he'd pressed her against the wall, devouring, taking, giving.

He drew his thumb across her lower lip and she snapped back to the present. "You must stop looking at me like that," he said.

"Like what?"

"Like you're frightened of me." There was an underlying note to his voice that she couldn't guess at, a frayed edge to his control that made his words gritty.

"I'm not."

"You look at me like I'm the very devil sometimes."

"You act like the very devil sometimes."

"True enough. But there are other times..."

"What other times?"

"You didn't used to look at me that way."

"How did I look at you?" she asked, her chest tightening, her stomach pulling in on itself.

"When you were a girl? With curiosity. At the hotel? Like you were hungry."

"You looked at me the same way."

"And how do you think I look at you now?"

"You don't," she whispered. "When you can help it, you don't look at me at all."

He moved his other hand up to cup her cheek, his

thumb still stroking her lower lip. "I'm looking at you now."

And there was heat in his eyes. Heat like there had been their night together, the night that had started all of this. The night that had changed the course of her life.

"Because you have to," she said. "For the guests."

"Oh, yes, the guests," he said.

Suddenly, a flash pierced the dim light, interrupting their moment. They both looked in the direction of the photographer, who was still snapping pictures in spite of the fact that the moment was completely broken.

"Shall we go in?" he asked. Any evidence of frayed control was gone now, the rawness, the intensity, covered by a mask. And now her husband was replaced with a smooth, cool stranger.

She'd love to say it wasn't the man she'd married, but this was exactly the man she'd married. This guarded man with more layers of artifice than anyone she'd ever met. She had been so convinced she'd seen the man behind the fiction, that the night in the hotel she'd seen the real Matteo. That in those stolen glances they'd shared when they were young, she'd seen the truth.

That in the moment of unrestrained violence, when

he'd put himself in harm's way to keep her from getting hurt, she'd seen the real man.

Now she realized what small moments those were in the entirety of Matteo's life. And for the first time, she wondered if she was simply wrong about him.

A feeling that settled sickly in her stomach, a leaden weight, as they continued up the stairs and into the entrance to the hotel's main ballroom.

There were more photographers inside, capturing photographs of the well-dressed crème de la crème of Sicilian society. And Alessia did her best to keep a smile on her face. This was her strength, being happy no matter what was going on. Keeping a smile glued to her face at whatever event she was at on behalf of her father, making sure she showed her brothers and sisters she was okay even if she'd just taken a slap to the face from their father.

But this wasn't so simple. She was having a harder time finding a place to go to inside of herself. Having a harder time finding that false feeling of hope that she'd become so good at creating for herself to help preserve her sanity.

No one could live in total hopelessness, so she'd spent her life creating hope inside of herself. She'd managed to do it through so many difficult scenarios. Why was it so hard now? So hard with Matteo?

She knew she'd already answered that question. It

was too hard to retreat to a much-loved fantasy when that much-loved fantasy was standing beside you, the source of most of your angst.

Though she couldn't blame it all on Matteo. The night of her bachelorette party was the first night she'd stopped trying to find solace in herself, had stopped just trying to be happy no matter what, and had gone for what she wanted, in spite of possible consequences.

She spent the night with Matteo's arm wrapped around her waist, his touch keeping her entire body strung tight, on a slow burn. She also turned down champagne more times than she could count. Was she normally offered alcohol so much at a party? She'd never been conscious of it when she was allowed to drink it. Right now it just seemed a cruelty, since she could use the haze, but couldn't take the chance with her baby's health.

Anyway, for some reason it all smelled sour and spoiled to her now. The pregnancy was making her nose do weird things.

Although Matteo smelled just as good as he ever had. The thought made her draw a little closer to him, breathe in the scent of him, some sort of spicy cologne mingling with the scent of his skin. She was especially tuned into the scent of his skin now, the scent of his sweat.

Dio, even his sweat turned her on. Because it reminded her of his bare skin, slick from exertion, her hands roaming over his back as he thrust hard into her, his dark eyes intent on hers. And there were no walls. Not then.

She blinked and came back to the present. She really had to stop with the sexual fantasies, they did her no good.

A photographer approached them. "Smile for me?" he asked.

Matteo drew her in close to his body, and she put her hand on his chest. She knew her smile looked perfect. She had perfected her picture smile for events such as these, to put on a good front for the Battaglia family. She was an expert.

Matteo should have been, as well, but he looked like he was trying to smile around a rock in his mouth, his expression strained and unnatural.

"A dance for the new bride and groom?" the photographer asked while taking their picture, and she was sure that in that moment her smile faltered a bit.

"Of course," Matteo said, his grin widening. Was she the only one who could see the totally feral light in his eyes, who could see that none of this was real?

The photographer was smiling back, as were some of the guests standing in their immediate area, so they must not be able to tell. Must not be able to see how completely disingenuous the expression of warmth was.

"Come. Dance with me."

And so she followed him out onto the glossy marble dance floor, where other couples were holding each other close, slow dancing to a piece of piano music.

It was different from when they'd danced in New York. The ballroom was bright, crystal chandeliers hanging overhead, casting shimmering light onto caramel-colored walls and floors. The music was as bright as the lighting, nothing darkly sensual or seductive.

And yet when Matteo drew her into his hold, his arms tight, strong around her, they might as well have been the only two people in the room. Back again, shrouded in darkness in the corner of a club, stealing whatever moments together they could have before fate would force them to part forever.

Except fate had had other ideas.

She'd spent a lot of her life believing in fate, believing that the right thing would happen in the end. She questioned that now. Now she just wondered if she'd let her body lead her into an impossible situation all for the sake of assuaging rioting hormones.

"This will make a nice headline, don't you think?"

he asked, swirling her around before drawing her back in tight against him.

"I imagine it will. You're a great dancer, by the way. I don't know if I mentioned that…last time."

"You didn't, but your mouth was otherwise occupied."

Her cheeks heated. "Yes, I suppose it was."

"My mother made sure I had dance lessons starting at an early age. All a part of grooming me to take my place at the helm of Benito's empire."

"But you haven't really. Taken the helm of your father's empire, I mean."

"Not as such. We've all taken a piece of it, but in the meantime we've been working to root out the shadier elements of the business. It's one thing my brothers and I do not suffer. We're not criminals."

"A fact I appreciate. And for the record, neither is Alessandro. I would never have agreed to marry him otherwise."

"Is that so?"

"I've had enough shady dealings to last me a lifetime. My father, for all that he puts on the front of being an honorable citizen, is not. At least your fathers and your grandfather had the decency to be somewhat open about the fact that they weren't playing by the rules."

"Gentleman thugs," he said, his voice hard. "But

I'll let you in on a little secret—no matter how good you are at dancing, no matter how nicely tailored your suit is, it doesn't change the fact that when you hit a man in the legs with a metal cane, his knees shatter. And he doesn't care what you're wearing. Neither do the widows of the men you kill."

Alessia was stunned by his words, not by the content of them, not as shocked as she wished she were. People often assumed that she was some naive, cosseted flower. Her smile had that effect. They assumed she must not know how organized crime worked. But she did. She knew the reality of it. She knew her father was bound up so tightly in all of it he could hardly escape it even if he wanted to.

He was addicted to the power, and being friendly with the mob bosses was what kept him in power. He couldn't walk away easily. Not with his power, possibly not even with his life.

And yet, the Correttis had disentangled themselves from it. The Corretti men and women had walked away from it.

No, it wasn't the content of his words that had surprised her. It was the fact that he'd said them at all. Because Matteo played his cards close to his chest. Because Matteo preferred not to address the subject of his family, of that part of his past.

"You aren't like that, though."

"No?" he asked. "I'm in a suit."

"And you wouldn't do that to someone."

"Darling Alessia, you are an eternal optimist," he said, and there was something in his words she didn't like. A hard edge that made her stomach tighten. "I don't know how you manage it."

"Survival. I have to protect myself."

"I thought that was where cynics came from?"

"Perhaps a good number of them. But no matter how I feel about a situation, I've never had any control over the outcome. My mother died in childbirth, and no amount of feeling good or bad about it would have changed that. My father is a criminal, no matter the public mask he wears, who has no qualms about slapping my face to keep me in line." They swirled in a fast circle, Matteo's hold tightening on her, something dangerous flickering in his eyes. "No matter how I feel about the situation, that is the situation. If I didn't choose to be happy no matter what, I'm not sure I would have ever stopped crying, and I didn't want to live like that, either."

"And why didn't you leave?" he asked.

"Without Marco, Giana, Eva and Pietro? Never. I couldn't do it."

"With them, then."

"With no money? With my father and his men bearing down on us? If it were only myself, then I would have left. But it was never only me. I think we were why my mother stayed, too." She swallowed hard. "And if she could do it for us, how could I do any less?"

"Your mother was good to you?"

"So good," Alessia said, remembering her beautiful, dark-haired mother, the gentle smile that had always put her at ease when her father was in the other room shouting. The sweet, soothing touch, a hand on her forehead to help her fall asleep. "I wanted to give them all what she gave to me. I was the oldest, the only one who remembered her very well. It seemed important I try to help them remember. That I give them the love I received, because I knew they would never get it from my father."

"And in New York? With me?"

"What do you mean?"

"You toed the line all of your life, Alessia. You were prepared to marry to keep your brothers and sisters safe and cared for. Why did you even chance ruining it by sleeping with me?" His hold tightened on her, his voice getting back that rough edge. That genuine quality it had been missing since they'd stepped inside the hotel.

It was a good question. It was *the* question, really.

"Tell me, *cara*," he said, and she glimpsed something in his eyes as he spoke. A desperation.

And she couldn't goad him. Couldn't lie to him. Not now.

"Did you ever want something, Matteo, with all of yourself? So much that it seemed like it was in your blood? I did. For so many years. When we were children, I wanted to cross that wall between our families' estates and take your hand, make you run with me in the grass, make you smile. And when I got older…well, I wanted something different from you, starting about the time you rescued me, and I don't want to hear about how much you regret that. It mattered to me. I dreamed of what it would be like to kiss you, and then, I dreamed of what it would be like to make love with you. So much so that by the time I saw you in New York, when you finally did kiss me, I felt like I knew the steps to the dance. And following your lead seemed the easiest thing. How could I not follow?"

"I am a man, Alessia, so I fear there is very little romance to my version of your story. From the time you started to become a woman, I dreamed of your skin against mine. Of kissing you. Of being inside you. I could not have stopped myself that night any more than you could have."

"That's good to know," she said, heat rushing through her, settling over her skin. It made her dress, so lovely and formfitting a few moments ago, feel tight. Far too tight.

"I don't understand what it is you do to me."

"I thought... I was certain that I must not be so different from all your other women."

"There weren't that many," he said. "And you are different."

It was a balm to her soul that he felt that way. That she truly hadn't been simply one in a lineup. It was easy for her, she realized, to minimize the experience on his end. It had been easy for her to justify being with him, not being honest with him, giving him a one-night stand, because she'd assumed he'd had them before. It had been easy to believe she was the only one who'd stood to be hurt or affected, because she was the virgin.

That had been unfair. And she could see now, looking into his eyes, that it wasn't true, either.

"Kiss me," he said, all of the civility gone now.

She complied, closing the short distance between them, kissing him, really kissing him, for the first time in three months. Their wedding kiss had been nothing. A pale shadow of the passion they'd shared before. A mockery of the desire that was like a living beast inside of them both.

She parted her lips for him, sucked his tongue deep inside of her mouth, not caring that it would be obvious to the people around them. Matteo was hers now, her husband. She wouldn't hide it, not from anyone. Wouldn't hide her desire.

He growled low in his throat, the sound vibrating through his body. "Careful, Alessia, or I will not be responsible for what happens."

"I don't want you to be responsible," she said, kissing his neck. Biting him lightly. There was something happening to her, something that had happened once before. A total loss of control. At the hands of Matteo Corretti.

It was like she was possessed, possessed by the desire to have him, to take him, make him hers. Make him understand what she felt. Make herself understand what she felt.

"We can't do this here," he said.

"This sounds familiar."

"It does," he said. He shifted, pulled her away from his body, twining his fingers with hers. "Come with me."

"Where?"

"Somewhere," he said.

He led her out of the ballroom, ignoring everyone who tried to talk to them. A photographer followed them and Matteo cursed, leading them a different way, down a corridor and to the elevators.

He pushed the up button and they both waited. It

only took a moment for the elevator doors to slide open, and the moment they did, she was being tugged inside, tugged up against the hard wall of his chest and kissed so hard, so deep, she was afraid she would drown in it.

She heard the doors slide closed behind them, was dimly aware of the elevator starting to move. Matteo shifted their positions, put her back up against the wall, his lips hungry on hers.

"I need you," he said, his voice shaking.

"I need *you*," she said.

Her entire body had gone liquid with desire, her need for him overshadowing everything. Common sense, self-protection, everything. There was no time for thought. This was Matteo. The man she wanted with everything she had in her, the man who haunted her dreams. This was her white knight, but he was different than she'd imagined.

There was a darkness to him. An edge she'd never been able to imagine. And she found she liked it. Found she wanted a taste of it. She didn't know what that said about her, didn't know what it meant, but at the moment, she didn't care, either.

"This is a beautiful dress," he said, tracing the deep V of the neckline with his fingertip, skimming silk and skin with the movement. Her breath hitched, her entire body on edge, waiting for what he would do next. Needing it more than she needed air. "But it is not as beautiful as you. And right now, I need to see you."

He reached around, tugging on the zipper, jerking it down.

"Careful," she said, choking on the word. "You'll snag the fabric."

"I'll tear it if I have to," he said.

The top fell around her waist, revealing her breasts, covered only by a whisper-thin bra that showed the outline of her nipples beneath the insubstantial fabric.

He lifted his hand and cupped her, slid his thumb over the tightened bud. "Hot for me?" he asked.

"Yes."

"Wet for me?" He put his other hand on her hip, flexed his fingers.

She couldn't speak, she just nodded. And he closed his eyes, his expression one of pained relief like she'd never seen before.

She put her hand between her breasts, flicked the front clasp on her bra, letting it fall to the elevator floor. He looked at her, lowering his head, sucking her deep into his mouth. An arrow of pleasure shot from there down to her core. She tightened her fingers in his hair, then suddenly became conscious of the continued movement of the elevator.

"Hit the stop button," she said, her voice breathless.

"What?" he asked, lifting his head, his cheeks flushed, his hair in disarray. Her heart nearly stopped. Matteo Corretti undone was the most amazing thing she'd ever seen.

"The elevator," she said.

He cursed and turned around, hitting the red button on the wall, the elevator coming to a halt. He cursed again and reached into his pocket, taking out his cell phone. "Just a second."

"You better not be texting," she said.

He pushed a few buttons, his eyes not straying to her. "Not exactly." He turned the screen toward her and she saw him. And her. And her breasts.

"Oh."

He pushed a few more buttons. "I have disabled the security camera now. Unless you like the idea of being on film."

She had to admit, she had a certain amount of curiosity as to what it looked like when Matteo Corretti made love to her. It was a video she wouldn't mind owning, in all honesty. But she didn't want it on security footage, either.

"Not in the mood to provide security with any early-evening jollies."

"No worries, I have now deleted that little stretch of footage. There are advantages to being a control freak. Having an app on your phone that lets you see all the security at your hotels, and do as you please with the cameras, is one of them."

He discarded his suit jacket and tie then, throwing them onto the floor of the elevator, tossing his phone down on top of them.

"Have you used that trick before?" she asked, before he lowered his head to kiss her again.

"With a woman?"

"Yes."

"Jealous?"

"Hell, yes," she said, not worried if he knew it. She wanted this moment, this desperation that was beyond anything she'd known, to be as foreign to him as it was to her.

"No, I haven't." He kissed her again, his tongue sliding against hers, and she forgot her lingering concerns.

Forgot about everything but what it felt like to have Matteo kissing her. Caressing her.

"Later—" he kissed the hollow of her throat "—I will do this right—" lowered his head and traced the line of her collarbone with his tongue. "I'll taste every inch of you. Take time to savor you. Take your clothes off slowly. Look at those gorgeous curves." He kissed her neck, bit her lightly like she'd done to him earlier. "Now, though...now I just need to be inside you."

He started to gather her skirt up in his hands, the slippery fabric sliding up her legs easily. "Take your panties off," he said.

She complied, her hands trembling as she worked her underwear down, kicking them to the side with her heels. He pushed her dress up around her hips, his hand hot on her thigh. He tugged her leg up around his, her back pinned against the wall of the elevator.

He tested her with his other hand, teasing her clitoris, sending streaks of white heat through her body with each pass his fingers made through her slick folds. "You didn't lie," he said. "You do want me."

"Yes," she said.

"Tell me," he said.

"I want you."

"My name."

"I want you, Matteo."

He abandoned her body for a moment, working at his belt, shoving his slacks and underwear down, just enough to free his erection so that he could sink into her. It was a shock, all those weeks without him, and she'd forgotten just how big he was. Just how much he filled her. She let her head fall back against the wall of the elevator, pleasure building deep inside her, her internal muscles tightening around his length.

And then there was no more talking. There was nothing but their ragged breathing, Matteo moving hard and fast inside her, blunt fingertips digging into her hips as he held her steady, thrusting into her.

He lowered his head, capturing her nipple in his mouth again. A raw sound of pleasure escaped her lips and she didn't even care. She wasn't embarrassed at all.

Because this was Matteo. The man she'd always wanted. Wanted enough to break out of what was expected of her for the first time in her life. The man who had saved her, the man who made her angry and hurt her, the man who made her feel things she'd never felt before.

Matteo scared her. He confused her. He made her feel more than anyone else ever had.

And right now he was driving her to a point she'd never even imagined, to the edge of a cliff so high she couldn't see the bottom of the chasm below.

She was afraid to fall, afraid to let the pleasure that was building in her break, because she didn't know what would greet her on the other side. Didn't know what would happen. And something *would* happen. Something would change. There was no question. None at all.

And then he looked at her, those dark eyes meeting hers, and she saw him. Not the mask, the man. Raw need, desperation and a fear that mirrored her own.

He lowered his head, his lips pressing against her

neck, his thrusts losing their measured rhythm. And something in her broke, released. And she was falling, falling into that endless chasm. But she wasn't afraid anymore.

Release rolled through her in waves, stealing every breath, every thought, everything but the moment.

And when she finally did reach bottom, Matteo was there, his strong arms around her. He was breathing hard, too, sweat on his brow, the back of his shirt damp, his heartbeat raging, so hard that, with his body pressed so tightly against hers, she could feel it against her own chest.

He stepped away from her slowly, running his hand over his hair, erasing the evidence that she'd ever speared her fingers through it. That she'd messed with his well-ordered control.

He adjusted his pants. Bent and collected his jacket, putting his phone back into his pocket. And she just stood there, her back to the wall, her dress still pushed partway up around her hips, the top resting at her waist, her underwear on the floor by her feet.

Matteo put his tie around his neck and started straightening it, too, before he looked at her. "Get dressed," he said.

"What?"

"Get dressed," he said. "We have to go back to the party."

"W-we do?"

"It's my charity," he said. "I have a speech to make." He checked his wristwatch. "And it seems I'm not too late for it so I really should try to manage it."

"I…"

"Turn around," he ordered, his voice harsh.

She did as he asked. He put her straps back into place, zipped the dress back up.

"My bra…"

"You don't need it," he said.

"What should I do with it?"

He opened up his jacket and indicated his inner pocket. She bent and scooped up her bra and panties and handed them to him, and he put both tiny garments into his pocket.

"Solved," he said.

She looked down at her chest, cupped her breasts for a moment. "I'm sagging."

"You are not."

He hit the button on the elevator and it started moving again, the doors sliding open. Then he hit the button for the first floor and they waited for the doors to close again.

Alessia felt…used. No, not even that. She just felt sad. Angry, because he was able to do that with her and then go back to his purely unruffled self.

Maybe she'd been making more out of them, and

the sex, than she should have. Maybe she was wrong. Maybe it didn't mean anything to him. Nothing more than just sex, anyway, and a man like Matteo surely had it quite a bit.

They rode in silence, and the doors opened again. The photographer was still out there, wandering the halls. Looking for a photo op, no doubt.

Matteo put his arm around her waist and led her through the hall, that false smile back on his face. They started back toward the ballroom and she had the strangest feeling of déjà vu. Like they were back at the beginning of the night. Like their interlude in the elevator hadn't happened at all. But it had. She knew it had.

The photographer snapped a picture. And Alessia didn't bother to smile.

CHAPTER EIGHT

MATTEO WASN'T SURE how he managed to get up and speak in front of the large crowd of people. Not when he could see Alessia in the audience, her face smooth, serene, her dark eyes the only window to the storm that lurked beneath.

A storm he was certain would boil over and onto him once they were alone.

He found he didn't mind. That he welcomed the chance to take her on because it was better than the overwhelming, biting need to take her back to the elevator and have her again. To let the elevator continue up to his suite where he would have her again. And again. Tasting her this time, truly savoring her.

Yes, fighting was infinitely better than that. He would rather have her yelling at him than sighing his name in his ear.

Because he didn't know what to do with her, what to do about his desire for her.

It wasn't what he was used to. Wasn't normal in any way.

Sex was simply a need to be met, like eating or breathing. Yes, he liked some food better than he liked others, but he wasn't a slave to cravings. He believed in moderation, in exercising control in all areas of life.

Alessia was the one craving he didn't seem to be able to fight, and that meant he had to learn how.

Anything else was inexcusable.

"Thank you all for coming tonight, and for your generous donations. I am happy to announce that I am personally matching all of the donations given tonight. And that thanks to your generosity, it is now possible for the Corretti Education Foundation to branch out into college grants. It is my belief that a good education can overcome any circumstance, and it is my goal that every person be given that chance. Thank you again, enjoy the rest of the evening."

He stepped down from the podium, not paying attention to the applause that was offered up for his speech. He could hardly hear anything over the roar of blood in his ears. Could hardly see anything but Alessia. Which was one reason he allowed himself to be pulled to the side by some of the guests, interrupted on his way back to where his wife was standing.

He stopped and talked to everyone who approached him, using it as a tactic to keep himself from having to face Alessia without his guard firmly back in place. Cowardly? Perhaps. But he found he didn't care. Not much, at least.

Alessia didn't make a move to approach him; instead, she made conversation with the people around her. And every so often she flicked him a glare with those beautiful eyes of hers, eyes that glittered beneath the lights of the chandeliers. Eyes that made promises of sensual heaven, the kind of heaven he could hardly risk trying to enter again.

Every time he touched Alessia, she tore down another piece of the wall, that very necessary wall of control he'd built around himself.

People started to disperse, and as they both went along the natural line of people that wanted to converse with them, the space between them started to close. Matteo's blood started to flow hotter, faster, just getting nearer to Alessia.

No matter there were still five hundred people in the room. No matter that he'd had her against a wall an hour earlier. Still she challenged him. Still she made him react like a teenage boy with no control over his baser urges.

Yes, think about that. Remember what that looks like.

Blind rage. Two young men, still and unmoving, blood everywhere. And then a calm. A cold sort of emptiness. If he felt anything at all it was a kind of distant satisfaction.

And then he'd looked at Alessia. At the terror in her eyes.

And he'd done what he'd sworn he would never do.

He'd wrapped his arms around her and pulled her into his chest, brushing away her tears. He'd made her cry. Horrified her, and he couldn't blame her for being horrified. It wasn't the kind of thing a girl of fourteen, or any age, should ever have to see.

When he pulled away, when he looked down at her face, her cheeks were streaked with blood. The blood from his hands. Not the only blood he had on his hands.

He breathed in sharply, taking himself back to the present. Away from blood-soaked memories.

Except it was still so easy to see them when he looked at Alessia's face. A face that had been marred with tears and blood. Because of him.

The gap between them continued to shrink, the crowd thinning, until they met in the middle, in the same group. And there was no excuse now for him not to pull her against his side, his arm wrapped around her waist. So he did.

Alessia's body was stiff at his side, but her expression was still relaxed, her smile easy. A lie. Why had he never noticed before that Alessia's smile wasn't always genuine?

He'd assumed that it was. That Alessia displayed and felt emotion with ease and honesty. Now he wondered.

The last of the guests started to file out, leaving Alessia and Matteo standing in the empty ballroom.

He looked around, at the expansive room. This was his hotel, separate from his family dynasty, and often, looking at it, at the architecture, the expanse of it, filled him with a sense of pride. He had hotels all over the world, but this one, back in Sicily, a hotel that belonged to him and not to his family in any part, had always filled him with a particular amount of satisfaction.

Now it just seemed like a big empty room.

He picked up his phone and punched in a number. "Delay cleaning until further notice, I require the ballroom for personal use for a while."

Alessia looked at him, her dark eyes wide. "What do you need the ballroom for?"

He shrugged. "Anything I want." He walked over to the edge of the stage and sat, gripping the edge. "It is my hotel, after all."

"Yes, and you're a man who takes great pride in the ownership of whatever he can possess," she said.

"And why not?" he asked, loosening his tie, trying not to think of Alessia's fingers on the knot, trying not to imagine her fingers at the buttons of his dress shirt as he undid the collar. "That's what it's always been about in my family. I go out of town—" and off the grid "—and my bastard cousin has taken over my office. My younger brother has managed to charm his way into the top seat of the fashion houses for Corretti. So you see? In my family, ownership is everything. And if you have to stab someone to get it, all the better."

"Metaphorical stabbing?" she asked, wrapping her arms around her waist, as if holding herself together. He hated that. Hated that he might cause her pain in any way.

"Or literal stabbing. I told you, my family has a colorful history."

"You said you and your brothers weren't criminals."

"We're not. Not convicted, anyway," he added, not sure why. Maybe because, in his heart, he knew he was one.

Knew he could be convicted for assault several times over if evidence was brought before a court.

"Why are you saying this?"

"What do you mean, why am I saying this? I'm telling you the truth. Was what I did that day near your father's gardens legal? Answer me," he said, his words echoing in the empty room.

"You saved me."

"Maybe."

"They would have raped me," she said.

He remembered it so clearly. And yet so differently.

Because he remembered coming upon Alessia, backed up against a tree, a stone wall behind her, two men in front of her, pressing her back to the tree, touching her, jeering at her. They had her shirt torn. They were pushing her skirt up. And he'd known what they intended to do. The evil they meant for his angel.

And then he remembered seeing red.

He pushed off from the stage, standing and pacing, trying to relieve the restless energy moving through him. Trying to ease the tightness in his chest.

He hadn't simply stopped when he'd gotten those men away from Alessia. Hadn't stopped when they quit fighting back. He hadn't stopped until Alessia had touched his back. And then he'd turned, a rock held tightly in his hand, ready to finish what he'd started. Ready to make sure they never got up again, ready to make sure they could never hurt another woman again. Any other woman, but most especially Alessia.

But then he'd looked into her eyes. Seen the fear. Seen the tears.

And he'd dropped his hand back to his side, letting the rock fall to the ground. Letting the rage drain from his body.

That was when he'd realized what he had done. What he had been about to do. And what it had done to Alessia to see it. More than that, it confirmed what he'd always known. That if he ever let himself go, if he ever allowed himself more than his emotionless existence, he would become a man he hated.

"I did more than save you," he said. "A lot more."

"You did what you had to."

"You say it as if I gave it some thought. I didn't. What I did was a reaction. Blind rage. As I was, if you were not there, I wouldn't have ended it until they were dead."

"You don't know that."

"That's the thing, Alessia, I do know that. I know exactly what my next move was going to be, and trust me, it's not something people get back up from."

"I wish you could see what I saw."

"And I wish like hell you hadn't seen any of it," he said, his voice rough.

"You were... I thought...I thought they were going

to get away with it. That no one would hear me scream. No one would stop them. I thought that they would do it. And then you came and you didn't let them. Do you have any idea what that meant to me? Do you know what you stopped?"

"I know what I stopped."

"Then why do you regret it so much?"

"I don't regret it, not like you mean." He could remember his father's face still, as he'd administered punishment to men in his debt. The calm. The absolute calm. But worse, he could remember his father's face when someone had enraged him. Could remember how volatile, how beyond reason, he became in those situations.

And always, the old man had a smug sense that he had done what must be done. Full and complete justification for every action.

Just as Matteo had felt after Alessia's attack. How he had felt after the fire.

"To me you were just a hero," she said, her words soft.

They hit him hard, like a bullet, twisted inside of him, blooming outward and touching him everywhere, scraping his heart, his lungs. For a moment, he couldn't breathe.

"It's so much more complicated than that," he said.

"Not to me. Not to the girl you rescued. You were

like… You were every unfulfilled dream from my entire life, showing up when I needed you most. How can you not understand that?"

"Maybe that," he said, "is our problem now. You know a dream, a fantasy, and I am not that man. I'm not the hero of the story."

She shook her head. "You were the hero of my story that day. And nothing will change that."

Coldness invaded him. "Is that what led you to my bed that night?"

She didn't look away. "Yes."

He swore, the word loud in the empty expanse of the ballroom. "So that was my thank-you?"

"No!" she said, the exclamation reverberating around them. "It's not like that at all. Don't make it into something like that it's… No."

"Then what, Alessia? Your fantasy of a knight?" Her cheeks turned pink and then she did look away. "*Dio*, is that what it is? You expected me to be your chivalrous knight in shining armor? What a disappointment this must be for you. You would have likely been better off with Alessandro."

"I didn't want Alessandro."

"Only because you lied to yourself about who I am."

"Who are you, then?" she asked. "You're my husband. I think you should tell me."

"I thought we went over this already."

"Yeah, you gave me that internet bio of a rundown on who you are. We told each other things we already knew."

"Why do we have to know each other?"

"Because it seems like we should. We're...married."

"Not really."

"You took me into an elevator and had me against the wall—what would make it more real for you?" she asked, the words exploding from her, crude and true, and nothing he could deny.

"That's sex, Alessia, and what we have is great, explosive sex. But that kind of thing isn't sustainable. It's not meant to be. It's not good for it to be."

"And you know this because you're constantly having spontaneous, explosive sex with strangers?"

"No."

"Then how do you know?"

"There's no control in it. No sense. We nearly let it get filmed, nearly let the elevator go to the next floor. Neither of us think when sex is involved."

"Maybe you think too much."

"And maybe you don't think enough. You feel, and look where all of that feeling has gotten you."

Her lip curled into a sneer. "Don't you dare blame this on me! Don't you dare act like it was me and my

girlish feelings that led us here. That's far too innocent of a take on it, first of all. Yes, I might have built
you up as a hero in my head, but what I wanted that
night in New York had nothing to do with you being
some kind of paragon and everything to do with me
wanting you as a woman wants a man. I didn't want
hearts and flowers, I wanted sex. And that was what
I got. That wasn't led by my feelings," she said, her
words cold, "that was led by my body and I was quite
happy with the results."

"Too bad the price was so steep."

"Wasn't it?"

Alessia looked at Matteo and, for a moment, she
almost hated him. Because he was fighting so hard,
against her, against everything. Or maybe she was
the one fighting. And she was just mad at him for
not being who she'd thought he was.

And that wasn't fair, not really. He couldn't help
it if he didn't line up with the fantasy she'd created
about him in her head. It wasn't even fair to expect
him to come close.

But no one in her life had ever been there for her,
not since her mother. It had all been about her giving. And then he'd been there, and he'd put it all on
the line for her, he'd given her all of himself in that
moment. And yes, what he'd done had been violent,
and terrifying in a way, but it was hard for her to feel

any sadness for the men who would have stolen her last bit of innocence from her.

She'd grown up in a house with a criminal father who lied and stole on a regular basis. She knew about the ugliness of life. She'd lost her mother, spent her days walking on eggshells to try to avoid incurring any of her father's wrath.

But in all that time, at least, no one had forced themselves on her sexually, and considering the kind of company her father kept, it had always seemed kind of an amazing thing.

And then someone had tried to take that from her, too. But Matteo had stopped it.

"Do you understand how much of my life has been decided for me?" she asked.

"Yes," he said slowly, obviously unwilling to admit to not understanding something.

"I don't think you do. I spent my days mothering my siblings, and I don't regret it, because it had to be done, but that meant I didn't go away to school. It meant I stayed at home when a lot of girls my age would have been moving out, going to university. I went to events my father wanted me to go to, hosted parties in dresses he deemed appropriate. That day... that day on the road, those two men tried to take another choice from me. They tried to choose how I would learn about sex, how I would be introduced to it. With violence and pain and force. They tried to take something from me, and I don't just mean virginity, I mean the way I saw myself. The way I saw men. The way I saw people. And you stopped them. So I'm sorry if you don't want to have been my hero, but you were. You let me hold on to some of my innocence. You let me keep some parts of life a fantasy. I know about how harsh life can be. I know about reality, but I don't need to have every horrible thing happen to me. And it was going to." Her voice was rough, raw with tears she needed to shed.

She turned away from him, trying to catch her breath.

"And then my father told me that I was going to marry Alessandro. And I could see more choices being taken from me but this time I didn't see a way out. Then my friend Carolina said she would host a bachelorette party for me. And for once my father didn't deny me. I didn't know you would be there. And Carolina suggested we go to your hotel and I... well, then I hoped you'd be there. And you were. And I saw another chance to make a choice. So don't ask me to regret it."

His eyes were black, endless, unreadable. "I won't ask you to regret it, because then I would have to regret it, and I don't. When I found out I was your first...I can't tell you how that satisfied me, and I don't care if that's not the done thing, if I shouldn't care, because I did. I still care. I'm still glad it was me."

"I am, too," she said, her voice a whisper. The honesty cost them both, she knew.

His eyes met hers, so bleak, so filled with need. And she hoped she could fill it. Hoped she could begin to understand the man that he was and not just the man she'd created a fiction about in her head.

She nearly went to him then. Nearly touched him. Asked him to lie her down on the cold marble of the ballroom floor and make love to her again. But then she remembered. Remembered the question he hadn't answered. The one she'd been determined to get the answer to before she ever let him touch her again.

She'd messed up earlier. She hadn't been able to think clearly enough to have a conversation with him. But now, she would ask now. Again. And she would get her answer.

"Will you be faithful to me?" she asked.

He pushed his fingers through his hair. "Why do you keep asking me this?"

"Because it's a simple question and one I deserve the answer to. I'm not sleeping with you if you won't promise I'm the only woman in your life."

"I can't love you," he said, the words pulled from

him. Not *I don't love you*, like he'd said earlier, but *I can't*.

"I'm not asking you to love me, I'm asking you to not have sex with other women."

His jaw tightened, his hands clenching into fists at his sides. "To answer that question, I would have to know how I planned on conducting our relationship, and I do not know the answer to that yet."

"Were you planning on asking me?"

He shook his head. "I already told you we won't have a normal marriage."

"Why?" She knew she shouldn't ask, not in such a plaintive, needy tone, but she couldn't help herself, couldn't hide the hurt that was tearing through her. How was it she'd managed to get her dream, only to have it turn to ash the moment her fingers touched it?

"Because I cannot be a husband to you. I can't. I won't love you. I won't... I can't give what a husband is supposed to give. I don't know where to begin. I have an empire to run, my hotels, plus I have my bastard cousin installed in my offices at the family corporation, with his ass in my chair, sitting at my desk like he's the one who worked so hard for any of it. I don't have time to deal with you. If you took me on as a husband you would have me in your bed and nowhere else. And I'm not sure I want to put either of us through that."

"But you are my husband. Whether or not you want to be doesn't come into it at this point. You are my husband. You're the father of my baby."

"And our baby has the protection of my name, the validity of having married parents. I'm able to strike the deal for the docklands with your father thanks to this marriage and your siblings will be cared for. I'm sending them all to school, I don't think I told you."

Her throat closed, her body trembling. "I… No, you didn't."

"My point is, regardless of what happens behind closed doors, our marriage was a necessity, but what we choose to do in our own home rests squarely on us. And there are decisions to be made."

Decisions. She'd imagined that if she married Matteo her time for decision making would be over before it ever started. But he was telling her there was still a chance to make choices. That them legally being husband and wife didn't mean it was settled.

In some ways, the opportunity to make decisions was a heady rush of power she'd only experienced on a few occasions. In other ways…well, she wanted him to want to be married to her, if she was honest.

You're still chasing the fantasy when you have reality to contend with.

She had to stop that. She had to put it away now, the haze of fantasy. Had to stop trying to create a happy place where there wasn't one and simply stand up and face reality.

"So…if I say I don't want to be in a normal marriage, and if you can't commit to being faithful to me, does that mean that I have my choice of other lovers, too?"

Red streaked his cheekbones, his fists tightening further, a muscle in his jaw jerking. "Of course," he said, tight. Bitter.

"As long as there are no double standards," she said, keeping her words smooth and calm.

"If I release my hold on you, then I release it. We'll have to be discreet in public, naturally, but what happens behind closed doors is no one's business but our own."

"Ours and the elevator security cameras," she said.

"That will not happen again."

"It won't?"

"An unforgivable loss of control on my part."

"You've had a few of those recently."

She'd meant to spark an angry reply, to keep the fight going, because as long as they were fighting, she didn't ache for him. Wasn't so conscious of the tender emotions he made her feel. And she wasn't so overwhelmed by the need to be skin to skin to him when they were fighting. But she didn't get anger. Instead, she got a bleak kind of pain that echoed in her soul, a hopelessness in his dark eyes that shocked her.

"Yes," he said. "I have. Always with you."

"I don't know how you are in other areas of your life. I only know how you are with me," she said.

His eyes grew darker. "A pity for you. I'm much more pleasant than this, usually."

"I make you misbehave."

He chuckled, no humor in the sound. "You could say that. We should go home."

She nodded. "Yes, we should."

They were in an empty ballroom, and she really would have loved a romantic moment with him here. The chance to dance as the only two people in the room. To go up to his suite and make love. To share a moment with each other that was out of time, apart from reality.

But they'd had their fantasy. Reality was here now, well and truly.

She still didn't want to leave.

Matteo picked up his phone and dialed. "Yes, you can send in the crew now."

She swallowed hard, feeling like they'd missed a key moment. Feeling like she'd missed one.

"Let's go," he said. There was no press now, no one watching to see if he would put his arm around her.

So he didn't. He turned and walked ahead, and she followed behind him, her heart sinking.

Matteo didn't know what he wanted. And she didn't, either.

No, that was a lie, she knew what she wanted. But it would require her to start dealing with Matteo as he was, and at some point, it would require him to meet her in the middle, it would require him to drop his guard.

She wasn't sure if either of them could do what needed to be done. Wasn't sure if they ever had a hope of fixing the tangled mess that they'd created.

She wasn't even sure if Matteo wanted to.

CHAPTER NINE

MATTEO WAS TEMPTED to drink again. He hated the temptation. He hated the feeling of temptation full stop. Before Alessia there had been no temptation.

No, that was a lie. The first temptation had been to break the rules and see what the Battaglias were really like. And so he had looked.

And from there, every temptation, every failing, had been tied to Alessia. She was his own personal road to ruin and there were some days he wondered why he bothered to stay off it.

At least he might go up in flames in her arms. At least then heat and fire might be connected with her, instead of that night his father had died.

Yes, he should just embrace it. He should just follow to road to hell and be done with it.

And bring her with you. Bring the baby with you.
Porca miseria. The baby.

He could scarcely think of the baby. He'd hardly had a moment. He felt a little like he was going crazy sometimes, in all honesty. There was everything that was happening with Corretti Enterprises, and he had to handle it. He should go in and try to wrench the reins back from Angelo, should kick Luca out of his position and expose whatever lie he'd told to get there because he was sure the feckless playboy hadn't gotten there on merit alone.

Instead, Matteo was tied up in knots over his wife. Bewitched by a dark-haired vixen who seemed to have him in a death grip.

She was the reason he'd left, the reason he'd gone up to a remote house he owned in Germany that no one knew about. The reason he hadn't answered calls or returned emails. The reason he hadn't known or cared he was being usurped in his position as head of his branch of the family business.

He had to get a handle on it, and he had no idea how. Not when he felt like he was breaking apart from the inside out.

The business stuff, the Corretti stuff, he could handle that. But he found he didn't care to, and that was the thing that got to him.

He didn't even want to think about the baby. But he had to. Didn't want to try to figure out what to do with Alessia, who was still sleeping in the guest bedroom in the palazzo, for heaven's sake.

Something had to be done. Action had to be taken, and for the first time in his life, he felt frozen.

He set his shot glass down on the counter and tilted it to the side before pushing the bottom back down onto the tile, the sound of glass on ceramic loud and decisive. He stalked out of the bar and into the corridor, taking a breath, trying to clear his head.

Alcohol was not the answer. A loss of control was not the answer.

He had to get a grip. On his thoughts. On his actions. He had a business to try to fix, deals to cement. And all he could think about was Alessia.

He turned and faced the window that looked out on the courtyard. Moonlight was spilling over the grass, a pale shade of gray in the darkness of night.

And then he saw a shadow step into the light. The brightness of the moon illuminated the figure's hair, wild and curling in the breeze. A diaphanous gown, so sheer the light penetrated it, showed the body beneath, swirled around her legs as she turned in a slow circle.

An angel.

And then he was walking, without even thinking, he was heading outside, out to the courtyard, out to the woman who woke something deep in his soul.

Something he hadn't known existed before she'd come into his life.

Something he wished he'd never discovered.

But it was too late now.

He opened the back door and stepped out onto the terrace, walking to the balustrade and grasping the stone with his hands, leaning forward, his attention fixed on the beauty before him.

On Alessia.

She was in his system, beneath his skin. So deep he wondered if he could ever be free of her. It would be harder now, all things considered. She was his wife, the mother of his child.

He could send her to live in the *palazzolo* with his mother. Perhaps his mother would enjoy a grandchild.

He sighed and dismissed that idea almost the moment it hit. A grandchild would only make his mother feel old. And would quite possibly give her worry lines thanks to all the crying.

And you would send your child to live somewhere else?

Yes. He was considering it, in all honesty.

What did he know about children? What did he know about love? Giving it. Receiving it. The kind of nurturing, the father-son bond fostered by his father was one he would just as soon forget.

A bond forged, and ended, by fire.

He threw off the memories and started down the steps that led to the grass. His feet were bare and in that moment he realized he never went outside without his shoes. A strange realization, but he became conscious of the fact when he felt the grass beneath his feet.

Alessia turned sharply, her dark hair cascading over her shoulder in waves. "Matteo."

"What are you doing out here?"

"I needed some air."

"You like being outdoors."

She nodded. "I always have. I hated being cooped up inside my father's house. I liked to take long walks in the sun, away from the...staleness of the estate."

"You used to walk by yourself a lot."

"I still do."

"Even after the attack?" The words escaped without his permission, but he found he couldn't be sorry he'd spoken them.

"Even then."

"How?" he asked, his voice rough. "How did you keep doing that? How did you go on as if nothing had changed?"

"Life is hard, Matteo. People you love die, I know you know about that. People who should love you don't treat you any better than they'd treat a piece of property they were trying to sell for a profit. I've just always tried to see the good parts of life, because what else could I do? I could sit and feel sorry for myself, but it wouldn't change anything. And I've made the choice to stay, so that would be silly. I made the choice to stay and be there for my brothers and sisters, and I can't regret it. That means I have to find happiness in it. And that means I can't cut out my walks just because a couple of horrible men tried to steal them from me."

"And it's that simple?"

"It's not simple at all, but I do it. Because I have to find a way to live my life. My life. It's the only one I have. And I've just learned to try to love it as it is."

"And do you?" he asked. "Do you love it?"

She shook her head. "No." Her voice was a whisper. "But I'm not unhappy all the time. And I think that's something. I mean, it has to count for something."

"What about now? With this?"

"Are you happy?"

"Happiness has never been one of my primary goals. I don't know that I've ever thought about it too closely."

"Everybody wants to be happy," she said.

Matteo put his hands into his pockets and looked over the big stone wall that partitioned his estate from the rest of the world, looked up at the moon. "I want to make something different out of my family. I want to do something more than threaten and terrorize the people in Palermo. Beyond that...does it matter?"

"It does matter. Your happiness matters."

"I haven't been unhappy," he said, and then he wondered if he was lying. "What about you, Alessia?"

"I made a decision, Matteo, and it landed me in a situation that hasn't been entirely comfortable. It was my first big mistake. My first big fallout. And no, not all of it has been happy. But I can't really regret it, either."

"I'm glad you don't regret me."

"Do you regret me?"

"I should. I should regret my loss of control more than I do—" a theme in his life, it seemed "—but I find I cannot."

"What about tonight? In the elevator? Why did you just walk away?"

"I don't know what to do with us," he said, telling the truth, the honest, raw truth.

"Why do we have to know what we're doing?"

"Because this isn't some casual affair, and it never can be." Because of how she made him feel, how she challenged him. But he wouldn't say that. His honesty had limits, and that was a truth he disliked admitting even to himself. "You're my wife. We're going to have a child."

"And if we don't try, then we're going to spend years sniping at each other and growing more and more bitter, is that better?"

"Better than hurting you? I think so."

"You've hurt me already."

"I did?"

"You won't promise to be faithful to me, you clearly hate admitting that you want me, even though as soon as we touch...Matteo, we catch fire, and you can't deny that. You know I don't have a lot of experience with men, but I know this isn't just normal. I know people don't just feel this way."

"And that's exactly why we have to be careful."

"So we'll be careful. But we're husband and wife, and I think we should try...try for the sake of our child, for our families, to make this marriage work. And I think we owe it to each other to not be unhappy."

"Alessia..."

"Let's keep taking walks, Matteo," she said, her voice husky. She took a step toward him, her hair shimmering in the dim light.

He caught her arm and pulled her in close, his heart pounding hard and fast. "I can't love you."

"You keep saying."

"You need to understand. There is a limit to what

we can share. I'll have you in my bed, but that's as far as it goes. This wasn't my choice."

"I wasn't your choice?"

Her words hit him hard, and they hurt. Because no, he hadn't chosen to marry her without being forced into it. But it wasn't for lack of wanting her. If there was no family history. If he had not been the son of one of Sicily's most notorious crime bosses, if there was nothing but him and Alessia and every other woman on earth, he would choose her every time.

But he couldn't discount those things. He couldn't erase what was. He couldn't make his heart anything but cold, not just toward her, but toward anyone. And he couldn't afford to allow a change.

Alessia had no idea. Not of the real reasons why. Not the depth he was truly capable of sinking to. The man underneath the iron control was the very devil, as she had once accused him of being. There was no hero beneath his armor. Only ugliness and death. Only anger, rage, and the ability and willingness to mete out destruction and pain to those who got in his way.

If he had to choose between a life without feeling or embracing the darkness, he would take the blessed numbness every time.

"You know it wasn't."

She thrust her chin into the air. "And that's how

you want to start? By reminding me you didn't choose me?"

"It isn't to hurt you, or even to say that I don't want you. But I would never have tied you to me if it wasn't a necessity, and that is not a commentary on you, but on me, and what I'm able to give. There are reasons I never intended to take a wife. I know who I am, but you don't."

"Show me," she said. And he could tell she meant it, with utter conviction. But she didn't know what she was asking. She had no way of knowing. He had given her a window into his soul, a glimpse of the monster that lurked beneath his skin, but she didn't know the half of it.

Didn't know what he was truly capable of. What his father had trained him for.

And what it had all led to seven years ago during the fire that had taken Benito's and Carlo's lives.

That was when he discovered that he truly was the man his father had set out to make him. That was when he'd discovered just how deep the chill went.

He was cold all the way down. And it was only control that held it all in check.

There was only one place he had heat. Only one way he could get warm. But it was a fine line, because he needed the cold. Needed his control, even with it...even with it he was capable of things most men would never entertain thoughts of. But without it he knew the monster would truly be unleashed. That it would consume him.

"I know what I'd like to show you," he said, taking a step toward her, putting his hand on her cheek. She warmed his palm. The heat, the life, that came from her, pouring into him. She shivered beneath his hand, as though his touch had frozen her, and he found it oddly appropriate.

If he kissed her, if he moved nearer to her now, he was making the choice to drag her into the darkness with him. To take what he wanted and use her to his own selfish ends.

He could walk away from her now and he could do the right thing. Protect her, protect their child. Give them both his name and a home, his money. Everything they would need.

She didn't need him in his bed, taking his pleasure in her body, using her to feel warm.

To court the fire and passion that could burn down every last shred of his control. It would be a tightrope walk. Trying to keep the lusts of his body from turning into a desire that overwhelmed his heart.

If he wanted Alessia, there was no other choice.

It was easy with her, to focus on his body. What he wanted from her. Because she called to him, reached him, made him burn in a way no other woman ever had.

With her, though, there was always something else. Something more.

He shut it down. Severed the link. Focused on his body. The burn in his chest, his gut. Everywhere. He was so hard it hurt. Hard with the need for her. To be in her. To taste her.

He could embrace that, and that only. And consign her to a life with a man who would never give her what she deserved.

In this case, he would embrace the coldness in him. Only an utter bastard would do this to her. So it was a good thing that was what he was.

He bent his head and pressed his lips to hers. It wasn't a deep kiss, it was a test. A test for him. To see if he could touch her without losing his mind.

She was soft. So soft. So alive. A taste of pure beauty in a world so filled with ugliness and filth. She reached into him and shone a light on him. On the darkest places in him.

No. He could not allow that. This was only about sex. Only about lust.

"Only me," she said when they parted.

"What?"

"You either have only me, or every other woman you might want, but before you kiss me again, Matteo, you have to make that decision."

His lips still tasted of her skin. "You." It was an easy answer, he found.

She put her hands on his face and drew up on her tiptoes. Her kiss was deep. Filled with the need and passion that echoed inside of his body. He wrapped his arm around her waist and relished every lush detail of holding her. Her soft curves, those generous breasts pressed against his chest. He slipped his hand over her bottom, squeezed her tightly. She was everything a woman should be. Total perfection.

She kissed his jaw, her lips light on his skin, hot and so very tempting. She made him want more, stripped him of his patience. He had always been a patient lover, the kind of lover who worked to ensure his partner's pleasure before taking his own. Because he could. Because even if he took pleasure with his body, his actions were dictated by his mind.

But she challenged that. Made him want so badly to lose himself. To think of nothing but her. Alessia. He was hungry for her in a way he had never hungered for anyone or anything.

He slid his hands over the bodice of her nightgown, cupped her breasts through the thin fabric and found she had nothing on underneath. He could feel her nipples, hard and scarcely veiled by the gauzy material.

He lowered his head and circled one of the tightened buds with his tongue, drew it deep into his mouth. It wasn't enough. He needed to taste her.

Her name pounded through his head in time with the beat of his heart. His need a living, breathing thing.

He gripped the straps of her gown and tugged hard, the top giving way. It fell around her waist, exposing her to him. He smoothed his hand over her bare skin, then lowered his head again, tasting her, filling himself with her.

He dropped to his knees and took the fabric in his hands, tugging it down the rest of the way, ignoring the sound of tearing fabric.

"I liked that nightgown," she said.

"It was beautiful." He kissed her stomach. "But it was not as beautiful as you are."

"You could have asked me to take it off."

"No time," he said, tracing a line from her belly button down to the edge of her panties. "I needed to taste you."

Her response was a strangled "Oh."

"Everywhere." He tugged at the sides of her underwear and drew them down her legs, tossing them to the side. He kissed her hip bone and she shuddered. "I think you should lay down for me, *cara*."

"Why is that?"

"All the better to taste you, *cara mia*."

"Can't you do it from where you are?"

"Not the way I want to."

She complied, her movements slow, shaky. It was a sharp reminder of how innocent she still was.

You let me hold on to some of my innocence.

Her words echoed in his mind as she sank to the ground in front of him, lying back, resting on her elbows, her legs bent at the knees.

No, he would not allow himself to be painted as some kind of hero. He might have saved her innocence then, but he had spent the past months ensuring that what remained was stripped from her. And tonight, he would continue it.

Keeping her bound to him would continue it.

It was too late to turn back now. Too late to stop. He put his hand on her thigh and parted her legs gently, sliding his fingers over the slickness at the entrance of her body. "Yes," he said, unable to hold the word back, a tremor of need racking his body.

He lowered his head to take in her sweetness, to try to satiate the need he felt for her. A need that seemed to flow through his veins along with his blood, until he couldn't tell which one was sustaining him. Until he was sure he needed both to continue breathing.

He was lost in Alessia. Her flavor, her scent.

He pushed one finger deep inside her while he continued to lavish attention on her with his lips and tongue. She arched up against him, a raw cry escaping her lips. And he took it as her approval, making his strokes with mouth and hands firmer, more insistent.

She drove her fingers deep into his hair, tugging hard, the pain giving him the slight distraction he needed to continue. Helping him hold back his own need.

He slipped a second finger inside of her and her muscles pulsed around him, her body getting stiff beneath him, her sound of completion loud, desperate. Satisfying to him on a level so deep he didn't want to examine it too closely.

He didn't have time to examine it because now he needed her. Needed his own release, a ferocity that had him shaking. He rose up, pausing to kiss her breasts again, before taking possession of her mouth.

He sat up and tugged his shirt over his head, shrugging his slacks down as quickly as possible, freeing his aching erection.

"Are you ready?" he asked. He needed the answer to be yes.

"Yes."

He looked at her face, at Alessia, and as he did, he pushed inside the tight heat of her body. He nearly lost it then, a cold sweat breaking out over his skin, his muscles tense, pain coursing through him, everything in him trying to hold back. To make this last.

"Matteo."

It was her voice that broke him. Her name on his lips. He started to thrust hard into her, and no matter how he told himself to take it slow, take it gentle, he couldn't. He was a slave to her, to his need.

Finesse was lost. Control was lost.

She arched against him every time he slid home, a small sigh of pleasure on her lips. He lowered his head, buried his face in her neck, breathing her in. Lilacs and skin. And the one woman he would always know. The one woman who mattered.

Sharp nails dug into the flesh on his shoulder, but this time, the pain didn't bring him back. He lost himself, let his orgasm take him over, a rush of completion that took him under completely. He was lost in a wave, and burning. Burning hot and bright, nothing coming to put him out. To give him any relief. All he could do was hang on and weather it. Try to survive a pleasure so intense it bordered on destructive.

And when it was over, she was there, soft arms wrapped around him, her scent surrounding him.

"Will it always be like this?" Alessia's voice was broken with sharp, hard breaths.

He didn't have an answer for her. He couldn't speak. Couldn't think. And he hoped to God it wouldn't always be like this because there was no way his control could withstand it. And at the same time he knew he couldn't live with her and deny himself her body.

He would keep it under control. He would keep his heart separate from his body. He'd done it with women all his life. He'd done it when his father had asked him to learn the family business. The night his father had forced him to dole out punishment to a man in debt to the Corretti family.

He had locked his heart in ice and kept himself from feeling. His actions unconnected to anything but his mind.

He could do it again. He would.

"We should go inside," he said, sitting up, his breathing still ragged.

"Yeah. I'm pretty sure I have grass stains in… places."

He turned to her, a shocked laugh bursting from him. A real laugh. He couldn't remember the last time he'd laughed and meant it. "Well, you should be glad I made quick work of your gown, then."

"You tore it," she said, moving into a standing position and picking up her shredded garment.

"You liked it."

He could see her smile, even in the dim light. "A little."

There was a strange lightness in his chest now, a

feeling that was completely foreign to him. As though a rock had been taken off his shoulders.

"I'm hungry," she said.

She started walking back toward the house, and he kept his eyes trained on her bare backside, on the twin dimples low on her back. She was so sexy he was hard again already.

He bent and picked his underwear up from the ground, tugging the black boxer briefs on quickly and following her inside. "Do you want to eat?" he asked.

"Yes, I do." She wandered through the maze of rooms, still naked, and he followed.

"And what would you like?"

"Pasta. Have you got an apron?"

"Have I got an apron?"

"You have a cook, yes?"

"Yes."

"Does he have an apron?"

"She." He opened the pantry door and pulled a short red apron off a hook.

Alessia smiled and slipped the apron over her head, tying it tight. She was a lot taller than the little round woman he'd hired to cook his meals. The apron came down just to the tops of her thighs and it tied in the back, exposing her body to him from that angle.

"Dinner and a show," he said.

She tossed him a playful glare, then started riffling through the cabinets. "What kind of pasta have you got?"

"Fresh in the fridge," he said.

She opened up the stainless-steel fridge and bent down, searching for a few moments before popping up with a container that held pappardelle pasta and another that had marinara sauce.

She put a pan of water on the stove, then put the sauce in another pan to reheat, and leaned back against the counter, her arms crossed beneath her breasts.

"Didn't you ever hear that a watched pot never boils?"

"No. Who says that?"

"People do," he said.

"Did your mom say it to you?"

"No. A cook we had, I think."

"Oh. It's the kind of thing my mother probably would have said to me someday. If she had lived."

"You miss her still."

"I always will. But you lost your father."

Guilt, ugly, strangling guilt, tightened in his chest. "Yes."

"So you understand."

He shook his head slowly. "I'm not sure I do."

"You don't miss him?"

"Never."

"I know your father was hard to deal with. I know he was…I know he was shady like my father but surely you must—"

"No," he said.

"Oh."

"Will you miss your father?"

"I think so. He's not a wonderful man, but he's the only father I have."

"I would have been better off without one than the one that I had."

Alessia moved to put the pasta into the pan. "You say that with a lot of certainty."

"Trust me on this, Alessia."

They stood in silence until the pasta was done. Matteo got bowls out of the cupboard and set them on the counter and Alessia dished them both a bowl of noodles and sauce.

"Nothing like a little post…you know, snack," she said, lifting her bowl to her lips, her eyes glued to his chest. "You're barely dressed."

"You should talk," he said.

She looked down. "I'm dressed."

"Turn around." She complied, flashing her bare butt to him. "That's not dressed, my darling wife."

"Are you issuing a formal complaint?"

"Not in the least. I prefer you this way."

"Well, the apron is practical. Don't go tearing it off

me if you get all impatient." She took a bit of pasta and smiled, her grin slightly impish. It made it hard to breathe.

There was something so normal about this. But it wasn't a kind of normal he knew. Not the kind he'd ever known. He wasn't the sort of man who walked barefoot in the grass and then ate pasta at midnight in his underwear.

He'd never had a chance to be that man. He wondered again at what it would be like if all the things of the world could simply fall away.

"Matteo?"

"Yes?"

"I lost you for a second. Where were you?"

"Just thinking."

"Mmm." She nodded. "I'm tempted to ask you what about but I sort of doubt you'd want to tell me."

"About my father," he said, before he could stop himself.

"You really don't miss him?"

"No." A wall of flame filled his mind. An image of the warehouse, burning. "Never."

"My father has mainly ignored my existence. The only time he's ever really acknowledged me is if he needs something, or if he's angry."

Rage churned in Matteo's stomach. "Did he hit you?"

"Yes. Not beatings or anything, but if I said something that displeased him, he would slap my face."

"He should feel very fortunate he never did so in front of me."

Alessia was surprised at the sudden change in Matteo's demeanor. At the ice in his tone. For a moment, they'd actually been getting along. For a moment, they'd been connecting with clothes on, and that was a rarity for the two of them.

He was willing to try. He'd told her that. And he would be faithful. Those were the only two promises she required from him. Beyond that, she was willing to take her chances.

Willing to try to know the man she'd married. Past her fantasy of him as a hero, as her white knight, and as the man he truly was. No matter what that might mean.

"I handled it," she said.

"It was wrong of him."

She nodded. "I know. But I was able to keep him from ever hitting one of the other kids and that just reinforced why I was there. Yes, I bore the brunt of a lot of it. I had to plan parties and play hostess, I had to take the wrath. But I've been given praise, too."

"I was given praise by my father sometimes, too," Matteo said. There was a flatness to his tone, a darkness in his words that made her feel cold. "He spent some time, when I was a bit older, teaching me how to do business like a Corretti. Not the business we presented to the world. The clean, smooth front. Hotels, fashion houses. All of that was a cover then. A successful cover in its own right, but it wasn't the main source of industry for our family."

"I think…I mean, I think everyone knows that."

"Yes, I'm sure they do. But do you have any idea how far-reaching it was? How much power my father possessed? How he chose to exercise it?"

She shook her head, a sick weight settling in her stomach. "What did he do, Matteo? What did he do to you?"

"To me? Nothing. In the sense that he never physically harmed me."

"There are other kinds of harm."

"Remember I told you I wasn't a criminal? That's on a technicality. It's only because I was never convicted of my crimes."

"What did he do to you, Matteo?" Her stomach felt sick now, and she pushed her bowl of food across the counter, making her way to where Matteo was standing.

"When I was fifteen he started showing me the ropes. The way things worked. He took me on collection calls. We went to visit people who owed him money. Now, my father was only ever involved on the calls where people owed him a lot of money. People who were in serious trouble with him. Otherwise, his men, his hired thugs, paid the visits."

"And he took you on these...visits?"

Matteo nodded, his arms crossed over his bare chest. There was a blankness in his eyes that hurt, a total detachment that froze her inside.

"For the first few weeks I just got to watch. One quick hit to the legs. A warning. A bone-breaking warning, but much better than the kind of thing he and his thugs were willing to do."

"*Dio.* You should never have... He should never have let you see..." She stopped talking then, because she knew there was more. And that it was worse. She could feel the anxiety coming off him in waves.

She took a step toward him, put her hand on his forearm. It was damp with sweat, his muscles shaking beneath her touch.

"One night he asked me to do it," he said.

His words were heavy in the room, heavy on her. They settled over her skin, coating her, making her feel what he felt. Dirty. Ashamed. She didn't know how she was so certain that was what he felt, but she was.

"What happened?" She tried to keep her voice steady, tried to sound ready to hear it. Tried to be ready to hear it. Because he needed to say it without fear of recrimination from her. Without fear of being told there was something wrong with him.

She knew that as deeply, as innately, as she knew his other feelings.

"I did it," he said. "My father asked me to break a man's legs because he owed the family money. And I did."

CHAPTER TEN

MATTEO WAITED FOR the horror of his admission to sink in. Waited for Alessia to turn from him, to run away in utter terror and disgust. She should. He wouldn't blame her.

He also desperately wanted her to stay.

"Matteo…"

"These hands," he said, holding them out, palms up, "that have touched you, have been used in ways that a man should never use his hands."

"But you aren't like that."

He shook his head. "Clearly I am."

"But you didn't enjoy it."

"No. I didn't enjoy it." He could remember very vividly how it had felt, how the sweat had broken out on his skin. How he had vomited after. His father's men had found that terribly amusing. "But I did it."

"What would your father have done to you if you hadn't?"

He shook his head. "It doesn't matter."

"Yes, it does, Matteo, you were a boy."

"I was a boy, but I was old enough to know that what my father did, what he was, was wrong."

"And you were trapped in it."

"Maybe. And maybe that would be an acceptable excuse for some people, but it's not for me."

"Why not? You were a boy and he abused you. Tell me, and be honest, what did he say he would do to you if you didn't do it?"

Matteo was afraid for one moment that his stomach might rebel against him. "He told me if I couldn't do it to a grown man, there were some children in the village I might practice on."

Alessia's face contorted with utter horror. "Would he have done that?"

"I don't know. But I wasn't going to find out, either."

"He made you do it."

"He manipulated me into doing it, but I did it."

"How?" she asked, her voice a whisper.

"It's easy to do things, anything, when you can shut the emotion down inside yourself. I learned to do that. I learned that there was a place inside of myself as cold as any part of my father's soul. If I went there, it wasn't so hard to do." It was only after that he had broken. In the end, it was both the brokenness, and the cold, that had saved him.

His father had decided he wasn't ready. Didn't want his oldest son, the one poised to take over his empire, undermining his position by showing such weakness.

And after, the way he'd dealt with the knowledge that he'd lived with a monster, the way he'd dealt with knowing that he was capable of the very same atrocities, was to freeze out every emotion. He would not allow himself to want, to crave power or money in the way his father did. Passion, need, greed, were the enemy.

Then he'd seen Alessia. And he had allowed her a place inside him, a place that was warm and bright, one that he could retreat to. He saw happiness through her eyes when he watched her. His attraction to her not physical, but emotional. He let a part of himself live through her.

And that day when he'd seen those men attacking her, the monster inside him had met up against passion that had still existed in the depths of him, and had combined to create a violence that was beyond his control. One that frightened him much more than that moment of controlled violence in his father's presence had.

More even than that final act, the one that had re-moved his father from his life forever.

Because it had been a choice he'd made. It had been fueled by his emotion, by his rage, and no matter how deserving those men had been...it was what it said about himself that made him even more certain that it must never happen again. That he must never be allowed to feel like that.

"Do you see?" he asked. "Do you see what kind of man I am?"

She nodded slowly. "Yes. You're a good man, with a tragic past. And the things that happened weren't your fault."

"When I went back home the day of your attack, there was still blood all over me. I walked in, and my father was there. He looked at me, saw the evidence of what had happened. Then he smiled, and he laughed," Matteo spat. "And he said to me, 'Looks like you're ready now. I always knew you were my son.'"

That moment was burned into his brain, etched into his chest. Standing there, shell-shocked by what had happened, by what he had done. By what had nearly happened to Alessia. And having his father act as though he'd made some sort of grand passage into manhood. Having him be proud.

"He was wrong, Matteo, you aren't like him. You

were protecting me, you weren't trying to extort money out of those men. It's not the same thing."

"But it's the evidence of what I'm capable of. My father had absolute conviction in what he did. He could justify it. He believed he was right, Alessia, do you understand that? He believed with conviction that he had a right to this money, that he had the right to harm those who didn't pay what he felt he was owed. All it takes is a twist of a man's convictions."

"But yours wouldn't be…"

"They wouldn't be?" He almost told her then, but he couldn't. The words he could never say out loud. The memory he barely allowed himself to have. "You honestly believe that? Everyone is corruptible, *cara*. The only way around it is to use your head, to learn what is right, and to never ever let your desire change wrong to right in your mind. Because that's what desire does. My father's desire for money, your father's desire for power, made them men who will do whatever it takes to have those things. Regardless of who they hurt. And I will never be that man."

"You aren't that man. You acted to save me, and you did it without thought to your own safety. Can't you see how good that is? How important?"

"I don't regret what I did," he said, choosing his words carefully. "I had a good reason to do it. But how many more good reasons could I find? If it suited me, if I was so immersed in my own needs, in my own desires, what else might I consider a good reason? So easily, Alessia, I could be like Benito was."

"No, that isn't true."

"Why do you think that?"

"Because you're…good."

He laughed. "You are so certain?"

"Yes. Yes, Matteo, I'm certain you're good. Do you know what I remember from that day? The way you held me after. Do you know how long it had been since someone had tried to comfort me? Since someone had wiped away my tears? Not since my mother. Before that, I had done all of the comforting, and then when I needed someone? You were there. And you told me it would be okay. More than that, you made it okay. So don't tell me you aren't good. You are."

He didn't believe her, because she didn't know the whole truth. But he wanted to hold her words tightly inside of him, wanted to cling to her vision of him, didn't want her to see him any other way.

"I got blood on your face," he said, his voice rough. "That day when I wiped your tears."

She looked at him with those dark, beautiful eyes. "It was worth it." She took a step toward him, taking his hand in hers. "Come on. Let's go to bed."

And he was powerless to do anything but follow her.

* * *

Alessia woke the next morning with a bone-deep feeling of contentment. She noticed because she'd never felt anything like it before. Had never felt like things were simply right in the world. That there wasn't anything big left to accomplish. That she just wanted to stay and live in the moment. A moment made sweeter by the fact that there was nothing pressing or horrible looming in the future.

Then she became conscious of a solid, warm weight at her back, a hand resting on her bare hip. And she was naked, which was unusual because she normally slept in a nightgown.

A nightgown that was torn.

A smile stretched across her face and she rolled over to face Matteo. Her lover. Her husband. He was still sleeping, the lines on his forehead smoothed, his expression much more relaxed than it ever was when he was awake.

She leaned over and kissed his cheek, the edge of his mouth. She wanted him again. It didn't matter how many times he'd turned to her in the middle of the night, she wanted him again. It didn't matter if they had sex, or if he just touched her, but she wanted him. His presence, his kiss, him breathing near her.

This moment was one she'd dreamed of for half

of her life. This moment with Matteo Corretti. Not with any other man.

She'd woken up next to him once before, but she hadn't been able to savor it. Her wedding had been looming in the not-too-distant future and guilt and fear had had her running out the door before Matteo had woken up.

But not this morning. This morning, she would stay with him until he woke. And maybe she would share his bed again tonight. And every night after that. He was her husband, after all, and it only seemed right that they sleep together.

They were going to try to make a real marriage out of a legal one.

He'll never love you.

She ignored the chill that spread through her veins when that thought invaded her mind. It didn't matter. She wouldn't dwell on it. Right now, she had a hope at a future she could be happy with. Matteo in her bed. In her life.

And she was having his baby. At some point, that would sink in and not just be a vague, sort of frightening, sort of wonderful thought.

But right now, she was simply lingering in the moment. Not wondering if Matteo's feelings would ever change, not worrying about changing diapers.

He shifted then, his eyes fluttering open. "Good

morning," he said. So much different than his greeting the morning after their wedding.

"Good morning, handsome."

"Handsome?"

"You are. And I've always wanted to say that." *To you*.

"Alessia…you are something."

"I know, right?" Matteo rolled over onto his back and she followed him, resting her breasts on his chest, her chin propped up on her hands. "Last night was wonderful."

He looked slightly uncomfortable. Well, she imagined she wasn't playing the part of blasé sophisticate very well, but in her defense…she wasn't one. She was a women with very little sexual experience having the time of her life with a man who'd spent years as the star attraction in her fantasies. It was sort of hard to be cool in those circumstances.

He kissed her, cupping her chin with his thumb and forefinger. She closed her eyes and hummed low in her throat. "You're so good at that," she said when they parted. "I feel like I have a post-orgasm buzz. Is that a thing?"

He rolled onto his side again and moved into a sitting position, not bothering to cover himself with the blankets.

"I don't know," he said. "I can't say I've ever experienced it."

"Oh." That hurt more than it should have. Not because she wanted him to have experienced post-orgasm buzz with anyone else, but because she wished he'd experienced it with her.

"What is it, *cara*?"

"Nothing." She put her palm flat on his chest and leaned in, her lips a whisper from his. Then his phone started vibrating on the nightstand.

"I have to take that," he said, moving away from her. He turned away from her and picked it up. "Corretti." Every muscle in his back went rigid. "What the hell do you want, Alessandro?"

Alessia's stomach rolled. Alessandro. She would rather not think about him right at the moment. She felt bad for the way things had ended. He'd been nice enough to her, distant, and there had been no attraction, but he'd been decent. And she'd sort of waited until the last minute to change her mind.

She got out of bed and started hunting for some clothes. There was nothing. Only a discarded red apron that she knew from last night didn't cover a whole lot.

"I'm busy, you can't just call a meeting and expect me to drop everything and come to you like a lap-dog. Maybe you're used to your family treating you that way, but you don't get that deference from me."

Alessia picked the apron up and put it on. It was better than nothing.

Matteo stood from the bed, completely naked, pacing the room. She stood for a moment and just watched. The play of his muscles beneath sleek, olive skin was about the sexiest thing she'd ever seen.

"Angelo?" The name came out like a curse. "What are you doing meeting with that bastard?" A pause. "It was a commentary on his character, not his birth. Fine. Noon. Salvatore's."

He pushed the end-call button and tossed the phone down on the bed, continuing to prowl the room. "That was Alessandro."

"I got that."

"He wants me to come to a meeting at our grandfather's. With Angelo, of all people."

"He is your cousin. He's family, and so is Alessandro."

"I have enough family that I don't like. Why would I add any more?"

"You don't even like your brothers?"

"No."

"Why don't you like your brothers?"

"Because if I ever do seem to be in danger of being

sucked into the Corretti mind-set it's when we start playing stupid business games."

"But they're your family."

"My family is a joke. We're nothing but criminals and selfish assholes who would sell each other out for the right price. And we've all done it."

"So maybe someone needs to stop," she said, her voice soft.

"I don't know if we can."

"Maybe you should be the first one?"

"Alessia..."

"Look, I know I'm not a business mind, and I know I don't understand the dynamics of your family, but if you hate this part of it so much, then end it."

"I need to get dressed."

"I'll go make breakfast," she said. "I'm dressed for it."

"You might give my staff a shock."

"Oh—" her cheeks heated "—right, on second thought I might go back to my room."

"That's fine. And after that, you can ask Giancarlo if he would have your things moved into the master suite."

"You want me to move in?"

"Yes. You tramping back to your room in an apron is going to get inconvenient quickly, don't you think?"

Alessia felt her little glow of hope grow. "Yeah.

Definitely it would be a little bit inconvenient. I would love to move into your room."

"Good." He leaned in and dropped a kiss on her lips. "Now, I have to get ready."

When Salvatore had been alive, Matteo had avoided going to his grandparents' home as often as he could. The old man was a manipulator and Matteo was rarely in the mood for his kind of mind games.

Still, whenever his grandmother had needed him, he had been there. They all had. This had long been neutral ground for that very reason. For Teresa. Which made it a fitting setting for what they were doing today.

Matteo walked over the threshold and was ushered back toward the study. He didn't see his grandmother, or any of the staff. Only a hostile-looking Alessandro, and Angelo sitting in a chair, a drink in hand.

"What was so important that you needed to speak to me?"

"Sorry to interrupt the blissful honeymoon stage with your new bride. I assume she actually went through with your wedding," Alessandro said.

"She did," he said.

Angelo leaned back in one of the high-backed chairs, scanning the room. "So this is what old Corretti money buys. I think I prefer my homes."

"We all prefer not to be here," Matteo said. "Which begs the question again, why are we?"

"You married Alessia, I can only assume that means you've cut a deal with her father?"

"Trade in and out of Sicily is secured for the Correttis and the docklands are ours. The revitalization project is set to move forward."

"Handy," Angelo said, leaning forward, "because I secured a deal with Battaglia, as well." Angelo explained the details of the housing development he was working on, eased by Battaglia's connections.

"And what does that have to do with us?"

"Well," Angelo continued, "it can have a lot to do with you. Assuming you want to take steps to unify the company."

"We need to unify," Alessandro said, his tone uncompromising. "Otherwise, we'll just spend the next forty years tearing everything apart. Like our fathers did."

Matteo laughed, a black, humorless sound. "You are my cousin, Alessandro, but I have no desire to die in a warehouse fire with you."

"That's why this has to end," Alessandro said. "I have a proposal to make. One that will see everyone in the family with an equal share of power. It will put us in the position to make the company, the family, strong again. Without stooping to criminal activity to accomplish it."

Alessandro outlined his plan. It would involve everyone, including their sisters, giving everyone equal share in the company and unifying both sides for the first time.

"This will work as long as this jackass is willing to put some of the extra shares he's acquired back into the pot," Alessandro said, indicating Angelo.

"I said I would," Angelo responded, his acquiescence surprising. Equally surprising was the lack of venom and anger coming from the other man. Or maybe not. Matteo had to wonder if Angelo had met a woman. He knew just the kind of change a woman could effect on a man.

"There you are," Alessandro said. "Are you with us?"

Matteo thought of the fire. Of the last time he'd seen his father. Of all that greed had cost. This was his chance to put an end to that. To start fresh. The past could never be erased, it would always be there. But the future could be new. For him. For Alessia. For their child.

He had too many other things in his life, good things, to waste any effort holding on to hatred he didn't even have the energy to feel.

He extended his hand and Alessandro took it, shaking it firmly. Then Matteo extended his hand to Angelo and, for the first time, shook his hand. "I guess that means you're one of us now," he said to Angelo. "I don't know if you should be happy about that or not."

"I'll let you know," Angelo said. "But so far, it doesn't seem so bad."

"All right, where do I sign?"

CHAPTER ELEVEN

MATTEO WAS EXHAUSTED by the time he got around to driving back to his palazzo. Dealing with Alessandro, going to his grandfather's house, had been draining in a way he had not anticipated. And yet, in some ways, there was a weight lifted. The promise of a future that held peace instead of violence. The first time his future had ever looked that way.

And he had Alessia to go home to. That thought sent a kick of adrenaline through him, made him feel like there was warmth in his chest. Made him feel like he wasn't so cold.

He left the car parked in front of his house with the keys in the ignition. One of his staff would park it for him later. And if not, he didn't mind it being there in the morning. But he couldn't put off seeing Alessia, not for another moment. He needed to see her for some reason, needed affirmation of who he was. To see her face light up. To have someone look at him like they didn't know who and what he was.

Alessandro and Angelo didn't know about his past, but they knew enough about the family to have an idea. Alessandro certainly hadn't escaped a childhood with Carlo without gaining a few scars of his own.

But Alessia looked at him like none of that mattered. Like she didn't know or believe any of it.

That isn't fair. She should know.

No, he didn't want her to know. He wanted to keep being her knight. To have one person look and see the man he might have been if it weren't for Benito Corretti.

He would change what it meant to be a Corretti for his child. He would never let them see the darkness. Never.

A fierce protectiveness surged through him, for the first time a true understanding of what it meant for Alessia to be pregnant.

A child. His child.

He prowled through the halls of the palazzo and found Alessia in a sitting room, a book in her hands, her knees drawn up to her chest. She was wearing a simple sundress that had slid high up her thighs. He wanted nothing more than to push it up the rest of the way, but he also found he didn't want to disturb her. He simply wanted to look.

She raised her focus then, and her entire countenance changed, her face catching the sunlight filtering through the window. Her dark eyes glittered, her smile bright. Had anyone else ever looked at him like that?

He didn't think they had.

"How did the meeting go?"

"We called each other names. Insulted each other's honor and then shook hands. So about as expected."

She laughed. "Good, I guess."

"Yes. We've come up with a way to divide Corretti Enterprises up evenly. A way for everyone to get their share. It's in everyone's best interests, really. Especially the generation that comes after us. Which I now have a vested interest in."

She smiled, the dimple on her left cheek deepening. "I suppose you do. And…I'm glad you do."

He moved to sit on the couch, at her feet, then he leaned in. "Can you feel the baby move yet?"

She shook her head. "No. The doctor said it will feel like a flutter, though."

"May I?" he asked, stretching his hand out, just over the small, rounded swell of her stomach.

"Of course."

He swallowed hard and placed his palm flat on her belly. It was the smallest little bump, but it was different than it had been. Evidence of the life that was growing inside her. A life they'd created.

She was going to be the mother of his child. She deserved to know. To really understand him. Not to simply look at him and see an illusion. He'd given her a taste of it earlier, but his need for that look, that one she reserved just for him, that look he only got from her, had prevented him from being honest. Had made him hold back the most essential piece of just why he was not the man to be her husband.

The depth to which he was capable of stooping.

Because no matter how bright the future had become, the past was still filled with shadows. And until they were brought into the sunlight, their power would remain.

"There is something else," he said, taking his hand from her stomach, curling it into a fist. His skin burned.

"About the meeting?"

"No," he said. "Not about the meeting."

"What about?"

"About me. About why…about why it might not be the best idea for you to try to make a marriage with me. About the limit of what I can give."

"Matteo, I already told you how I feel about what happened with your father."

"By that you mean when he took me on errands?"

"Well…yes."

"So, you don't mean what happened the night of the warehouse fire that killed him and Carlo."

"No. No one knows what happened that night."

"That isn't true," he said, the words scraping his throat raw. "Someone knows."

"Who?" she asked, but he could tell she already knew.

"I know."

"How?"

"Because, *cara mia*. I was there."

"You were there?"

He nodded slowly. Visions of fire filled his mind. Fire and brimstone, such an appropriate vision. "Yes. I was there to try to convince my father to turn over the holdings of Corretti to me entirely. I wanted to change things. To end the extortion and scams. All of it. But he wouldn't hear it. You see, at the time, he was still running criminal schemes, using the hotels, which I was managing, to help launder money. To help get counterfeit bills into circulation, into the right hands. Or wrong hands as the case may have been. I didn't want any part of it, but as long as my father was involved in the running of the corporation, that was never going to end. I wanted out."

"Oh," Alessia said, the word a whisper, as if she knew what was coming next. He didn't want her to guess at it, because he wanted, perversely, for her to believe it impossible. For her to cling to the white-knight image and turn away from the truth he was about to show her.

"I don't know how the fire started. But the warehouse was filled with counterfeiting plates, and their printing presses. That's one way to make money, right? Print your own."

He looked down at his hands, his heart pounding hard, his stomach so tight he could hardly breathe. "The fire spread quickly. I don't know where Carlo was when it broke out. But I was outside arguing with my father. And he turned and...and he looked at the blaze and he started to walk toward it."

Matteo closed his eyes, the impression of flames burning bright behind his eyelids. "I told him if he went back into that damned warehouse to rescue those plates, I would leave him to it. I told him to let it burn. To let us start over. I told him that if he went back, I would be happy to let him burn with it all, and then let him continue to burn in hell."

"Matteo...no." She shook her head, those dark eyes glistening with tears. She looked horrified. Utterly. Completely. The light was gone. His light.

"Yes," he said, his voice rough. "Can you guess what he did?"

"What?" The word was scarcely a whisper.

"He laughed. And he said, 'Just as I thought, you are my son.' He told me that no matter how I dressed it up, no matter how I pretended I had morals, I was just as bloodthirsty as he was. Just as hungry for vengeance and to have what I thought should be mine, in the fashion I saw fit. And then he walked back into the warehouse."

"What did you do?"

Matteo remembered the moment vividly. Remembered waiting for a minute, watching, letting his father's words sink in. Recognizing the truth of them. And embracing them fully. He was his father's son. And if he, or anyone else, stood a chance of ever breaking free, it had to end.

The front end of the warehouse had collapsed and Matteo had stood back, looking on, his hand curled around his phone. He could have called emergency services. He could have tried to save Benito.

But he hadn't. Instead, he'd turned his back, the heat blistering behind him, a spark falling onto his neck, singeing his flesh. And then he'd walked away. And he hadn't looked back, not once. And in that moment he was the full embodiment of everything his father had trained him to be.

He'd found out about Carlo's and Benito's deaths over the phone the next day. And there had been no more denial, no more hiding. No more believing that somewhere deep down he was good. That he had a hope of redemption.

He had let it burn in the warehouse.

"I let him die," he said. "I watched him go in, watched as the front end of the building collapsed. I could have called someone, and I didn't. I made the choice to be the man he always wanted me to be. The man I always was. I turned and I walked away. I did just as I promised I would do. I let him burn, with all of his damned money. And I can't regret the choice. He made his, I made mine. And everyone is free of him now. Of both of them."

Alessia was waxen, her skin pale, her lips tinged blue. "I don't know what to say."

"Do you see, Alessia? This is what I was trying to tell you. What you need to understand." He leaned forward, extending his hand to her, and she jerked back. Her withdrawal felt like a stab to the chest, but it was no less than he deserved. "I'm not the hero of the story. I am nothing less than the villain."

She understood now, he could see it, along with a dawning horror in her eyes that he wanted to turn away from. She was afraid. Afraid of him. He wasn't her knight anymore.

"I think maybe I should wait a few days to have my things moved into your room," she said after a long moment of silence.

He nodded. "That might be wise." Pain assaulted him and he tried to ignore it, tried to grit his teeth and sit with a neutral expression.

"I'll talk to you later?"

"Of course." He sat back on the couch and watched her leave. Then he closed his eyes and tried to picture her smile again. Tried to recapture the way she'd looked at him just a few moments before. But instead of her light, all he could see was a haunted expression, one he had put there.

Alessia was gasping for breath by the time she got to her bedroom. She closed the door behind her and put her hand on her chest, felt her heart hammering beneath her palm.

Matteo had let Benito and Carlo die.

She sucked in a shuddering breath and started pacing back and forth, fighting the tears that were threatening to spill down her cheeks.

She replayed what he had said again in her mind. He hadn't forced Benito or Carlo back into the burning building. Hadn't caused them harm with his own hands.

He had walked away. He had washed his hands and walked away, accepting in that moment whatever the consequences might be.

Alessia walked over to her bed and sat on the edge

of it. And she tried to reconcile the man downstairs with the man she'd always believed him to be.

The man beneath the armor wasn't perfect. He was wounded, damaged beyond reason. Hurting. And for the first time she really understood what that meant. Understood how shut down he was. How much it would take to reach him.

And she wasn't sure if she could do it. Wasn't sure she had the strength to do it.

It had been so much easier when he was simply the fantasy. When he was the man she'd made him be in her mind. When he was an ideal, a man sent to ride to her rescue.

She'd put him in that position. From the moment she'd first seen him. Then after he had rescued her, she'd assigned him that place even more so.

The night of her bachelorette party...

"Damn you, Alessia," she said to herself.

Because she'd done it then, too. She'd used Matteo as part of her fantasy, as part of the little world she'd built up in her mind to keep herself from crumbling. She had taken him on her own terms, used him to fill a void, and never once had she truly looked into his. Never once had she truly tried to fill it.

Being there for Matteo, knowing him, meant knowing this. Meant knowing that he had faced down a terrible decision, and that he had made a terrible choice.

The wrong choice, at least in traditional terms of right and wrong.

Very few people would hold it against him that he hadn't raced into the burning building after his father, but to know that he had also not called for help. That he had meant what he'd said to his father. That he would let him, and all of it, burn. In flame. In greed. And he had.

Her lover, her Matteo, had a core of ice and steel. Getting through it, finding his heart, might be impossible. She faced that, truly faced it, for the first time.

Matteo might never love. The ending might not really be happy. The truth was, she lived her life in denial. The pursuit of contentment at least, at all costs, and if that required denial, then she employed it, and she'd always done it quite effectively.

Walking down the aisle toward Alessandro had been the first time she'd truly realized that if she didn't do something, if she didn't stop it, it wouldn't stop itself.

She wrapped her arms around herself, cold driving through her. She had another choice to make. A choice about Matteo. And she wouldn't make it lightly.

There was no sugarcoating this. No putting on

blinders. It was what the wives of these Corretti men, of the Battaglia men, had always done. Looked the other way while their husbands sank into destruction and depravity, but she wouldn't do that.

If she was going to be Matteo's wife, in every sense, then she would face it all head-on.

It was empty to make a commitment to someone if you were pretending they were someone they weren't. It was empty to say you loved someone if you only loved a mirage.

Love. She had been afraid of that word in connection to Matteo for so long, and yet, she knew that was what it was. What it had always been. At least, she'd loved what she'd known about him.

Now she knew more. Now she was going to have to figure out whether she loved the idea, or the man.

Matteo lay in bed. It was past midnight. Hours since he'd last seen Alessia. Hours since they'd spoken.

His body ached, a bleeding wound in his chest where his heart should be. The absence of the heart was nothing new, but the pain was. He had lived in numbness for so long, and Alessia had come back into his life.

Then things had started to change. He'd started to want again. Started to feel again. And now he felt like he was torn open, like the healed, scarred-over, nerveless pieces of himself had been scrubbed raw again. Like he was starting over, starting back at the boy he'd been. The one who had been taken into his father's hands and molded, hard and cruel, into the image the older man had wanted to see.

He felt weak. Vulnerable in a way he could never recall feeling at any point in his life.

Alessia had walked away from him, and he couldn't blame her. In a way, it comforted him. Because at least she hadn't simply blithely walked on in her illusion of who she wanted him to be. She had heard his words. And she'd believed them.

He should be completely grateful for that. Should be happy that she knew. That she wasn't committed to a man who didn't truly exist.

But he couldn't be happy. Selfishly, he wanted her back. Wanted the light and heat and smiles. Wanted one person to look at him and see hope.

"Matteo?"

He looked up and saw Alessia standing in the doorway, her dark hair loose around her shoulders.

"Yes?" He pushed into a sitting position.

"I felt like I owed it to you to really think about what you said."

"And you owed it to you."

She nodded. "I suppose I did."

"And what conclusion have you come to?"

"You aren't the man I thought you were."

The words hit him with the force of a moving truck. "No. I'm sure in all of your fantasies about me you never once dreamed that I was a killer."

She shook her head. "I didn't. I still don't think you're that. I don't think you're perfect, either, but I don't think it was ever terribly fair of me to try to make you perfect. You had your own life apart from me. Your own experiences. My mistake was believing that everything began and ended during the times our eyes met over the garden wall. In my mind, when you held me after the attack, you went somewhere hazy, somewhere I couldn't picture. I didn't think about what you did after, not really. I didn't think of the reality of you returning home, covered in blood. I didn't think about what your father might have said to you. I knew Benito Corretti was a bad man, but for some reason I never imagined how it might have touched you. I only ever pictured you in the context of my world, my dreams and where you fit into them. It was my mistake, not yours."

"But I wouldn't have blamed you if you never imagined that. No one did. Not even my family, I'm certain of that."

"Still, I wasn't looking at you like you were a real person. And you were right to make me see."

"Alessia, if you want—"

"Let me finish. I see now. I see you, Matteo, not just the fantasy I created. And I don't want to walk away. I want to stay with you. I want to make a family with you."

"You trust me to help raise your child after you found out what I'm capable of?"

"That night of your life can't live in isolation. It's connected to the rest of your life, to all of it. To who your father was, the history of what he'd done to other people, to what he'd done to you."

"He never did anything to me, he just—"

"He forced you to do things you would never have done. He made you violate your conscience, over and over again until it was scarred. He would have turned you into a monster."

"He did, Alessia. That's the point. He did."

She shook her head. "You put a stop to it."

"I had to," he said, his voice rough. "I had to because you don't just walk away from the Correttis. It's not possible. My father would not have released his hold."

"I know. I understand."

"And you absolve me?"

"You don't need my absolution."

"But do I have it?" he asked, desperate for it, craving it more than his next breath.

She nodded. "If I have yours."

"For what?"

"For what I did. For not telling you about Alessandro. For agreeing to marry him in the first place. For trapping you in this marriage."

"You didn't trap me."

"You said—"

"Alessia, I have been manipulated into doing things far worse than marrying you, and I have done it with much greater coercion. A little news piece on what a jerk I am for not making your child legitimate was hardly going to force my hand."

"Then why did you do it?"

"To cement the deal. To give our child my name. All things I could have walked away from."

"Then forgive me, at least, for lying to you. For leaving you in the hotel room."

"I do. I was angry about it, but only because it felt so wrong to watch you walking toward him. To know that he would have you and not me. If I had known that there was a deal on the table that could be secured by marriage to you I would have been the one volunteering for the job."

A ghost of a smile touched her lips. "When my father first told me about the deal with the Correttis, that it would be sealed by marriage, I said yes immediately. I was so sure it would be you. And when it was Alessandro who showed up at the door to talk terms the next day I thought...I thought I would die."

"Waiting for your knight to rescue you?"

"Yes. I was. But I've stopped doing that now. I need to learn to rescue myself. To make my own decisions."

"You've certainly been doing that over the past couple of months."

"I have. And some of them have been bad, ill-timed decisions, but they've been mine. And I want you to know that I've made another decision."

"What is that?"

"You're my husband. And I'll take you as you are. Knowing your past, knowing the kind of man you can be. I want you to understand that I'm not sugar-coating it, or glossing over the truth. I understand what you did. I understand that...that you don't feel emotion the same way that I do. The same way most people do."

"Do you really understand that? I keep it on a leash for a reason, Alessia, a very important reason, and I won't compromise it."

She nodded. "I know."

"And still you want to try? You want to be my wife? To let me have a hand in raising our child?"

"Yes. No matter what, you're the father of my child,

Matteo, and there is no revelation that can change that. I don't want to change that."

"How can you say that with such confidence?"

"Because no matter what you might have done, you aren't cruel."

She leaned in and he took a strand of her hair between his thumb and forefinger. Soft like silk. He wanted to feel it brushing over his skin. Wanted to drown out this moment, drown out his pain, with physical pleasure.

"Am I not?" he asked.

"No."

"You're wrong there," he said. "So very wrong. I am selfish, a man who thinks of his own pleasure, his own comfort, above all else. No matter how I pretend otherwise."

"That isn't true."

"Yes, it is. Even now, all I can think about is what your bare skin will feel like beneath my hands. All I want is to lose myself in you."

"Then do it."

His every muscle locked up, so tight it was painful. "Alessia, don't."

"What?"

"Don't sacrifice yourself for me!" he roared. "Don't do this because you feel sorry for me."

"I'm not." She took a step toward him. "I want

this because I want to be close to you. To know you. To be your wife in every way." A smile tugged at the corners of her lips. "I'm also not opposed to the orgasms you're so good at giving me. This is by no means unselfish on my part, trust me."

His skin felt like it was burning. Or perhaps that was the blood beneath his skin. Either way, he felt like he would be consumed by his need. His desire. Passion he swore he would never allow himself to feel.

Emotion he swore he would never feel.

But in this moment with Alessia, her eyes so bright and intense, so honest, he could hold back nothing. Deny her nothing. Least of all this.

She knew the truth, and still she wanted him. Not as a perfect figure, a knight in shining armor, but as the man he was. It was a gift he didn't deserve, a gift he should turn away, because he had no right to it.

But he had spoken the truth. He was selfish. Far too selfish to do anything but take what was on offer.

"Show me you want me." His words were rough, forced through his tightened throat. "Show me you still want me." Those words echoed through his soul, tearing through him, leaving him raw and bleeding inside.

Alessia wrapped one arm around his neck, her fingers laced in his hair, and put the other on his cheek.

She pressed a kiss to his lips, soft, gentle. Purposeful. "Always."

There was no hope of him being noble, not now, not tonight. But then, that shouldn't be a surprise. He didn't do noble. He didn't do selfless. And it wouldn't start now.

He kissed her, deep and hard, his body throbbing, his heart raging. He wrapped his arms around her and pulled her in close, reveling in the feel of her. Touching Alessia was a thrill that he didn't think would ever become commonplace. He had hungered for her touch, for her closeness, for so many years, and he knew his desire for it would never fade.

If anything, it only grew.

He slid his hands down her waist, over her hips, her thighs, and gripped her hard, tugging her up into his arms, those long, lean legs wrapping around his waist as he walked them both to the bed.

Alessia started working on the knot on his tie, her movements shaky and clumsy and all the sexier for it. He sat on the bed, and Alessia remained on top of him, now resting on her knees. She tugged hard on the tie and managed to get it off, then started working at the buttons on his shirt.

He continued to kiss her, deep and desperate, pushing her dress up, past her hips, her waist, her breasts, and over her head. Her lips were swollen from kissing, her face flushed, her hair disheveled from where he'd run his fingers through it.

She looked wild, free, the most beautiful thing he'd ever seen. But then, Alessia had been, from the moment he'd seen her, the most beautiful sight he'd ever beheld. And then, when his vision of her had been one of innocence, protectiveness, it had been all about that glow that was inside of her.

He could see it, along with the outer beauty that drove him to madness. Now that their lives, their feelings, had no more innocence left, he could still see it. Still feel it deep inside of him, an ache that wouldn't ease.

She pushed his shirt off his shoulders, the buttoned cuffs snagging on his hands. A little growl escaped her lips. He wrapped one hand around her waist to hold her steady and lay back on the bed, leaving her perched over him, then he undid the buttons as quickly as possible and tossed the shirt to the side.

Alessia moved away from him, standing in front of the bed, in front of him. She met his eyes, and put her hands behind her back, her movement quick. Her bra loosened, then fell, baring her breasts to him. His stomach tightened, he could barely breathe.

She smiled, then hooked her fingers into the sides of her panties and tugged them off.

He wanted to say something. To tell her how beautiful she was, how perfect. But he couldn't speak. He could only watch, held completely under her spell.

She approached the bed, her fingers deft on his belt buckle, making quick work of his pants and underwear, and leaving him as naked as she was.

"You're so much more...just so much more than I ever imagined," she said. "I made fantasies about you, but they were a girl's fantasies. I'm not a girl, though, I'm a woman. And I'm glad you're not only that one-dimensional imagining I had of you. I'm glad you're you."

She leaned in, running the tip of her finger along the length of his rock-hard erection. Every thought ran from his head like water, his heart thundering in his ears.

Lush lips curved into a wicked smile and she leaned in, flicking her tongue over the head of his shaft. "I've never done this before. So you have to tell me if I do it wrong."

"You couldn't possibly do it wrong," he said, not sure how he managed to speak at all. It shouldn't be possible when he couldn't breathe.

And she proved him right. Her mouth on him hot, sweet torture that streaked through his veins like flame. But where other flames destroyed, this fire cleansed. He sifted his fingers through her hair, needing an anchor. Needing to touch her, to be a part of this. Not simply on the receiving end of the pleasure she was giving him.

He needed more. Needed to taste her, too.

"Get on the bed," he growled.

She complied, not abandoning her task as she got up onto the bed, onto her knees. He sat up and she raised her head, her expression confused. Then he grasped her hips and maneuvered her around so that she was over him, so that he could taste her like she was tasting him.

She gasped when his tongue touched her.

"Don't stop," he said, the command rough, firmer than he'd intended it to be, but she didn't seem to mind.

He slipped a finger inside of her while he pleasured her with his tongue, and she gasped again, freezing for a moment before taking him fully into her mouth. His head fell back, a harsh groan on his lips.

"I can't last much longer," he said.

"Neither can I," she panted, moving away from him, returning a moment later, her thighs on either side of his. She bent down and pressed a kiss to his lips. "Ready?" she asked.

"More than."

She positioned her body so that the head of his erection met with her slick entrance, then she lowered herself down onto him, so slowly he thought he would be consumed utterly by the white heat moving through him.

She moved over him, her eyes locked with his. He grasped her hips, meeting each of her thrusts, watching her face, watching her pleasure.

He moved his hand, pressed his palm flat over her stomach, then slid it upward to cup one of her breasts. He liked the view. Liked being able to see all of her as she brought them both to the brink.

She leaned forward, kissing his lips, her breath getting harsher, faster, her movements more erratic. He lowered his hand back to her hip and strengthened his own movements, pushing them farther, faster.

They both reached the edge at the same time, and when he tipped over into the abyss, all he could do was hold on to her as release rushed through him like a wave, leaving no part of him untouched. No part of him hidden.

When the storm passed, Alessia was with him.

She rested her head on his chest, her breath hot on his skin. He wrapped his arms tight around her, held her to him.

He would keep her with him, no matter what.

Yes, he was a selfish bastard.

But in this moment, he couldn't regret it. If it meant keeping Alessia, he never would.

CHAPTER TWELVE

ALESSIA WOKE UP a few hours later, feeling cold. She wasn't sure why. It was a warm evening, and she had blankets, and Matteo, to keep her warm.

Matteo.

He made her heart feel like it was cracking apart. She wanted to reach him. Wanted to touch him. Really touch him, not just with her hands on his skin, but to touch his heart.

This was so close to what she wanted. A baby. The man she loved. *Dio*, she loved him so much. It made her hurt. Not just for her, but for him. For what she knew they could have that he seemed determined to wall himself off from.

A tear slipped down her cheek and she sat up, getting out of bed and crossing to the window. Now she was crying. She wasn't really sure why she was crying, either.

But she was. Really crying. From somewhere deep inside of herself. From a bottomless well that seemed to have opened up in her.

Why did she never get what she wanted? Why was it always out of reach?

Her mother's love had been there, so briefly, long enough for her to have tasted it, to know what it was. Just so she could feel the ache keenly when it was gone? And then there was Matteo. The man she'd wanted all her life. Her hero. Her heart's desire.

And when her father said she would marry a Corretti, of course it was Matteo who had come to mind. But she'd been given to Alessandro instead. And then, one more chance, Matteo at the hotel. And she'd managed to mess that up.

In the end, she'd gotten Matteo, but in the clumsiest, most dishonest way imaginable. Not telling him she was engaged, announcing to the world she was pregnant, forcing him to marry her, in a sense.

And now there was this…this heat between them that didn't go deeper than skin on his side. This love that was burning a hole through her soul, that he would never, ever be able to return.

"Alessia?" She turned and saw Matteo sitting up, his voice filled with concern. "Are you okay? Did I hurt you?"

"No." She shook her head. And he hadn't. She'd

hurt herself. "I was just…thinking." There was no point in hiding the tears. Her voice was wobbly, watery. Too late to bother with the fiction that she was fine.

"About what?"

She bit her lip. Then opted for some form of honesty. "I've been pretending."

"What do you mean?"

"My whole life. I thought if I pretended to be happy, if I made the best of what I had, that I would be okay not having it all. That if I smiled enough I would get past my mother being gone. That my father's most recent slap to my face hadn't hurt me deeper than I wanted to admit. I had to, because someone had to show my brothers and sisters that you made a choice about how you handled life. We only had what we had, and I didn't want them…I didn't want them to be sad, or to see me sad. So I protected them from what I could. I made sure they didn't know how hard it was. How bad it was. I've been carrying around the burden of everyone's happiness and just trying to make what I had work. But I'm not happy." It burst from her, truer than any words she'd ever spoken. "I don't want to smile about my childhood. It was horrible. My father was horrible. And I had to care for my siblings and it was so hard." She wiped at a tear on her cheek, tried to stop her hands from shaking. But she couldn't.

She couldn't stop shaking.

"I love them, so much, so I hate to even admit this but…I was willing to give everything for them. And no one…no one has ever given even the smallest thing for me. And I'm sorry if that makes me a bad person but I want someone to care. I want someone to care about me."

"Alessia…"

"I'm sorry," she said, wiping at more tears. "This is…probably hormones talking."

"Is it?"

She nodded, biting her lip to keep a sob from escaping. "I'm feeling sorry for myself a little too late."

"Tell me what you want, Alessia."

It was a command, and since he was the first person to ever ask, she felt compelled to answer.

"I wish someone loved me."

"Your brothers and sisters do."

She nodded. "I know they do."

Matteo watched Alessia, her body bent in despair, her expression desolate, and felt like someone was stabbing him.

Her admission was so stark, so painful. He realized then that he had put her in a position, as his angel, his light, and he had never once sought out whether or not she needed something.

He was taking from her instead. Draining her light. Using it to illuminate the dark and void places in himself. Using her to warm his soul, and he was costing her. Just another person intent on taking from her for his own selfish needs.

"It's not the same as what you mean, though, is it?" he asked slowly.

"It's just…I can't really be myself around them," she said. "I can't show them my pain. I can't…I can't let my guard drop for a moment because then they might know, and they'll feel like they're a burden, and I just…don't want them to carry that. It's not fair."

"But what about you?"

"What about me?"

Matteo felt like someone had placed a rock in his stomach. Only hours ago, he had been content to hold Alessia tight against him. Content to keep her because she had accepted who he was, hadn't she?

But he saw now. He saw that Alessia accepted far less than she should. That she gave at the expense of herself. That she would keep doing it until the light in her had been used up. And he would be the worst offender. Because he was too closed off, too dark, to offer anything in return.

Sex wouldn't substitute, no matter how much he

wanted to pretend it might. That as long as he could keep her sleepy, and naked and satisfied, he was giving.

But they were having a baby, a child. She was his wife. And life, the need for support, for touch, for caring, went well outside the bedroom. He knew that, as keenly as he knew he couldn't give it.

"I have to go," he said, his words leaden.

"What?"

"I have to go down to my offices for a few hours."

"It's four in the morning."

"I know, but this cannot wait."

"Okay," she said.

Damn her for accepting it. Damn him for making her.

He bent down and started collecting his clothes, running his fingers over his silk tie, remembering how she'd undone it only hours before with shaking fingers. How she'd kissed him. How she'd given to him.

He dressed quickly, Alessia still standing by the window, frozen, watching him.

He did the buttons on his shirt cuffs and opened his closet, retrieving his suit jacket. Then he took a breath, and turned his back on Alessia.

"I should be back later today. Feel free to go back to bed."

"In here?"

"Perhaps it would be best if you went back to your room. You haven't had your things moved, after all."

"But I made my decision."

"Perhaps I haven't made mine."

"You said you had earlier."

"Yes, I did, and then you decided you needed more time to think about it. Now I would like an extension, as well. That seems fair, doesn't it?"

He took his phone off the nightstand and curled his fingers around it. A flashback assaulted him. Of how it had been when he'd turned his back on the burning warehouse, leaving the people inside of it to deal with the consequences of their actions without his help.

But this was different. He was walking away for different reasons. It wasn't about freeing himself. This was about freeing her.

And when he returned home later in the day, perhaps he would have the strength to do it. To do what needed to be done.

Alessia didn't go back to sleep. Instead, she wandered around the palazzo like a zombie, trying to figure out why she'd exploded all over Matteo like that. And why he'd responded like he had.

It was this love business. It sucked, in her opinion.

Suddenly she'd felt like she was being torn open,

like she was too full to hold everything in. Like she'd glossed over everything with that layer of contentment she'd become so good at cultivating.

She wanted more than that, and she wasn't sure why. Wasn't sure why she couldn't just keep making the best of things. She had Matteo. That should be enough.

But it wasn't.

Because you don't really have him.

She didn't. She had his name. She was married to him. She was having his baby, sharing his bed and his body, but she didn't really have him. Because the core of him remained off-limits to her. Not just her, but to everyone.

She wanted it all. Whether she should or not. Whether it made sense or not. But that was love. Which brought her back around to love sucking. Because if she could just put on a smile and deal with it, if she could just take what he was giving and not ask for any more, she was sure there could be some kind of happiness there.

But there wouldn't be joy. There wouldn't be anything deep and lasting. And she was tired of taking less than what she wanted to keep from making waves. She was so tired of it she thought she might break beneath the strain of it.

"Buongiorno."

Alessia turned and saw Matteo standing in the

doorway, his hair a mess, as though he'd run his fingers through it a few too many times, his tie undone, his shirt unbuttoned at the collar. His jacket had been discarded somewhere else.

"Hello, Matteo. Did you have a good day at work?"

"I didn't go to work," he said.

His admission hit her hard. "You didn't?"

"No. I was running again. Like I did the day of your first wedding. That was what I did, you know. You asked me to go to the airport, and I nearly went. But in the end I was too angry at you. For lying. For being ready to marry him. So I went to my house in Germany, mainly because no one knows about it. And I did my best to be impossible to reach, because I didn't want to deal with any accusations. I didn't want to hear from my family. And I didn't want to hear from you, because I knew you would be too much of a temptation for me to resist. That if I read your emails or listened to your messages, I would want you back. That I would come back to you."

"So you hid instead?"

"It was easier. And today I thought I might do the same thing. Because I don't like to see you cry. I don't like seeing you sad, knowing that it's my fault."

"It's not your fault."

"Mainly I just drove," he said, as if she hadn't spoken. "A little too fast, but that's what a Ferrari is for."

"I suppose so."

"I've come to a decision."

"Wait, before you say anything, I want to say something."

"Why is it your turn?"

"Because you left this morning before I could finish. All right, not really, I didn't know what I was going to say then. But I do now."

"And what are you going to say?"

"I love you, Matteo. I think, in some ways, I always have. But more over the past months, more still when you told me your story. I am in love with you, and I want you to love me back. I'm tired of not having everything, and I think you and I could have everything. But you have to let us."

"Alessia...I can't."

"You can, you just have to....you have to..."

"What? I have to forget a lifetime of conditioning? I have to ignore the fact that my losing control, that my embracing emotion, might have horrible, devastating consequences, not just for you, but for our child? I have to ignore what I know to be true about myself, about my blood, and just...let it all go? Do you want me to just forget that I'm the sort of man who walked away and left his father to die in a burning warehouse? To just take that off like old clothes and put on something new? It wouldn't work. Even if it did it would be dangerous. I can't forget. I have to keep control."

"I don't believe you," she said.

"You don't believe me? Did you not listen to what I told you? Did you not understand? All of that, breaking that man's legs, leaving my father, that was what I am capable of when I have the most rigid control of myself. What I did to those men who attacked you? That blind rage? I didn't know what I was doing. I had no control, and if you hadn't stopped me...I would have killed them. I would have killed them and never felt an ounce of guilt for it."

"So you would have killed rapists, am I supposed to believe that makes you a bad, horrible, irredeemable person? That you would have done what you had to do to save a young girl?"

"That isn't the point," he said. "As long as I control it...as long as I don't feel, I won't do something I regret. I won't do something beyond myself. Even with control, do you see what I can do? What I have done? I can never afford to let it go. I can't afford—"

"I don't believe it. That isn't it. You're running scared, Matteo. You aren't afraid of losing control, you're afraid that if you feel you're going to have to face the guilt. The grief. You're hiding from the consequences of your actions. Hiding behind this blessed wall of cold and ice, but you can't live there forever."

"Yes, I can."

"No, you can't. Because at least for the sake of our child, our baby, Matteo, you have to break out of it."

"Has it ever once occurred to you that I don't want to?" he roared. "I don't want to feel, Alessia, I damn well don't. I don't want to face what I've done. To feel the full impact of my life. Of what was done to me. I don't want it. I don't need it. And I don't want you."

She stepped back, her body going numb suddenly. Shock. It must be that. Her body's defense because if it allowed her to feel the pain, she would collapse at his feet.

"You don't want me?" she asked.

"No. I never did. Not outside the bedroom. I told you that if you didn't expect love we would be fine. It was the one thing I told you could never be. I said no love. I promised faithfulness, a place in my home, my bed, what more did you want? I offered everything!"

"You offered me nothing," she said, her voice quivering, a slow ache starting to break through the numbness, shards of pain pushing through. "None of that means anything if you're withholding the only thing I really want."

"My love is so important? When has love ever given you anything but pain, Alessia?"

"I don't know because I've never had it for long enough to see."

"Then why make it so important?"

"Because I deserve it!" She broke then, tears spilling down her cheeks. "Don't I deserve it, Matteo?"

Matteo's face paled, and he took a step back. "Yes."

She didn't take it as a sign that she had gotten what she wanted. No, Matteo looked like someone had died.

She didn't say anything. She just waited.

"You deserve that," he said finally. "And you won't get it from me."

"Can't you just try?"

He shook his head. "I can't."

"Stop being so bloody noble. Stop being so repressed. Fight for us. Fight for this."

"No. I won't hold you to me. I won't hold you to this. That is one thing I will do for you, one thing I'll do right."

"You really think removing yourself is the only way to fix something? Keeping yourself distant?" It broke her heart. More than his rejection, it was his view of himself that left her crippled with pain.

"It's a kindness, Alessia. The best thing I've ever done. Trust me."

He turned and walked out of the room, left her standing there in the massive sitting area by herself. She couldn't cry. Couldn't bring herself to make the sound of pain that was building inside her. Endless. Bereft.

She wanted to collapse. But she couldn't. Because she had to stand strong for her child. Matteo might have walked away, but it didn't change the fact that they were having a baby. Didn't change the fact that she would be a mother in under six months.

It didn't change the fact that, no matter what, she loved Matteo Corretti with everything she had in her.

But she would never go back and demand less. Would never undo what she'd said to him. Because she had a right to ask for more. Had a right to expect more. She was willing to give to Matteo. To love him no matter who he was. No matter what he had done.

But she needed his love in return. Because she wasn't playing at love, it was real. And she refused to play at happiness, to feign joy.

She sank into one of the plush love seats, the pain from her chest spreading to the rest of her body.

She had a feeling there would be no happiness, fake or genuine, for a very long time.

CHAPTER THIRTEEN

MATTEO DIDN'T BOTHER with alcohol this time. He didn't deserve to have any of the reality of the past few hours blunted for his own comfort. He deserved for it to cut him open.

He shifted into Fifth and pushed harder on the gas pedal. Driving always helped him sort through things. And it helped him get farther away from his problems while he did it. But Alessia didn't feel any farther away.

She was with him. In him. Beneath his skin and, he feared, past his defenses.

Those defenses he had just given all to protect.

You aren't afraid of losing control, you're afraid that if you feel you're going to have to face the guilt.

That was just what he was. Afraid. To his very core.

He was scared that if he reached a hand out and

asked for redemption it would truly be beyond his reach. He was afraid that if he let the door open on his emotions there would be nothing but pain, and grief, and the unending lash of guilt for all he had done, both under his father's influence, and the night of the fire.

He was afraid that he would expose himself, let himself feel it all, and he would still fall short for Alessia. That he wouldn't know how to be a real husband, or a real father.

He was afraid to want it. Afraid to try it.

She wanted him to fight for them. Nothing good came from him fighting.

Except the time you saved her.

Yes, there was that. He had always held that moment up as a banner displaying what happened when he lost control. A reminder that, as dangerous as he was in general, it was when he felt passion that he truly became a monster.

He pulled his car over to the side of the road, heart pounding, and he closed his eyes, let himself picture that day fully.

The fear in Alessia's eyes. The way those men had touched her. The rage that had poured through him.

And he knew one thing for certain in that moment. That no matter how blinded he was by anger, he would never hurt Alessia. He would never hurt his child. No, his emotions, not his mind, told him emphatically that he would die before he let any harm come to them.

That he would give everything to keep them safe.

He had been so certain, all this time, that his mind would protect him, but it had been his heart that had demanded he do whatever it took to save Alessia Battaglia from harm. It had been his heart that had demanded he spend that night in New York with her.

And it was his heart that was crumbling into pieces now. There was no protecting his defenses, because Alessia had slipped in beneath them years ago, before they had fully formed, and she was destroying them now from the inside out.

Matteo put his head on the steering wheel, his body shaking as pain worked its way through him, spreading through his veins like poison.

Something in him cracked open, every feeling, every desire, every deep need, suddenly acute and sharp. It was too much. Because it was everything all at once. Grief for the boy he'd been, for the man his father had become and what the end had done to both of them. Justification because he'd done what he had for his whole family. To free everyone. To free himself. Guilt, anguish, because in some ways he would always regret it.

And a desperate longing for redemption. A desperate wish he could go back to the beginning, to the start of it all, and take the path that would form him into Alessia's white knight. So that he could truly be the man she'd seen.

Alessia. He thought of her face. Her bright smile. Her tears.

Of meeting her eyes in the mirror at a bar, and feeling a sense of certainty, so deep, so true, he hadn't even tried to fight it.

And he felt something else. A light, flooding through his soul, touching everything. Only this time, it wasn't brief. Wasn't temporary. It stayed. It shone on everything, the ugly, the unfinished and the good. It showed him for what he was, what he could be.

Love. He loved Alessia. He had loved her all of his life.

And he wasn't the man that she should have. He wasn't the man he could have been if things had gone differently.

But with love came hope. A hope that he could try. A hope for redemption. A hope for the future.

For every dirty, broken feeling that he'd unleashed inside of him, he had let loose the good to combat it.

He had never imagined that. Had never believed that there was so much lightness in him.

It was Alessia. His love for her. His hope for their future.

He might not be the man she'd once imagined. He might not be the man he might have been in different circumstances. But that man was the one that Alessia deserved and no less.

So he would become that man. Because he loved Alessia too much to offer her less.

Matteo picked up his phone, and dialed a number he rarely used if he could help it. But this was the start. The start of changing. He was too tired to keep fighting, anyway. Too tired to continue a rivalry he simply didn't want to be involved in. A rivalry created by his father, by Alessandro's father. They both hated those bastards so what was the point of honoring a hatred created and fostered by them?

No more. It had to end.

"Corretti."

"It's Matteo."

"Ah, Matteo." Alessandro didn't sound totally thrilled to hear from him.

"How is everything going? In terms of unifying the business?"

"Fine."

"Great. That's not exactly why I called."

"Why did you call, then? I'm a little busy."

"I called because I want to make sure that as we unify the company, we unify the family, as well. I...I don't want to keep any of this rivalry alive. I've been holding on to some things for far too long that I need to let go. This is one of them."

"Accepting my superiority?"

"If that's what it takes."

Alessandro paused for a moment. "You aren't dying, are you?"

"It feels like it. But I think it will pass." It had to. "I don't want to carry things on like Carlo and Benito did, and I don't just mean the criminal activity. If we have a problem, I say we just punch each other in the face and get it over with, rather than creating a multi-generational feud."

"That works for me."

"Good. See you at the next meeting." He hung up. It wasn't like he needed to hug it out with his cousin or anything, but he was ready to start putting things behind him. To stop shielding himself from the past and embrace the future.

A future that would include Alessia.

Alessia looked up when the Ferrari roared back onto the grounds. She was standing in the garden, doing her best to at least enjoy the waning sunlight. It was better than the whole dissolving-into-never-ending-tears bit.

Matteo left the car in the middle of the drive and strode into the yard, his eyes fixed on hers. When he reached her, he pulled her into his arms, his expression fierce. Then he lowered his head and kissed her. Long. Deep. Intense.

She wrapped her arms around his neck and kissed him back, her face wet, tasting salt from tears. She didn't know whose. She didn't care.

She didn't want to ask questions now, she just wanted to live in this moment. When they parted, Matteo buried his face in her neck and held her tight. And she held him, too. Neither of them moved, neither of them spoke.

Emotion swelled in her chest, so big she wasn't sure she could stand it. Wasn't sure she could breathe around it.

"I love you," he said. "I have never said it before, Alessia. Not to anyone. Not to a woman, not to family. So when I say it, I mean it. With everything I have, such as it is. I love you."

A sob broke through her lips and she tightened her hold on him. "I love you, too."

"Still?"

"Always."

"You were right. I was afraid. I'm still afraid. But I can't hide anymore. You made it impossible. I want to be the man worthy of that look you used to give me. I want to be everything for you, I don't just want to take from you. I was content to just take that light you carry around in you, Alessia. To let it warm me. But you deserve more than that. So I'll be more than that. I'm not everything I should be. I'm broken. I've done things that were wrong. I've seen things no man should have to see. But I will give you everything that I have to give, and then I'll reach deep and find more, because you're right, you deserve it all. And I want you, so that means I have to figure out a way to be it all."

"Matteo, no, you don't. You just have to meet me in the middle. And love will cover our shortcomings."

"Just meet you in the middle?"

"Mainly, I just need you to love me."

"That I can do, Alessia Corretti. I've been doing it for most of my life."

"You might not believe this, Matteo, but as you are, you're my knight in shining armor. You are flawed. You've been through unimaginable things, and you love anyway. You're so strong, so brave, so utterly perfect. Well, not perfect, but perfect for me. You're the only man I've ever wanted, the only man I've ever loved. And that will never change."

"How is it that you see me, all of me, and love me, anyway?"

"That's what love is. And you know what? It's not hard to love you. You're brave, honorable. You were willing to cut off any chance at having your own happiness to try to protect the people around you. To try to do right. You're the most incredible man I've ever known."

"Quite the compliment coming from the most amazing woman. Your bravery, your willingness to love, in spite of all you've been through, that's what pulled me out of the darkness. Your light won. Your love won."

"I'm so glad it did."

He put his hand on Alessia's stomach. "This is what I want. You, me, our baby. I was too afraid before to admit how much I wanted it. Too afraid I didn't deserve it, that I would lose it. I'm still afraid I don't deserve it, but I want it so much." He leaned in and kissed her lips. "I'm not cold anymore."

"Never again," she said.

He wrapped his arms tight around her and spun them both in a circle. She laughed, and so did he. Genuine. Happy. Joy bloomed inside of her. Joy like she'd never felt before. Real, true. And for her. Not to keep those around her smiling.

"We agreed on one night. This is turning into a lot longer than one night," he said when they stopped spinning.

"It is," she said. "All things considered, I was thinking we might want to make it forever."

"Forever sounds about right."

EPILOGUE

THE CORRETTIS WERE all together. But unlike at the funerals that had been the most common reason for them to come together in the past, unlike Alessia and Alessandro's wedding-that-wasn't, there was no veiled animosity here at the celebration of Teresa's birthday. And not just Teresa's birthday, but the regeneration of the docklands. The culmination of a joint family effort. Of them coming together.

After the big ceremony down at the docklands, they'd returned to the family estate.

They had all sat down to dinner together. They had all talked, business and personal, and not a single punch had been thrown. And it wasn't only Correttis. Some of the Battaglias, Alessia's siblings, were there, as well.

Matteo considered it a resounding success.

After dinner, they all sat in the garden, lights

strung overhead, a warm breeze filtering through. And Matteo felt peace.

"Hey there." Alessia walked away from where she'd been talking to his sister Lia and came to stand beside him, their daughter, Luciana Battaglia-Corretti, on her hip.

"The most beautiful women here have graced me with their presence. I am content," he said, brushing his knuckles over Alessia's cheek and dropping a kiss onto Luciana's soft head.

Matteo looked at his wife and daughter, at his family, all of them, surrounding him. That word meant something new now. The Correttis were no longer at war.

He bent down and extracted Luciana from her mother's arms, pulling his daughter close, the warm weight of her, her absolute trust in him, something he would never take for granted.

Alessia smiled at him, her eyes shining, her face glowing. "The way you look at me," he said. "Like I'm your knight in shining armor."

"You are," she said. "You saved me, after all."

Matteo looked around one more time, at all of the people in his life. People that he loved. "No, Alessia. You saved me."

* * * * *

*Read on for an exclusive
interview with Maisey Yates!*

BEHIND THE SCENES OF SICILY'S CORRETTI DYNASTY
with Maisey Yates

It's such a huge world to create—an entire Sicilian dynasty. Did you discuss parts of it with the other writers?

Yes, we had a loop set up for discussion, and there were a *lot* of details to work out. And every so often messages would come in with the funniest subject lines I've ever seen.

How does being part of a continuity differ from when you are writing your own stories?

I think it takes a little bit to attach to characters you didn't create from scratch, but in the end, for me, I work so hard to find that attachment that I think continuity characters end up being my favorite.

What was the biggest challenge? And what did you most enjoy about it?

I think getting to the heart of my hero. Just because you've been given an outline with characters doesn't mean you've been given all the answers. In Matteo's case he was hiding something very dark and it was up to me to dig it out of him. I love a tortured hero, so this was right up my alley.

As you wrote your hero and heroine was there anything about them that surprised you?

Hee, hee… This goes with the above. Yes, Matteo surprised me with the depth of the darkness in him. I think Alessia surprised me with her strength. Every time she opened her mouth she had something sassy to say.

What was your favorite part of creating the world of Sicily's most famous dynasty?

I loved the family villas, the idea of old-world history and beauty. I love a country setting.

If you could have given your heroine one piece of advice before the opening pages of the book, what would it be?

It's never too late to try to claim your own independence…but next time maybe do it before you're walking down the aisle.

What was your hero's biggest secret?

Oh, now, see, I can't tell you that. I'd have to kill you. He's a very good dancer, though.

What does your hero love most about your heroine?

Her strength, her ability to love and feel in spite of everything she'd been through. He feels like he's on the outside, looking in at all that light and beauty, unable to touch it.

What does your heroine love most about your hero?

The man beneath the cold exterior. The man who has braved so much pain and come out the other side standing strong. The man who gave so much to free his family from their father.

Which of the Correttis would you most like to meet and why?

Matteo. Because he's a sexy beast. I can't lie.

The World of Mills & Boon®

There's a Mills & Boon® series that's perfect for you. We publish ten series and, with new titles every month, you never have to wait long for your favourite to come along.

Blaze®
Scorching hot, sexy reads
4 new stories every month

By Request
Relive the romance with the best of the best
9 new stories every month

Cherish™
Romance to melt the heart every time
12 new stories every month

Desire™
Passionate and dramatic love stories
8 new stories every month